THIS BOOK BELONGS TO

GARFIELD: © 1978 United Feature Syndicate, Inc.

8286

HIDEAWAY

Dean R. Koontz

HIDEAWAY

G. P. PUTNAM'S SONS
New York

This is a work of fiction. The events described are imaginary. The setting and characters are fictitious and not intended to represent specific places or persons.

G. P. Putnam's Sons
Publishers Since 1838
200 Madison Avenue
New York, NY 10016

Library of Congress Cataloging-in-Publication Data

Koontz, Dean R. (Dean Ray), date.
Hideaway / Dean R. Koontz.
p.   cm.
ISBN 0-399-13673-8
ISBN 0-399-13682-7 (Limited Edition)
I. Title.
PS3561.O55H5   1992   91-29786 CIP
813'.54—dc20

Book design by MaryJane DiMassi

Printed in the United States of America
1   2   3   4   5   6   7   8   9   10

TO GERDA.
FOREVER.

O, WHAT MAY MAN WITHIN HIM HIDE,
THOUGH ANGEL ON THE OUTWARD SIDE!

—*William Shakespeare*

Part I

JUST SECONDS FROM A CLEAN GETAWAY

Life is a gift that must be given back,
and joy should arise from its possession.
It's too damned short, and that's a fact.
Hard to accept, this earthly procession
to final darkness is a journey done,
circle completed, work of art sublime,
a sweet melodic rhyme, a battle won.

—THE BOOK OF COUNTED SORROWS

ONE

1

An entire world hummed and bustled beyond the dark ramparts of the mountains, yet to Lindsey Harrison the night seemed empty, as hollow as the vacant chambers of a cold, dead heart. Shivering, she slumped deeper in the passenger seat of the Honda.

Serried ranks of ancient evergreens receded up the slopes that flanked the highway, parting occasionally to accommodate sparse stands of winter-stripped maples and birches that poked at the sky with jagged black branches. However, that vast forest and the formidable rock formations to which it clung did not reduce the emptiness of the bitter March night. As the Honda descended the winding blacktop, the trees and stony outcroppings seemed to float past as if they were only dream images without real substance.

Harried by fierce wind, fine dry snow slanted through the headlight beams. But the storm could not fill the void, either.

The emptiness that Lindsey perceived was internal, not external. The night was brimming, as ever, with the chaos of creation. Her own soul was the only hollow thing.

She glanced at Hatch. He was leaning forward, hunched slightly over the steering wheel, peering ahead with an expression which might be flat and inscrutable to anyone else but which, after twelve years of marriage, Lindsey could easily read. An excellent driver, Hatch was not daunted by poor road conditions. His thoughts,

like hers, were no doubt on the long weekend they had just spent
at Big Bear Lake.

Yet again they had tried to recapture the easiness with each
other that they had once known. And again they had failed.

The chains of the past still bound them.

The death of a five-year-old son had incalculable emotional
weight. It pressed on the mind, quickly deflating every moment of
buoyancy, crushing each new blossom of joy. Jimmy had been
dead for more than four and a half years, nearly as long as he had
lived, yet his death weighed as heavily on them now as on the day
they had lost him, like some colossal moon looming in a low orbit
overhead.

Squinting through the smeared windshield, past snow-caked
wiper blades that stuttered across the glass, Hatch sighed softly.
He glanced at Lindsey and smiled. It was a pale smile, just a ghost
of the real thing, barren of amusement, tired and melancholy. He
seemed about to say something, changed his mind, and returned
his attention to the highway.

The three lanes of blacktop—one descending, two ascending—
were disappearing under a shifting shroud of snow. The road
slipped to the bottom of the slope and entered a short straightaway leading into a wide, blind curve. In spite of that flat stretch
of pavement, they were not out of the San Bernardino Mountains
yet. The state route eventually would turn steeply downward once
more.

As they followed the curve, the land changed around them: the
slope to their right angled upward more sharply than before, while
on the far side of the road, a black ravine yawned. White metal
guardrails marked that precipice, but they were barely visible in
the sheeting snow.

A second or two before they came out of the curve, Lindsey had
a premonition of danger. She said, "Hatch . . ."

Perhaps Hatch sensed trouble, too, for even as Lindsey spoke,
he gently applied the brakes, cutting their speed slightly.

A downgrade straightaway lay beyond the bend, and a beer
distributor's large truck was halted at an angle across two lanes,
just fifty or sixty feet in front of them.

Lindsey tried to say, *oh God,* but her voice was locked within her.

While making a delivery to one of the area ski resorts, the trucker evidently had been surprised by the blizzard, which had set in only a short while ago but half a day ahead of the forecasters' predictions. Without benefit of snow chains, the big truck tires churned ineffectively on the icy pavement as the driver struggled desperately to bring his rig around and get it moving again.

Cursing under his breath but otherwise as controlled as ever, Hatch eased his foot down on the brake pedal. He dared not jam it to the floor and risk sending the Honda into a deadly spin.

In response to the glare of the car headlights, the trucker looked through his side window. Across the rapidly closing gap of night and snow, Lindsey saw nothing of the man's face but a pallid oval and twin charry holes where the eyes should have been, a ghostly countenance, as if some malign spirit was at the wheel of that vehicle. Or Death himself.

Hatch was heading for the outermost of the two ascending lanes, the only part of the highway not blocked.

Lindsey wondered if other traffic was coming uphill, hidden from them by the truck. Even at reduced speed, if they collided head-on, they would not survive.

In spite of Hatch's best efforts, the Honda began to slide. The tail end came around to the left, and Lindsey found herself swinging away from the stranded truck. The smooth, greasy, out-of-control motion was like the transition between scenes in a bad dream. Her stomach twisted with nausea, and although she was restrained by a safety harness, she instinctively pressed her right hand against the door and her left against the dashboard, bracing herself.

"Hang on," Hatch said, turning the wheel where the car wanted to go, which was his only hope of regaining control.

But the slide became a sickening spin, and the Honda rotated three hundred and sixty degrees, as if it were a carousel without calliope: around . . . around . . . until the truck began to come into view again. For an instant, as they glided downhill, still turning, Lindsey was certain the car would slip safely past the other vehicle. She could see beyond the big rig now, and the road below was free of traffic.

Then the front bumper on Hatch's side caught the back of the truck. Tortured metal shrieked.

The Honda shuddered and seemed to *explode* away from the point of collision, slamming backward into the guardrail. Lindsey's teeth clacked together hard enough to ignite sparks of pain in her jaws, all the way into her temples, and the hand braced against the dashboard bent painfully at the wrist. Simultaneously, the strap of the shoulder harness, which stretched diagonally across her chest from right shoulder to left hip, abruptly cinched so tight that her breath burst from her.

The car rebounded from the guardrail, not with sufficient momentum to reconnect with the truck but with so much torque that it pivoted three hundred and sixty degrees again. As they spun-glided past the truck, Hatch fought for control, but the steering wheel jerked erratically back and forth, tearing through his hands so violently that he cried out as his palms were abraded.

Suddenly the moderate gradient appeared precipitously steep, like the water-greased spillway of an amusement-park flume ride. Lindsey would have screamed if she could have drawn breath. But although the safety strap had loosened, a diagonal line of pain still cut across her chest, making it impossible to inhale. Then she was rattled by a vision of the Honda skating in a long glissade to the next bend in the road, crashing through the guardrail, tumbling out into the void—and the image was so horrifying that it was like a blow, knocking breath back *into* her.

As the Honda came out of the second rotation, the entire driver's side slammed into the guardrail, and they slid thirty or forty feet without losing contact. To the accompaniment of a grinding-screeching-scraping of metal against metal, showers of yellow sparks plumed up, mingling with the falling snow, like swarms of summer fireflies that had flown through a time warp into the wrong season.

The car shuddered to a halt, canted up slightly at the front left corner, evidently hooked on a guard post. For an instant the resultant silence was so deep that Lindsey was half stunned by it; she shattered it with an explosive exhalation.

She had never before experienced such an overwhelming sense of relief.

Then the car moved again.

It began to tilt to the left. The guardrail was giving way, perhaps weakened by corrosion or by the erosion of the highway shoulder beneath it.

"Out!" Hatch shouted, frantically fumbling with the release on his safety harness.

Lindsey didn't even have time to pop loose of her own harness or grab the door handle before the railing cracked apart and the Honda slipped into the ravine. Even as it was happening, she couldn't believe it. The brain acknowledged the approach of death, while the heart stubbornly insisted on immortality. In almost five years she had not adjusted to Jimmy's death, so she was not easily going to accept the imminence of her own demise.

In a jangle of detached posts and railings, the Honda slid sideways along the ice-crusted slope, then flipped over as the embankment grew steeper. Gasping for breath, heart pounding, wrenched painfully from side to side in her harness, Lindsey hoped for a tree, a rock outcropping, anything that would halt their fall, but the embankment seemed clear. She was not sure how often the car rolled—maybe only twice—because up and down and left and right lost all meaning. Her head banged into the ceiling almost hard enough to knock her out. She didn't know if she'd been thrown upward or if the roof had caved in to meet her, so she tried to slump in her seat, afraid the roof might crumple further on the next roll and crush her skull. The head-lights slashed at the night, and from the wounds spouted torrents of snow. Then the windshield burst, showering her with minutely fragmented safety glass, and abruptly she was plunged into total darkness. Apparently the headlights blinked off, and the dashboard lights, reflected in Hatch's sweat-slicked face. The car rolled onto its roof again and stayed there. In that inverted posture it sledded farther into the seemingly bottomless ravine, with the thunderous noise of a thousand tons of coal pouring down a steel chute.

The gloom was utterly tenebrous, seamless, as if she and Hatch were not outdoors but in some windowless funhouse, rocketing down a roller-coaster track. Even the snow, which usually had a natural phosphorescence, was suddenly invisible. Cold flakes stung her face as the freezing wind drove them through the empty windshield frame, but she could not see them even as they frosted her lashes. Struggling to quell a rising panic, she wondered if she had been blinded by the imploding glass.

Blindness.

That was her special fear. She was an artist. Her talent took inspiration from what her eyes observed, and her wonderfully dexterous hands rendered inspiration into art with the critical judgment of those eyes to guide them. What did a blind painter paint? What could she hope to create if suddenly deprived of the sense that she relied upon the most?

Just as she started to scream, the car hit bottom and rolled back onto its wheels, landing upright with less impact than she had anticipated. It came to a halt almost gently, as if on an immense pillow.

"Hatch?" Her voice was hoarse.

After the cacophonous roar of their plunge down the ravine wall, she felt half deaf, not sure if the preternatural silence around her was real or only perceived.

"Hatch?"

She looked to her left, where he ought to have been, but she could not see him—or anything else.

She *was* blind.

"Oh, God, no. Please."

She was dizzy, too. The car seemed to be turning, wallowing like an airborne kite dipping and rising in the thermal currents of a summer sky.

"Hatch!"

No response.

Her lightheadedness increased. The car rocked and wallowed worse than ever. Lindsey was afraid she would faint. If Hatch was injured, he might bleed to death while she was unconscious and unable to help him.

She reached out blindly and found him crumpled in the driver's seat. His head was bent toward her, resting against his own shoulder. She touched his face, and he did not move. Something warm and sticky covered his right cheek and temple. Blood. From a head injury. With trembling fingers, she touched his mouth and sobbed with relief when she felt the hot exhalation of his breath between his slightly parted lips.

He was unconscious, not dead.

Fumbling in frustration with the release mechanism on her safety harness, Lindsey heard new sounds that she could not identify. A soft slapping. Hungry licking. An eerie, liquid chuckling. For a moment she froze, straining to identify the source of those unnerving noises.

Without warning the Honda tipped forward, admitting a cascade of icy water through the broken windshield onto Lindsey's lap. She gasped in surprise as the arctic bath chilled her to the marrow, and realized she was not lightheaded after all. The car *was* moving. It was afloat. They had landed in a lake or river. Probably a river. The placid surface of a lake would not have been so active.

The shock of the cold water briefly paralyzed her and made her wince with pain, but when she opened her eyes, she could see again. The Honda's headlights were, indeed, extinguished, but the dials and gauges in the dashboard still glowed. She must have been suffering from hysterical blindness rather than genuine physical damage.

She couldn't see much, but there was not much to see at the bottom of the night-draped ravine. Splinters of dimly glimmering glass rimmed the broken-out windshield. Outside, the oily water was revealed only by a sinuous, silvery phosphorescence that highlighted its purling surface and imparted a dark obsidian sparkle to the jewels of ice that floated in tangled necklaces atop it. The riverbanks would have been lost in absolute blackness but for the ghostly raiments of snow that cloaked the otherwise naked rocks, earth, and brush. The Honda appeared to be motoring through the river: water poured halfway up its hood before parting in a "V" and streaming away to either side as it might from the prow of a ship, lapping at the sills of the side windows. They were being swept downstream, where eventually the currents were certain to turn more turbulent, bringing them to rapids or rocks or worse. At a glance, Lindsey grasped the extremity of their situation, but she was still so relieved by the remission of her blindness that she was grateful for the sight of anything, even of trouble this serious.

Shivering, she freed herself from the entangling straps of the safety harness, and touched Hatch again. His face was ghastly in the queer backsplash of the instrument lights: sunken eyes, waxen skin, colorless lips, blood oozing—but, thank God, not spurting—from the gash on the right side of his head. She shook him gently, then a little harder, calling his name.

They wouldn't be able to get out of the car easily, if at all, while it was being borne down the river—especially as it now began to move faster. But at least they had to be prepared to scramble out if it came up against a rock or caught for a moment against one of the banks. The opportunity to escape might be short-lived.

Hatch could not be awakened.

Without warning the car dipped sharply forward. Again icy water gushed in through the shattered windshield, so cold that it had some of the effect of an electrical shock, halting Lindsey's heart for a beat or two and locking the breath in her lungs.

The front of the car did not rise in the currents, as it had done previously. It was settling deeper than before, so there was less river under it to provide lift. The water continued to pour in, quickly rising past Lindsey's ankles to mid-calf. They were sinking.

"Hatch!" She was shouting now, shaking him hard, heedless of his injuries.

The river gushed inside, rising to seat level, churning up foam that refracted the amber light from the instrument panel and looked like garlands of golden Christmas tinsel.

Lindsey pulled her feet out of the water, knelt on her seat, and splashed Hatch's face, desperately hoping to bring him around.

But he was sunk in deeper levels of unconsciousness than mere concussive sleep, perhaps in a coma as plumbless as a mid-ocean trench.

Swirling water rose to the bottom of the steering wheel.

Frantically Lindsey ripped at Hatch's safety harness, trying to strip it away from him, only half aware of the hot flashes of pain when she tore a couple of fingernails.

"Hatch, damn it!"

The water was halfway up the steering wheel, and the Honda all but ceased its forward movement. It was too heavy now to be budged by the persistent pressure of the river behind it.

Hatch was five-feet-ten, a hundred and sixty pounds, only average in size, but he might as well have been a giant. As dead weight, resistant to her every effort, he was virtually immovable. Tugging, shoving, wrenching, clawing, Lindsey struggled to free him, and by the time she finally managed to disentangle him from the straps, the water had risen over the top of the dashboard, more than halfway up her chest. It was even higher on Hatch, just under his chin, because he was slumped in his seat.

The river was unbelievably icy, and Lindsey felt the warmth pumping out of her body as if it were blood gushing from a severed artery. As body heat bled from her, the cold bled in, and her muscles began to ache.

Nevertheless, she welcomed the rising flood because it would make Hatch buoyant and therefore easier to maneuver out from under the wheel and through the shattered windshield. That was her theory, anyway, but when she tugged on him, he seemed heavier than ever, and now the water was at his lips.

"Come on, come on," she said furiously, "you're gonna drown, damn it!"

2

Finally pulling his beer truck off the road, Bill Cooper broadcast a Mayday on his CB radio. Another trucker responded and, equipped with a cellular telephone as well as a CB, promised to call the authorities in nearby Big Bear.

Bill hung up the citizen's-band handset, took a long-handled six-battery flashlight from under the driver's seat, and stepped out into the storm. The frigid wind cut through even his fleece-lined denim jacket, but the bitterness of the winter night was not half as icy as his stomach, which had turned sour and cold as he had watched the Honda spin its luckless occupants down the highway and over the brink of the chasm.

He hurried across the slippery pavement and along the shoulder to the missing section of guardrail. He hoped to see the Honda close below, caught up against the trunk of a tree. But there were no trees on that slope—just a smooth mantle of snow from previous storms, scarred by the passage of the car, disappearing beyond the reach of his flashlight beam.

An almost disabling pang of guilt stabbed through him. He'd been drinking again. Not much. A few shots out of the flask he carried. He had been certain he was sober when he'd started up the mountain. Now he wasn't so sure. He felt . . . fuzzy. And suddenly it seemed stupid to have tried to make a delivery with the weather turning ugly so fast.

Below him, the abyss appeared supernaturally bottomless, and the apparent extreme depth engendered in Bill the feeling that he was gazing into the damnation to which he'd be delivered when his own life ended. He was paralyzed by that sense of futility that sometimes overcame even the best of men—though usually when they were alone in a bedroom, staring at the meaningless patterns of shadows on the ceiling at three o'clock in the morning.

Then the curtains of snow parted for a moment, and he saw the floor of the ravine about a hundred or a hundred and fifty feet below, not as deep as he had feared. He stepped through the gap in the guardrail, intending to crab down the treacherous hillside and assist the survivors if there were any. Instead he hesitated on the narrow shelf of flat earth at the brink of the slope because he was whiskey-dizzy but also because he could not see where the car had come to rest.

A serpentine black band, like satin ribbon, curved through the snow down there, intersecting the tracks the car had made. Bill blinked at it uncomprehendingly, as if staring at an abstract painting, until he remembered that a river lay below.

The car had gone into that ebony ribbon of water.

Following a winter of freakishly heavy snow, the weather had turned warmer a couple of weeks ago, triggering a premature spring melt. The runoff continued, for winter had returned too recently to have locked the river in ice again. The temperature of the water would be only a few degrees above freezing. Any occupant of the car, having survived both the wreck and death by drowning, would perish swiftly from exposure.

If I'd been sober, he thought, I would've turned back in this weather. I'm a pathetic joke, a tanked-up beer deliveryman who didn't even have enough loyalty to get plastered on beer. Christ.

A joke, but people were dying because of him. He tasted vomit in the back of his throat, choked it down.

Frantically he surveyed the murky ravine until he spotted an eerie radiance, like an otherworldly presence, drifting spectrally with the river to the right of him. Soft amber, it faded in and out through the falling snow. He figured it must be the interior lights of the Honda, which was being borne downriver.

Hunched for protection against the biting wind, holding on to the guardrail in case he slipped and fell over the edge, Bill scuttled along the top of the slope, in the same direction as the waterswept car below, trying to keep it in sight. The Honda drifted swiftly at first, then slower, slower. Finally it came to a complete halt, perhaps stopped by rocks in the watercourse or by a projection of the riverbank.

The light was slowly fading, as if the car's battery was running out of juice.

3

Though Hatch was freed from the safety harness, Lindsey could not budge him, maybe because his clothes were caught on something she could not see, maybe because his foot was wedged under the brake pedal or bent back and trapped under his own seat.

The water rose over Hatch's nose. Lindsey could not hold his head any higher. He was breathing the river now.

She let go of him because she hoped that the loss of his air supply would finally bring him around, coughing and spluttering and splashing up from his seat, but also because she did not have the energy to continue struggling with him. The intense cold of the water sapped her strength. With frightening rapidity, her extremities were growing numb. Her exhaled breath seemed just as cold as every inhalation, as if her body had no heat left to impart to the used air.

The car had stopped moving. It was resting on the bottom of the river, completely filled and weighed down with water, except for a bubble of air under the shallow dome of the roof. Into that space she pressed her face, gasping for breath.

She was making horrid little sounds of terror, like the bleats of an animal. She tried to silence herself but could not.

The queer, water-filtered light from the instrument panel began to fade from amber to muddy yellow.

A dark part of her wanted to give up, let go of this world, and move on to someplace better. It had a small quiet voice of its own: *Don't fight, there's nothing left to live for anyway, Jimmy has been dead for so long, so very long, now Hatch is dead or dying, just let go, surrender, maybe you'll wake up in Heaven with them* . . . The voice possessed a lulling, hypnotic appeal.

The remaining air could last only a few minutes, if that long, and she would die in the car if she did not escape immediately.

Hatch is dead, lungs full of water, only waiting to be fish food, so let go, surrender, what's the point, Hatch is dead . . .

She gulped air that was swiftly acquiring a tart, metallic taste. She was able to draw only small breaths, as if her lungs had shriveled.

If any body heat was left in her, she was not aware of it. In reaction to the cold, her stomach knotted with nausea, and even the vomit that kept rising into her throat was icy; each time she choked it down, she felt as if she had swallowed a vile slush of dirty snow.

Hatch is dead, Hatch is dead . . .

"No," she said in a harsh, angry whisper. "No. No."

Denial raged through her with the fury of a storm: Hatch could not be dead. Unthinkable. Not Hatch, who never forgot a birthday or an anniversary, who bought her flowers for no reason at all, who never lost his temper and rarely raised his voice. Not Hatch, who always had time to listen to the troubles of others and sympathize with them, who never failed to have an open wallet for a friend in need, whose greatest fault was that he was too damn much of a soft touch. He could not be, must not be, *would* not be dead. He ran five miles a day, ate a low-fat diet with plenty of fruits and vegetables, avoided caffeine *and* decaffeinated beverages. Didn't that count for something, damn it? He lathered on sunscreen in the summer, did not smoke, never drank more than two beers or two glasses of wine in a single evening, and was too easy-going ever to develop heart disease due to stress. Didn't self-denial and self-control count for anything? Was creation so screwed up that there was *no* justice any more? Okay, all right, they said the good died young, which sure had been true of Jimmy, and Hatch was not yet forty, young by any standard, okay, agreed, but they also said that virtue was its own reward, and there was plenty of virtue here, damn it, a whole shitload of virtue, which ought to count for something, unless God wasn't listening, unless He didn't care, unless the world was an even crueler place than she had believed.

She refused to accept it.

Hatch. Was. Not. Dead.

She drew as deep a breath as she could manage. Just as the last of the light faded, plunging her into blindness again, she sank into the water, pushed across the dashboard, and went through the missing windshield onto the hood of the car.

Now she was not merely blind but deprived of virtually all five senses. She could hear nothing but the wild thumping of her own heart, for the water effectively muffled sound. She could smell and speak only at the penalty of death by drowning. The anesthetizing effect of the glacial river left her with a fraction of her sense of touch, so she felt as if she were a disembodied spirit suspended in whatever medium composed Purgatory, awaiting final judgment.

Assuming that the river was not much deeper than the car and that she would not need to hold her breath long before she reached the surface, she made another attempt to free Hatch. Lying on the hood of the car, holding fast to the edge of the windshield frame with one numb hand, straining against her body's natural buoyancy, she reached back inside, groped in the blackness until she located the steering wheel and then her husband.

Heat rose in her again, at last, but it was not a sustaining warmth. Her lungs were beginning to burn with the need for air.

Gripping a fistful of Hatch's jacket, she pulled with all her might—and to her surprise he floated out of his seat, no longer immovable, suddenly buoyant and unfettered. He caught on the steering wheel, but only briefly, then bobbled out through the windshield as Lindsey slid backward across the hood to make way for him.

A hot, pulsing pain filled her chest. The urge to breathe grew overpowering, but she resisted it.

When Hatch was out of the car, Lindsey embraced him and kicked for the surface. He was surely drowned, and she was clinging to a corpse, but she was not repulsed by that macabre thought. If she could get him ashore, she would be able to administer artificial respiration. Although the chance of reviving him was slim, at least some hope remained. He was not truly dead, not really a corpse, until all hope had been exhausted.

She burst through the surface into a howling wind that made the marrow-freezing water seem almost warm by comparison. When that air hit her burning lungs, her heart stuttered, her chest clenched with pain, and the second breath was harder to draw than the first.

Treading water, holding tight to Hatch, Lindsey swallowed mouthfuls of the river as it splashed her face. Cursing, she spat it out. Nature seemed alive, like a great hostile beast, and she found herself irrationally angry with the river and the storm, as if they were conscious entities willfully aligned against her.

She tried to orient herself, but it was not easy in the darkness and shrieking wind, without solid ground beneath her. When she saw the riverbank, vaguely luminous in its coat of snow, she attempted a one-arm sidestroke toward it with Hatch in tow, but the current was too strong to be resisted, even if she'd been able to swim with both arms. She and Hatch were swept downstream, repeatedly dragged beneath the surface by an undertow, repeatedly thrust back into the wintry air, battered by fragments of tree branches and chunks of ice that were also caught up in the current, moving helplessly and inexorably toward whatever sudden fall or deadly phalanx of rapids marked the river's descent from the mountains.

4

He had started drinking when Myra left him. He never could handle being womanless. Yeah, and wouldn't God Almighty treat that excuse with contempt when it came time for judgment?

Still holding the guardrail, Bill Cooper crouched indecisively on the brink of the slope and stared intently down at the river. Beyond the screen of falling snow, the lights of the Honda had gone out.

He didn't dare take his eyes off the obscured scene below to check the highway for the ambulance. He was afraid that when he looked back into the ravine again, he would misremember the exact spot where the light had disappeared and would send the rescuers to the wrong point along the riverbank. The dim black-and-white world below offered few prominent landmarks.

"Come on, hurry up," he muttered.

The wind—which stung his face, made his eyes water, and pasted snow in his mustache—was keening so loudly that it masked the approaching sirens of the emergency vehicles until they rounded the bend uphill, enlivening the night with their head-lights and red flashers. Bill rose, waving his arms to draw their attention, but he still did not look away from the river.

Behind him, they pulled to the side of the road. Because one of their sirens wound down to silence faster than the other, he knew there were two vehicles, probably an ambulance and a police cruiser.

They would smell the whiskey on his breath. No, maybe not in all that wind and cold. He felt that he deserved to die for what he'd done—but if he wasn't going to die, then he didn't think he deserved to lose his job. These were hard times. A recession. Good jobs weren't easy to find.

Reflections of the revolving emergency beacons lent a strobo-scopic quality to the night. Real life had become a choppy and technically inept piece of stop-motion animation, with the scarlet snow like a spray of blood falling haltingly from the wounded sky.

5

Sooner than Lindsey could have hoped, the surging river shoved her and Hatch against a formation of water-smoothed rocks that rose like a series of worn teeth in the middle of its course, wedging them into a gap sufficiently narrow to prevent them from being swept farther downstream. Water foamed and gurgled around them, but with the rocks behind her, she was able to stop strug-gling against the deadly undertow.

She felt limp, every muscle soft and unresponsive. She could barely manage to keep Hatch's head from tipping forward into the water, though doing so should have been a simple task now that she no longer needed to fight the river.

Though she was incapable of letting go of him, keeping his head above water was a pointless task: he had drowned. She could not kid herself that he was still alive. And minute by minute he was less likely to be revived with artificial respiration. But she would not give up. Would not. She was astonished by her fierce refusal to relinquish hope, though just before the accident she had thought she was devoid of hope forever.

The chill of the water had thoroughly penetrated Lindsey, numbing mind as well as flesh. When she tried to concentrate on forming a plan that would get her from the middle of the river to the shore, she could not bring her thoughts into focus. She felt drugged. She knew that drowsiness was a companion of hypothermia, that dozing off would invite deeper unconsciousness and ultimately death. She was determined to keep awake and alert at all costs—but suddenly she realized that she had closed her eyes, giving in to the temptation of sleep.

Fear twisted through her. Renewed strength coiled in her muscles.

Blinking feverishly, eyelashes frosted with snow that no longer melted from her body heat, she peered around Hatch and along the line of water-polished boulders. The safety of the bank was only fifteen feet away. If the rocks were close to one another, she might be able to tow Hatch to shore without being sucked through a gap and carried downriver.

Her vision had adapted sufficiently to the gloom, however, for her to see that centuries of patient currents had carved a five-foot-wide hole in the middle of the granite span against which she was wedged. It was halfway between her and the river's edge. Dimly glistening under a lacework shawl of ice, the ebony water quickened as it was funneled toward the gap; no doubt it exploded out the other side with tremendous force.

Lindsey knew she was too weak to propel herself across that powerful affluxion. She and Hatch would be swept through the breach and, at last, to certain death.

Just when surrender to an endless sleep began, again, to look more appealing than continued pointless struggle against nature's hostile power, she saw strange lights at the top of the ravine, a couple of hundred yards upriver. She was so disoriented and her mind so anesthetized by the cold that for a while the pulsing crimson glow seemed eerie, mysterious, supernatural, as if she were staring upward at the wondrous radiance of a hovering, divine presence.

Gradually she realized that she was seeing the throb of police or ambulance beacons on the highway far above, and then she spotted the flashlight beams nearer at hand, like silver swords slashing the darkness. Rescuers had descended the ravine wall. They were maybe a hundred yards upriver, where the car had sunk.

She called to them. Her shout issued as a whisper. She tried again, with greater success, but they must not have heard her above the keening wind, for the flashlights continued to sweep back and forth over the same section of riverbank and turbulent water.

Suddenly she realized that Hatch was slipping out of her grasp again. His face was underwater.

With the abruptness of a switch being thrown, Lindsey's terror became anger again. She was angry with the truck driver for being caught in the mountains during a snowstorm, angry with herself for being so weak, angry with Hatch for reasons she could not define, angry with the cold and insistent river, and *enraged* at God for the violence and injustice of His universe.

Lindsey found greater strength in anger than in terror. She flexed her half-frozen hands, got a better grip on Hatch, pulled his head out of the water again, and let out a cry for help that was louder than the banshee voice of the wind. Upstream, the flashlight beams, as one, swung searchingly in her direction.

6

The stranded couple looked dead already. Targeted by the flashlights, their faces floated on the dark water, as white as apparitions—translucent, unreal, lost.

Lee Reedman, a San Bernardino County Deputy Sheriff with emergency rescue training, waded into the water to haul them ashore, bracing himself against a rampart of boulders that extended out to midstream. He was on a half-inch, hawser-laid nylon line with a breaking strength of four thousand pounds, secured to the trunk of a sturdy pine and belayed by two other deputies.

He had taken off his parka but not his uniform or boots. In those fierce currents, swimming was impossible anyway, so he did not have to worry about being hampered by clothes. And even sodden garments would protect him from the worst bite of the frigid water, reducing the rate at which body heat was sucked out of him.

Within a minute of entering the river, however, when he was only halfway toward the stranded couple, Lee felt as if a refrigerant had been injected into his bloodstream. He couldn't believe that he would have been any colder had he dived naked into those icy currents.

He would have preferred to wait for the Winter Rescue Team that was on its way, men who had experience pulling skiers out of avalanches and retrieving careless skaters who had fallen through thin ice. They would have insulated wetsuits and all the necessary gear. But the situation was too desperate to delay; the people in the river would not last until the specialists arrived.

He came to a five-foot-wide gap in the rocks, where the river gushed through as if being drawn forward by a huge suction pump. He was knocked off his feet, but the men on the bank kept the line taut, paying it out precisely at the rate he was moving, so he was not swept into the breach. He flailed forward through the surging river, swallowing a mouthful of water so bitterly cold that it made his teeth ache, but he got a grip on the rock at the far side of the gap and pulled himself across.

A minute later, gasping for breath and shivering violently, Lee reached the couple. The man was unconscious, but the woman was alert. Their faces bobbled in and out of the overlapping flashlight beams directed from shore, and they both looked in terrible shape. The woman's flesh seemed to have both shriveled and blanched of all color, so the natural phosphorescence of bone shone like a light within, revealing the skull beneath her skin. Her lips were as white as her teeth; other than her sodden black hair, only her eyes were dark, as sunken as the eyes of a corpse and bleak with the pain of dying. Under the circumstances he could not guess her age within fifteen years and could not tell if she was ugly or attractive, but he could see, at once, that she was at the limit of her resources, holding on to life by willpower alone.

"Take my husband first," she said, pushing the unconscious man into Lee's arms. Her shrill voice cracked repeatedly. "He's got a head injury, needs help, hurry up, go on, go on, damn you!"

Her anger didn't offend Lee. He knew it was not directed against him, really, and that it gave her the strength to endure.

"Hold on, and we'll all go together." He raised his voice above the roar of the wind and the racing river. "Don't fight it, don't try to grab on to the rocks or keep your feet on the bottom. They'll have an easier time reeling us in if we let the water buoy us."

She seemed to understand.

Lee glanced back toward shore. A light focused on his face, and he shouted, "Ready! Now!"

The team on the riverbank began to reel him in, with the unconscious man and the exhausted woman in tow.

7

After Lindsey was hauled out of the water, she drifted in and out of consciousness. For a while life seemed to be a videotape being fast-forwarded from one randomly chosen scene to another, with gray-white static in between.

As she lay gasping on the ground at the river's edge, a young paramedic with a snow-caked beard knelt at her side and directed a penlight at her eyes, checking her pupils for uneven dilation. He said, "Can you hear me?"

"Of course. Where's Hatch?"

"Do you know your name?"

"Where's my husband? He needs . . . CPR."

"We're taking care of him. Now, do you know your name?"

"Lindsey."

"Good. Are you cold?"

That seemed like a stupid question, but then she realized she was no longer freezing. In fact, a mildly unpleasant heat had arisen in her extremities. It was not the sharp, painful heat of flames. Instead, she felt as if her feet and hands had been dipped in a caustic fluid that was gradually dissolving her skin and leaving raw nerve ends exposed. She knew, without having to be told, that her inability to feel the bitter night air was an indication of physical deterioration.

Fast forward . . .

She was being moved on a stretcher. They were heading along the riverbank. With her head toward the front of the litter, she could look back at the man who was carrying the rear of it. The snow-covered ground reflected the flashlight beams, but that soft eerie glow was only bright enough to reveal the basic contours of the stranger's face and add a disquieting glimmer to his iron-hard eyes.

As colorless as a charcoal drawing, strangely silent, full of dreamlike motion and mystery, that place and moment had the quality of a nightmare. She felt her heartbeat accelerate as she squinted back and up at the almost faceless man. The illogic of a dream shaped her fear, and suddenly she was certain that she was dead and that the shadowy men carrying her stretcher were not men at all but carrion-bearers delivering her to the boat that would convey her across the Styx to the land of the dead and damned.

Fast forward . . .

Lashed to the stretcher now, tilted almost into a standing position, she was being pulled along the snow-covered slope of the ravine wall by unseen men reeling in a pair of ropes from above. Two other men accompanied her, one on each side of the stretcher, struggling up through the knee-deep drifts, guiding her and making sure she didn't flip over.

She was ascending into the red glow of the emergency beacons. As that crimson radiance completely surrounded her, she began to hear the urgent voices of the rescuers above and the crackle of police-band radios. When she could smell the pungent exhaust fumes of their vehicles, she knew that she was going to survive.

33

Just seconds from a clean getaway, she thought.

Though in the grip of a delirium born of exhaustion, confused and fuzzy-minded, Lindsey was alert enough to be unnerved by that thought and the subconscious longing it represented. Just seconds from a clean getaway? The only thing she had been seconds away from was death. Was she still so depressed from the loss of Jimmy that, even after five years, her own death was an acceptable release from the burden of her grief?

Then why didn't I surrender to the river? she wondered. Why not just let go?

Hatch, of course. Hatch had needed her. She'd been ready to step out of this world in hope of setting foot into a better one. But she had not been able to make that decision for Hatch, and to surrender her own life under those circumstances would have meant forfeiting his as well.

With a clatter and a jolt, the stretcher was pulled over the brink of the ravine and lowered flat onto the shoulder of the mountain highway beside an ambulance. Red snow swirled into her face.

A paramedic with a weather-beaten face and beautiful blue eyes leaned over her. "You're going to be all right."

"I didn't want to die," she said.

She was not really speaking to the man. She was aruging with herself, trying to deny that her despair over the loss of her son had become such a chronic emotional infection that she had been secretly longing to join him in death. Her self-image did not include the word "suicidal," and she was shocked and repulsed to discover, under extreme stress, that such an impulse might be a part of her.

Just seconds from a clean getaway . . .

She said, "Did I want to die?"

"You aren't going to die," the paramedic assured her as he and another man untied the ropes from the handles of the litter, preparatory to loading her into the ambulance. "The worst is over now. The worst is over."

TWO

1

Half a dozen police and emergency vehicles were parked across two lanes of the mountain highway. Uphill and downhill traffic shared the third lane, regulated by uniformed deputies. Lindsey was aware of people gawking at her from a Jeep Wagoneer, but they vanished beyond shatters of snow and heavy plumes of crystallized exhaust fumes.

The ambulance van could accommodate two patients. They loaded Lindsey onto a wheeled gurney that was fixed to the left wall by two spring clamps to prevent it from rolling while the vehicle was in motion. They put Hatch on another identical gurney along the right wall.

Two paramedics crowded into the rear of the ambulance and pulled the wide door shut behind them. As they moved, their white, insulated nylon pants and jackets produced continuous frictional sounds, a series of soft whistles that seemed to be electronically amplified in those close quarters.

With a short burst of its siren, the ambulance started to move. The paramedics swayed easily with the rocking motion. Experience had made them surefooted.

Side by side in the narrow aisle between the gurneys, both men turned to Lindsey. Their names were stitched on the breast pockets of their jackets: David O'Malley and Jerry Epstein. With a curious combination of professional detachment and concerned attentiveness, they began to work on her, exchanging medical information with each other in crisp emotionless voices but speaking to her in soft, sympathetic, encouraging tones.

That dichotomy in their behavior alarmed rather than soothed Lindsey, but she was too weak and disoriented to express her fear. She felt infuriatingly delicate. Shaky. She was reminded of a surrealistic painting titled *This World and the Next,* which she had done last year, because the central figure in that piece had been a wire-walking circus acrobat plagued by uncertainty. Right now consciousness was a high wire on which she was precariously perched. Any effort to speak to the paramedics, if sustained for more than a word or two, might unbalance her and send her into a long, dark fall.

Although her mind was too clouded to find any sense in most of what the two men were saying, she understood enough to know that she was suffering from hypothermia, possibly frostbite, and that they were worried about her. Blood pressure too low. Heartbeat slow and irregular. Slow and shallow respiration.

Maybe that clean getaway was still possible.

If she really wanted it.

She was ambivalent. If she actually had hungered for death on a subconscious level since Jimmy's funeral, she had no special appetite for it now—though neither did she find it particularly unappealing. Whatever happened to her would happen, and in her current condition, with her emotions as numb as her five senses, she did not much care about her fate. Hypothermia switched off the survival instinct with a narcotizing pall as effective as that produced by an alcoholic binge.

Then, between the two muttering paramedics, she caught a glimpse of Hatch lying on the other gurney, and abruptly she was jolted out of her half-trance by her concern for him. He looked so pale. But not just white. Another, less healthy shade of pale with a lot of gray in it. His face—turned toward her, eyes closed, mouth open slightly—looked as if a flash fire had swept through it, leaving nothing between bone and skin except the ashes of flesh consumed.

"Please," she said, "my husband." She was surprised that her voice was just a low, rough croak.

"You first," O'Malley said.

"No. Hatch. Hatch . . . needs . . . help."

"You first," O'Malley repeated.

His insistence reassured her somewhat. As bad as Hatch looked, he must be all right, must have responded to CPR, must be in better shape than she was, or otherwise they would have tended to him first. Wouldn't they?

Her thoughts grew fuzzy again. The sense of urgency that had gripped her now abated. She closed her eyes.

2

Later . . .

In Lindsey's hypothermic torpor, the murmuring voices above her seemed as rhythmic, if not as melodic, as a lullaby. But she was kept awake by the increasingly painful stinging sensation in her extremities and by the rough handling of the medics, who were packing small pillowlike objects against her sides. Whatever the things were—electric or chemical heating pads, she supposed— they radiated a soothing warmth far different from the fire burning within her feet and hands.

"Hatch needs warmed up, too," she said thickly.

"He's fine, don't you worry about him," Epstein said. His breath puffed out in small white clouds as he spoke.

"But he's cold."

"That's what he needs to be. That's just how we want him."

O'Malley said, "But not too cold, Jerry. Nyebern doesn't want a Popsicle. Ice crystals form in the tissue, there'll be brain damage."

Epstein turned to the small half-open window that separated the rear of the ambulance from the forward compartment. He called loudly to the driver: "Mike, turn on a little heat maybe."

Lindsey wondered who Nyebern might be, and she was alarmed by the words "brain damage." But she was too weary to concentrate and make sense of what they said.

Her mind drifted to recollections from childhood, but they were so distorted and strange that she must have slipped across the border of consciousness into a half-sleep where her subconscious could work nightmarish tricks on her memories.

. . . she saw herself, five years of age, at play in a meadow behind her house. The sloped field was familiar in its contours, but some hateful influence had crept into her mind and meddled with the details, wickedly recoloring the grass a spider-belly black. The petals of all the flowers were blacker still, with crimson stamens that glistened like fat drops of blood. . . .

. . . she saw herself, at seven, on the school playground at twilight, but alone as she had never been in real life. Around her stood the usual array of swings and seesaws and jungle gyms and slides, casting crisp shadows in the peculiar orange light of day's end. Those machineries of joy seemed curiously ominous now. They loomed malevolently, as if they might begin to move at any second, with much creaking and clanking, blue St. Elmo's fire glowing on their flanks and limbs, seeking blood for a lubricant, robotic vampires of aluminum and steel. . . .

3

Periodically Lindsey heard a strange and distant cry, the mournful bleat of some great, mysterious beast. Eventually, even in her semi-delirious condition, she realized that the sound did not originate either in her imagination or in the distance but directly overhead. It was no beast, just the ambulance siren, which was needed only in short bursts to clear what little traffic had ventured onto the snowswept highways.

The ambulance came to a stop sooner than she had expected, but that might be only because her sense of time was as out of whack as her other perceptions. Epstein threw the rear door open while O'Malley released the spring clamps that fixed Lindsey's gurney in place.

When they lifted her out of the van, she was surprised to see that she was not at a hospital in San Bernardino, as she expected to be, but in a parking lot in front of a small shopping center. At that late hour the lot was deserted except for the ambulance and, astonishingly, a large helicopter on the side of which was emblazoned a red cross in a white circle and the words AIR AMBULANCE SERVICE.

The night was still cold, and wind hooted across the blacktop. They were now below the snow line, although just at the base of the mountains and still far from San Bernardino. The ground was bare, and the wheels of the gurney creaked as Epstein and O'Malley rushed Lindsey into the care of the two men waiting beside the chopper.

The engine of the air ambulance was idling. The rotors turned sluggishly.

The mere presence of the craft—and the sense of extreme urgency that it represented—was like a flare of sunlight that burned off some of the dense fog in Lindsey's mind. She realized that either she or Hatch was in worse shape than she had thought, for only a critical case could justify such an unconventional and expensive method of conveyance. And they obviously were going farther than to a hospital in San Bernardino, perhaps to a treatment center specializing in state-of-the-art trauma medicine of one kind or another. Even as that light of understanding came to her, she wished that it could be extinguished, and she despairingly sought the comfort of that mental fog again.

As the chopper medics took charge of her and lifted her into the aircraft, one of them shouted above the engine noise, "But she's alive."

"She's in bad shape," Epstein said.

"Yeah, okay, she looks like shit," the chopper medic said, "but she's still alive. Nyebern's expecting a stiff."

O'Malley said, "It's the other one."

"The husband," Epstein said.

"We'll bring him over," O'Malley said.

Lindsey was aware that a monumental piece of information had been revealed in those few brief exchanges, but she was not clear-headed enough to understand what it was. Or maybe she simply did not want to understand.

As they moved her into the spacious rear compartment of the helicopter, transferred her onto one of their own litters, and strapped her to the vinyl-covered mattress, she sank back into frighteningly corrupted memories of childhood:

. . . she was nine years old, playing fetch with her dog, Boo, but when the frisky labrador brought the red rubber ball back to her and dropped it at her feet, it was not a ball any longer. It was a throbbing heart, trailing torn arteries and veins. It was pulsing not because it was alive but because a mass of worms and sarcophagus beetles churned within its rotting chambers . . .

4

The helicopter was airborne. Its movement, perhaps because of the winter wind, was less reminiscent of an aircraft than of a boat tumbling in a bad tide. Nausea uncoiled in Lindsey's stomach.

A medic bent over her, his face masked in shadows, applying a stethoscope to her breast.

Across the cabin, another medic was shouting into a radio headset as he bent over Hatch, talking not to the pilot in the forward compartment but perhaps to a receiving physician at whatever hospital awaited them. His words were sliced into a series of thin sounds by the air-carving rotors overhead, so his voice fluttered like that of a nervous adolescent.

". . . minor head injury . . . no mortal wounds . . . apparent cause of death . . . seems to be . . . drowning . . ."

On the far side of the chopper, near the foot of Hatch's litter, the sliding door was open a few inches, and Lindsey realized the door on her side was not fully closed, either, creating an arctic cross-draught. That also explained why the roar of the wind outside and the clatter of the rotors was so deafening.

Why did they want it so cold?

The medic attending to Hatch was still shouting into his headset: ". . . mouth-to-mouth . . . mechanical resuscitator . . . O-2 and CO-2 without results . . . epinephrine was ineffective . . ."

The real world had become too real, even viewed through her delirium. She didn't like it. Her twisted dreamscapes, in all their mutant horror, were more appealing than the inside of the air ambulance, perhaps because on a subconscious level she was able to exert at least *some* control on her nightmares but none at all on real events.

. . . she was at her senior prom, dancing in the arms of Joey Delvecchio, the boy with whom she had been going steady in those days. They were under a vast canopy of crepe-paper streamers. She was speckled with sequins of blue and white and yellow light cast off by the revolving crystal-and-mirror chandelier above the dance floor. It was the music of a better age, before rock-'n'-roll started to lose its soul, before disco and New Age and hip-hop, back when Elton John and the Eagles were at their peak, when the Isley Brothers were still recording, the Doobie Brothers, Stevie Wonder, Neil Sedaka making a major comeback, the music still alive, *everything and everyone so alive, the world filled with hope and possibilities now long since lost. They were slow-dancing to a Freddy Fender tune reasonably well rendered by a local band, and she was suffused with happiness and a sense of well-being—until she lifted her head from Joey's shoulder and looked up and saw not Joey's face but the rotting countenance of a cadaver, yellow teeth exposed between shriveled black lips, flesh pocked and blistered and oozing, bloodshot eyes bulging and weeping vile fluid from lesions of decay. She tried to scream and pull away from him, but she could only continue to dance, listening to the overly sweet romantic strains of "Before the Next Teardrop Falls," aware that she was seeing Joey as he would be in a few years, after he had died in the Marine-barracks explosion in Lebanon. She felt death leeching from his cold flesh into hers. She knew she had to tear herself from his embrace before that mortal tide filled her. But when she looked desperately around for someone who might help her, she saw that Joey was not the only dead dancer. Sally Ontkeen, who in eight years would succumb to cocaine poisoning, glided by in an advanced stage of decomposition, in the arms of her*

boyfriend who smiled down on her as if unaware of the corruption of her flesh. Jack Winslow, the school football star who would be killed in a drunken driving accident in less than a year, spun his date past them; his face was swollen, purple tinged with green, and his skull was crushed along the left side as it would be after the wreck. He spoke to Lindsey and Joey in a raspy voice that didn't belong to Jack Winslow but to a creature on holiday from a graveyard, vocal cords withered into dry strings: "What a night! Man, what a night!"

Lindsey shuddered, but not solely because of the frigid wind that howled through the partly open chopper doors.

The medic, his face still in shadows, was taking her blood pressure. Her left arm was no longer under the blanket. The sleeves of her sweater and blouse had been cut away, exposing her bare skin. The cuff of the sphygmomanometer was wound tightly around her biceps and secured by Velcro strips.

Her shudders were so pronounced that they evidently looked, to the paramedic, as if they might be the muscle spasms that accompanied convulsions. He plucked a small rubber wedge from a nearby supply tray and started to insert it in her mouth to prevent her from biting or swallowing her tongue.

She pushed his hand away. "I'm going to die."

Relieved that she was not having convulsions, he said, "No, you're not that bad, you're okay, you're going to be fine."

He didn't understand what she meant. Impatiently, she said, "We're *all* going to die."

That was the meaning of her dream-distorted memories. Death had been with her from the day she'd been born, always at her side, constant companion, which she had not understood until Jimmy's death five years ago, and which she had not *accepted* until tonight when death took Hatch from her.

Her heart seemed to clutch up like a fist within her breast. A new pain filled her, separate from all the other agonies and more profound. In spite of terror and delirium and exhaustion, all of which she had used as shields against the awful insistence of reality, truth came to her at last, and she was helpless to do anything but accept it.

Hatch had drowned.

Hatch was dead. CPR had not worked.

Hatch was gone forever.

. . . she was twenty-five years old, propped against bed pillows in the maternity ward at St. Joseph's Hospital. The nurse was bringing her a small blanket-wrapped bundle, her baby, her son, James Eugene Harrison, whom she had carried for nine months but had not met, whom she loved with all her heart but had not seen. The smiling nurse gently conveyed the bundle into Lindsey's arms, and Lindsey tenderly lifted aside the satin-trimmed edge of the blue cotton blanket. She saw that she cradled a tiny skeleton with hollow eye sockets, the small bones of its fingers curled in the wanting-needing gesture of an infant. Jimmy had been born with death in him, as everyone was, and in less than five years cancer would claim him. The small, bony mouth of the skeleton-child eased open in a long, slow, silent cry . . .

5

Lindsey could hear the chopper blades carving the night air, but she was no longer inside the craft. She was being wheeled across a parking lot toward a large building with many lighted windows. She thought she ought to know what it was, but she couldn't think clearly, and in fact she didn't care what it was or where she was going or why.

Ahead, a pair of double doors flew open, revealing a space warmed by yellow light, peopled by several silhouettes of men and women. Then Lindsey was rushed into the light and among the silhouettes . . . a long hallway . . . a room that smelled of alcohol and other disinfectants . . . the silhouettes becoming people with faces, then more faces appearing . . . soft but urgent voices . . . hands gripping her, lifting . . . off the gurney, onto a bed . . . tipped back a little, her head below the level of her body . . . rhythmic beeps and clicks issuing from electronic equipment of some kind. . . .

She wished they would just all go away and leave her alone, in peace. Just go away. Turn off the lights as they went. Leave her in darkness. She longed for silence, stillness, peace.

A vile odor with an edge of ammonia assaulted her. It burned her nasal passages, made her eyes pop open and water.

A man in a white coat was holding something under her nose and peering intently into her eyes. As she began to choke and gag on the stench, he took the object away and handed it to a brunette in a white uniform. The pungent odor quickly faded.

Lindsey was aware of movement around her, faces coming and going. She knew that she was the center of attention, an object of urgent inquiry, but she did not—could not manage to—care. It was all more like a dream than her actual dreams had been. A soft tide of voices rose and fell around her, swelling rhythmically like gentle breakers whispering on a sandy shore:

". . . marked paleness of the skin . . . cyanosis of lips, nails, fingertips, lobes of the ears . . ."

". . . weak pulse, very rapid . . . respiration quick and shallow . . ."

". . . blood pressure's so damned low I can't get a reading . . ."

"Didn't those assholes treat her for shock?"

"Sure, all the way in."

"Oxygen, CO-2 mix. And make it fast!"

"Epinephrine?"

"Yeah, prepare it."

"Epinephrine? But what if she has internal injuries? You can't see a hemorrhage if one's there."

"Hell, I gotta take a chance."

Someone put a hand over her face, as if trying to smother her. Lindsey felt something plugging up her nostrils, and for a moment she could not breathe. The curious thing was that she didn't care. Then cool dry air hissed into her nose and seemed to force an expansion of her lungs.

A young blonde, dressed all in white, leaned close, adjusted the inhalator, and smiled winningly. "There you go, honey. Are you getting that?"

The woman was beautiful, ethereal, with a singularly musical voice, backlit by a golden glow.

A heavenly apparition. An angel.

Wheezing, Lindsey said, "My husband is dead."

"It'll be okay, honey. Just relax, breathe as deeply as you can, everything will be all right."

"No, he's dead," Lindsey said. "Dead and gone, gone forever. Don't you lie to me, angels aren't allowed to lie."

On the other side of the bed, a man in white was swabbing the inside of Lindsey's left elbow with an alcohol-soaked pad. It was icy cold.

To the angel, Lindsey said, "Dead and gone."

Sadly, the angel nodded. Her blue eyes were filled with love, as an angel's eyes should be. "He's gone, honey. But maybe this time that isn't the end of it."

Death was always the end. How could death not be the end?

A needle stung Lindsey's left arm.

"This time," the angel said softly, "there's still a chance. We've got a special program here, a real—"

Another woman burst into the room and interrupted excitedly: "Nyebern's in the hospital!"

A communal sigh of relief, almost a quiet cheer, swept those gathered in the room.

"He was at dinner in Marina Del Rey when they reached him. He must've driven like a bat out of Hell to get back here this fast."

"You see, dear?" the angel said to Lindsey. "There's a chance. There's still a chance. We'll be praying."

So what? Lindsey thought bitterly. Praying never works for me. Expect no miracles. The dead stay dead, and the living only wait to join them.

THREE

1

Guided by procedures outlined by Dr. Jonas Nyebern and kept on file in the Resuscitation Medicine Project office, the Orange County General Hospital emergency staff had prepared an operating room to receive the body of Hatchford Benjamin Harrison. They had gone into action the moment the on-site paramedics in the San Bernardino Mountains had reported, by police-band radio, that the victim had drowned in near-freezing water but had suffered only minor injuries in the accident itself, which made him a perfect subject for Nyebern. By the time the air ambulance was touching down in the hospital parking lot, the usual array of operating-room instruments and devices had been augmented with a bypass machine and other equipment required by the resuscitation team.

Treatment would not take place in the regular emergency room. Those facilities offered insufficient space to deal with Harrison in addition to the usual influx of patients. Though Jonas Nyebern was a cardiovascular surgeon and the project team was rich with surgical skills, resuscitation procedures seldom involved surgery. Only the discovery of a severe internal injury would require them to cut Harrison, and their use of an operating room was more a matter of convenience than necessity.

When Jonas entered from the surgical hallway after preparing himself at the scrub sinks, his project team was waiting for him.

47

Because fate had deprived him of his wife, daughter, and son, leaving him without family, and because an innate shyness had always inhibited him from making friends beyond the boundaries of his profession, these were not merely his colleagues but the only people in the world with whom he felt entirely comfortable and about whom he cared deeply.

Helga Dorner stood by the instrument cabinets to Jonas's left, in the penumbra of the light that fell from the array of halogen bulbs over the operating table. She was a superb circulating nurse with a broad face and sturdy body reminiscent of any of countless steroid-saturated female Soviet track stars, but her eyes and hands were those of the gentlest Raphaelite Madonna. Patients initially feared her, soon respected her, eventually adored her.

With solemnity that was characteristic in moments like this, Helga did not smile but gave Jonas a thumbs-up sign.

Near the bypass machine stood Gina Delilo, a thirty-year-old RN and surgical technician who chose, for whatever reasons, to conceal her extraordinary competence and sense of responsibility behind a pert, cute, ponytailed exterior that made her seem to be an escapee from one of those old Gidget or beach-party movies that had been popular decades ago. Like the others, Gina was dressed in hospital greens and a string-tied cotton cap that concealed her blond hair, but bright-pink ankle socks sprouted above the elastic-edged cloth boots that covered her shoes.

Flanking the operating table were Dr. Ken Nakamura and Dr. Kari Dovell, two hospital-staff physicians with successful local private practices. Ken was a rare double threat, holding advanced degrees in internal medicine and neurology. Daily experience with the fragility of human physiology drove some doctors to drink and caused others to harden their hearts until they were emotionally isolated from their patients; Ken's healthier defense was a sense of humor that was sometimes twisted but always psychologically healing. Kari, a first-rate specialist in pediatric medicine, was four inches taller than Ken's five-feet-seven, reed-thin where he was slightly pudgy, but she was as quick to laugh as the internist. Sometimes, though, a profound sadness in her eyes troubled Jonas and led him to believe that a cyst of loneliness lay so deep within her that friendship could never provide a scalpel long or sharp enough to excise it.

Jonas looked at each of his four colleagues in turn, but none of them spoke. The windowless room was eerily quiet.

For the most part the team had a curiously passive air, as if disinterested in what was about to happen. But their eyes gave them away, for they were the eyes of astronauts who were standing in the exit bay of an orbiting shuttle on the brink of a space walk: aglow with excitement, wonder, a sense of adventure—and a little fear.

Other hospitals had emergency-room staffs skilled enough at resuscitation medicine to give a patient a fighting chance at recovery, but Orange County General was one of only three centers in all of southern California that could boast a separately funded, cutting-edge project aimed at maximizing the success of reanimation procedures. Harrison was the project's forty-fifth patient in the fourteen months since it had been established, but the manner of his death made him the most interesting. Drowning. Followed by rapidly induced hypothermia. Drowning meant relatively little physical damage, and the chill factor dramatically slowed the rate at which postmortem cell deterioration took place.

More often than not, Jonas and his team had treated victims of catastrophic stroke, cardiac arrest, asphyxiation due to tracheal obstruction, or drug overdose. Those patients usually had suffered at least some irreversible brain damage prior to or at the moment of death, before coming under the care of the Resuscitation Project, compromising their chances of being brought back in perfect condition. And of those who had died from violent trauma of one kind or another, some had been too severely injured to be saved even after being resuscitated. Others had been resuscitated and stabilized, only to succumb to secondary infections that swiftly developed into toxic shock. Three had been dead so long that, once resuscitated, brain damage was either too severe to allow them to regain consciousness or, if they were conscious, too extensive to allow them to lead anything like a normal life.

With sudden anguish and a twinge of guilt, Jonas thought of his failures, of life incompletely restored, of patients in whose eyes he had seen the tortured awareness of their own pathetic condition. . . .

"This time will be different." Kari Dovell's voice was soft, only a whisper, but it shattered Jonas's reverie.

Jonas nodded. He felt considerable affection for these people. For their sake more than his own, he wanted the team to have a major, unqualified success.

"Let's do it," he said.

Even as he spoke, the double doors to the operating room crashed open, and two surgical orderlies rushed in with the dead man on a gurney. Swiftly and skillfully, they transferred the body onto the slightly tilted operating table, treating it with more care and respect than they might have shown a corpse in other circumstances, and then exited.

The team went to work even as the orderlies were heading out of the room. With speed and economy of movement, they scissored the remaining clothes off the dead man, leaving him naked on his back, and attached to him the leads of an electrocardiograph, an electroencephalograph, and a skin-patch digital-readout thermometer.

Seconds were golden. Minutes were beyond price. The longer the man remained dead, the less chance they had of bringing him back with any degree of success whatsoever.

Kari Dovell adjusted the controls of the EKG, sharpening the contrast. For the benefit of the tape recording that was being made of the entire procedure, she repeated what all of them could see: "Flat line. No heartbeat."

"No alpha, no beta," Ken Nakamura added, confirming the absence of all electrical activity in the patient's brain.

Having wrapped the pressure cuff of a sphygmomanometer around the patient's right arm, Helga reported the reading they expected: "No measurable blood pressure."

Gina stood beside Jonas, monitoring the digital-readout thermometer. "Body temperature's forty-six degrees."

"So low!" Kari said, her green eyes widening with surprise as she stared down at the cadaver. "And he must've warmed up at least ten degrees since they pulled him out of that stream. We keep it cool in here, but not *that* cool."

The thermostat was set at sixty-four degrees to balance the comfort of the resuscitation team against the need to prevent the victim from warming too fast.

Looking up from the dead man to Jonas, Kari said, "Cold is good, okay, we want him cold, but not too damned cold. What if his tissues froze and he sustained massive cerebral-cell damage?"

Examining the dead man's toes and then his fingers, Jonas was almost embarrassed to hear himself say, "There's no indication of vesicles—"

"That doesn't prove anything," Kari said.

Jonas knew that what she said was true. They all knew it. There would not have been time for vesicles to form in the dead flesh of frost-bitten fingertips and toes before the man, himself, had died. But, damn it, Jonas did not want to give up before they had even started.

He said, "Still, there's no sign of necrotic tissue—"

"Because the entire patient is necrotic," Kari said, unwilling to let go of it. Sometimes she seemed as ungainly as a spindly-legged bird that, although a master of the air, was out of its element on the land. But at other times, like now, she used her height to advantage, casting an intimidating shadow, looking down at an adversary with a hard gaze that seemed to say better-listen-to-me-or-I-might-peck-your-eyes-out-mister. Jonas was two inches taller than Kari, so she couldn't actually look down at him, but few women were that close to being able to give him even a level-eyed stare, and the effect was the same as if he had been five-feet-two.

Jonas looked at Ken, seeking support.

The neurologist was having none of it. "In fact the body temperature could have fallen below freezing *after* death, then warmed up on the trip here, and there'd be no way for us to tell. You know that, Jonas. The only thing we can say for sure about this guy is that he's deader than Elvis has ever been."

"If he's only forty-six degrees *now* . . . ," Kari said.

Every cell in the human body is composed primarily of water.

The percentage of water differs from blood cells to bone cells, from skin cells to liver cells, but there is always more water than anything else. And when water freezes, it expands. Put a bottle of soda in the freezer to quick-chill it, leave it too long, and you're left with just the exploded contents bristling with shattered glass. Frozen water bursts the walls of brain cells—all body cells—in a similar fashion.

No one on the team wanted to revive Harrison from death if they were assured of bringing back something dramatically less than a whole person. No good physician, regardless of his passion to heal, wanted to battle and defeat death only to wind up with a conscious patient suffering from massive brain damage or one who could be sustained "alive" only in a deep coma with the aid of machines.

Jonas knew that his own greatest weakness as a physician was the extremity of his hatred for death. It was an anger he carried at all times. At moments like this the anger could swell into a quiet fury that affected his judgment. Every patient's death was a personal affront to him. He tended to err on the side of optimism, proceeding with a resuscitation that could have more tragic consequences if it succeeded than if it failed.

The other four members of the team understood his weakness, too. They watched him expectantly.

If the operating room had been tomb-still before, it was now as silent as the vacuum of any lonely place between the stars where God, if He existed, passed judgment on His helpless creations.

Jonas was acutely aware of the precious seconds ticking past.

The patient had been in the operating room less than two minutes. But two minutes could make all the difference.

On the table, Harrison was as dead as any man had ever been. His skin was an unhealthy shade of gray, lips and fingernails and toenails a cyanotic blue, lips slightly parted in an eternal exhalation. His flesh was utterly devoid of the tension of life.

However, aside from the two-inch-long shallow gash on the right side of his forehead, an abrasion on his left jaw, and abrasions on the palms of his hands, he was apparently uninjured. He had been in excellent physical condition for a man of thirty-eight, carrying no more than five extra pounds, with straight bones and well-defined musculature. No matter what might have happened to his brain cells, he *looked* like a perfect candidate for resuscitation.

A decade ago, a physician in Jonas's position would have been guided by the Five-Minute Limit, which then had been acknowledged as the maximum length of time the human brain could go without blood-borne oxygen and suffer no diminution of mental faculties. During the past decade, however, as resuscitation medicine had become an exciting new field, the Five-Minute Limit had been exceeded so often that it was eventually disregarded. With new drugs that acted as free-radical scavengers, machines that could cool and heat blood, massive doses of epinephrine, and other tools, doctors could step well past the Five-Minute Limit and snatch some patients back from deeper regions of death. And hypothermia—extreme cooling of the brain which blocked the swift and ruinous chemical changes in cells following death— could extend the length of time a patient might lie dead yet be successfully revived. Twenty minutes was common. Thirty was not hopeless. Cases of triumphant resuscitation at forty and fifty minutes were on record. In 1988, a two-year-old girl in Utah, plucked from an icy river, was brought back to life without any apparent brain damage after being dead at least sixty-six minutes, and only last year a twenty-year-old woman in Pennsylvania had been revived with all faculties intact seventy minutes after death.

The other four members of the team were still staring at Jonas.

Death, he told himself, is just another pathological state.

Most pathological states could be reversed with treatment.

Dead was one thing. But *cold* and dead was another.

To Gina, he said, "How long's he been dead?"

Part of Gina's job was to serve as liaison, by radio, with the on-site paramedics and make a record of the information most vital to the resuscitation team at this moment of decision. She looked at her watch—a Rolex on an incongruous pink leather band to match her socks—and did not even have to pause to calculate: "Sixty minutes, but they're only guessing how long he was dead in the water before they found him. Could be longer."

"Or shorter," Jonas said.

While Jonas made his decision, Helga rounded the table to Gina's side and, together, they began to study the flesh on the cadaver's left arm, searching for the major vein, just in case Jonas decided to resuscitate. Locating blood vessels in the slack flesh of a corpse was not always easy, since applying a rubber tourniquet would not increase systemic pressure. There *was* no pressure in the system.

"Okay, I'm going to call it," Jonas said.

He looked around at Ken, Kari, Helga, and Gina, giving them one last chance to challenge him. Then he checked his own Timex wristwatch and said, "It's nine-twelve P.M., Monday night, March fourth. The patient, Hatchford Benjamin Harrison, is dead . . . but retrievable."

To their credit, whatever their doubts might have been, no one on the team hesitated once the call had been made. They had the right—and the duty—to advise Jonas as he was making the decision, but once it was made, they put all of their knowledge, skill, and training to work to insure that the "retrievable" part of his call proved correct.

Dear God, Jonas thought, I hope I've done the right thing.

Already Gina had inserted an exsanguination needle into the vein that she and Helga had located. Together they switched on and adjusted the bypass machine, which would draw the blood out of Harrison's body and gradually warm it to one hundred degrees. Once warmed, the blood would be pumped back into the still-blue patient through another tube feeding a needle inserted in a thigh vein.

With the process begun, more urgent work awaited than time to do it. Harrison's vital signs, currently nonexistent, had to be monitored for the first indications of response to therapy. The treatment already provided by the paramedics needed to be reviewed to determine if a previously administered dose of epinephrine—a heart-stimulating hormone—was so large as to rule out giving more of it to Harrison at this time. Meanwhile Jonas pulled up a wheeled cart of medications, prepared by Helga before the body had arrived, and began to calculate the variety and quantity of ingredients for a chemical cocktail of free-radical scavengers designed to retard tissue damage.

"Sixty-one minutes," Gina said, updating them on the estimated length of time that the patient had been dead. "Wow! That's a long time talking to the angels. Getting this one back isn't going to be a weenie roast, boys and girls."

"Forty-eight degrees," Helga reported solemnly, noting the cadaver's body temperature as it slowly rose toward the temperature of the room around it.

Death is just an ordinary pathological state, Jonas reminded himself. Pathological states can usually be reversed.

With her incongruously slender, long-fingered hands, Helga folded a cotton surgical towel over the patient's genitals, and Jonas recognized that she was not merely making a concession to modesty but was performing an act of kindness that expressed an important new attitude toward Harrison. A dead man had no interest in modesty. A dead man did not require kindness. Helga's consideration was a way of saying that she believed this man would once more be one of the living, welcomed back to the brotherhood and sisterhood of humanity, and that he should be treated henceforth with tenderness and compassion and not just as an interesting and challenging prospect for reanimation.

2

The weeds and grass were as high as his knees, lush from an unusually rainy winter. A cool breeze whispered through the meadow. Occasionally bats and night birds passed overhead or swooped low off to one side, briefly drawn to him as if they recognized a fellow predator but immediately repelled when they sensed the terrible difference between him and them.

He stood defiantly, gazing up at the stars shining between the steadily thickening clouds that moved eastward across the late-winter sky. He believed that the universe was a kingdom of death, where life was so rare as to be freakish, a place filled with countless barren planets, a testament not to the creative powers of God but to the sterility of His imagination and the triumph of the forces of darkness aligned against Him. Of the two realities that coexisted in this universe—life and death—life was the smaller and less consequential. As a citizen in the land of the living, your existence was limited to years, months, weeks, days, hours. But as a citizen in the kingdom of the dead, you were immortal.

He lived in the borderland.

He hated the world of the living, into which he had been born. He loathed the pretense to meaning and manners and morals and virtue that the living embraced. The hypocrisy of human interaction, wherein selflessness was publicly championed and selfishness privately pursued, both amused and disgusted him. Every act of kindness seemed, to him, to be performed only with an eye to the payback that might one day be extracted from the recipient.

His greatest scorn—and sometimes fury—was reserved for those who spoke of love and made claims to feeling such a thing. Love, he knew, was like all the other high-minded virtues that family, teachers, and priests blathered about. It didn't exist. It was a sham, a way to control others, a con.

He cherished, instead, the darkness and strange anti-life of the world of the dead in which he belonged but to which he could not yet return. His rightful place was with the damned. He felt at home among those who despised love, who knew that the pursuit of pleasure was the sole purpose of existence. Self was primary. There were no such things as "wrong" and "sin."

The longer he stared at the stars between the clouds, the brighter they appeared, until each pinpoint of light in the void seemed to prick his eyes. Tears of discomfort blurred his vision, and he lowered his gaze to the earth at his feet. Even at night, the land of the living was too bright for the likes of him. He didn't need light to see. His vision had adapted to the perfect blackness of death, to the catacombs of Hell. Light was not merely superfluous to eyes like his; it was a nuisance and, at times, an abomination.

Ignoring the heavens, he walked out of the field, returning to the cracked pavement. His footsteps echoed hollowly through this place that had once been filled with the voices and laughter of multitudes. If he had wanted, he could have moved with the silence of a stalking cat.

The clouds parted and the lunar lamp beamed down, making him wince. On all sides, the decaying structures of his hideaway cast stark and jagged shadows in moonlight that would have seemed wan to anyone else but that, to him, shimmered on the pavement as if it were luminous paint.

He took a pair of sunglasses from an inside pocket of his leather jacket and put them on. That was better.

For a moment he hesitated, not sure what he wanted to do with the rest of the night. He had two basic choices, really: spend the remaining pre-dawn hours with the living or with the dead. This time it was even an easier choice than usual, for in his current mood, he much preferred the dead.

He stepped out of a moon-shadow that resembled a giant, canted, broken wheel, and he headed toward the moldering structure where he kept the dead. His collection.

3

"Sixty-four minutes," Gina said, consulting her Rolex with the pink leather band. "This one could get messy."

Jonas couldn't believe how fast time was passing, just speeding by, surely faster than usual, as if there had been some freak acceleration of the continuum. But it was always the same in situations like this, when the difference between life and death was measured in minutes and seconds.

He glanced at the blood, more blue than red, moving through the clear-plastic exsanguination tube into the purring bypass machine. The average human body contained five liters of blood. Before the resuscitation team was done with Harrison, his five liters would have been repeatedly recycled, heated, and filtered.

Ken Nakamura was at a light board, studying head and chest X rays and body-sonograms that had been taken in the air ambulance during its hundred-eighty-mile-per-hour journey from the base of the San Bernardinos to the hospital in Newport Beach. Kari was bent close to the patient's face, examining his eyes through an ophthalmoscope, checking for indications of dangerous cranial pressure from a buildup of fluid on the brain.

With Helga's assistance, Jonas had filled a series of syringes with large doses of various free-radical neutralizers. Vitamins E and C were effective scavengers and had the advantage of being natural substances, but he also intended to administer a lazeroid—tirilazad mesylate—and phenyl tertiary butyl nitrone.

Free radicals were fast-moving, unstable molecules that ricocheted through the body, causing chemical reactions that damaged most cells with which they came into contact. Current theory held that they were the primary cause of human aging, which explained why natural scavengers like vitamins E and C boosted the immune system and, in long-term users, promoted a more youthful appearance and higher energy levels. Free radicals were a by-product of ordinary metabolic processes and were always present in the system. But when the body was deprived of oxygenated blood for an extended period, even with the protection of hypothermia, huge pools of free radicals were created in excess of anything the body had to deal with normally. When the heart was started again, renewed circulation swept those destructive molecules through the brain, where their impact was devastating.

The vitamin and chemical scavengers would deal with the free radicals before they could cause any irreversible damage. At least that was the hope.

Jonas inserted the three syringes in different ports that fed the main intravenous line in the patient's thigh, but he did not yet inject the contents.

"Sixty-five minutes," Gina said.

A long time dead, Jonas thought.

It was very near the record for a successful reanimation.

In spite of the cool air, Jonas felt sweat breaking out on his scalp, under his thinning hair. He always got too involved, emotional. Some of his colleagues disapproved of his excessive empathy; they believed a judicious perspective was insured by the

58

maintenance of a professional distance between the doctor and those he treated. But no patient was *just* a patient. Every one of them was loved and needed by someone. Jonas was acutely aware that if he failed a patient, he was failing more than one person, bringing pain and suffering to a wide network of relatives and friends. Even when he was treating someone like Harrison, of whom Jonas knew virtually nothing, he began to *imagine* the lives interlinking with that of the patient, and he felt responsible to them as much as he would have if he had known them intimately.

"The guy looks clean," Ken said, turning away from the X rays and sonograms. "No broken bones. No internal injuries."

"But those sonograms were taken after he was dead," Jonas noted, "so they don't show *functioning* organs."

"Right. We'll snap some pictures again when he's reanimated, make sure nothing's ruptured, but it looks good so far."

Straightening up from her examination of the dead man's eyes, Kari Dovell said, "There might be concussion to deal with. Hard to say from what I can see."

"Sixty-six minutes."

"Seconds count here. Be ready, people," Jonas said, although he knew they were ready.

The cool air couldn't reach his head because of his surgical cap, but the sweat on his scalp felt icy. Shivers cascaded through him.

Blood, heated to one hundred degrees, began to move through the clear plastic IV line and into the body through a thigh vein, surging rhythmically to the artificial pulse of the bypass machine.

Jonas depressed the plungers halfway on each of the three syringes, introducing heavy doses of the free-radical scavengers into the first blood passing through the line. He waited less than a minute, then swiftly depressed the plungers all the way.

Helga had already prepared three more syringes according to his instructions. He removed the depleted ones from the IV ports and introduced the full syringes without injecting any of their contents.

Ken had moved the portable defibrillation machine next to the patient. Subsequent to reanimation, if Harrison's heart began to beat erratically or chaotically—fibrillation—it might be coerced

59

into a normal rhythm by the application of an electric shock. That
was a last-hope strategy, however, for violent defibrillation could
also have a serious adverse effect on a patient who, having been
recently brought back from the dead, was in an exceptionally
fragile state.

Consulting the digital thermometer, Kari said, "His body temperature's up to only fifty-six degrees."

"Sixty-seven minutes," Gina said.

"Too slow," Jonas said.

"External heat?"

Jonas hesitated.

"Let's go for it," Ken advised.

"Fifty-seven degrees," Kari said.

"At this rate," Helga said worriedly, "we're going to be past
eighty minutes before he's anywhere near warm enough for the
heart to kick in."

Heating pads had been placed under the operating-table sheet
before the patient had been brought into the room. They extended
the length of his spine.

"Okay," Jonas said.

Kari clicked the switch on the heating pads.

"But easy," Jonas advised.

Kari adjusted the temperature controls.

They needed to warm the body, but potential problems could
arise from a too-rapid reheating. Every resuscitation was a tight-
rope walk.

Jonas tended to the syringes in the IV ports, administering
additional doses of vitamins E and C, tirilazad mesylate, and
phenyl tertiary butyl nitrone.

The patient was motionless, pale. He reminded Jonas of a figure
in a life-size tableau in some old cathedral: the supine body of
Christ sculpted from white marble, rendered by the artist in the
position of entombment as He would have rested just prior to the
most successful resurrection of all time.

Because Kari Dovell had peeled back Harrison's eyelids for the
ophthalmoscopic examination, his eyes were open, staring sight-

lessly at the ceiling, and Gina was putting artificial tears in them with a dropper to insure that the lenses did not dry out. She hummed "Little Surfer Girl" as she worked. She was a Beach Boys fan.

No shock or fear was visible in the cadaver's eyes, as one might have expected. Instead, they held an expression that was almost peaceful, almost touched by wonder. Harrison looked as if he had seen something, in the moment of death, to lift his heart.

Finishing with the eyedrops, Gina checked her watch. "Sixty-eight minutes."

Jonas had the crazy urge to tell her to shut up, as though time would halt as long as she was not calling it out, minute by minute.

Blood pumped in and out of the bypass machine.

"Sixty-two degrees." Helga spoke so sternly that she might have been chastising the dead man for the laggardly pace of his reheating.

Flat lines on the EKG.

Flat lines on the EEG.

"Come on," Jonas urged. "Come on, come on."

4

He entered the museum of the dead not through one of its upper doors but through the waterless lagoon. In that shallow depression, three gondolas still lay on the cracked concrete. They were ten-passenger models that had long ago been tipped off the heavy chain-drive track along which they'd once carried their happy passengers. Even at night, wearing sunglasses, he could see they did not have the swan-neck prows of real gondolas in Venice, but sported leering gargoyles as figureheads, hand-carved from wood, garishly painted, perhaps fearsome at one time but now cracked, weathered, and peeling. The lagoon doors, which in better days had swung smoothly out of the way at the approach of each gondola, were no longer motorized. One of them was frozen open;

the other was closed, but it was hanging from only two of its four corroded hinges. He walked through the open door into a passageway that was far blacker than the night behind him.

He took off the sunglasses. He didn't need them in that gloom.

Neither did he require a flashlight. Where an ordinary man would have been blind, he could see.

The concrete sluiceway, along which the gondolas had once moved, was three feet deep and eight feet wide. A much narrower channel in the sluiceway floor contained the rusted chain-drive mechanism—a long series of blunt, curved, six-inch-high hooks that had pulled the boats forward by engaging the steel loops on the bottoms of their hulls. When the ride had been in operation, those hooks had been concealed by water, contributing to the illusion that the gondolas were actually adrift. Now, dwindling into the dreary realm ahead, they looked like a row of stubby spines on the back of an immense prehistoric reptile.

The world of the living, he thought, is always fraught with deception. Beneath the placid surface, ugly mechanisms grind away at secret tasks.

He walked deeper into the building. The gradual downward slope of the sluiceway was at first barely perceptible, but he was aware of it because he had passed that way many times before.

Above him, to either side of the channel, were concrete service walks, about four feet wide. Beyond them were the tunnel walls, which had been painted black to serve as a non-reflective backdrop for the moments of half-baked theater performed in front of them.

The walkways widened occasionally to form niches, in some places even whole rooms. When the ride had been in operation, the niches had been filled with tableaus meant to amuse or horrify or both: ghosts and goblins, ghouls and monsters, ax-wielding madmen standing over the prostrate bodies of their beheaded victims. In one of the room-sized areas, there had been an elaborate graveyard filled with stalking zombies; in another, a large and convincing flying saucer had disgorged blood-thirsty aliens with a shark's profusion of teeth in their huge heads. The robotic figures had moved, grimaced, reared up, and threatened all passersby with tape-recorded voices, eternally repeating the same brief programmed dramas with the same menacing words and snarls.

No, not eternally. They were gone now, carted away by the official salvagers, by agents of the creditors, or by scavengers.

Nothing was eternal.

Except death.

A hundred feet beyond the entrance doors, he reached the end of the first section of the chain-drive. The tunnel floor, which had been sloping imperceptibly, now tilted down sharply, at about a thirty-five-degree angle, falling away into flawless blackness. Here, the gondolas had slipped free of the blunt hooks in the channel floor and, with a stomach-wrenching lurch, sailed down a hundred-and-fifty-foot incline, knifing into the pool below with a colossal splash that drenched the passengers up front, much to the delight of those fortunate—or smart—enough to get a seat in the back.

Because he was not like ordinary men and possessed certain special powers, he could see part of the way down the incline, even in that utterly lightless environment, although his perception did not extend to the very bottom. His catlike night vision was limited: within a radius of ten or fifteen feet, he could see as clearly as if he stood in daylight; thereafter, objects grew blurry, steadily less distinct, shadowy, until darkness swallowed everything at a distance of perhaps forty or fifty feet.

Leaning backward to retain his balance on the steep slope, he headed down into the bowels of the abandoned funhouse. He was not afraid of what might wait below. Nothing could frighten him any more. After all, he was deadlier and more savage than anything with which this world could threaten him.

Before he descended half the distance to the lower chamber, he detected the odor of death. It rose to him on currents of cool dry air. The stench excited him. No perfume, regardless of how exquisite, even if applied to the tender throat of a lovely woman, could ever thrill him as profoundly as the singular, sweet fragrance of corrupted flesh.

5

Under the halogen lamps, the stainless-steel and white-enameled surfaces of the operating room were a little hard on the eyes, like the geometric configurations of an arctic landscape polished by the glare of a winter sun. The room seemed to have gotten chillier, as if the heat flowing into the dead man was pushing the cold out of him, thereby lowering the air temperature. Jonas Nyebern shivered.

Helga checked the digital thermometer that was patched to Harrison. "Body temperature's up to seventy degrees."

"Seventy-two minutes," Gina said.

"We're going for the brass ring now," Ken said. "Medical history, the *Guinness Book of World Records,* TV appearances, books, movies, T-shirts with our faces on 'em, novelty hats, plastic lawn ornaments in our images."

"Some dogs have been brought back after ninety minutes," Kari reminded him.

"Yeah," Ken said, "but they were *dogs*. Besides, they were so screwed up, they chased bones and buried cars."

Gina and Kari laughed softly, and the joke seemed to break the tension for everyone except Jonas. He could never relax for a moment in the process of a resuscitation, although he knew that it was possible for a physician to get so tightly wound that he was no longer performing at his peak. Ken's ability to vent a little nervous energy was admirable, and in the service of the patient; however, Jonas was incapable of doing likewise in the midst of a battle.

"Seventy-two degrees, seventy-three."

It *was* a battle. Death was the adversary: clever, mighty, and relentless. To Jonas, death was not *just* a pathological state, not merely the inevitable fate of all living things, but actually an entity that walked the world, perhaps not always the robed figure of myth with its skeletal face hidden in the shadows of a cowl, but a very real presence nonetheless, Death with a capital D.

"Seventy-four degrees," Helga said.

Gina said, "Seventy-three minutes."

Jonas introduced more free-radical scavengers into the blood that surged through the IV line.

He supposed that his belief in Death as a supernatural force with a will and consciousness of its own, his certainty that it sometimes walked the earth in an embodied form, his awareness of its presence right now in this room in a cloak of invisibility, would seem like silly superstition to his colleagues. It might even be regarded as a sign of mental imbalance or incipient madness. But Jonas was confident of his sanity. After all, his belief in Death was based on empirical evidence. He had *seen* the hated enemy when he was only seven years old, had heard it speak, had looked into its eyes and smelled its fetid breath and felt its icy touch upon his face.

"Seventy-five degrees."

"Get ready," Jonas said.

The patient's body temperature was nearing a threshold beyond which reanimation might begin at any moment. Kari finished filling a hypodermic syringe with epinephrine, and Ken activated the defibrillation machine to let it build up a charge. Gina opened the flow valve on a tank containing an oxygen–carbon dioxide mixture that had been formulated to the special considerations of resuscitation procedures, and picked up the mask of the pulmonary machine to make sure it was functioning.

"Seventy-six degrees," Helga said, "seventy-seven."

Gina checked her watch. "Coming up on . . . seventy-four minutes."

6

At the bottom of the long incline, he entered a cavernous room as large as an airplane hangar. Hell had once been re-created there, according to the unimaginative vision of an amusement-park designer, complete with gas-jet fires lapping at formed-concrete rocks around the perimeter.

The gas had been turned off long ago. Hell was tar-black now. But not to him, of course.

He moved slowly across the concrete floor, which was bisected by a serpentine channel housing another chain-drive. There, the gondolas had moved through a lake of water made to look like a lake of fire by clever lighting and bubbling air hoses that simulated boiling oil. As he walked, he savored the stench of decay, which grew more exquisitely pungent by the second.

A dozen mechanical demons had once stood on higher formations, spreading immense bat wings, peering down with glowing eyes that periodically raked the passing gondolas with harmless crimson laser beams. Eleven of the demons had been hauled away, peddled to some competing park or sold for scrap. For unknown reasons, one devil remained—a silent and unmoving agglomeration of rusted metal, moth-eaten fabric, torn plastic, and grease-caked hydraulic mechanisms. It was still perched on a rocky spire two-thirds of the way toward the high ceiling, pathetic rather than frightening.

As he passed beneath that sorry funhouse figure, he thought, *I am the only real demon this place has ever known or ever will,* and that pleased him.

Months ago he stopped thinking of himself by his Christian name. He adopted the name of a fiend that he had read about in a book on Satanism. Vassago. One of the three most powerful demon princes of Hell, who answered only to His Satanic Majesty. Vassago. He liked the sound of it. When he said it aloud, the name rolled from his tongue so easily that it seemed as if he'd never answered to anything else.

"Vassago."

In the heavy subterranean silence, it echoed back to him from the concrete rocks: *"Vassago."*

7

"Eighty degrees."

"It should be happening," Ken said.

Surveying the monitors, Kari said, "Flat lines, just flat lines."

Her long, swanlike neck was so slender that Jonas could see her pulse pounding rapidly in her carotid artery.

He looked down at the dead man's neck. No pulse there.

"Seventy-five minutes," Gina announced.

"If he comes around, it's officially a record now," Ken said. "We'll be obligated to celebrate, get drunk, puke on our shoes, and make fools of ourselves."

"Eighty-one degrees."

Jonas was so frustrated that he could not speak—for fear of uttering an obscenity or a low, savage snarl of anger. They had made all the right moves, but they were losing. He hated losing. He hated Death. He hated the limitations of modern medicine, all circumscriptions of human knowledge, and his own inadequacies.

"Eighty-two degrees."

Suddenly the dead man gasped.

Jonas twitched and looked at the monitors.

The EKG showed spastic movement in the patient's heart.

"Here we go," Kari said.

8

The robotic figures of the damned, more than a hundred in Hell's heyday, were gone with eleven of the twelve demons; gone, as well, were the wails of agony and the lamentations that had been broadcast through their speaker-grille mouths. The desolate chamber, however, was not without lost souls. But now it housed something more appropriate than robots, more like the real thing: Vassago's collection.

At the center of the room, Satan waited in all his majesty, fierce and colossal. A circular pit in the floor, sixteen to eighteen feet in diameter, housed a massive statue of the Prince of Darkness himself. He was not shown from the waist down; but from his navel to the tips of his segmented horns, he measured thirty feet. When the funhouse had been in operation, the monstrous sculpture waited in a thirty-five-foot pit, hidden beneath the lake, then periodically surged up out of its lair, water cascading from it, huge eyes afire, monstrous jaws working, sharp teeth gnashing, forked tongue flickering, thundering a warning—"Abandon hope all ye who enter here!"—and then laughing malevolently.

Vassago had ridden the gondolas several times as a boy, when he had been one of the wholly alive, before he had become a citizen of the borderland, and in those days he had been spooked by the handcrafted devil, affected especially by its hideous laugh. If the machinery had overcome years of corrosion and suddenly brought the cackling monster to life again, Vassago would not have been impressed, for he was now old enough and sufficiently experienced to know that Satan was incapable of laughter.

He halted near the base of the towering Lucifer and studied it with a mixture of scorn and admiration. It was corny, yes, a funhouse fake meant to test the bladders of small children and give teenage girls a reason to squeal and cuddle for protection in the arms of their smirking boyfriends. But he had to admit that it was also an inspired creation, because the designer had not opted for the traditional image of Satan as a lean-faced, sharp-nosed, thin-lipped Lothario of troubled souls, hair slicked back from a widow's peak, goatee sprouting absurdly from a pointed chin. Instead, this was a Beast worthy of the title: part reptile, part insect, part humanoid, repulsive enough to command respect, just familiar enough to seem real, alien enough to be awesome. Several years of dust, moisture, and mold had contributed a patina that softened the garish carnival colors and lent it the authority of one of those gigantic stone statues of Egyptian gods found in ancient sand-covered temples, far beneath the desert dunes.

Although he didn't know what Lucifer actually looked like, and though he assumed that the Father of Lies would be far more heart-chilling and formidable than this funhouse version, Vassago found the plastic and polyfoam behemoth sufficiently impressive to make it the center of the secret existence that he led within his hideaway. At the base of it, on the dry concrete floor of the drained lake, he had arranged his collection partly for his own pleasure and amusement but also as an offering to the god of terror and pain.

The naked and decaying bodies of seven women and three men were displayed to their best advantage, as if they were ten exquisite sculptures by some perverse Michelangelo in a museum of death.

9

A single shallow gasp, one brief spasm of the heart muscles, and an involuntary nerve reaction that made his right arm twitch and his fingers open and close like the curling legs of a dying spider—those were the only signs of life the patient exhibited before settling once more into the still and silent posture of the dead.

"Eighty-three degrees," Helga said.

Ken Nakamura wondered: "Defibrillation?"

Jonas shook his head. "His heart's not in fibrillation. It's not beating at all. Just wait."

Kari was holding a syringe. "More epinephrine?"

Jonas stared intently at the monitors. "Wait. We don't want to bring him back only to overmedicate him and precipitate a heart attack."

"Seventy-six minutes," Gina said, her voice as youthful and breathless and perkily excited as if she were announcing the score in a game of beach volleyball.

"Eighty-four degrees."

Harrison gasped again. His heart stuttered, sending a series of spikes across the screen of the electrocardiograph. His whole body shuddered. Then he went flatline again.

Grabbing the handles on the positive and negative pads of the defibrillation machine, Ken looked expectantly at Jonas.

"Eighty-five degrees," Helga announced. "He's in the right thermal territory, and he wants to come back."

Jonas felt a bead of sweat trickle with centipede swiftness down his right temple and along his jaw line. The hardest part was waiting, giving the patient a chance to kick-start himself before risking more punishing techniques of forced reanimation.

A third spasm of heart activity registered as a shorter burst of spikes than the previous one, and it was not accompanied by a pulmonary response as before. No muscle contractions were visible, either. Harrison lay slack and cold.

"He's not able to make the leap," Kari Dovell said.

Ken agreed. "We're gonna lose him."

"Seventy-seven minutes," Gina said.

Not four days in the tomb, like Lazarus, before Jesus had called him forth, Jonas thought, but a long time dead nevertheless.

"Epinephrine," Jonas said.

Kari handed the hypodermic syringe to Jonas, and he quickly administered the dosage through one of the same IV ports that he had used earlier to inject free-radical scavengers into the patient's blood.

Ken lifted the negative and positive pads of the defibrillation machine, and positioned himself over the patient, ready to give him a jolt if it came to that.

Then the massive charge of epinephrine, a powerful hormone extracted from the adrenal glands of sheep and cattle and referred to by some resuscitation specialists as "reanimator juice," hit Harrison as hard as any electrical shock that Ken Nakamura was prepared to give him. The stale breath of the grave exploded from him, he gasped air as if he were still drowning in that icy river, he shuddered violently, and his heart began to beat like that of a rabbit with a fox close on its tail.

10

Vassago had arranged each piece in his macabre collection with more than casual contemplation. They were not simply ten corpses dumped unceremoniously on the concrete. He not only respected death but loved it with an ardor akin to Beethoven's passion for music or Rembrandt's fervent devotion to art. Death, after all, was the gift that Satan had brought to the inhabitants of the Garden, a gift disguised as something prettier; he was the Giver of Death, and his was the kingdom of death everlasting.

Any flesh that death had touched was to be regarded with all the reverence that a devout Catholic might reserve for the Eucharist. Just as their god was said to live within that thin wafer of unleavened bread, so the face of Vassago's unforgiving god could be seen everywhere in the patterns of decay and dissolution.

The first body at the base of the thirty-foot Satan was that of Jenny Purcell, a twenty-two-year-old waitress who had worked the evening shift in a re-creation of a 1950s diner, where the jukebox played Elvis Presley and Chuck Berry, Lloyd Price and the Platters, Buddy Holly and Connie Francis and the Everly Brothers. When Vassago had gone in for a burger and a beer, Jenny thought he looked cool in his black clothes, wearing sunglasses indoors at night and making no move to take them off. With his baby-faced good looks given interest by a contrastingly firm set to his jaw and a slight cruel twist to his mouth, and with thick black hair falling across his forehead, he looked a little like a young Elvis. *What's your name,* she asked, and he said, *Vassago,* and she said, *What's your first name,* so he said, *That's it, the whole thing, first and last,* which must have intrigued her, got her imagination going, because she said, *What, you mean like Cher only has one name or Madonna or Sting?* He stared hard at her from behind his heavily tinted sunglasses and said, *Yeah—you have a problem with that?* She didn't have a problem. In fact she was attracted to him. She said he was "different," but only later did she discover just *how* different he really was.

Everything about Jenny marked her as a slut in his eyes, so after killing her with an eight-inch stiletto that he drove under her rib cage and into her heart, he arranged her in a posture suitable for a sexually profligate woman. Once he had stripped her naked, he braced her in a sitting position with her thighs spread wide and knees drawn up. He bound her slender wrists to her shins to keep her upright. Then he used strong lengths of cord to pull her head forward and down farther than she could have managed to do while alive, brutally compressing her midriff; he anchored the cords around her thighs, so she was left eternally looking up the cleft between her legs, contemplating her sins.

Jenny had been the first piece in his collection. Dead for about nine months, trussed up like a ham in a curing barn, she was withered now, a mummified husk, no longer of interest to worms or other agents of decomposition. She did not stink as she had once stunk.

Indeed, in her peculiar posture, having contracted into a ball as she had decayed and dried out, she resembled a human being so little that it was difficult to think of her as ever having been a living person, therefore equally difficult to think of her as a dead person. Consequently, death seemed no longer to reside in her remains. To Vassago, she had ceased to be a corpse and had become merely a curious object, an impersonal thing that might always have been inanimate. As a result, although she was the start of his collection, she was now of minimal interest to him.

He was fascinated solely with death and the dead. The living were of interest to him only insofar as they carried the ripe promise of death within them.

11

The patient's heart oscillated between mild and severe tachycardia, from a hundred and twenty to over two hundred and thirty beats per minute, a transient condition resulting from the epinephrine and hypothermia. Except it wasn't acting like a transient condition. Each time the pulse rate declined, it did not subside as far as it had previously, and with each new acceleration, the EKG showed escalating arrhythmia that could lead only to cardiac arrest.

No longer sweating, calmer now that the decision to fight Death had been made and was being acted upon, Jonas said, "Better hit him with it."

No one doubted to whom he was speaking, and Ken Nakamura pressed the cold pads of the defibrillation machine to Harrison's chest, bracketing his heart. The electrical discharge caused the patient to bounce violently against the table, and a sound like an iron mallet striking a leather sofa—*wham!*—slammed through the room.

Jonas looked at the electrocardiograph just as Kari read the meaning of the spikes of light moving across the display: "Still two hundred a minute but the rhythm's there now . . . steady . . . steady."

Similarly, the electroencephalograph showed alpha and beta brain waves within normal parameters for an unconscious man.

"There's self-sustained pulmonary activity," Ken said.

"Okay," Jonas decided, "let's respirate him and make sure he's getting enough oxygen in those brain cells."

Gina immediately put the oxygen mask on Harrison's face.

"Body temperature's at ninety degrees," Helga reported.

The patient's lips were still somewhat blue, but that same deathly hue had faded from under his fingernails.

Likewise, his muscle tone was partially restored. His flesh no longer had the flaccidity of the dead. As feeling returned to Harrison's deep-chilled extremities, his punished nerve endings excited a host of tics and twitches.

His eyes rolled and jiggled under his closed lids, a sure sign of REM sleep. He was dreaming.

"One hundred and twenty beats a minute," Kari said, "and declining . . . completely rhythmic now . . . very steady."

Gina consulted her watch and let her breath out in a *whoosh* of amazement. "Eighty minutes."

"Sonofabitch," Ken said wonderingly, "that beats the record by ten."

Jonas hesitated only a brief moment before checking the wall clock and making the formal announcement for the benefit of the tape recorder: "Patient successfully resuscitated as of nine-thirty-two Monday evening, March fourth."

A murmur of mutual congratulations accompanied by smiles of relief was as close as they would get to a triumphant cheer of the sort that might have been heard on a real battleground. They were not restrained by modesty but by a keen awareness of Harrison's tenuous condition. They had won the battle with Death, but their patient had not yet regained consciousness. Until he was awake and his mental performance could be tested and evaluated, there was a chance that he had been reanimated only to live out a life of anguish and frustration, his potential tragically circumscribed by irreparable brain damage.

12

Enraptured by the spicy perfume of death, at home in the subterranean bleakness, Vassago walked admiringly past his collection. It encircled one-third of the colossal Lucifer.

Of the male specimens, one had been taken while changing a flat tire on a lonely section of the Ortega Highway at night. Another had been asleep in his car in a public-beach parking lot. The third had tried to pick up Vassago at a bar in Dana Point. The dive hadn't even been a gay hangout; the guy had just been drunk, desperate, lonely—and careless.

Nothing enraged Vassago more than the sexual needs and excitement of others. He had no interest in sex any more, and he never raped any of the women he killed. But his disgust and anger, engendered by the mere perception of sexuality in others, were not a result of jealousy, and did not spring from any sense that his impotency was a curse or even an unfair burden. No, he was glad to be free of lust and longing. Since becoming a citizen of the borderland and accepting the promise of the grave, he did not regret the loss of desire. Though he was not entirely sure *why* the very thought of sex could sometimes throw him into a rage, why a flirtatious wink or a short skirt or a sweater stretched across a full bosom could incite him to torture and homicide, he suspected that it was because sex and life were inextricably entwined. Next to self-preservation, the sex drive was, they said, the most powerful human motivator. Through sex, life was created. Because he hated life in all its gaudy variety, hated it with such intensity, it was only natural that he would hate sex as well.

He preferred to kill women because society encouraged them,

more than men, to flaunt their sexuality, which they did with the assistance of makeup, lipstick, alluring scents, revealing clothes, and coquettish behavior. Besides, from a woman's womb came new life, and Vassago was sworn to destroy life wherever he could. From women came the very thing he loathed in himself: the spark of life that still sputtered in him and prevented him from moving on to the land of the dead, where he belonged.

Of the remaining six female specimens in his collection, two had been housewives, one a young attorney, one a medical secretary, and two college students. Though he had arranged each corpse in a manner fitting the personality, spirit, and weaknesses of the person who had once inhabited it, and though he had considerable talent for cadaver art, making especially clever use of a variety of props, he was far more pleased by the effect he had achieved with one of the students than with all of the others combined.

He stopped walking when he reached her.

He regarded her in the darkness, pleased by his work. . . .

Margaret . . .

He first saw her during one of his restless late-night rambles, in a dimly lighted bar near the university campus, where she was sipping diet cola, either because she was not old enough to be served beer along with her friends or because she was not a drinker. He suspected the latter.

She looked singularly wholesome and uncomfortable in the smoke and din of the tavern. Even from halfway across the room, judging by her reactions to her friends and her body language, Vassago could see that she was a shy girl struggling hard to fit in with the crowd, even though in her heart she knew that she would never entirely belong. The roar of liquor-amplified conversation, the clink and clatter of glasses, the thunderous jukebox music of Madonna and Michael Jackson and Michael Bolton, the stink of cigarettes and stale beer, the moist heat of college boys on the make—none of that touched her. She sat in the bar but existed apart from it, unstained by it, filled with more secret energy than that entire roomful of young men and women combined.

She was so vital, she seemed to glow. Vassago found it hard to believe that the ordinary, sluggish blood of humanity moved through her veins. Surely, instead, her heart pumped the distilled essence of life itself.

Her vitality drew him. It would be enormously satisfying to snuff such a brightly burning flame of life.

To learn where she lived, he followed her home from the bar. For the next two days, he stalked the campus, gathering information about her as diligently as a real student might have researched a term paper.

Her name was Margaret Ann Campion. She was a senior, twenty years old, majoring in music. She could play the piano, flute, clarinet, guitar, and almost any other instrument she took a fancy to learn. Perhaps the best-known and most-admired student in the music program, she was also widely considered to possess an exceptional talent for composition. An essentially shy person, she made a point of forcing herself out of her shell, so music was not her only interest. She was on the track team, the second-fastest woman in their lineup, a spirited competitor; she wrote about music and movies for the student paper; and she was active in the Baptist church.

Her astonishing vitality was evident not merely in the joy with which she wrote and played music, not just in the almost spiritual aura that Vassago had seen in the bar, but also in her physical appearance. She was incomparably beautiful, with the body of a silver-screen sex goddess and the face of a saint. Clear skin. Perfect cheekbones. Full lips, a generous mouth, a beatific smile. Limpid blue eyes. She dressed modestly in an attempt to conceal the sweet fullness of her breasts, the contrasting narrowness of her waist, the firmness of her buttocks, and the long supple lines of her legs. But he was certain that when he stripped her, she would be revealed for what he had known her to be when he had first glimpsed her: a prodigious breeder, a hot furnace of life in which eventually other life of unparalleled brightness would be conceived and shaped.

He wanted her dead.

He wanted to stop her heart and then hold her for hours, feeling the heat of life radiate out of her, until she was cold.

This one murder, it seemed to him, might at last earn him

passage out of the borderland in which he lived and into the land of the dead and damned, where he belonged, where he longed to be.

Margaret made the mistake of going alone to a laundry room in her apartment complex at eleven o'clock at night. Many of the units were leased to financially comfortable senior citizens and, because they were near the University of California at Irvine, to pairs and trios of students who shared the rent. Maybe the tenant mix, the fact that it was a safe and friendly neighborhood, and the abundance of landscape and walkway lighting all combined to give her a false sense of security.

When Vassago entered the laundry room, Margaret had just begun to put her dirty clothes into one of the washing machines. She looked at him with a smile of surprise but with no apparent concern, though he was dressed all in black and wearing sunglasses at night.

She probably thought he was just another university student who favored an eccentric look as a way of proclaiming his rebellious spirit and intellectual superiority. Every campus had a slew of the type, since it was easier to *dress* as a rebellious intellectual than *be* one.

"Oh, I'm sorry, Miss," he said, "I didn't realize anyone was in here."

"That's okay. I'm only using just one washer," she said. "There're two others."

"No, I already did my laundry, then back at the apartment when I took it out of the basket, I was missing one sock, so I figure it's got to be in one of the washers or dryers. But I didn't mean to get in your way. Sorry about that."

She smiled a little broader, maybe because she thought it funny that a would-be James Dean, black-clad rebel without a cause, would choose to be so polite—or would do his own laundry and chase down lost socks.

By then he was beside her. He hit her in the face—two hard, sharp punches that knocked her unconscious. She crumpled onto the vinyl-tile floor as if she were a pile of laundry.

Later, in the dismantled Hell under the moldering funhouse,

when she regained consciousness and found herself naked on the concrete floor and effectively blind in those lightless confines, tied hand and foot, she did not attempt to bargain for her life as some of the others had done. She didn't offer her body to him, didn't pretend to be turned on by his savagery or the power that he wielded over her. She didn't offer him money, or claim to understand and sympathize with him in a pathetic attempt to convert him from nemesis to friend. Neither did she scream nor weep nor wail nor curse. She was different from the others, for she found hope and comfort in a quiet, dignified, unending chain of whispered prayers. But she never prayed to be delivered from her tormentor and returned to the world out of which she had been torn—as if she knew that death was inevitable. Instead, she prayed that her family would be given the strength to cope with the loss of her, that God would take care of her two younger sisters, and even that her murderer would receive divine grace and mercy.

Vassago swiftly came to loathe her. He knew that love and mercy were nonexistent, just empty words. *He* had never felt love, neither during his time in the borderland nor when he had been one of the living. Often, however, he had pretended to love someone—father, mother, a girl—to get what he wanted, and they had always been deceived. Being deceived into believing that love existed in others, when it didn't exist in you, was a sign of fatal weakness. Human interaction was nothing but a game, after all, and the ability to see through deception was what separated the good players from the inept.

To show her that he could not be deceived and that her god was powerless, Vassago rewarded her quiet prayers with a long and painful death. At last she *did* scream. But her screams were not satisfying, for they were only the sounds of physical agony; they did not reverberate with terror, rage, or despair.

He thought he would like her better when she was dead, but even then he still hated her. For a few minutes he held her body against him, feeling the heat drain from it. But the chilly advance of death through her flesh was not as thrilling as it should have been. Because she had died with an unbroken faith in life everlasting, she had cheated Vassago of the satisfaction of seeing the awareness of death in her eyes. He pushed her limp body aside in disgust.

Now, two weeks after Vassago had finished with her, Margaret Campion knelt in perpetual prayer on the floor of that dismantled Hell, the most recent addition to his collection. She remained upright because she was lashed to a length of steel rebar which he had inserted into a hole he had drilled in the concrete. Naked, she faced away from the giant, funhouse devil. Though she had been Baptist, a crucifix was clasped in her dead hands because Vassago liked the image of the crucifix better than a simple cross; it was turned upside down, with Christ's thorn-prickled head toward the floor. Margaret's own head had been cut off then resewn to her neck with obsessive care. Even though her body was turned away from Satan, she faced toward him in denial of the crucifix held irreverently in her hands. Her posture was symbolic of hypocrisy, mocking her pretense to faith, love, and life everlasting.

Although Vassago hadn't received nearly as much pleasure from murdering Margaret as from what he had done to her after she was dead, he was still pleased to have made her acquaintance. Her stubbornness, stupidity, and self-deception had made her death less satisfying for him than it should have been, but at least the aura he had seen around her in the bar was quenched. Her irritating vitality was drained away. The only energy her body harbored was that of the multitudinous carrion-eaters that teemed within her, consuming her flesh and bent on reducing her to a dry husk like Jenny, the waitress, who rested at the other end of the collection.

As he studied Margaret, a familiar need arose in him. Finally the need became a compulsion. He turned away from his collection, retracing his path across the huge room, heading for the ramp that led up to the entrance tunnel. Ordinarily, selecting another acquisition, killing it, and arranging it in the most aesthetically satisfying pose would have left him quiescent and sated for as much as a month. But after less than two weeks, he was compelled to find another worthy sacrifice.

Regretfully, he ascended the ramp, out of the purifying scent of death, into air tainted with the odors of life, like a vampire driven to hunt the living though preferring the company of the dead.

13

At ten-thirty, almost an hour after Harrison was resuscitated, he remained unconscious. His body temperature was normal. His vital signs were good. And though the patterns of alpha and beta brain waves were those of a man in a profound sleep, they were not obviously indicative of anything as deep as a coma.

When Jonas finally declared the patient out of immediate danger and ordered him moved to a private room on the fifth floor, Ken Nakamura and Kari Dovell elected to go home. Leaving Helga and Gina with the patient, Jonas accompanied the neurologist and the pediatrician to the scrub sinks, and eventually as far as the door to the staff parking lot. They discussed Harrison and what procedures might have to be performed on him in the morning, but for the most part they shared inconsequential small talk about hospital politics and gossip involving mutual acquaintances, as if they had not just participated in a miracle that should have made such banalities impossible.

Beyond the glass door, the night looked cold and inhospitable. Rain had begun to fall. Puddles were filling every depression in the pavement, and in the reflected glow of the parking-lot lamps, they looked like shattered mirrors, collections of sharp silvery shards.

Kari leaned against Jonas, kissed his cheek, clung to him for a moment. She seemed to want to say something but was unable to find the words. Then she pulled back, turned up the collar of her coat, and went out into the wind-driven rain.

Lingering after Kari's departure, Ken Nakamura said, "I hope you realize she's a perfect match for you."

Through the rain-streaked glass door, Jonas watched the woman as she hurried toward her car. He would have been lying if he had said that he never looked at Kari as a woman. Though tall, rangy, and a formidable presence, she was also feminine.

Sometimes he marveled at the delicacy of her wrists, at her swan-like neck that seemed too gracefully thin to support her head. Intellectually and emotionally she was stronger than she looked. Otherwise she couldn't have dealt with the obstacles and challenges that surely had blocked her advance in the medical profession, which was still dominated by men for whom—in some cases—chauvinism was less a character trait than an article of faith.

Ken said, "All you'd have to do is ask her, Jonas."

"I'm not free to do that," Jonas said.

"You can't mourn Marion forever."

"It's only been two years."

"Yeah, but you have to step back into life sometime."

"Not yet."

"Ever?"

"I don't know."

Outside, halfway across the parking lot, Kari Dovell had gotten into her car.

"She won't wait forever," Ken said.

"Goodnight, Ken."

"I can take a hint."

"Good," Jonas said.

Smiling ruefully, Ken pulled open the door, letting in a gust of wind that spat jewel-clear drops of rain on the gray tile floor. He hurried out into the night.

Jonas turned away from the door and followed a series of hallways to the elevators. He went up to the fifth floor.

He hadn't needed to tell Ken and Kari that he would spend the night in the hospital. They knew he always stayed after an apparently successful reanimation. To them, resuscitation medicine was a fascinating new field, an interesting sideline to their primary work, a way to expand their professional knowledge and keep their minds flexible; every success was deeply satisfying, a reminder of why they had become physicians in the first place—to heal. But it was more than that to Jonas. Each reanimation was a battle won in an endless war with Death, not just a healing act but an act of defiance, an angry fist raised in the face of fate.

81

Resuscitation medicine was his love, his passion, his definition of himself, his only reason for arising in the morning and getting on with life in a world that had otherwise become too colorless and purposeless to endure.

He had submitted applications and proposals to half a dozen universities, seeking to teach in their medical schools in return for the establishment of a resuscitation-medicine research facility under his supervision, for which he felt able to raise a sizable part of the financing. He was well-known and widely respected both as a cardiovascular surgeon and a reanimation specialist, and he was confident that he would soon obtain the position he wanted. But he was impatient. He was no longer satisfied with supervising reanimations. He wanted to study the effects of short-term death on human cells, explore the mechanisms of free-radicals and free-radical scavengers, test his own theories, and find new ways to evict Death from those in whom it had already taken up tenancy.

On the fifth floor, at the nurses' station, he learned that Harrison had been taken to 518. It was a semi-private room, but an abundance of empty beds in the hospital insured that it would be effectively maintained as a private unit as long as Harrison was likely to need it.

When Jonas entered 518, Helga and Gina were finishing with the patient, who was in the bed farthest from the door and nearest the rain-spotted window. They had gotten him into a hospital gown and hooked him to another electrocardiograph with a telemetry function that would reproduce his heart rhythms on a monitor at the nurses' station. A bottle of clear fluid hung from a rack beside the bed, feeding an IV line into the patient's left arm, which was already beginning to bruise from other intravenous injections administered by the paramedics earlier in the evening; the clear fluid was glucose enriched with an antibiotic to prevent dehydration and to guard against one of the many infections that could undo everything that had been achieved in the resuscitation room. Helga had smoothed Harrison's hair with a comb that she was now tucking away in the nightstand drawer. Gina was delicately applying a lubricant to his eyelids to prevent them from sticking together, a danger with comatose patients who spent long periods of time without opening their eyes or even blinking and who sometimes suffered from diminished lachrymal-gland secretion.

"Heart's still steady as a metronome," Gina said when she saw Jonas. "I have a hunch, before the end of the week, this one's going to be out playing golf, dancing, doing whatever he wants." She brushed at her bangs, which were an inch too long and hanging in her eyes. "He's a lucky man."

"One hour at a time," Jonas cautioned, knowing too well how Death liked to tease them by pretending to retreat, then returning in a rush to snatch away their victory.

When Gina and Helga left for the night, Jonas turned off all the lights. Illuminated only by the faint fluorescent wash from the corridor and the green glow of the cardiac monitor, room 518 was replete with shadows.

It was silent, too. The audio signal on the EKG had been turned off, leaving only the rhythmically bouncing light endlessly making its way across the screen. The only sounds were the soft moans of the wind at the window and the occasional faint tapping of rain against the glass.

Jonas stood at the foot of the bed, looking at Harrison for a moment. Though he had saved the man's life, he knew little about him. Thirty-eight years old. Five-ten, a hundred and sixty pounds. Brown hair, brown eyes. Excellent physical condition.

But what of the inner person? Was Hatchford Benjamin Harrison a good man? Honest? Trustworthy? Faithful to his wife? Was he reasonably free of envy and greed, capable of mercy, aware of the difference between right and wrong?

Did he have a kind heart?

Did he love?

In the heat of a resuscitation procedure, when seconds counted and there was too much to be done in too short a time, Jonas never dared to think about the central ethical dilemma facing any doctor who assumed the role of reanimator, for to think of it then might have inhibited him to the patient's disadvantage. Afterward, there was time to doubt, to wonder. . . . Although a physician was morally committed and professionally obligated to saving lives wherever he could, were all lives worth saving? When Death took an evil man, wasn't it wiser—and more ethically correct—to let him stay dead?

If Harrison was a bad man, the evil that he committed upon resuming his life after leaving the hospital would in part be the responsibility of Jonas Nyebern. The pain Harrison caused others would to some extent stain Jonas's soul, as well.

Fortunately, this time the dilemma seemed moot. Harrison appeared to be an upstanding citizen—a respected antique dealer, they said—married to an artist of some reputation, whose name Jonas recognized. A good artist had to be sensitive, perceptive, able to see the world more clearly than most people saw it. Didn't she? If she was married to a bad man, she would know it, and she wouldn't remain married to him. This time there was every reason to believe that a life had been saved that *should* have been saved.

Jonas only wished his actions had always been so correct.

He turned away from the bed and took two steps to the window. Five stories below, the nearly deserted parking lot lay under hooded pole lamps. The falling rain churned the puddles, so they appeared to be boiling, as if a subterranean fire consumed the blacktop from underneath.

He could pick out the spot where Kari Dovell's car had been parked, and he stared at it for a long time. He admired Kari enormously. He also found her attractive. Sometimes he dreamed of being with her, and it was a surprisingly comforting dream. He could admit to wanting her at times, as well, and to being pleased by the thought that she might also want him. But he did not *need* her. He needed nothing but his work, the satisfaction of occasionally beating Death, and the—

"Something's . . . out . . . there . . ."

The first word interrupted Jonas's thoughts, but the voice was so thin and soft that he didn't immediately perceive the source of it. He turned around, looking toward the open door, assuming the voice had come from the corridor, and only by the third word did he realize that the speaker was Harrison.

The patient's head was turned toward Jonas, but his eyes were focused on the window.

Moving quickly to the side of the bed, Jonas glanced at the electrocardiograph and saw that Harrison's heart was beating fast but, thank God, rhythmically.

"Something's . . . out there," Harrison repeated.

His eyes were not, after all, focused on the window itself, on nothing so close as that, but on some distant point in the stormy night.

"Just rain," Jonas assured him.

"No."

"Just a little winter rain."

"Something bad," Harrison whispered.

Hurried footsteps echoed in the corridor, and a young nurse burst through the open door, into the nearly dark room. Her name was Ramona Perez, and Jonas knew her to be competent and concerned.

"Oh, Doctor Nyebern, good, you're here. The telemetry unit, his heartbeat—"

"Accelerated, yes, I know. He just woke up."

Ramona came to the bed and switched on the lamp above it, revealing the patient more clearly.

Harrison was still staring beyond the rain-spotted window, as if oblivious of Jonas and the nurse. In a voice even softer than before, heavy with weariness, he repeated: "Something's out there." Then his eyes fluttered sleepily, and fell shut.

"Mr. Harrison, can you hear me?" Jonas asked.

The patient did not answer.

The EKG showed a quickly de-accelerating heartbeat: from one-forty to one-twenty to one hundred beats a minute.

"Mr. Harrison?"

Ninety per minute. Eighty.

"He's asleep again," Ramona said.

"Appears to be."

"Just sleeping, though," she said. "No question of it being a coma now."

"Not a coma," Jonas agreed.

"And he was speaking. Did he make sense?"

"Sort of. But hard to tell," Jonas said, leaning over the bed railing to study the man's eyelids, which fluttered with the rapid movement of the eyes under them. REM sleep. Harrison was dreaming again.

Outside, the rain suddenly began to fall harder than before. The wind picked up, too, and keened at the window.

Ramona said, "The words I heard were clear, not slurred."

"No. Not slurred. And he spoke some complete sentences."

"Then he's not aphasic," she said. "That's terrific."

Aphasia, the complete inability to speak or understand spoken or written language, was one of the most devastating forms of brain damage resulting from disease or injury. Thus affected, a patient was reduced to using gestures to communicate, and the inadequacy of pantomime soon cast him into deep depression, from which there was sometimes no coming back.

Harrison was evidently free of that curse. If he was also free of paralysis, and if there were not *too* many holes in his memory, he had a good chance of eventually getting out of bed and leading a normal life.

"Let's not jump to conclusions," Jonas said. "Let's not build up any false hopes. He still has a long way to go. But you can enter on his record that he regained consciousness for the first time at eleven-thirty, two hours after resuscitation."

Harrison was murmuring in his sleep.

Jonas leaned over the bed and put his ear close to the patient's lips, which were barely moving. The words were faint, carried on his shallow exhalations. It was like a spectral voice heard on an open radio channel, broadcast from a station halfway around the world, bounced off a freak inversion layer high in the atmosphere and filtered through so much space and bad weather that it sounded mysterious and prophetic in spite of being less than half-intelligible.

"What's he saying?" Ramona asked.

With the howl of the storm rising outside, Jonas was unable to catch enough of Harrison's words to be sure, but he thought the man was repeating what he'd said before: "Something's . . . out there. . . ."

Abruptly the wind shrieked, and rain drummed against the window so hard that it seemed certain to shatter the glass.

14

Vassago liked the rain. The storm clouds had plated over the sky, leaving no holes through which the too-bright moon could gaze. The downpour also veiled the glow of streetlamps and the head-lights of oncoming cars, moderated the dazzle of neon signs, and in general softened the Orange County night, making it possible for him to drive with more comfort than could be provided by his sunglasses alone.

He had traveled west from his hideaway, then north along the coast, in search of a bar where the lights might be low and a woman or two available for consideration. A lot of places were closed Mondays, and others didn't appear too active that late at night, between the half-hour and the witching hour.

At last he found a lounge in Newport Beach, along the Pacific Coast Highway. It was a tony joint with a canopy to the street, rows of miniature white lights defining the roof line, and a sign advertising DANCING WED THRU SAT/JOHNNY WILTON'S BIG BAND. Newport was the most affluent city in the county, with the world's largest private yacht harbor, so almost any establishment that pretended to a monied clientele most likely had one. Beginning mid-week, valet parking was probably provided, which would not have been good for his purposes, since a valet was a potential witness, but on a rainy Monday no valet was in sight.

He parked in the lot beside the club, and as he switched off the engine, the seizure hit him. He felt as if he'd received a mild but sustained electrical shock. His eyes rolled back in his head, and for a moment he thought he was having convulsions, because he was unable breathe or swallow. An involuntary moan escaped him. The attack lasted only ten or fifteen seconds, and ended with three words that seemed to have been spoken *inside* his head: *Something's . . . out . . . there . . .* It was not just a random thought sparked by some short-circuiting synapse in his brain, for it came to him in a distinct *voice,* with the timbre and inflection of spoken words as distinguished from thoughts. Not his own voice, either, but that of a stranger. He had an overpowering sense of another presence in the car, as well, as if a spirit had passed through some curtain between worlds to visit with him, an alien presence that was real in spite of being invisible. Then the episode ended as abruptly as it had begun.

He sat for a while, waiting for a reoccurrence.

Rain hammered on the roof.

The car ticked and pinged as the engine cooled down.

Whatever had happened, it was over now.

He tried to understand the experience. Had those words—*Something's out there*—been a warning, a psychic premonition? A threat? To what did it refer?

Beyond the car, there seemed to be nothing special about the night. Just rain. Blessed darkness. The distorted reflections of electric lights and signs shimmered on the wet pavement, in puddles, and in the torrents pouring along the overflowing gutters. Sparse traffic passed on Pacific Coast Highway, but as far as he could see, no one was on foot—and he could see as well as any cat.

After a while he decided that he would understand the episode when he was *meant* to understand it. Nothing was to be gained by brooding over it. If it was a threat, from whatever source, it did not trouble him. He was incapable of fear. That was the best thing about having left the world of the living, even if he was temporarily stuck in the borderland this side of death: nothing in existence held any terror for him.

Nevertheless, that inner voice had been one of the strangest things he had ever experienced. And he was not exactly without a store of strange experiences with which to compare it.

He got out of his silver Camaro, slammed the door, and walked to the club entrance. The rain was cold. In the blustering wind, the fronds of the palm trees rattled like old bones.

15

Lindsey Harrison was also on the fifth floor, at the far end of the main corridor from her husband. Little of the room was revealed when Jonas entered and approached the side of the bed, for there was not even the green light from a cardiac monitor. The woman was barely visible.

He wondered if he should try to wake her, and was surprised when she spoke:

"Who're you?"

He said, "I thought you were asleep."

"Can't sleep."

"Didn't they give you something?"

"It didn't help."

As in her husband's room, the rain drove against the window with sullen fury. Jonas could hear torrents cascading through the confines of a nearby aluminum downspout.

"How do you feel?" he asked.

"How the hell do you think I feel?" She tried to infuse the words with anger, but she was too exhausted and too depressed to manage it.

He put down the bed railing, sat on the edge of the mattress, and held out one hand, assuming that her eyes were better adapted to the gloom than his were. "Give me your hand."

"Why?"

"I'm Jonas Nyebern. I'm a doctor. I want to tell you about your husband, and somehow I think it'll be better if you'll just let me hold your hand."

She was silent.

"Humor me," he said.

Although the woman believed her husband to be dead, Jonas did not mean to torment her by withholding his report of the resuscitation. From experience, he knew that good news of this sort could be as shocking to the recipient as bad news; it had to be delivered with care and sensitivity. She had been mildly delirious upon admission to the hospital, largely as a result of exposure and shock, but that condition had been swiftly remedied with the administration of heat and medication. She had been in possession of all her faculties for a few hours now, long enough to absorb her husband's death and to begin to find her way toward a tentative accommodation of her loss. Though deep in grief and far from adjusted to her widowhood, she had by now found a ledge on the emotional cliff down which she had plunged, a narrow perch, a precarious stability—from which he was about to knock her loose.

Still, he might have been more direct with her if he'd been able to bring her unalloyed good news. Unfortunately, he could not promise that her husband was going to be entirely his former self, unmarked by his experience, able to reenter his old life without a hitch. They would need hours, perhaps days, in which to examine and evaluate Harrison before they could hazard a prediction as to the likelihood of a full recovery. Thereafter, weeks or months of physical and occupational therapy might lie ahead for him, with no guarantee of effectiveness.

Jonas was still waiting for her hand. At last she offered it diffidently.

In his best bedside manner, he quickly outlined the basics of resuscitation medicine. When she began to realize why he thought she needed to know about such an esoteric subject, her grip on his hand suddenly grew tight.

16

In room 518, Hatch foundered in a sea of bad dreams that were nothing but disassociated images melding into one another without even the illogical narrative flow that usually shaped nightmares. Wind-whipped snow. A huge Ferris wheel sometimes bedecked with festive lights, sometimes dark and broken and ominous in a night seething with rain. Groves of scarecrow trees, gnarled and coaly, stripped leafless by winter. A beer truck angled across a snowswept highway. A tunnel with a concrete floor that sloped down into perfect blackness, into something unknown that filled him with heart-bursting dread. His lost son, Jimmy, lying sallow-skinned against hospital sheets, dying of cancer. Water, cold and deep, impenetrable as ink, stretching to all horizons, with no possible escape. A naked woman, her head on backwards, hands clasping a crucifix . . .

Frequently he was aware of a faceless and mysterious figure at the perimeter of the dreamscapes, dressed in black like some grim reaper, moving in such fluid harmony with the shadows that he might have been only a shadow himself. At other times, the reaper was not part of the scene but seemed to be the viewpoint through which it was observed, as if Hatch was looking out through the eyes of another—eyes that beheld the world with all the compassionless, hungry, calculating practicality of a graveyard rat.

For a time, the dream took on more of a narrative quality, wherein Hatch found himself running along a train-station platform, trying to catch up with a passenger car that was slowly pulling away on the outbound track. Through one of the train windows, he saw Jimmy, gaunt and hollow-eyed in the grip of his disease, dressed only in a hospital gown, peering sadly at Hatch, one small hand raised as he waved goodbye, goodbye, goodbye. Hatch reached desperately for the vertical railing beside the boarding steps at the end of Jimmy's car, but the train picked up speed; Hatch lost ground; the steps slipped away. Jimmy's pale, small face lost definition and finally vanished as the speeding passenger car dwindled into the terrible nothingness beyond the station platform, a lightless void of which Hatch only now became aware. Then another passenger car began to glide past him *(clackety-clack, clackety-clack),* and he was startled to see Lindsey seated at one of the windows, looking out at the platform, a lost expression on her face. Hatch called to her—"Lindsey!"—but she did not hear or see him, she seemed to be in a trance, so he began to run again, trying to board her car *(clackety-clack, clackety-clack),* which drew away from him as Jimmy's had done. "Lindsey!" His hand was inches from the railing beside the boarding stairs. . . . Suddenly the railing and stairs vanished, and the train was not a train any more. With the eerie fluidity of all changes in all dreams, it became a roller coaster in an amusement park, heading out on the start of a thrill ride. *(Clackety-clack.)* Hatch came to the end of the platform without being able to board Lindsey's car, and she rocketed away from him, up the first steep hill of the long and undulant track. Then the last car in the caravan passed him, close behind Lindsey's. It held a single passenger. The figure in black—around whom shadows clustered like ravens on a cemetery fence—sat in front of the car, head bowed, his face concealed by thick hair that fell forward in the fashion of a monk's hood. *(Clackety-clack!)* Hatch shouted at Lindsey, warning her to look back and be aware of what rode in the car behind her, pleading with her to be careful and hold on tight, for God's sake, *hold on tight!* The caterpillar procession of linked cars reached the crest of the hill, hung there for a moment as if time had been suspended, then disappeared in a scream-filled plummet down the far side.

Ramona Perez, the night nurse assigned to the fifth-floor wing that included room 518, stood beside the bed, watching her patient. She was worried about him, but she was not sure that she should go looking for Dr. Nyebern yet.

According to the heart monitor, Harrison's pulse was in a highly fluctuant state. Generally it ranged between a reassuring seventy to eighty beats per minute. Periodically, however, it raced as high as a hundred and forty. On the positive side, she observed no indications of serious arrhythmia.

His blood pressure was affected by his accelerated heartbeat, but he was in no apparent danger of stroke or cerebral hemorrhage related to spiking hypertension, because his systolic reading was never dangerously high.

He was sweating profusely, and the circles around his eyes were so dark, they appeared to have been applied with actors' greasepaint. He was shivering in spite of the blankets piled on him. The fingers of his left hand—exposed because of the intravenous feed—spasmed occasionally, though not forcefully enough to disturb the needle inserted just below the crook of his elbow.

In a whisper he repeated his wife's name, sometimes with considerable urgency: "Lindsey . . . Lindsey . . . *Lindsey, no!*"

Harrison was dreaming, obviously, and events in a nightmare could elicit physiological responses every bit as much as waking experiences.

Finally Ramona decided that the accelerated heartbeat was solely the result of the poor man's bad dreams, not an indication of genuine cardiovascular destabilization. He was in no danger. Nevertheless, she remained at his bedside, watching over him.

17

Vassago sat at a window table overlooking the harbor. He had been in the lounge only five minutes, and already he suspected it was not good hunting grounds. The atmosphere was all wrong. He wished he had not ordered a drink.

No dance music was provided on Monday nights, but a pianist was at work in one corner. He played neither gutless renditions of '30s and '40s songs nor the studiedly bland arrangements of easy-listening rock-'n'-roll that rotted the brains of regular lounge patrons. But he spun out the equally noxious repetitive melodies of New Age numbers composed for those who found elevator music too complex and intellectually taxing.

Vassago preferred music with a hard beat, fast and driving, something that put his teeth on edge. Since becoming a citizen of the borderland, he could not take pleasure in most music, for its orderly structures irritated him. He could tolerate only music that was atonal, harsh, unmelodious. He responded to jarring key changes, thunderously crashing chords, and squealing guitar riffs that abraded the nerves. He enjoyed discord and broken patterns of rhythm. He was excited by music that filled his mind with images of blood and violence.

To Vassago, the scene beyond the big windows, because of its beauty, was as displeasing as the lounge music. Sailboats and motor yachts crowded one another at the private docks along the harbor. They were tied up, sails furled, engines silent, wallowing only slightly because the harbor was well protected and the storm was not particularly ferocious. Few of the wealthy owners actually lived aboard, regardless of the size of the craft or amenities, so lights glowed at only a few of the portholes. Rain, here and there transmuted into quicksilver by the dock lights, hammered the boats, beaded on their brightwork, drizzled like molten metal down their masts and across their decks and out of their scuppers. He had no tolerance for prettiness, for postcard scenes of harmonious composition, because they seemed false, a lie about what the world was really like. He was drawn, instead, to visual discord, jagged shapes, malignant and festering forms.

With its plush chairs and low amber lighting, the lounge was too soft for a hunter like him. It dulled his killing instincts.

He surveyed the patrons, hoping to spot an object of the quality suitable for his collection. If he saw something truly superb that excited his acquisitional fever, even the stultifying atmosphere would not be able to sap his energy.

A few men sat at the bar, but they were of no interest to him. The three men in his collection had been his second, fourth, and fifth acquisitions, taken because they had been vulnerable and in lonely circumstances that allowed him to overpower them and take them away without being seen. He had no aversion to killing men, but preferred women. Young women. He liked to get them before they could breed more life.

The only really young people among the customers were four women in their twenties who were seated by the windows, three tables away from him. They were tipsy and a little giddy, hunched over as if sharing gossip, talking intently, periodically bursting into gales of laughter.

One of them was lovely enough to engage Vassago's hatred of beautiful things. She had enormous chocolate-brown eyes, and an animal grace that reminded him of a doe. He dubbed her "Bambi." Her raven hair was cut into short wings, exposing the lower halves of her ears.

They were exceptional ears, large but delicately formed. He thought he might be able to do something interesting with them, and he continued to watch her, trying to decide if she was up to his standards.

Bambi talked more than her friends, and she was the loudest of the group. Her laugh was the loudest, as well, a jackass braying. She *was* exceptionally attractive, but her incessant chatter and annoying laughter spoiled the package. Clearly, she loved the sound of her own voice.

She'd be vastly improved, he thought, if she were to be stricken deaf and mute.

Inspiration seized him, and he sat up straighter in his chair. By removing her ears, tucking them into her dead mouth, and sewing her lips shut, he would be neatly symbolizing the fatal flaw in her beauty. It was a vision of such simplicity, yet such power, that—

"One rum and Coke," the waitress said, putting a glass and paper cocktail napkin on the table in front of Vassago. "You want to run a tab?"

He looked up at her, blinking in confusion. She was a stout middle-aged woman with auburn hair. He could see her quite clearly through his sunglasses, but in his fever of creative excitement, he had difficulty placing her.

Finally he said, "Tab? Uh, no. Cash, thank you, ma'am."

When he took out his wallet, it didn't feel like a wallet at all but like one of Bambi's ears might feel. When he slid his thumb back and forth across the smooth leather, he felt not what was there but what might soon be available for his caress: delicately shaped ridges of cartilage forming the auricula and pinna, the graceful curves of the channels that focused sound waves inward toward the tympanic membrane. . . .

He realized the waitress had spoken to him again, stating the price of his drink, and then he realized that it was the second time she had done so. He had been fingering his wallet for long, delicious seconds, daydreaming of death and disfigurement.

He fished out a crisp bill without looking at it, and handed it to her.

"This is a hundred," she said. "Don't you have anything smaller?"

"No, ma'am, sorry," he said, impatient now to be rid of her, "that's it."

"I'll have to go back to the bar to get this much change."

"Okay, yeah, whatever. Thank you, ma'am."

As she started away from his table, he returned his attention to the four young women—only to discover that they were leaving. They were nearing the door, pulling on their coats as they went.

He started to rise, intending to follow them, but he froze when he heard himself say, "Lindsey."

He didn't call out the name. No one in the bar heard him say it. He was the only one who reacted, and his reaction was one of total surprise.

For a moment he hesitated with one hand on the table, one on the arm of his chair, halfway to his feet. While he was paralyzed in that posture of indecisiveness, the four young women left the lounge. Bambi became of less interest to him than the mysterious name—"Lindsey"—so he sat down.

He did not know anyone named Lindsey.

He had *never* known anyone named Lindsey.

It made no sense that he would suddenly speak the name aloud.

He looked out the window at the harbor. Hundreds of millions of dollars of ego-gratification rose and fell and wallowed side to side on the rolling water. The sunless sky was another sea above, as cold and merciless as the one below. The air was full of rain like millions of gray and silver threads, as if nature was trying to sew the ocean to the heavens and thereby obliterate the narrow space between, where life was possible. Having been one of the living, one of the dead, and now one of the living dead, he had seen himself as the ultimate sophisticate, as experienced as any man born of woman could ever hope to be. He had assumed that the world held nothing new for him, had nothing to teach him. Now this. First the seizure in the car: *Something's out there!* And now Lindsey. The two experiences were different, because he heard no voice in his head the second time, and when he spoke it was with his own familiar voice and not that of a stranger. But both events were so peculiar that he knew they were linked. As he gazed at the moored boats, the harbor, and the dark world beyond, it began to seem more mysterious to him than it had in ages.

He picked up his rum and Coke. He took a long swallow of it.

As he was putting the drink down, he said, "Lindsey."

The glass rattled against the table, and he almost knocked it over, because the name surprised him again. He hadn't spoken it aloud to ponder the meaning of it. Rather, it had burst from him as before, a bit more breathlessly this time and somewhat louder.

Interesting.

The lounge seemed to be a magical place for him.

He decided to settle down for a while and wait to see what might happen next.

When the waitress arrived with his change, he said, "I'd like another drink, ma'am." He handed her a twenty. "This'll take care of it, and please keep the change."

Happy with the tip, she hurried back to the bar.

Vassago turned to the window again, but this time he looked at his own reflection in the glass instead of at the harbor beyond. The dim lights of the lounge threw insufficient glare on the pane to provide him with a detailed image. In that murky mirror, his sunglasses did not register well. His face appeared to have two gaping eye sockets like those of a fleshless skull. The illusion pleased him.

In a husky whisper not loud enough to draw the attention of anyone else in the lounge, but with more urgency than before, he said, "Lindsey, no!"

He had not anticipated that outburst any more than the previous two, but it did not rattle him. He had quickly adapted to the fact of these mysterious events, and had begun to try to understand them. Nothing could surprise him for long. After all, he had been to Hell and back, both to the real Hell and the one beneath the funhouse, so the intrusion of the fantastic into real life did not frighten or awe him.

He drank a third rum and Coke. When more than an hour passed without further developments, and when the bartender announced the last round of the night, Vassago left.

The need was still with him, the need to murder and create. It was a fierce heat in his gut that had nothing to do with the rum, such a steely tension in his chest that his heart might have been a clockwork mechanism with its spring wound to the breaking point. He wished that he had gone after the doe-eyed woman whom he had named Bambi.

Would he have removed her ears when she was dead at last—or while she was still alive?

Would she have been capable of understanding the artistic statement he was making as he sewed her lips shut over her full mouth? Probably not. None of the others had the wit or insight to appreciate his singular talent.

In the nearly deserted parking lot, he stood in the rain for a while, letting it soak him and extinguish some of the fire of his obsession. It was nearly two in the morning. Not enough time remained, before dawn, to do any hunting. He would have to return to his hideaway without an addition to his collection. If he were to get any sleep during the coming day and be prepared to hunt with the next nightfall, he had to dampen his blazing creative drive.

Eventually he began to shiver. The heat within him gave way to a relentless chill. He raised one hand, touched his cheek. His face felt cold, but his fingers were colder, like the marble hand of a statue of David that he'd admired in a memorial garden at Forest Lawn Cemetery when he had still been one of the living.

That was better.

As he opened the car door, he looked around once more at the rain-riven night. This time of his own volition, he said, "Lindsey?"

No answer.

Whoever she might be, she was not yet destined to cross his path.

He would have to be patient. He was mystified, therefore fascinated and curious. But whatever was happening would happen at its own pace. One of the virtues of the dead was patience, and though he was still half-alive, he knew he could find within himself the strength to match the forbearance of the deceased.

18

Early Tuesday morning, an hour after dawn, Lindsey could sleep no more. She ached in every muscle and joint, and what sleep she'd gotten had not lessened her exhaustion by any noticeable degree. She did not want sedatives. Unable to bear any further delay, she insisted they take her to Hatch's room. The charge nurse cleared it with Jonas Nyebern, who was still in the hospital, then wheeled Lindsey down the hall to 518.

Nyebern was there, red-eyed and rumpled. The sheets on the bed nearest the door were not turned back, but they were wrinkled, as if the doctor had stretched out to rest at least once during the night.

By now Lindsey had learned enough about Nyebern—some of it from him, much of it from the nurses—to know that he was a local legend. He had been a busy cardiovascular surgeon, but over the past two years, after losing his wife and two children in some kind of horrible accident, he had devoted steadily less time to surgery and more to resuscitation medicine. His commitment to his work was too strong to be called mere dedication. It was more of an obsession. In a society that was struggling to emerge from three decades of self-indulgence and me-firstism, it was easy to admire a man as selflessly committed as Nyebern, and everyone did seem to admire him.

Lindsey, for one, admired the hell out of him. After all, he had saved Hatch's life.

His weariness betrayed only by his bloodshot eyes and the rumpled condition of his clothes, Nyebern moved swiftly to pull back the privacy curtain that surrounded the bed nearest the window. He took the handles of Lindsey's wheelchair and rolled her to her husband's bedside.

The storm had passed during the night. Morning sun slanted through the slats of the Levolor blinds, striping the sheets and blankets with shadow and golden light.

Hatch lay beneath that faux tiger skin, only one arm and his face exposed. Although his skin was painted with the same jungle-cat camouflage as the bedding, his extreme pallor was evident. Seated in the wheelchair, regarding Hatch at an odd angle through the bed railing, Lindsey grew queasy at the sight of an ugly bruise that spread from the stitched gash on his forehead. But for the proof of the cardiac monitor and the barely perceptible rise-and-fall of Hatch's chest as he breathed, she would have assumed he was dead.

But he was alive, *alive,* and she felt a tightness in her chest and throat that presaged tears as surely as lightning was a sign of oncoming thunder. The prospect of tears surprised her, quickening her breath.

From the moment their Honda had gone over the brink and into the ravine, through the entire physical and emotional ordeal of the night just passed, Lindsey had never cried. She didn't pride herself on stoicism; it was just the way she was.

No, strike that.

It was just the way she had to become during Jimmy's bout with cancer. From the day of diagnosis until the end, her boy had taken nine months to die, as long as she had taken to lovingly shape him within her womb. Every day of that dying, Lindsey had wanted nothing more than to curl up in bed with the covers over her head and cry, just let the tears pour forth until all the moisture in her body was gone, until she dried up and crumbled into dust and ceased to exist. She *had* wept, at first. But her tears frightened Jimmy, and she realized that any expression of her inner turmoil was an unconscionable self-indulgence. Even when she cried in private, Jimmy knew it later; he had always been perceptive and sensitive beyond his years, and his disease seemed to make him more acutely aware of everything. Current theory of immunology gave considerable weight to the importance of a positive attitude, laughter, and confidence as weapons in the battle against life-threatening illness. So she had learned to suppress her terror at the prospect of losing him. She had given him laughter, love, confidence, courage—and never a reason to doubt her conviction that he would beat the malignancy.

By the time Jimmy died, Lindsey had become so successful at

100

repressing her tears that she could not simply turn them on again. Denied the release that easy tears might have given her, she spiraled down into a lost time of despair. She dropped weight—ten pounds, fifteen, twenty—until she was emaciated. She could not be bothered to wash her hair or look after her complexion or press her clothes. Convinced that she had failed Jimmy, that she had encouraged him to rely on her but then had not been special enough to help him reject his disease, she did not believe she deserved to take pleasure from food, from her appearance, a book, a movie, music, from anything. Eventually, with much patience and kindness, Hatch helped her see that her insistence on taking responsibility for an act of blind fate was, in its way, as much a disease as Jimmy's cancer had been.

Though she had still not been able to cry, she had climbed out of the psychological hole she'd dug for herself. Ever since, however, she had lived on the rim of it, her balance precarious.

Now, her first tears in a long, long time were surprising, unsettling. Her eyes stung, became hot. Her vision blurred. Disbelieving, she raised one shaky hand to touch the warm tracks on her cheeks.

Nyebern plucked a Kleenex from a box on the nightstand and gave it to her.

That small kindness affected her far out of proportion to the consideration behind it, and a soft sob escaped her.

"Lindsey . . ."

Because his throat was raw from his ordeal, his voice was hoarse, barely more than a whisper. But she knew at once who had spoken to her, and that it was not Nyebern.

She wiped hastily at her eyes with the Kleenex and leaned forward in the wheelchair until her forehead touched the cold bed railing. Hatch's head was turned toward her. His eyes were open, and they looked clear, alert.

"Lindsey . . ."

He had found the strength to push his right hand out from under the blankets, stretching it toward her.

She reached between the railings. She took his hand in hers.

His skin was dry. A thin bandage was taped over his abraded

palm. He was too weak to give her hand more than the faintest squeeze, but he was warm, blessedly warm, and alive.

"You're crying," Hatch said.

She was, too, harder than ever, a storm of tears, but she was smiling through them. Grief had not been able to free her first tears in five terrible years but joy *had* at last unleashed them. She was crying for joy, which seemed right, seemed healing. She felt a loosening of long-sustained tensions in her heart, as if the knotted adhesions of old wounds were dissolving, all because Hatch was alive, had been dead but was now alive.

If a miracle couldn't lift the heart, what could?

Hatch said, "I love you."

The storm of tears became a flood, ohgod, an ocean, and she heard herself blubber "I love you" back at him, then she felt Nyebern put a hand on her shoulder comfortingly, another small kindness that seemed huge, which only made her cry harder. But she was laughing even as she was weeping, and she saw that Hatch was smiling, too.

"It's okay," Hatch said hoarsely. "The worst . . . is over. The worst is . . . behind us now. . . ."

19

During the daylight hours, when he stayed beyond the reach of the sun, Vassago parked the Camaro in an underground garage that had once been filled with electric trams, carts, and lorries used by the park-maintenance crew. All of those vehicles were long gone, reclaimed by creditors. The Camaro stood alone in the center of that dank, windowless space.

From the garage, Vassago descended wide stairs—the elevators had not operated in years—to an even deeper subterranean level. The entire park was built on a basement that had once contained the security headquarters with scores of video monitors able to reveal every niche of the grounds, a ride-control center that had been an even more complex high-tech nest of computers and monitors, carpentry and electrical shops, a staff cafeteria, lockers and changing rooms for the hundreds of costumed employees working each shift, an emergency infirmary, business offices, and much more.

Vassago passed the door to that level without hesitating and continued down to the sub-basement at the very bottom of the complex. Even in the dry sands of southern California, the concrete walls exuded a damp lime smell at that depth.

No rats fled before him, as he had expected during his first descent into those realms many months ago. He had seen no rats at all, anywhere, in all the weeks he had roamed the tenebrous corridors and silent rooms of that vast structure, though he would not have been averse to sharing space with them. He liked rats. They were carrion-eaters, revelers in decay, scurrying janitors that cleaned up in the wake of death. Maybe they had never invaded the cellars of the park because, after its closure, the place had been pretty much stripped bare. It was all concrete, plastic, and metal, nothing biodegradable for rats to feed on, a little dusty, yes, with some crumpled paper here and there, but otherwise as sterile as an orbiting space station and of no interest to rodents.

Eventually rats might find his collection in Hell at the bottom of the funhouse and, having fed, spread out from there. Then he would have some suitable company in the bright hours when he could not venture out in comfort.

At the bottom of the fourth and last flight of stairs, two levels below the underground garage, Vassago passed through a doorway. The door was missing, as were virtually all the doors in the complex, hauled off by the salvagers and resold for a few bucks apiece.

Beyond was an eighteen-foot-wide tunnel. The floor was flat with a yellow stripe painted down the center, as if it were a highway—which it had been, of sorts. Concrete walls curved up to meet and form the ceiling.

Part of that lowest level was comprised of storerooms that had once held huge quantities of supplies. Styrofoam cups and burger packages, cardboard popcorn boxes and french-fry holders, paper napkins and little foil packets of ketchup and mustard for the many snack stands scattered over the grounds. Business forms for the offices. Packages of fertilizer and cans of insecticide for the landscape crew. All of that—and everything else a small city might need—had been removed long ago. The rooms were empty.

A network of tunnels connected the storage chambers to elevators that led upward into all the main attractions and restaurants. Goods could be delivered—or repairmen conveyed—throughout the park without disturbing the paying customers and shattering the fantasy they had paid to experience. Numbers were painted on the walls every hundred feet, to mark routes, and at intersections there were even signs with arrows to provide better directions:

◄ HAUNTED HOUSE
◄ ALPINE CHALET RESTAURANT
COSMIC WHEEL ►
BIG FOOT MOUNTAIN ►

Vassago turned right at the next intersection, left at the one after that, then right again. Even if his extraordinary vision had not permitted him to see in those obscure byways, he would have been able to follow the route he desired, for by now he knew the desiccated arteries of the dead park as well as he knew the contours of his own body.

Eventually he came to a sign—FUNHOUSE MACHINERY—beside an elevator. The doors of the elevator were gone, as were the cab and the lift mechanism, sold for reuse or for scrap. But the shaft remained, dropping about four feet below the floor of the tunnel, and leading up through five stories of darkness to the level that housed security and ride-control and park offices, on to the lowest level of the funhouse where he kept his collection, then to the second and third floors of that attraction.

He slipped over the edge, into the bottom of the elevator shaft. He sat on the old mattress he had brought in to make his hideaway more comfortable.

When he tilted his head back, he could see only a couple of floors into the unlighted shaft. The rusted steel bars of a service ladder dwindled up into the gloom.

If he climbed the ladder to the lowest level of the funhouse, he would come out in a service room behind the walls of Hell, from which the machinery operating the gondola chain-drive had been accessed and repaired—before it had been carted away forever.

A door from that chamber, disguised on the far side as a concrete boulder, opened into the now-dry lake of Hades, from which Lucifer towered.

He was at the deepest point of his hideaway, four feet more than two stories below Hell. There, he felt at home as much as it was possible for him to feel at home anywhere. Out in the world of the living, he moved with the confidence of a secret master of the universe, but he never felt as if he belonged there. Though he was not actually afraid of anything any more, a trace current of anxiety buzzed through him every minute that he spent beyond the stark, black corridors and sepulchral chambers of his hideaway.

After a while he opened the lid of a sturdy plastic cooler with a Styrofoam lining, in which he kept cans of root beer. He had always liked root beer. It was too much trouble to keep ice in the cooler, so he just drank the soda warm. He didn't mind.

He also kept snack foods in the cooler: Mars bars, Reese's peanut butter cups, Clark Bars, a bag of potato chips, packages of peanut-butter-and-cheese crackers, Mallomars, and Oreo cookies. When he had crossed into the borderland, something had happened to his metabolism; he seemed to be able to eat anything he wanted and burn it off without gaining weight or turning soft. And what he wanted to eat, for some reason he didn't understand, was what he had liked when he'd been a kid.

He opened a root beer and took a long, warm swallow.

He withdrew a single cookie from the bag of Oreos. He carefully separated the two chocolate wafers without damaging them. The circle of white icing stuck entirely to the wafer in his left hand. That meant he was going to be rich and famous when he grew up. If it had stuck to the one in his right hand, it would have meant that he was going to be famous but not necessarily rich, which could mean just about anything from being a rock-'n'-roll star to an assassin who would take out the President of the United States.

If some of the icing stuck to both wafers, that meant you had to eat another cookie or risk having no future at all.

As he licked the sweet icing, letting it dissolve slowly on his tongue, he stared up the empty elevator shaft, thinking about how interesting it was that he had chosen the abandoned amusement park for his hideaway when the world offered so many dark and lonely places from which to choose. He had been there a few times as a boy, when the park was still in operation, most recently eight years ago, when he had been twelve, little more than a year before the operation closed down. On that most special evening of his childhood, he had committed his first murder there, beginning his long romance with death. Now he was back.

He licked away the last of the icing.

He ate the first chocolate wafer. He ate the second.

He took another cookie out of the bag.

He sipped the warm root beer.

He wished he were dead. Fully dead. It was the only way to begin his existence on the Other Side.

"If wishes were cows," he said, "we'd eat steak every day, wouldn't we?"

He ate the second cookie, finished the root beer, then stretched out on his back to sleep.

Sleeping, he dreamed. They were peculiar dreams of people he had never seen, places he had never been, events that he had never witnessed. Water all around him, chunks of floating ice, snow sheeting through a hard wind. A woman in a wheelchair, laughing and weeping at the same time. A hospital bed, banded by shadows and stripes of golden sunlight. The woman in the wheelchair, laughing and weeping. The woman in the wheelchair, laughing. The woman in the wheelchair. The woman.

Part II

ALIVE AGAIN

In the fields of life, a harvest
sometimes comes far out of season,
when we thought the earth was old
and could see no earthly reason
to rise for work at break of dawn,
and put our muscles to the test.
With winter here and autumn gone,
it just seems best to rest, to rest.
But under winter fields so cold,
wait the dormant seeds of seasons
unborn, and so the heart does hold
hope that heals all bitter lesions.
In the fields of life, a harvest.

—THE BOOK OF COUNTED SORROWS

FOUR

1

Hatch felt as if time had slipped backward to the fourteenth century, as if he were an accused infidel on trial for his life during the Inquisition.

Two priests were present in the attorney's office. Although only of average height, Father Jiminez was as imposing as any man a foot taller, with jet-black hair and eyes even darker, in a black clerical suit with a Roman collar. He stood with his back to the windows. The gently swaying palm trees and blue skies of Newport Beach behind him did not lighten the atmosphere in the mahogany-paneled, antique-filled office where they were gathered, and in silhouette Jiminez was an ominous figure. Father Duran, still in his twenties and perhaps twenty-five years younger than Father Jiminez, was thin, with ascetic features and a pallid complexion. The young priest appeared to be enthralled by a collection of Meiji Period Satsuma vases, incensers, and bowls in a large display case at the far end of the office, but Hatch could not escape the feeling that Duran was faking interest in the Japanese porcelains and was actually furtively observing him and Lindsey where they sat side by side on a Louis XVI sofa.

Two nuns were present, as well, and they seemed, to Hatch, more threatening than the priests. They were of an order that favored the voluminous, old-fashioned habits not seen so often these days. They wore starched wimples, their faces framed in ovals of white linen that made them look especially severe. Sister Immaculata, who was in charge of St. Thomas's Home for Children, looked like a great black bird of prey perched on the armchair to the right of the sofa, and Hatch would not have been surprised if she had suddenly let out a screaky cry, leapt into flight with a great flap of her robes, swooped around the room, and dive-bombed him with the intention of pecking off his nose. Her executive assistant was a somewhat younger, intense nun who paced ceaselessly and had a stare more penetrating than a steel-cutting laser beam. Hatch had temporarily forgotten her name and thought of her as The Nun with No Name, because she reminded him of Clint Eastwood playing The *Man* with No Name in those old spaghetti Westerns.

He was being unfair, more than unfair, a little irrational due to a world-class case of nerves. Everyone in the attorney's office was there to help him and Lindsey. Father Jiminez, the rector of St. Thomas's Church, who raised much of the annual budget of the orphanage headed by Sister Immaculata, was really no more ominous than the priest in *Going My Way,* a Latino Bing Crosby, and Father Duran seemed sweet-tempered and shy. In reality, Sister Immaculata looked no more like a bird of prey than she did a stripper, and The Nun with No Name had a genuine and almost constant smile that more than compensated for whatever negative emotions one might choose to read into her piercing stare. The priests and nuns tried to keep a light conversation going; Hatch and Lindsey were, in fact, the ones who were too tense to be as sociable as the situation required.

So much was at stake. That was what made Hatch jumpy, which was unusual, because he was ordinarily the most mellow man to be found outside of the third hour of a beer-drinking contest. He wanted the meeting to go well because his and Lindsey's happiness, their future, the success of their new life depended on it.

Well, that was not true, either. That was overstating the case again.

He couldn't help it.

Since he had been resuscitated more than seven weeks ago, he and Lindsey had undergone an emotional sea change together.

The long, smothering tide of despair, which had rolled over them upon Jimmy's death, abruptly abated. They realized they were still together only by virtue of a medical miracle. Not to be thankful for that reprieve, not to fully enjoy the borrowed time they had been given, would have made them ungrateful to both God and their physicians. More than that—it would have been stupid. They had been right to mourn Jimmy, but somewhere along the way, they had allowed grief to degenerate into self-pity and chronic depression, which had not been right at all.

They had needed Hatch's death, reanimation, and Lindsey's near death to jolt them out of their deplorable habit of gloom, which told him that they were more stubborn than he had thought. The important thing was that they *had* been jolted and were determined to get on with their lives at last.

To both of them, getting on with life meant having a child in the house again. The desire for a child was not a sentimental attempt to recapture the mood of the past, and it wasn't a neurotic need to replace Jimmy in order to finish getting over his death. They were just good with kids; they liked kids; and giving of themselves to a child was enormously satisfying.

They had to adopt. That was the hitch. Lindsey's pregnancy had been troubled, and her labor had been unusually long and painful. Jimmy's birth was a near thing, and when at last he made it into the world, the doctors informed Lindsey that she would not be capable of having any more children.

The Nun with No Name stopped pacing, pulled up the voluminous sleeve of her habit, and looked at her wristwatch. "Maybe I should go see what's keeping her."

"Give the child a little more time," Sister Immaculata said quietly. With one plump white hand, she smoothed the folds of her habit. "If you go to check on her, she'll feel you don't trust her to be able to take care of herself. There's nothing in the ladies' restroom that she can't deal with herself. I doubt she even had the need to use it. She probably just wanted to be alone a few minutes before the meeting, to settle her nerves."

To Lindsey and Hatch, Father Jiminez said, "Sorry about the delay."

"That's okay," Hatch said, fidgeting on the sofa. "We understand. We're a little nervous ourselves."

Initial inquiries made it clear that a lot—a veritable *army*—of couples were waiting for children to become available for adoption. Some had been kept in suspense for two years. After being childless for five years already, Hatch and Lindsey didn't have the patience to go on the bottom of anyone's waiting list.

They were left with only two options, the first of which was to attempt to adopt a child of another race, black or Asian or Hispanic. Most would-be adoptive parents were white and were waiting for a white baby that might conceivably pass for their own, while countless orphans of various minority groups were destined for institutions and unfulfilled dreams of being part of a family. Skin color meant nothing to either Hatch or Lindsey. They would have been happy with any child regardless of its heritage. But in recent years, misguided do-goodism in the name of civil rights had led to the imposition of an array of new rules and regulations designed to inhibit interracial adoption, and vast government bureaucracies enforced them with mind-numbing exactitude. The theory was that no child could be truly happy if raised outside of its ethnic group, which was the kind of elitist nonsense—and reverse racism—that sociologists and academics formulated without consulting the lonely kids they purported to protect.

The second option was to adopt a disabled child. There were far fewer disabled than minority orphans—even including technical orphans whose parents were alive somewhere but who'd been abandoned to the care of the church or state because of their differentness. On the other hand, though fewer in number, they were in even less demand than minority kids. They had the tremendous advantage of being currently beyond the interest of any pressure group eager to apply politically correct standards to their care and handling. Sooner or later, no doubt, a marching moron army would secure the passage of laws forbidding adoption of a green-eyed, blond, deaf child by anyone but green-eyed, blond, deaf parents, but Hatch and Lindsey had the good fortune to have submitted an application before the forces of chaos had descended.

Sometimes, when he thought about the troublesome bureaucrats they had dealt with six weeks ago, when they had first decided to adopt, he wanted to go back to those agencies and throttle the social workers who had thwarted them, just choke a little common sense into them. And wouldn't the expression of *that* desire make the good nuns and priests of St. Thomas's Home eager to commend one of their charges to his care!

"You're still feeling well, no lasting effects from your ordeal, eating well, sleeping well?" Father Jiminez inquired, obviously just to pass the time while they waited for the subject of the meeting to arrive, not meaning to impugn Hatch's claim to a full recovery and good health.

Lindsey—by nature more nervous than Hatch, and usually more prone to overreaction than he was—leaned forward on the sofa. Just a touch sharply, she said, "Hatch is at the top of the recovery curve for people who've been resuscitated. Dr. Nyebern's ecstatic about him, given him a clean bill of health, totally clean. It was all in our application."

Trying to soften Lindsey's reaction lest the priests and nuns start to wonder if she was protesting too much, Hatch said, "I'm terrific, really. I'd recommend a brief death to everyone. It relaxes you, gives you a calmer perspective on life."

Everyone laughed politely.

In truth, Hatch *was* in excellent health. During the four days following reanimation, he had suffered weakness, dizziness, nausea, lethargy, and some memory lapses. But his strength, memory, and intellectual functions returned one hundred percent. He had been back to normal for almost seven weeks.

Jiminez's casual reference to sleeping habits had rattled Hatch a little, which was probably what had also put Lindsey on edge. He had not been fully honest when he had implied he was sleeping well, but his strange dreams and the curious emotional effects they had on him were not serious, hardly worth mentioning, so he did not feel that he had actually lied to the priest.

They were so close to getting their new life started that he did not want to say the wrong thing and cause any delays. Though Catholic adoption services took considerable care in the place-

113

ment of children, they were not pointlessly slow and obstructive, as were public agencies, especially when the would-be adopters were solid members of the community like Hatch and Lindsey, and when the adoptee was a disabled child with no option except continued institutionalization. The future could begin for them this week, as long as they gave the folks from St. Thomas's, who were already on their side, no reason to reconsider.

Hatch was a little surprised by the piquancy of his desire to be a father again. He felt as if he had been only half-alive, at best, during the past five years. Now suddenly all the unused energies of that half-decade flooded into him, overcharging him, making colors more vibrant and sounds more melodious and feelings more intense, filling him with a passion to go, do, see, *live*. And be somebody's dad again.

"I was wondering if I could ask you something," Father Duran said to Hatch, turning away from the Satsuma collection. His wan complexion and sharp features were enlivened by owlish eyes, full of warmth and intelligence, enlarged by thick glasses. "It's a little personal, which is why I hesitate."

"Oh, sure, anything," Hatch said.

The young priest said, "Some people who've been clinically dead for short periods of time, a minute or two, report . . . well . . . a certain similar experience. . . ."

"A sense of rushing through a tunnel with an awesome light at the far end," Hatch said, "a feeling of great peace, of going home at last?"

"Yes," Duran said, his pale face brightening. "That's what I meant exactly."

Father Jiminez and the nuns were looking at Hatch with new interest, and he wished he could tell them what they wanted to hear. He glanced at Lindsey on the sofa beside him, then around at the assemblage, and said, "I'm sorry, but I didn't have the experience so many people have reported."

Father Duran's thin shoulders sagged a little. "Then what *did* you experience?"

Hatch shook his head. "Nothing. I wish I had. It would be . . . comforting, wouldn't it? But in that sense, I guess I had a boring death. I don't remember anything whatsoever from the time I was knocked out when the car rolled over until I woke up hours later in a hospital bed, looking at rain beating on a window-pane—"

He was interrupted by the arrival of Salvatore Gujilio in whose office they were waiting. Gujilio, a huge man, heavy *and* tall, swung the door wide and entered as he always did—taking big strides instead of ordinary steps, closing the door behind him in a grand sweeping gesture. With the unstoppable determination of a force of nature—rather like a disciplined tornado—he swept around the room, greeting them one by one. Hatch would not have been surprised to see furniture spun aloft and artwork flung off walls as the attorney passed, for he seemed to radiate enough energy to levitate anything within his immediate sphere of influence.

Keeping up a continuous line of patter, Gujilio gave Jiminez a bear hug, shook hands vigorously with Duran, and bowed to each of the nuns with the sincerity of a passionate monarchist greeting members of the royal family. Gujilio bonded with people as quickly as one piece of pottery to another under the influence of super glue, and by their second meeting he'd greeted and said goodbye to Lindsey with a hug. She liked the man and didn't mind the hugging, but as she had told Hatch, she felt like a very small child embracing a sumo wrestler. "He lifts me off my feet, for God's sake," she'd said. Now she stayed on the sofa instead of rising, and merely shook hands with the attorney.

Hatch rose and extended his right hand, prepared to see it engulfed as if it were a speck of food in a culture dish filled with hungry amoebas, which is exactly what happened. Gujilio, as always, took Hatch's hand in both of his, and since each of his mitts was half-again the size of any ordinary man's, it wasn't so much a matter of shaking as being shaken.

"What a wonderful day," Gujilio said, "a special day. I hope for everyone's sake it goes as smooth as glass."

The attorney donated a certain number of hours a week to St. Thomas's Church and the orphanage. He appeared to take great satisfaction in connecting adoptive parents with disabled kids.

"Regina's on her way from the ladies," Gujilio told them. "She stopped to chat a moment with my receptionist, that's all. She's nervous, I think, trying to delay a little longer until she has her courage screwed up as far as it'll go. She'll be here in a moment."

Hatch looked at Lindsey. She smiled nervously and took his hand.

"Now, you understand," Salvatore Gujilio said, looming over them like one of those giant balloons in a Macy's Thanksgiving Day parade, "that the point of this meeting is for you to get to know Regina and for her to get to know you. Nobody makes a decision right here, today. You go away, think about it, and let us know tomorrow or the day after whether this is the one. The same goes for Regina. She has a day to think about it."

"It's a big step," Father Jiminez said.

"An enormous step," Sister Immaculata concurred.

Squeezing Hatch's hand, Lindsey said, "We understand."

The Nun with No Name went to the door, opened it, and peered down the hallway. Evidently Regina was not in sight.

Rounding his desk, Gujilio said, "She's coming, I'm sure."

The attorney settled his considerable bulk into the executive office chair beside his desk, but because he was six-feet-five, he seemed almost as tall seated as standing. The office was furnished entirely with antiques, and the desk was actually a Napoleon III table so fine that Hatch wished he had something like it in the front window of his shop. Banded by ormolu, the exotic woods of the marquetry top depicted a central cartouche with a detailed musical trophy over a conforming frieze of stylized foliage. The whole was raised on circular legs with acanthus-leaf ormolu joined by a voluted X stretcher centered with an ormolu urn finial, on toupie feet. At every meeting, Gujilio's size and dangerous levels of kinetic energy initially made the desk—and all the antiques— seem fragile, in imminent jeopardy of being knocked over or smashed to smithereens. But after a few minutes, he and the room seemed in such perfect harmony, you had the eerie feeling that he had recreated a decor he had lived with in another—thinner—life.

A soft, distant, but peculiar *thud* drew Hatch's attention away from the attorney and the desk.

The Nun with No Name turned from the door and hurried back into the room, saying, "Here she comes," as if she didn't want Regina to think she had been looking for her.

The sound came again. Then again. And again.

It was rhythmic and getting louder.

Thud. Thud.

Lindsey's hand tightened on Hatch's.

Thud. Thud!

Someone seemed to be keeping time to an unheard tune by rapping a lead pipe against the hardwood floor of the hallway beyond the door.

Puzzled, Hatch looked at Father Jiminez, who was staring at the floor, shaking his head, his state of mind not easy to read. As the sound grew louder and closer, Father Duran stared at the half-open hall door with astonishment, as did The Nun with No Name. Salvatore Gujilio rose from his chair, looking alarmed. Sister Immaculata's pleasantly ruddy cheeks were now as white as the linen band that framed her face.

Hatch became aware of a softer scraping between each of the hard sounds.

Thud! Sccccuuuurrrr . . . Thud! Sccccuuuurrrr . . .

As the sounds grew nearer, their effect rapidly increased, until Hatch's mind was filled with images from a hundred old horror films: the-thing-from-out-of-the-lagoon hitching crablike toward its prey; the-thing-from-out-of-the-crypt shuffling along a grave-yard path under a gibbous moon; the-thing-from-another-world propelling itself on God-knows-what sort of arachnoid-reptilian-horned feet.

THUD!

The windows seemed to rattle.

Or was that his imagination?

Sccccuuuurrrr . . .

A shiver went up his spine.

THUD!

He looked around at the alarmed attorney, the head-shaking priest, the wide-eyed younger priest, the two pale nuns, then quickly back at the half-open door, wondering just exactly what

117

sort of disability this child had been born with, half expecting a
startlingly tall and twisted figure to appear with a surprising re-
semblance to Charles Laughton in *The Hunchback of Notre Dame*
and a grin full of fangs, whereupon Sister Immaculata would turn
to him and say, *You see, Mr. Harrison, Regina came under the care
of the good sisters at Saint Thomas's not from ordinary parents but
from a laboratory where the scientists are doing some really interesting genetic research. . . .*

A shadow tilted across the threshold.

Hatch realized that Lindsey's grip on his hand had become
downright painful. And his palm was damp with sweat.

The weird sounds stopped. A hush of expectation had fallen
over the room.

Slowly the door to the hall was pushed all the way open.

Regina took a single step inside. She dragged her right leg as if
it were a dead weight: *sccccuuuurrrr*. Then she slammed it down:
THUD!

She stopped to look around at everyone. Challengingly.

Hatch found it difficult to believe that she had been the source
of all that ominous noise. She was small for a ten-year-old girl, a
bit shorter and more slender than the average kid her age. Her
freckles, pert nose, and beautiful deep-auburn hair thoroughly
disqualified her for the role of the-thing-from-the-lagoon or any
other shudder-making creature, although there was something in
her solemn gray eyes that Hatch did not expect to see in the eyes
of a child. An adult awareness. A heightened perceptivity. But for
those eyes and an aura of iron determination, the girl seemed
fragile, almost frighteningly delicate and vulnerable.

Hatch was reminded of an exquisite 18th-century Mandarin-
pattern Chinese-export porcelain bowl currently for sale in his
Laguna Beach shop. It rang as sweetly as any bell when pinged
with one finger, raising the expectation that it would shatter into
thousands of pieces if struck hard or dropped. But when you
studied the bowl as it stood on an acrylic display base, the hand-
painted temple and garden scenes portrayed on its sides and the
floral designs on its inner rim were of such high quality and
possessed such power that you became acutely aware of the piece's

age, the weight of the history behind it. And you were soon convinced, in spite of its appearance, that it would bounce when dropped, cracking whatever surface it struck but sustaining not even a small chip itself.

Aware that the moment was hers and hers alone, Regina hitched toward the sofa where Hatch and Lindsey waited, making less noise as she limped off the hardwood floor onto the antique Persian carpet. She was wearing a white blouse, a Kelly-green skirt that fell two inches above her knees, green kneesocks, black shoes—and on her right leg a metal brace that extended from the ankle to above the knee and looked like a medieval torture device. Her limp was so pronounced that she rocked from side to side at the hips with each step, as if in danger of toppling over.

Sister Immaculata rose from her armchair, scowling at Regina in disapproval. "Exactly what is the reason for these theatrics, young lady?"

Ignoring the true meaning of the nun's question, the girl said, "I'm sorry I'm so late, Sister. But some days it's harder for me than others." Before the nun could respond, the girl turned to Hatch and Lindsey, who had stopped holding hands and had risen from the sofa. "Hi, I'm Regina. I'm a cripple."

She reached out in greeting. Hatch reached out, too, before he realized that her right arm and hand were not well formed. The arm was almost normal, just a little thinner than her left, until it got to the wrist, where the bones took an odd twist. Instead of a full hand, she possessed just two fingers and the stub of a thumb that all seemed to have limited flexibility. Shaking hands with the girl felt strange—distinctly strange—but not unpleasant.

Her gray eyes were fixed intently on his eyes. Trying to read his reaction. He knew at once that it would be impossible ever to conceal true feelings from her, and he was relieved that he had not been in the least repelled by her deformity.

"I'm so happy to meet you, Regina," he said. "I'm Hatch Harrison, and this is my wife, Lindsey."

The girl turned to Lindsey and shook hands with her, as well, saying, "Well, I know I'm a disappointment. You child-starved women usually prefer babies young enough to cuddle—"

The Nun with No Name gasped in shock. "Regina, really!"

Sister Immaculata looked too apoplectic to speak, like a penguin that had frozen solid, mouth agape and eyes bulging in protest, hit by an arctic chill too cold even for Antarctic birds to survive.

Approaching from the windows, Father Jiminez said, "Mr. and Mrs. Harrison, I apologize for—"

"No need to apologize for anything," Lindsey said quickly, evidently sensing, as Hatch did, that the girl was testing them and that to have any hope of passing the test, they must not let themselves be co-opted into an adults-against-the-kid division of sympathies.

Regina hopped-squirmed-wriggled into the second armchair, and Hatch was fairly certain she was making herself appear a lot more awkward than she really was.

The Nun with No Name gently touched Sister Immaculata on the shoulder, and the older nun eased back into her chair, still with the frozen-penguin look. The two priests brought the client chairs from in front of the attorney's desk, and the younger nun pulled up a side chair from a corner, so they could all join the group. Hatch realized he was the only one still standing. He sat on the sofa beside Lindsey again.

Now that everyone had arrived, Salvatore Gujilio insisted on serving refreshments—Pepsi, ginger ale, or Perrier—which he did without calling for the assistance of his secretary, fetching everything from a wet bar discreetly tucked into one mahogany-paneled corner of the genteel office. As the attorney bustled about, quiet and quick in spite of his immensity, never crashing into a piece of furniture or knocking over a vase, never coming even close to obliterating one of the two Tiffany lamps with hand-blown trumpet-flower shades, Hatch realized that the big man was no longer an overpowering figure, no longer the inevitable center of attention: he could not compete with the girl, who was probably less than one-fourth his size.

"Well," Regina said to Hatch and Lindsey, as she accepted a glass of Pepsi from Gujilio, holding it in her left hand, the good one, "you came here to learn all about me, so I guess I should tell you about myself. First thing, of course, is that I'm a cripple." She tilted her head and looked at them quizzically. "Did you know I was a cripple?"

"We do now," Lindsey said.

"But I mean before you came."

"We knew you had—some sort of problem," Hatch said.

"Mutant genes," Regina said.

Father Jiminez let out a heavy sigh.

Sister Immaculata seemed about to say something, glanced at Hatch and Lindsey, then decided to remain silent.

"My parents were dope fiends," the girl said.

"Regina!" The Nun with No Name protested. "You don't know that for sure, you don't know any such a thing."

"Well, but it figures," the girl said. "For at least twenty years now, illegal drugs have been the cause of most birth defects. Did you know that? I read it in a book. I read a lot. I'm book crazy. I don't want to say I'm a bookworm. That sounds icky—don't you think? But if I were a worm, I'd rather be curled up in a book than in any apple. It's good for a crippled kid to like books, because *they* won't let you do the things ordinary people do, even if you're pretty sure you can do them, so books are like having a whole other life. I like adventure stories where they go to the north pole or Mars or New York or somewhere. I like good mysteries, too, most anything by Agatha Christie, but I especially like stories about animals, and most especially about talking animals like in *The Wind in the Willows.* I had a talking animal once. It was just a goldfish, and of course it was really me not the fish who talked, because I read this book on ventriloquism and learned to throw my voice, which is neat. So I'd sit across the room and throw my voice into the goldfish bowl." She began to talk squeakily, without moving her lips, and the voice seemed to come out of The Nun with No Name: *"Hi, my name's Binky the Fish, and if you try to put me in a sandwich and eat me, I'll shit on the mayonnaise."* She returned to her normal voice and talked right over the flurry of reactions from the religiosities around her. "There you have an-

121

other problem with cripples like me. We tend to be smart-mouthed sometimes because we know nobody has the guts to whack us on the ass."

Sister Immaculata looked as if *she* might have the guts, but in fact all she did was mumble something about no TV privileges for a week.

Hatch, who had found the nun as frightening as a pterodactyl when he'd first met her, was not impressed by her glower now, even though it was so intense that he registered it with his peripheral vision. He could not take his eyes off the girl.

Regina went blithely on without pause: "Besides being smart-mouthed sometimes, what you should know about me is, I'm so clumsy, hitching around like Long John Silver—now *there* was a good book—that I'll probably break everything of value in your house. Never meaning to, of course. It'll be a regular destruction derby. Do you have the patience for that? I'd hate to be beaten senseless and locked in the attic just because I'm a poor crippled girl who can't always control herself. This leg doesn't look so bad, really, and if I keep exercising it, I think it's going to turn out pretty enough, but I don't really have much strength in it, and I don't feel too damned much in it, either." She balled up her deformed right hand and smacked it so hard against the thigh of her right leg that she startled Gujilio, who was trying to convey a ginger ale into the hand of the younger priest, who was staring at the girl as if mesmerized. She smacked herself again, so hard that Hatch winced, and she said, "You see? Dead meat. Speaking of meat, I'm also a fussy eater. I simply can't stomach dead meat. Oh, I don't mean I eat live animals. What I am is, I'm a vegetarian, which makes things harder for you, even supposing you didn't mind that I'm not a cuddly baby you can dress up cute. My only virtue is that I'm very bright, practically a genius. But even that's a drawback as far as some people are concerned. I'm smart beyond my years, so I don't act much like a child—"

"You're certainly acting like one now," Sister Immaculata said, and seemed pleased at getting in that zinger.

But Regina ignored it: "—and what you want, after all, is a child, a precious and ignorant blob, so you can show her the

122

world, have the fun of watching her learn and blossom, whereas
I have already done a lot of my blossoming. Intellectual blossoming, that is. I still don't have boobs. I'm also bored by TV, which
means I wouldn't be able to join in a jolly family evening around
the tube, and I'm allergic to cats in case you've got one, and I'm
opinionated, which some people find infuriating in a ten-year-old
girl." She paused, sipped her Pepsi, and smiled at them. "There.
I think that pretty much covers it."

"She's never like this," Father Jiminez mumbled, more to himself or to God than to Hatch and Lindsey. He tossed back half of
his Perrier as if chugging hard liquor.

Hatch turned to Lindsey. Her eyes were a little glazed. She
didn't seem to know what to say, so he returned his attention to
the girl. "I suppose it's only fair if I tell you something about us."

Putting aside her drink and starting to get up, Sister Immaculata said, "Really, Mr. Harrison, you don't have to put
yourself through—"

Politely waving the nun back into her seat, Hatch said, "No, no.
It's all right. Regina's a little nervous—"

"Not particularly," Regina said.

"Of course, you are," Hatch said.

"No, I'm not."

"A little nervous," Hatch insisted, "just as Lindsey and I are.
It's okay." He smiled at the girl as winningly as he could. "Well,
let's see . . . I've had a lifelong interest in antiques, an affection for
things that endure and have real character about them, and I have
my own antique shop with two employees. That's how I earn my
living. I don't like television much myself or—"

"What kind of a name is Hatch?" the girl interrupted. She
giggled as if to imply that it was too funny to be the name of
anyone except, perhaps, a talking goldfish.

"My full first name is Hatchford."

"It's still funny."

"Blame my mother," Hatch said. "She always thought my dad
was going to make a lot of money and move us up in society, and
she thought Hatchford sounded like a really upper-crust name:
Hatchford Benjamin Harrison. The only thing that would've

made it a better name in her mind was if it was Hatchford Benja-min Rockefeller."

"Did he?" the girl asked.

"Who he, did what?"

"Did your father make a lot of money?"

Hatch winked broadly at Lindsey and said, "Looks like we have a gold digger on our hands."

"If you were rich," the girl said, "of course, that would be a consideration."

Sister Immaculata let a hiss of air escape between her teeth, and The Nun with No Name leaned back in her chair and closed her eyes with an expression of resignation. Father Jiminez got up and, waving Gujilio away, went to the wet bar to get something stronger than Perrier, Pepsi, or ginger ale. Because neither Hatch nor Lindsey seemed obviously offended by the girl's behavior, none of the others felt authorized to terminate the interview or even further reprimand the child.

"I'm afraid we're not rich," Hatch told her. "Comfortable, yes. We don't want for anything. But we don't drive a Rolls-Royce, and we don't wear caviar pajamas."

A flicker of genuine amusement crossed the girl's face, but she quickly suppressed it. She looked at Lindsey and said, "What about you?"

Lindsey blinked. She cleared her throat. "Uh, well, I'm an artist. A painter."

"Like Picasso?"

"Not that style, no, but an artist like him, yes."

"I saw a picture once of a bunch of dogs playing poker," the girl said. "Did you paint that?"

Lindsey said, "No, I'm afraid I didn't."

"Good. It was stupid. I saw a picture once of a bull and a bullfighter, it was on velvet, very bright colors. Do you paint in very bright colors on velvet?"

"No," Lindsey said. "But if you like that sort of thing, I could paint any scene you wanted on velvet for your room."

Regina crinkled up her face. "Puh-leeese. I'd rather put a dead cat on the wall."

Nothing surprised the folks from St. Thomas's any more. The younger priest actually smiled, and Sister Immaculata murmured "dead cat," not in exasperation but as if agreeing that such a bit of macabre decoration would, indeed, be preferable to a painting on velvet.

"My style," Lindsey said, eager to rescue her reputation after offering to paint something so tacky, "is generally described as a blending of neoclassicism and surrealism. I know that's quite a big mouthful—"

"Well, it's not my favorite sort of thing," Regina said, as if she had a hoot-owl's idea in hell what those styles were like and what a blend of them might resemble. "If I came to live with you, and if I had a room of my own, you wouldn't make me hang a lot of *your* paintings on my walls, would you?" The "your" was emphasized in such a way as to imply that she still preferred a dead cat even if velvet was not involved.

"Not a one," Lindsey assured her.

"Good."

"Do you think you might like living with us?" Lindsey asked, and Hatch wondered whether that prospect excited or terrified her.

Abruptly the girl struggled up from the chair, wobbling as she reached her feet, as if she might topple headfirst into the coffee table. Hatch rose, ready to grab her, even though he suspected it was all part of the act.

When she regained her balance, she put down her glass, from which she'd drunk all the Pepsi, and she said, "I've got to go pee, I've got a weak bladder. Part of my mutant genes. I can never hold myself. Half the time I feel like I'm going to burst in the most embarrassing places, like right here in Mr. Gujilio's office, which is another thing you should probably consider before taking me into your home. You probably have a lot of nice things, being in the antiques and art business, nice things you wouldn't want messed up, and here I am lurching into everything and breaking it or, worse, I get a bursting bladder attack all over something priceless. Then you'd ship me back to the orphanage, and I'd be so emotional about it, I'd clump up to the roof and throw myself off, a most tragic suicide, which none of us really would want to see happen. Nice meeting you."

She turned and wrenched herself across the Persian carpet and out of the room in that most unlikely gait—*sccccuuuurrrr . . . THUD!*—which no doubt sprang from the same well of talent out of which she had drawn her goldfish ventriloquism. Her deep-auburn hair swayed and glinted like fire.

They all stood in silence, listening to the girl's slowly fading footsteps. At one point, she bumped against the wall with a solid *thunk!* that must have hurt, then bravely scrape-thudded onward.

"She does *not* have a weak bladder," Father Jiminez said, taking a swallow from a glassful of amber liquid. He seemed to be drinking bourbon now. "That is *not* part of her disability."

"She's not really like that," Father Duran said, blinking his owlish eyes as if smoke had gotten in them. "She's a delightful child. I know that's hard for you to believe right now—"

"And she can walk much better than that, immeasurably better," said The Nun with No Name. "I don't know what's gotten into her."

"I do," Sister Immaculata said. She wiped one hand wearily down her face. Her eyes were sad. "Two years ago, when she was eight, we managed to place her with adoptive parents. A couple in their thirties who were told they could never have children of their own. They convinced themselves that a disabled child would be a special blessing. Then, two weeks after Regina went to live with them, while they were in the pre-adoption trial phase, the woman became pregnant. Suddenly they were going to have their own child, after all, and the adoption didn't seem so wise."

"And they just brought Regina back?" Lindsey asked. "Just dumped her at the orphanage? How terrible."

"I can't judge them," Sister Immaculata said. "They may have felt they didn't have enough love for a child of their own and poor Regina, too, in which case they did the right thing. Regina doesn't deserve to be raised in a home where every minute of every day she knows she's second best, second in love, something of an outsider. Anyway, she was broken up by the rejection. She took a long time to get her self-confidence back. And now I think she doesn't want to take another risk."

They stood in silence.

The sun was very bright beyond the windows. The palm trees swayed lazily. Between the trees lay glimpses of Fashion Island, the Newport Beach shopping center and business complex at the perimeter of which Gujilio's office was located.

"Sometimes, with the sensitive ones, a bad experience ruins any chance for them. They refuse to try again. I'm afraid our Regina is one of those. She came in here determined to alienate you and wreck the interview, and she succeeded in singular style."

"It's like somebody who's been in prison all his life," said Father Jiminez, "gets paroled, is all excited at first, then finds he can't make it on the outside. So he commits a crime just to get back in. The institution might be limiting, unsatisfying—but it's known, it's safe."

Salvatore Gujilio bustled around, relieving people of their empty glasses. He was still an enormous man by any standard, but even with Regina gone from the room, Gujilio no longer dominated it as he had done before. He had been forever diminished by that single comparison with the delicate, pert-nosed, gray-eyed child.

"I'm so sorry," Sister Immaculata said, putting a consoling hand on Lindsey's shoulder. "We'll try again, my dear. We'll go back to square one and match you up with another child, the perfect child this time."

2

Lindsey and Hatch left Salvatore Gujilio's office at ten past three that Thursday afternoon. They had agreed not to talk about the interview until dinner, giving themselves time to contemplate the encounter and examine their reactions to it. Neither wanted to make a decision based on emotion, or influence the other to act on initial impressions—then live to regret it.

Of course, they had never expected the meeting to progress remotely along the lines it had gone. Lindsey was eager to talk about it. She assumed that their decision was already made, had been made for them by the girl, and that there was no point in further contemplation. But they had agreed to wait, and Hatch did not seem disposed to violate that agreement, so she kept her mouth shut as well.

She drove their new sporty-red Mitsubishi. Hatch sat in the passenger seat with his shades on, one arm out his open window, tapping time against the side of the car as he listened to golden oldie rock-'n'-roll on the radio. "Please Mister Postman" by the Marvelettes.

She passed the last of the giant date palms along Newport Center Drive and turned left onto Pacific Coast Highway, past vine-covered walls, and headed south. The late-April day was warm but not hot, with one of those intensely blue skies that, toward sunset, would acquire an electric luminescence reminiscent of skies in Maxfield Parrish paintings. Traffic was light on the Coast Highway, and the ocean glimmered like a great swatch of silver- and gold-sequined cloth.

A quiet exuberance flowed through Lindsey, as it had done for seven weeks. It was exhilaration over just being alive, which was in every child but which most adults lost during the process of growing up. She'd lost it, too, without realizing. A close encounter with death was just the thing to give you back the *joie de vivre* of extreme youth.

More than two floors below Hell, naked beneath a blanket on his stained and sagging mattress, Vassago passed the daylight hours in sleep. His slumber was usually filled with dreams of violated flesh and shattered bone, blood and bile, vistas of human skulls. Sometimes he dreamed of dying multitudes writhing in agony on barren ground beneath a black sky, and he walked among them as a prince of Hell among the common rabble of the damned.

The dreams that occupied him on that day, however, were strange and remarkable for their ordinariness. A dark-haired, dark-eyed woman in a cherry-red car, viewed from the perspective of an unseen man in the passenger seat beside her. Palm trees. Red bougainvillea. The ocean spangled with light.

Harrison's Antiques was at the south end of Laguna Beach, on Pacific Coast Highway. It was in a stylish two-story Art Deco building that contrasted interestingly with the 18th- and 19th-century merchandise in the big display windows.

Glenda Dockridge, Hatch's assistant and the store manager, was helping Lew Booner, their general handyman, with the dusting. In a large antique store, dusting was akin to the painting of the Golden Gate Bridge: once you reached the far end, it was time to come back to the beginning and start all over again. Glenda was in a great mood because she had sold a Napoleon III ormolu-mounted black-lacquered cabinet with Japanned panels *and,* to the same customer, a 19th-century Italian polygonal, tilt-top table with elaborate marquetry inlay. They were excellent sales—especially considering that she worked on salary against a commission.

While Hatch looked through the day's mail, attended to some correspondence, and examined a pair of 18th-century rosewood palace pedestals with inlaid jade dragons that had arrived from a scout in Hong Kong, Lindsey helped Glenda and Lew with the dusting. In her new frame of mind, even that chore was a pleasure. It gave her a chance to appreciate the details of the antiques—the turn of a finial on a bronze lamp, the carving on a table leg, the delicately pierced and hand-finished rims on a set of 18th-century English porcelains. Contemplating the history and cultural meaning of each piece as she happily dusted it, she realized that her new attitude had a distinctly Zen quality.

At twilight, sensing the approach of night, Vassago woke and sat up in the approximation of a grave that was his home. He was filled with a hunger for death and a need to kill.

The last image he remembered from his dream was of the woman from the red car. She was not in the car any more, but in a chamber he could not quite see, standing in front of a Chinese screen, wiping it with a white cloth. She turned, as if he had spoken to her, and she smiled.

Her smile was so radiant, so full of life, that Vassago wanted to smash her face in with a hammer, break out her teeth, shatter her jaw bones, make it impossible for her to smile ever again.

He had dreamed of her two or three times over the past several weeks. The first time she had been in a wheelchair, weeping and laughing simultaneously.

Again, he searched his memory, but he could not recall her face among those he had ever seen outside of dreams. He wondered who she was and why she visited him when he slept.

Outside, night fell. He sensed it coming down. A great black drape that gave the world a preview of death at the end of every bright and shining day.

He dressed and left his hideaway.

By seven o'clock that early-spring night, Lindsey and Hatch were at Zov's, a small but busy restaurant in Tustin. The decor was mainly black and white, with lots of big windows and mirrors. The staff, unfailingly friendly and efficient, were dressed in black and white to complement the long room. The food they served was such a perfect sensual experience that the monochromatic bistro seemed ablaze with color.

The noise level was congenial rather than annoying. They did not have to raise their voices to hear each other, and felt as if the background buzz provided a screen of privacy from nearby tables.

Through the first two courses—calamari; black-bean soup—they spoke of trivial things. But when the main course was served— swordfish for both of them—Lindsey could no longer contain herself.

She said, "Okay, all right, we've had all day to brood about it. We haven't colored each other's opinions. So what do you think of Regina?"

"What do *you* think of Regina?"

"You first."

"Why me?"

Lindsey said, "Why not?"

He took a deep breath, hesitated. "I'm crazy about the kid."

Lindsey felt like leaping up and doing a little dance, the way a cartoon character might express uncontainable delight, because her joy and excitement were brighter and bolder than things were supposed to be in real life. She had hoped for just that reaction from him, but she hadn't known what he would say, really hadn't had a clue, because the meeting had been . . . well, one apt word would be "daunting."

"Oh, God, I love her," Lindsey said. "She's so sweet."

"She's a tough cookie."

"That's an act."

"She was putting on an act for us, yeah, but she's tough just the same. She's had to be tough. Life didn't give her a choice."

"But it's a good tough."

"It's a great tough," he agreed. "I'm not saying it put me off. I admired it, I loved her."

"She's so bright."

"Struggling so hard to make herself unappealing," Hatch said, "and that only made her *more* appealing."

"The poor kid. Afraid of being rejected again, so she took the offensive."

"When I heard her coming down the hall, I thought it was—"

"Godzilla!" Lindsey said.

"At least. And how'd you like Binky the talking goldfish?"

"Shit on the mayonnaise!" Lindsey said.

They both laughed, and people around them turned to look,

either because of their laughter or because some of what Lindsey said was overheard, which only made them laugh harder.

"She's going to be a handful," Hatch said.

"She'll be a dream."

"Nothing's that easy."

"She will be."

"One problem."

"What's that?"

He hesitated. "What if she doesn't want to come with us?"

Lindsey's smile froze. "She will. She'll come."

"Maybe not."

"Don't be negative."

"I'm only saying we've got to be prepared for disappointment."

Lindsey shook her head adamantly. "No. It's going to work out. It has to. We've had more than our share of bad luck, bad times. We deserve better. The wheel has turned. We're going to put a family together again. Life is going to be good, it's going to be so fine. The worst is behind us now."

3

That Thursday night, Vassago enjoyed the conveniences of a motel room.

Usually he used one of the fields behind the abandoned amusement park as a toilet. He also washed each evening with bottled water and liquid soap. He shaved with a straight razor, an aerosol can of lather, and a piece of a broken mirror that he had found in a corner of the park.

When rain fell at night, he liked to bathe in the open, letting the downpour sluice over him. If lightning accompanied the storm, he sought the highest point on the paved midway, hoping that he was about to receive the grace of Satan and be recalled to the land of the dead by one scintillant bolt of electricity. But the rainy season in southern California was over now, and most likely would not come around again until December. If he earned his way back into the fold of the dead and damned before then, the means of his deliverance from the hateful world of the living would be some other force than lightning.

Once a week, sometimes twice, he rented a motel room to use the shower and make a better job of grooming than he could in the primitive conditions of his hideaway, though not because hygiene was important to him. Filth had its powerful attractions. The air and water of Hades, to which he longed to return, were filth of infinite variety. But if he was to move among the living and prey upon them, building the collection that might win him readmission to the realm of the damned, there were certain conventions that had to be followed in order not to draw undue attention to himself. Among them was a certain degree of cleanliness.

Vassago always used the same motel, the Blue Skies, a seedy hole toward the southern end of Santa Ana, where the unshaven desk clerk accepted only cash, asked for no identification, and never looked guests in the eyes, as if afraid of what he might see in theirs or they in his. The area was a swamp of drug dealers and streetwalkers. Vassago was one of the few men who did not check in with a whore in tow. He stayed only an hour or two, however, which was in keeping with the duration of the average customer's use of the accommodations, and he was allowed the same anonymity as those who, grunting and sweating, noisily rocked the headboards of their beds against the walls in rooms adjoining his.

He could not have lived there full time, if only because his awareness of the frenzied coupling of the sluts and their johns filled him with anger, anxiety, and nausea at the urgent needs and frenetic rhythms of the living. The atmosphere made it difficult to think clearly and impossible to rest, even though the perversion and dementia of the place was the very thing in which he had reveled when he had been one of the fully alive.

No other motel or boarding house would have been safe. They would have wanted identification. Besides, he could pass among the living as one of them only as long as their contact with him was casual. Any motel clerk or landlord who took a deeper interest in his character and encountered him repeatedly would soon realize that he was different from them in some indefinable yet deeply disturbing way.

Anyway, to avoid drawing attention to himself, he preferred the amusement park as primary quarters. The authorities looking for him would be less likely to find him there than anywhere else. Most important, the park offered solitude, graveyard stillness, and regions of perfect darkness to which he could escape during daylight hours when his sensitive eyes could not tolerate the insistent brightness of the sun.

Motels were tolerable only between dusk and dawn.

That pleasantly warm Thursday night, when he came out of the Blue Skies Motel office with his room key, he noticed a familiar Pontiac parked in shadows at the back of the lot, beyond the end unit, not nose-in to the motel but facing the office. The car had been there on Sunday, the last time Vassago had used the Blue Skies. A man was slumped behind the wheel, as if sleeping or just passing time while he waited for someone to meet him. He had been there Sunday night, features veiled by the night and the haze of reflected light on his windshield.

Vassago drove the Camaro to unit six, about in the middle of the long arm of the L-shaped structure, parked in front, and let himself into his room. He carried only a change of clothes—all black like the clothes he was wearing.

Inside the room, he did not turn on the light. He never did.

For a while he stood with his back against the door, thinking about the Pontiac and the man behind the steering wheel. He might have been just a drug dealer working out of his car. The number of dealers crawling the neighborhood was even greater than the number of cockroaches swarming inside the walls of that decaying motel. But where were his customers with their quick nervous eyes and greasy wads of money?

Vassago dropped his clothes on the bed, put his sunglasses in his jacket pocket, and went into the small bathroom. It smelled of hastily sloshed disinfectant that could not mask a mélange of vile biological odors.

A rectangle of pale light marked a window above the back wall of the shower. Sliding open the glass door, which made a scraping noise as it moved along the corroded track, he stepped into the stall. If the window had been fixed, or if it had been divided vertically into two panes, he would have been foiled. But it swung outward from the top on rusted hinges. He gripped the sill above his head, pulled himself through the window, and wriggled out into the service alley behind the motel.

He paused to put on his sunglasses again. A nearby sodium-vapor streetlamp cast a urine-yellow glare that scratched like windblown sand at his eyes. The glasses mellowed it to a muddy amber and clarified his vision.

He went right, all the way to the end of the block, turned right on the side street, then right again at the next corner, circling the motel. He slipped around the end of the short wing of the L-shaped building and moved along the covered walkway in front of the last units until he was behind the Pontiac.

At the moment that end of the motel was quiet. No one was coming or going from any of the rooms.

The man behind the wheel was sitting with one arm out of the open car window. If he had glanced at the side mirror, he might have seen Vassago coming up on him, but his attention was focused on room six in the other wing of the L.

Vassago jerked open the door, and the guy actually started to fall out because he'd been leaning against it. Vassago hit him hard in the face, using his elbow like a battering ram, which was better than a fist, except he didn't hit him squarely enough. The guy was rocked but not finished, so he pushed up and out of the Pontiac, trying to grapple with Vassago. He was overweight and slow. A knee driven hard into his crotch slowed him even more. The guy went into a prayer posture, gagging, and Vassago stepped back far enough to kick him. The stranger fell over onto his side, so Vassago kicked him again, in the head this time. The guy was out cold, as still as the pavement on which he was sprawled.

Hearing a startled intake of breath, Vassago turned and saw a frizzy-haired blond hooker in a miniskirt and a middle-aged guy in a cheap suit and a bad toupee. They were coming out of the nearest room. They gaped at the man on the ground. At Vassago.

135

He stared back at them until they reentered their room and quietly pulled the door shut behind them.

The unconscious man was heavy, maybe two hundred pounds, but Vassago was more than strong enough to lift him. He carried the guy around to the passenger side and loaded him into the other front seat. Then he got behind the wheel, started the Pontiac, and departed the Blue Skies.

Several blocks away, he turned onto a street of tract homes built thirty years ago and aging badly. Ancient Indian laurels and coral trees flanked the canted sidewalks and lent a note of grace in spite of the neighborhood's decline. He pulled the Pontiac to the curb. He switched off the engine and the lights.

As no streetlamps were nearby, he removed his sunglasses to search the unconscious man. He found a loaded revolver in a shoulder holster under the guy's jacket. He took it for himself.

The stranger was carrying two wallets. The first, and thicker, contained three hundred dollars in cash, which Vassago confiscated. It also held credit cards, photographs of people he didn't know, a receipt from a dry cleaner, a buy-ten-get-one-free punch card from a frozen-yogurt shop, a driver's license that identified the man as Morton Redlow of Anaheim, and insignificant odds and ends. The second wallet was quite thin, and it proved to be not a real wallet at all but a leather ID holder. In it were Redlow's license to operate as a private investigator and another license to carry a concealed weapon.

In the glove compartment, Vassago found only candy bars and a paperback detective novel. In the console between seats, he found chewing gum, breath mints, another candy bar, and a bent Thomas Brothers map book of Orange County.

He studied the map book for a while, then started the car and pulled away from the curb. He headed for Anaheim and the address on Redlow's driver's license.

When they were more than halfway there, Redlow began to groan and twitch, as if he might come to his senses. Driving with one hand, Vassago picked up the revolver he had taken off the man and clubbed him alongside the head with it. Redlow was quiet again.

4

One of the five other kids who shared Regina's table in the dining hall was Carl Cavanaugh, who was eight years old and acted every bit of it. He was a paraplegic, confined to a wheelchair, which you would have thought was enough of a handicap, but he made his lot in life worse by being a complete nerd. Their plates had no sooner been put on the table than Carl said, "I really like Friday afternoons, and you know why?" He didn't give anyone a chance to express a lack of interest. "Because Thursday night we always have beans *and* pea soup, so by Friday afternoon you can really cut some ripe farts."

The other kids groaned in disgust. Regina just ignored him.

Nerd or not, Carl was right: Thursday dinner at St. Thomas's Home for Children was always split-pea soup, ham, green beans, potatoes in herb butter sauce, and a square of fruited Jell-O with a blob of fake whipped cream for dessert. Sometimes the nuns got into the sherry or just went wild from too many years in their suffocating habits, and if they lost control on a Thursday, you might get corn instead of green beans or, if they were really over the top, maybe a pair of vanilla cookies with the Jell-O.

That Thursday the menu held no surprises, but Regina would not have cared—and might not have noticed—if the fare had included filet mignon or, conversely, cow pies. Well, she probably would have noticed a cow pie on her plate, though she wouldn't have cared if it was substituted for the green beans because she didn't like green beans. She liked ham. She had lied when she'd told the Harrisons she was a vegetarian, figuring they would find dietary fussiness one more reason to reject her flat-out, at the start, instead of later when it would hurt more. But even as she ate, her attention was not on her food and not on the conversation of the other kids at her table, but on the meeting in Mr. Gujilio's office that afternoon.

She had screwed up.

They were going to have to build a Museum of Famous Screw-ups just to have a place for a statue of her, so people could come from all over the world, from France and Japan and Chile, just to see it. Schoolkids would come, whole classes at a time with their teachers, to study her so they could learn what *not* to do and how *not* to act. Parents would point at her statue and ominously warn their children, "Anytime you think you're so smart, just remember her and think how you might wind up like *that,* a figure of pity and ridicule, laughed at and reviled."

Two thirds of the way through the interview, she had realized the Harrisons were special people. They probably would never treat her as badly as she had been treated by the Infamous Dotterfields, the couple who accepted her and took her home and then rejected her in two weeks when they discovered they were going to have a child of their own, Satan's child, no doubt, who would one day destroy the world and turn against even the Dotterfields, burning them alive with a flash of fire from his demonic little pig eyes. (Uh-oh. Wishing harm to another. The thought is as bad as the deed. Remember that for confession, Reg.) Anyway, the Harrisons were different, which she began to realize slowly—such a screwup—and which she knew for sure when Mr. Harrison made the crack about caviar pajamas and showed he had a sense of humor. But by then she was so *into* her act that somehow she couldn't stop being obnoxious—screwup that she was—couldn't find a way to retreat and start over. Now the Harrisons were probably getting drunk, celebrating their narrow escape, or maybe down on their knees in a church, weeping with relief and fervently saying the Rosary, thanking the Holy Mother for interceding to spare them the mistake of adopting that awful girl sight-unseen. Shit. (Oops. Vulgarity. But not as bad as taking the Lord's name in vain. Even worth mentioning in the confessional?)

In spite of having no appetite and in spite of Carl Cavanaugh and his crude humor, she ate all of her dinner, but only because God's policemen, the nuns, would not let her leave the table until she cleaned her plate. The fruit in the lime Jell-O was peaches, which made dessert an ordeal. She couldn't understand how anyone could think that lime and peaches went together.

Okay, so nuns were not very worldly, but she wasn't asking them to learn which rare wine to serve with roast tenderloin of platypus, for God's sake. (Sorry, God.) Pineapple and lime Jell-O, certainly. Pears and lime Jell-O, okay. Even bananas and lime Jell-O. But putting peaches in lime Jell-O was, to her way of thinking, like leaving the raisins out of rice pudding and replacing them with chunks of watermelon, for God's sake. (Sorry, God.) She managed to eat the dessert by telling herself that it could have been worse; the nuns could have served dead mice dipped in chocolate—though why nuns, of all people, would want to do that, she had no idea. Still, imagining something worse than what she had to face was a trick that worked, a technique of self-persuasion that she had used many times before. Soon the hated Jell-O was gone, and she was free to leave the dining hall.

After dinner most kids went to the recreation room to play Monopoly and other games, or to the TV room to watch whatever slop was on the boob tube, but as usual she returned to her room. She spent most evenings reading. Not tonight, though. She planned to spend this evening feeling sorry for herself and contemplating her status as a world-class screwup (good thing stupidity isn't a sin), so she would never forget how dumb she had been and would remember never to make such a jackass of herself again.

Moving along the tile-floored hallways nearly as fast as a kid with two good legs, she remembered how she had clumped into the attorney's office, and she began to blush. In her room, which she shared with a blind girl named Winnie, as she jumped into bed and flopped on her back, she recalled the calculated clumsiness with which she had levered herself into the chair in front of Mr. and Mrs. Harrison. Her blush deepened, and she put both hands over her face.

"Reg," she said softly against the palms of her own hands, "you are the biggest asshole in the world." (One more item on the list for the next confession, besides lying and deceiving and taking God's name in vain: the repeated use of a vulgarity.) "Shit, shit, shit!" (Going to be a long confession.)

5

When Redlow regained consciousness, his assorted pains were so bad, they took one hundred percent of his attention. He had a violent headache to which he could have testified with such feeling in a television commercial that they would have been forced to open new aspirin factories to meet the consumer response. One eye was puffed half shut. His lips were split and swollen; they were numb and felt huge. His neck hurt, and his stomach was sore, and his testicles throbbed so fiercely from the knee he had taken in the crotch that the idea of getting up and walking sent a paroxysm of nausea through him.

Gradually he remembered what had happened to him, that the bastard had taken him by surprise. Then he realized he was not lying on the motel parking lot but sitting in a chair, and for the first time he was afraid.

He was not merely sitting in the chair. He was tied in it. Ropes bound him at chest and waist, and more ropes wound across his thighs, securing him to the seat. His arms were fixed to the arms of the chair just below his elbows and again at the wrists.

Pain had muddied his thought processes. Now fear clarified them.

Simultaneously squinting his good right eye and trying to widen his swollen left eye, he studied the darkness. For a moment he assumed he was in a room at the Blue Skies Motel, outside of which he had been running a surveillance in hope of spotting the kid. Then he recognized his own living room. He couldn't see much. No lights were on. But having lived in that house for eighteen years, he could identify the patterns of ambient night-glow at the windows, the dim shapes of the furniture, shadows among shadows of differing intensity, and the subtle but singular smell of home, which was as special and instantly identifiable to him as the odor of any particular lair to any particular wolf in the wild.

He did not feel much like a wolf tonight. He felt like a rabbit, shivering in recognition of its status as prey.

For a few seconds he thought he was alone, and he began to

140

strain at the ropes. Then a shadow rose from other shadows and approached him.

He could see nothing more of his adversary than a silhouette. Even that seemed to melt into the silhouettes of inanimate objects, or to change as if the kid were a polymorphous creature that could assume a variety of forms. But he knew it was the kid because he sensed that difference, that *alienness* he had perceived the first time he had laid eyes on the bastard on Sunday, just four nights ago, at the Blue Skies.

"Comfortable, Mr. Redlow?"

Over the past three months, as he had searched for the creep, Redlow had developed a deep curiosity about him, trying to puzzle out what he wanted, what he needed, how he thought. After showing countless people the various photographs of the kid, and after spending more than a little of his own time in contemplation of them, he had been especially curious about what the voice would be like that went with that remarkably handsome yet forbidding face. It sounded nothing like he had imagined it would be, neither cold and steely like the voice of a machine designed to pass for human nor the guttural and savage snarling of a beast. Rather, it was soothing, honey-toned, with an appealing reverberant timbre.

"Mr. Redlow, sir, can you hear me?"

More than anything else, the kid's politeness and the natural formality of his speech disconcerted Redlow.

"I apologize for having been so rough with you, sir, but you really didn't give me much choice."

Nothing in the voice indicated that the kid was being snide or mocking. He was just a boy who had been raised to address his elders with consideration and respect, a habit he could not cast off even under circumstances such as these. The detective was gripped by a primitive, superstitious feeling that he was in the presence of am entity that could imitate humanity but had nothing whatsoever in common with the human species.

Speaking through split lips, his words somewhat slurred, Morton Redlow said, "Who are you, what the hell do you want?"

"You know who I am."

141

"I haven't a fucking clue. You blindsided me. I haven't seen your face. What—are you a bat or something? Why don't you turn on a light?"

Still only a black form, the kid moved closer, to within a few feet of the chair. "You were hired to find me."

"I was hired to run surveillance on a guy named Kirkaby. Leonard Kirkaby. Wife thinks he's cheating on her. And he is. Brings his secretary to the Blue Skies every Thursday for some in-and-out."

"Well, sir, that's a little hard for me to believe, you know? The Blue Skies is for low-life guys and cheap whores, not business executives and their secretaries."

"Maybe he gets off on the sleaziness of it, treating the girl like a whore. Who the hell knows, huh? Anyway, you sure aren't Kirkaby. I know his voice. He doesn't sound anything like you. Not as young as you, either. Besides, he's a piece of puff pastry. He couldn't have handled me the way you did,"

The kid was quiet for a while. Just staring down at Redlow. Then he began to pace. In the dark. Unhesitating, never bumping into furniture. Like a restless cat, except his eyes didn't glow.

Finally he said, "So what're you saying, sir? That this is all just a big mistake?"

Redlow knew his only chance of staying alive was to convince the kid of the lie—that a guy named Kirkaby had a letch for his secretary, and a bitter wife seeking evidence for a divorce. He just didn't know what tone to take to sell the story. With most people, Redlow had an unerring sense of which approach would beguile them and make them accept even the wildest proposition as the truth. But the kid was different; he didn't think or react like ordinary people.

Redlow decided to play it tough. "Listen, asshole, I wish I did know who you are or at least what the hell you look like, 'cause once this was finished, I'd come after you and bash your fuckin' head in."

The kid was silent for a while, mulling it over.

Then he said, "All right, I believe you."

Redlow sagged with relief, but sagging made all of his pains worse, so he tensed his muscles and sat up straight again.

"Too bad, but you just aren't right for my collection," the kid said.

"Collection?"

"Not enough life in you."

"What're you talking about?" Redlow asked.

"Burnt out."

The conversation was taking a turn Redlow didn't understand, which made him uneasy.

"Excuse me, sir, no offense meant, but you're getting too old for this kind of work."

Don't I know it, Redlow thought. He realized that, aside from one initial tug, he had not again tested the ropes that bound him. Only a few years ago, he would have quietly but steadily strained against them, trying to stretch the knots. Now he was passive.

"You're a muscular man, but you've gone a little soft, you've got a gut on you, and you're slow. From your driver's license, I see you're fifty-four, you're getting up there. Why do you still do it, keep hanging in there?"

"It's all I've got," Redlow said, and he was alert enough to be surprised by his own answer. He had meant to say, *It's all I know.*

"Well, yessir, I can see that," the kid said, looming over him in the darkness. "You've been divorced twice, no kids, and no woman lives with you right now. Probably hasn't been one living with you for years. Sorry, but I was snooping around the house while you were out cold, even though I knew it wasn't really right of me. Sorry. But I just wanted to get a handle on you, try to understand what you get out of this."

Redlow said nothing because he couldn't understand where all of this was leading. He was afraid of saying the wrong thing, and setting the kid off like a bottle rocket. The son of a bitch was insane. You never knew what might light the fuse on a nutcase like him. The kid had been through some analysis of his own over the years, and now he seemed to want to analyze Redlow, for reasons even he probably could not have explained. Maybe it was best to just let him rattle on, get it out of his system.

"Is it money, Mr. Redlow?"

"You mean, do I make any?"

"That's what I mean, sir."

"I do okay."

"You don't drive a great car or wear expensive clothes."

"I'm not into flash," Redlow said.

"No offense, sir, but this house isn't much."

"Maybe not, but there's no mortgage on it."

The kid was right over him, slowly leaning farther in with each question, as if he could see Redlow in the lightless room and was intently studying facial tics and twitches as he questioned him. Weird. Even in the dark, Redlow could sense the kid bending closer, closer, closer.

"No mortgage on it," the kid said thoughtfully. "Is that your reason for working, for living? To be able to say you paid off a mortgage on a dump like this?"

Redlow wanted to tell him to go fuck himself, but suddenly he was not so sure that playing tough was a good idea, after all.

"Is that what life's all about, sir? Is that all it's about? Is that why you find it so precious, why you're so eager to hold on to it? Is that why you life-lovers struggle to go on living—just to acquire a pitiful pile of belongings, so you can go out of the game a winner? I'm sorry, sir, but I just don't understand that. I don't understand at all."

The detective's heart was pounding too hard. It slammed painfully against his bruised ribs. He hadn't treated his heart well over the years, too many hamburgers, too many cigarettes, too much beer and bourbon. What was the crazy kid trying to do—talk him to death, scare him to death?

"I'd imagine you have some clients who don't want it on record that they ever hired you, they pay in cash. Would that be a valid assumption, sir?"

Redlow cleared his throat and tried not to sound frightened. "Yeah. Sure. Some of them."

"And part of winning the game would be to keep as much of

that money as you could, avoiding taxes on it, which would mean never putting it in a bank."

The kid was so close now that the detective could smell his breath. For some reason he had expected it to be sour, vile. But it smelled sweet, like chocolate, as if the kid had been eating candy in the dark.

"So I'd imagine you have a nice little stash here in the house somewhere. Is that right, sir?"

A warm quiver of hope caused a diminishment of the cold chills that had been chattering through Redlow for the past few minutes. If it was about money, he could deal with that. It made sense. He could understand the kid's motivation, and could see a way to get through the evening alive.

"Yeah," the detective said. "There's money. Take it. Take it and go. In the kitchen, there's a waste can with a plastic bag for a liner. Lift out the bag of trash, there's a brown paper bag full of cash under it, in the bottom of the can."

Something cold and rough touched the detective's right cheek, and he flinched from it.

"Pliers," the kid said, and the detective felt the jaws take a grip on his flesh.

"What're you doing?"

The kid twisted the pliers.

Redlow cried out in pain. "Wait, wait, stop it, shit, please, stop it, no!"

The kid stopped. He took the pliers away. He said, "I'm sorry, sir, but I just want you to understand that if there isn't any cash in the trash can, I won't be happy. I'll figure if you lied to me about this, you lied to me about everything."

"It's there," Redlow assured him hastily.

"It's not nice to lie, sir. It's not good. Good people don't lie. That's what they teach you, isn't it, sir?"

"Go, look, you'll see it's there," Redlow said desperately.

The kid went out of the living room, through the dining room archway. Soft footsteps echoed through the house from the tile floor of the kitchen. A clatter and rustle arose as the garbage bag was pulled out of the waste can.

145

Already damp with perspiration, Redlow began to gush sweat as he listened to the kid return through the pitch-black house. He appeared in the living room again, partly silhouetted against the pale-gray rectangle of a window.

"How can you see?" the detective asked, dismayed to hear a faint note of hysteria in his voice when he was struggling so hard to maintain control of himself. He *was* getting old. "What—are you wearing night-vision glasses or something, some military hardware? How in the hell would you get your hands on anything like that?"

Ignoring him, the kid said, "There isn't much I want or need, just food and changes of clothes. The only money I get is when I make an addition to my collection, whatever she happens to be carrying. Sometimes it's not much, only a few dollars. This is really a help. It really is. This much should last me as long as it takes for me to get back to where I belong. Do you know where I belong, Mr. Redlow?"

The detective did not answer. The kid had dropped down below the windows, out of sight. Redlow was squinting into the gloom, trying to detect movement and figure where he had gone.

"You know where I belong, Mr. Redlow?" the kid repeated.

Redlow heard a piece of furniture being shoved aside. Maybe an end table beside the sofa.

"I belong in Hell," the kid said. "I was there for a while. I want to go back. What kind of life have you led, Mr. Redlow? Do you think, when I go back to Hell, that maybe I'll see you over there?"

"What're you doing?" Redlow asked.

"Looking for an electrical outlet," the kid said as he shoved aside another piece of furniture. "Ah, here we go."

"Electrical outlet?" Redlow asked agitatedly. "Why?"

A frightening noise cut through the darkness: *zzzzrrrrrrrrr.*

"What was that?" Redlow demanded.

"Just testing, sir."

"Testing what?"

"You've got all sorts of pots and pans and gourmet utensils out there in the kitchen, sir. I guess you're really into cooking, are you?" The kid rose up again, appearing against the backdrop of

146

the dim ash-gray glow in the window glass. "The cooking—was that an interest before the second divorce, or more recent?"

"What were you testing?" Redlow asked again.

The kid approached the chair.

"There's more money," Redlow said frantically. He was soaked in sweat now. It was running down him in rivulets. "In the master bedroom." The kid loomed over him again, a mysterious and inhuman form. He seemed to be darker than anything around him, a black hole in the shape of a man, blacker than black. "In the c-closet. There's a w-w-wooden floor." The detective's bladder was suddenly full. It had blown up like a balloon all in an instant. Bursting. "Take out the shoes and crap. Lift up the back f-f-floorboards." He was going to piss himself. "There's a cash box. Thirty thousand dollars. Take it. Please. Take it and go."

"Thank you, sir, but I really don't need it. I've got enough, more than enough."

"Oh, Jesus, help me," Redlow said, and he was despairingly aware that this was the first time he had spoken to God—or even thought of Him—in decades.

"Let's talk about who you're *really* working for, sir."

"I told you—"

"But I lied when I said I believed you."

Zzzzrrrrrrrrrrrrr.

"What *is* that?" Redlow asked.

"Testing."

"Testing what, damn it?"

"It works real nice."

"What, what is it, what've you got?"

"An electric carving knife," the kid said.

6

Hatch and Lindsey drove home from dinner without getting on a freeway, taking their time, using the coast road from Newport Beach south, listening to K-Earth 101.1 FM, and singing along with golden oldies like "New Orleans," "Whispering Bells," and "California Dreamin'." She couldn't remember when they had last harmonized with the radio, though in the old days they had done it all the time. When he'd been three, Jimmy had known all the words to "Pretty Woman." When he was four he could sing "Fifty Ways to Leave Your Lover" without missing a line. For the first time in five years, she could think of Jimmy and still feel like singing.

They lived in Laguna Niguel, south of Laguna Beach, on the eastern side of the coastal hills, without an ocean view but with the benefit of sea breezes that moderated summer heat and winter chill. Their neighborhood, like most south-county developments, was so meticulously laid out that at times it seemed as if the planners had come to community design with a military background. But the gracefully curving streets, iron streetlamps with an artificial green patina, just-so arrangements of palms and jacarandas and ficus benjaminas, and well-maintained greenbelts with beds of colorful flowers were so soothing to the eye and soul that the subliminal sense of regimentation was not stifling.

As an artist, Lindsey believed that the hands of men and women were as capable of creating great beauty as nature was, and that discipline was fundamental to the creation of real art because art was meant to reveal meaning in the chaos of life. Therefore, she understood the impulse of the planners who had labored countless hours to coordinate the design of the community all the way down to the configuration of the steel grilles in the street drains that were set in the gutters.

Their two-story house, where they had lived only since Jimmy's death, was an Italian-Mediterranean model—the whole community was Italian Mediterranean—with four bedrooms and den, in cream-colored stucco with a Mexican tile roof. Two large ficus trees flanked the front walk. Malibu lights revealed beds of impatiens and petunias in front of red-flowering azalea bushes. As they pulled into the garage, they finished the last bars of "You Send Me."

Between taking turns in the bathroom, Hatch started a gas-log fire in the family-room fireplace, and Lindsey poured Baileys Irish

Cream on the rocks for both of them. They sat on the sofa in front of the fire, their feet on a large, matching ottoman.

All the upholstered furniture in the house was modern with soft lines and in light natural tones. It made a pleasing contrast with—and good backdrop for—the many antique pieces and Lindsey's paintings.

The sofa was also hugely comfortable, good for conversation and, as she discovered for the first time, a great spot to snuggle. To her surprise, snuggling turned into necking, and their necking escalated into petting, as if they were a couple of teenagers, for God's sake. Passion overwhelmed her as it had not done in years.

Their clothes came off slowly, as in a series of dissolves in a motion picture, until they were naked without quite knowing how they had gotten that way. Then they were just as mysteriously coupled, moving together in a silken rhythm, bathed in flickering firelight. The joyful naturalness of it, escalating from a dreamy motion to breathless urgency, was a radical departure from the stilted and dutiful lovemaking they had known during the past five years, and Lindsey could almost believe it really was a dream patterned on some remembered scrap of Hollywood eroticism. But as she slid her hands over the muscles of his arms and shoulders and back, as she rose to meet each of his thrusts, as she climaxed, then again, and as she felt him loose himself within her and dissolve from iron to molten flow, she was wonderfully, acutely aware that it was not a dream. In fact, she had opened her eyes at last from a long twilight sleep and was, with this release, only now fully awake for the first time in years. The true dream was real life during the past half-decade, a nightmare that had finally drawn to an end.

Leaving their clothes scattered on the floor and hearth behind them, they went upstairs to make love again, this time in the huge Chinese sleigh bed, with less urgency than before, more tenderness, to the accompaniment of murmured endearments that seemed almost to comprise the lyrics and melody of a quiet song. The less insistent rhythm allowed a keener awareness of the exquisite textures of skin, the marvelous flexibility of muscle, the firmness of bone, the pliancy of lips, and the syncopated beating of their hearts. When the tide of ecstasy crested and ebbed, in the stillness that followed, the words "I love you" were superfluous but nonetheless musical to the ear, and cherished.

That April day, from first awareness of the morning light until surrender to sleep, had been one of the best of their lives. Ironically, the night that followed was one of Hatch's worst, so frightening and so strange.

By eleven o'clock Vassago had finished with Redlow and disposed of the body in a most satisfying fashion. He returned to the Blue Skies Motel in the detective's Pontiac, took the long hot shower that he had intended to take earlier in the night, changed into clean clothes, and left with the intention of never going there again. If Redlow had made the place, it was not safe any longer.

He drove the Camaro a few blocks and abandoned it on a street of decrepit industrial buildings where it might sit undisturbed for weeks before it was either stolen or hauled off by the police. He had been using it for a month, after taking it from one of the women whom he had added to his collection. He had changed license plates on it a few times, always stealing the replacements from parked cars in the early hours before dawn.

After walking back to the motel, he drove away in Redlow's Pontiac. It was not as sexy as the silver Camaro, but he figured it would serve him well enough for a couple of weeks.

He went to a neo-punk nightclub named Rip It, in Huntington Beach, where he parked at the darkest end of the lot. He found a pouch of tools in the trunk and used a screwdriver and pliers to remove the plates, which he swapped with those on a battered gray Ford parked beside him. Then he drove to the other end of the lot and reparked.

Fog, with the clammy feel of something dead, moved in from the sea. Palm trees and telephone poles disappeared as if dissolved by the acidity of the mist, and the streetlamps became ghost lights adrift in the murk.

Inside, the club was everything he liked. Loud, dirty, and dark.

Reeking of smoke, spilled liquor, and sweat. The band hit the chords harder than any musicians he'd ever heard, rammed pure rage into each tune, twisting the melody into a squealing mutant voice, banging the numbingly repetitious rhythms home with savage fury, playing each number so loud that, with the help of huge amplifiers, they rattled the filthy windows and almost made his eyes bleed.

The crowd was energetic, high on drugs of every variety, some of them drunk, many of them dangerous. In clothing, the preferred color was black, so Vassago fit right in. And he was not the only one wearing sunglasses. Some of them, both men and women, were skinheads, and some wore their hair in short spikes, but none of them favored the frivolous flamboyancy of huge spikes and cock's combs and colorful dye jobs that had been a part of early punk. On the jammed dance floor, people seemed to be shoving each other and roughing each other up, maybe feeling each other up in some cases, but no one there had ever taken lessons at an Arthur Murray studio or watched "Soul Train."

At the scarred, stained, greasy bar, Vassago pointed to the Corona, one of six brands of beer lined up on a shelf. He paid and took the bottle from the bartender without the need to exchange a word. He stood there, drinking and scanning the crowd.

Only a few of the customers at the bar and tables, or those standing along the walls, were talking to one another. Most were sullen and silent, not because the pounding music made conversation difficult but because they were the new wave of alienated youth, estranged not only from society but from one another. They were convinced that nothing mattered except self-gratification, that nothing was worth talking about, that they were the last generation on a world headed for destruction, with no future.

He knew of other neo-punk bars, but this was one of only two in Orange and Los Angeles counties—the area that so many chamber of commerce types liked to call the Southland—that were the real thing. Many of the others catered to people who wanted to play at the lifestyle the same way some dentists and accountants liked to put on hand-tooled boots, faded jeans, checkered shirts, and ten-gallon hats to go to a country-and-western bar and pretend they were cowboys. At Rip It, there was no pretense in anyone's eyes, and everyone you encountered met you with a challenging stare, trying to decide whether they wanted sex or violence from you and whether you were likely to give them either. If it was an either-or situation, many of them would have chosen violence over sex.

A few were looking for something that transcended violence and sex, without a clear idea of what it might be. Vassago could have shown them precisely that for which they were searching.

The problem was, he did not at first see anyone who appealed to him sufficiently to consider an addition to his collection. He was not a crude killer, piling up bodies for the sake of piling them up. Quantity had no appeal to him; he was more interested in quality. A connoisseur of death. If he could earn his way back into Hell, he would have to do so with an exceptional offering, a collection that was superior in both its overall composition and in the character of each of its components.

He had made a previous acquisition at Rip It three months ago, a girl who insisted her name was Neon. In his car, when he tried to knock her unconscious, one blow didn't do the job, and she fought back with a ferocity that was exhilarating. Even later, in the bottom floor of the funhouse, when she regained consciousness, she resisted fiercely, though bound at wrists and ankles. She squirmed and thrashed, biting him until he repeatedly bashed her skull against the concrete floor.

Now, just as he finished his beer, he saw another woman who reminded him of Neon. Physically they were far different, but spiritually they were the same: hard cases, angry for reasons they didn't always understand themselves, worldly beyond their years, with all the potential violence of tigresses. Neon had been five-four, brunette, with a dusky complexion. This one was a blonde in her early twenties, about five-seven. Lean and rangy. Riveting eyes the same shade of blue as a pure gas flame, yet icy. She was wearing a ragged black denim jacket over a tight black sweater, a short black skirt, and boots.

In an age when attitude was admired more than intelligence, she knew how to carry herself for the maximum impact. She moved with her shoulders back and her head lifted almost haughtily. Her self-possession was as intimidating as spiked armor. Although every man in the room looked at her in a way that said he wanted her, none of them dared to come on to her, for she appeared to be able to emasculate with a single word or look.

Her powerful sexuality, however, was what made her of interest to Vassago. Men would always be drawn to her—he noticed that those flanking him at the bar were watching her even now—and some would not be intimidated. She possessed a savage vitality that made even Neon seem timid. When her defenses were penetrated, she would be lubricious and disgustingly fertile, soon fat with new life, a wild but fruitful brood mare.

He decided that she had two great weaknesses. The first was her clear conviction that she was superior to everyone she met and was, therefore, untouchable and safe, the same conviction that had made it possible for royalty, in more innocent times, to walk among commoners in complete confidence that everyone they passed would draw back respectfully or drop to their knees in awe. The second weakness was her extreme anger, which she stored in such quantity that Vassago seemed to be able to see it crackling off her smooth pale skin, like an overcharge of electricity.

He wondered how he might arrange her death to best symbolize her flaws. Soon he had a couple of good ideas.

She was with a group of about six men and four women, though she did not seem to be attached to any one of them. Vassago was trying to decide on an approach to her when, not entirely to his surprise, *she* approached *him*. He supposed their encounter was inevitable. They were, after all, the two most dangerous people at the dance.

Just as the band took a break and the decibel level fell to a point at which the interior of the club would no longer have been lethal to cats, the blonde came to the bar. She pushed between Vassago and another man, ordered and paid for a beer. She took the bottle from the bartender, turned sideways to face Vassago, and looked at him across the top of the open bottle, from which wisps of cold vapor rose like smoke.

She said, "You blind?"

"To some things, Miss."

She looked incredulous. "Miss?"

He shrugged.

"Why the sunglasses?" she asked.

"I've been to Hell."

"What's that supposed to mean?"

"Hell is cold, dark."

"That so? I still don't get the sunglasses."

"Over there, you learn to see in total darkness."

"This is an interesting line of bullshit."

"So now I'm sensitive to light."

"A real *different* line of bullshit."

He said nothing.

She drank some beer, but her eyes never left him.

He liked the way her throat muscles worked when she swallowed.

After a moment she said, "This your usual line of crap, or do you just make it up as you go?"

He shrugged again.

"You were watching me," she said.

"So?"

"You're right. Every asshole in here is watching me most of the time."

He was studying her intensely blue eyes. What he thought he might do was cut them out, then reinsert them backward, so she was looking into her own skull. A comment on her self-absorbtion.

In the dream Hatch was talking to a beautiful but incredibly cold-looking blonde. Her flawless skin was as white as porcelain, and her eyes were like polished ice reflecting a clear winter sky. They were standing at a bar in a strange establishment he had never seen before. She was looking at him across the top of a beer bottle that she held—and brought to her mouth—as she might have held a phallus. But the taunting way she drank from it and licked the glass rim seemed to be as much a threat as it was an erotic invitation. He could not hear a thing she said, and he could hear only a few words that he spoke himself: ". . . been to Hell . . . cold, dark . . . sensitive to light . . ." The blonde was looking at him, and it was surely he who was speaking to her, yet the words were not in his own voice. Suddenly he found himself focusing more intently on her arctic eyes, and before he knew what he was doing, he produced a switchblade knife and flicked it open. As if she felt no pain, as if in fact she was dead already, the blonde did not react when, with a swift whip of the knife, he took her left eye from its socket. He rolled it over on his fingertips, and replaced it with the blind end outward and the blue lens gazing inward—

Hatch sat up. Unable to breathe. Heart hammering. He swung his legs out of bed and stood, feeling as if he had to run away from something. But he just gasped for breath, not sure where to run to find shelter, safety.

They had fallen asleep with a bedside lamp on, a towel draped over the shade to soften the light while they made love. The room was well enough lit for him to see Lindsey lying on her side of the bed in a tangle of covers.

She was so still, he thought she was dead. He had the crazy feeling that he'd killed her. With a switchblade.

Then she stirred and mumbled in her sleep.

He shuddered. He looked at his hands. They were shaking.

Vassago was so enamored of his artistic vision that he had the impulsive desire to reverse her eyes right there, in the bar, with everyone watching. He restrained himself.

"So what do you want?" she asked, after taking another swallow of beer.

He said, "Out of what—life?"

"Out of me."

"What do you think?"

"A few thrills," she said.

"More than that."

"Home and family?" she asked sarcastically.

He didn't answer right away. He wanted time to think. This one was not easy to play, a different sort of fish. He did not want to risk saying the wrong thing and letting her slip the hook. He got another beer, drank some of it.

Four members of a backup band approached the stage. They were going to play during the other musicians' break. Soon conversation would be impossible again. More important, when the crashing music began, the energy level of the club would rise, and it might exceed the energy level between him and the blonde. She might not be as susceptible to the suggestion that they leave together.

He finally answered her question, told her a lie about what he wanted to do with her: "You know anybody you wish was dead?"

"Who doesn't?"

"Who is it?"

"Half the people I've ever met."

"I mean, one person in particular."

She began to realize what he was suggesting. She took another sip of beer and lingered with her mouth and tongue against the rim of the bottle. "What—is this a game or something?"

"Only if you want it to be, Miss."

"You're weird."

"Isn't that what you like?"

"Maybe you're a cop."

"You really think so?"

She stared intently at his sunglasses, though she wouldn't have been able to see more than a dim suggestion of his eyes beyond the heavily tinted lenses. "No. Not a cop."

"Sex isn't a good way to start," he said.

"It isn't, huh?"

"Death is a better opener. Make a little death together, then make a little sex. You won't believe how intense it can get."

She said nothing.

The backup band was picking up the instruments on the stage. He said, "This one in particular you'd like dead—it's a guy?"

"Yeah."

156

"He live within driving distance?"

"Twenty minutes from here."

"So let's do it."

The musicians began to tune up, though it seemed a pointless exercise, considering the type of music they were going to play. They had better play the right stuff, and they had better be good at it, because it was the kind of club where the customers wouldn't hesitate to trash the band if they didn't like it.

At last the blonde said, "I've got a little PCP. Want to do some with me?"

"Angel dust? It runs in my veins."

"You got a car?"

"Let's go."

On the way out he opened the door for her.

She laughed. "You're one weird son of a bitch."

According to the digital clock on the nightstand, it was 1:28 in the morning. Although Hatch had been asleep only a couple of hours, he was wide awake and unwilling to lie down again.

Besides, his mouth was dry. He felt as if he had been eating sand. He needed a drink.

The towel-draped lamp provided enough light for him to make his way to the dresser and quietly open the correct drawer without waking Lindsey. Shivering, he took a sweatshirt from the drawer and pulled it on. He was wearing only pajama bottoms, but he knew that the addition of a thin pajama top would not quell his chills.

He opened the bedroom door and stepped into the upstairs hall. He glanced back at his slumbering wife. She looked beautiful there in the soft amber light, dark hair against the white pillow, her face relaxed, lips slightly parted, one hand tucked under her chin. The sight of her, more than the sweatshirt, warmed him. Then he thought about the years they had lost in their surrender to grief, and the residual fear from the nightmare was further diluted by a flood of regret. He pulled the door shut soundlessly behind him.

The second-floor hall was hung with shadows, but wan light rose along the stairwell from the foyer below. On their way from the family-room sofa to the sleigh bed, they had not paused to switch off lamps.

Like a couple of horny teenagers. He smiled at the thought.

On his way down the stairs, he remembered the nightmare, and his smile slipped away.

The blonde. The knife. The eye.

It had seemed so *real.*

At the foot of the stairs he stopped, listening. The silence in the house was unnatural. He rapped one knuckle against the newel post, just to hear a sound. The tap seemed softer than it should have been. The silence following it was deeper than before.

"Jesus, that dream really spooked you," he said aloud, and the sound of his own voice was reassuring.

His bare feet made an amusing slapping sound on the oak floor of the downstairs hall, and even more noise on the tile floor of the kitchen. His thirst growing more acute by the second, he took a can of Pepsi from the refrigerator, popped it open, tilted his head back, closed his eyes, and had a long drink.

It didn't taste like cola. It tasted like beer.

Frowning, he opened his eyes and looked at the can. It was not a can any more. It was a bottle of beer, the same brand as in the dream: Corona. Neither he nor Lindsey drank Corona. When they had a beer, which was rarely, it was a Heineken.

Fear went through him like vibrations through a wire.

Then he noticed that the tile floor of the kitchen was gone. He was standing barefoot on gravel. The stones cut into the balls of his feet.

As his heart began to race, he looked around the kitchen with a desperate need to reaffirm that he was in his own house, that the world had not just tilted into some bizarre new dimension. He let his gaze travel over the familiar white-washed birch cabinets, the dark granite countertops, the dishwasher, the gleaming face of the built-in microwave, and he willed the nightmare to recede. But the gravel floor remained. He was still holding a Corona in his right hand. He turned toward the sink, intent on splashing cold water in his face, but the sink was no longer there. One half of the kitchen had vanished, replaced by a roadside bar along which cars were parked in a row, and then—

—he was not in his kitchen at all. It was entirely gone. He was in the open air of the April night, where thick fog glowed with the reflection of red neon from a sign somewhere behind him. He was walking along a graveled parking lot, past the row of parked cars. He was not barefoot any more but wearing rubber-soled black Rockports.

He heard a woman say, "My name's Lisa. What's yours?"

He turned his head and saw the blonde. She was at his side, keeping pace with him across the parking lot.

Instead of answering her right away, he tipped the Corona to his mouth, sucked down the last couple of ounces, and dropped the empty bottle on the gravel. "My name—"

—he gasped as cold Pepsi foamed from the dropped can, and puddled around his bare feet. The gravel had disappeared. A spreading pool of cola glistened on the peach-colored Santa Fe tiles of his kitchen floor.

In Redlow's Pontiac, Lisa told Vassago to take the San Diego Freeway south. By the time he traveled eastward on fog-filled surface streets and eventually found a freeway entrance, she had extracted capsules of what she said was PCP from the pharmacopoeia in her purse, and they had washed them down with the rest of her beer.

PCP was an animal tranquilizer that often had the opposite of a tranquilizing effect on human beings, exciting them into destructive frenzies. It would be interesting to watch the impact of the drug on Lisa, who seemed to have the conscience of a snake, to whom the concept of morality was utterly alien, who viewed the world with unrelenting hatred and contempt, whose sense of personal power and superiority did not preclude a self-destructive streak, and who was already so full of tightly contained psychotic energy that she always seemed about to explode. He suspected that, with the aid of PCP, she'd be capable of highly entertaining extremes of violence, fierce storms of bloody destruction that he would find exhilarating to watch.

"Where are we going?" he asked as they cruised south on the freeway. The headlights drilled into a white mist that hid the world and made it seem as if they could invent any landscape and future they wished. Whatever they imagined might take substance from the fog and appear around them.

"El Toro," she said.

"That's where he lives?"

"Yeah."

"Who is he?"

"You need a name?"

"No, ma'am. Why do you want him dead?"

She studied him for a while. Gradually a smile spread across her face, as if it were a wound being carved by a slow-moving and invisible knife. Her small white teeth looked pointy. Piranha teeth. "You'll really do it, won't you?" she asked. "You'll just go in there and kill the guy to prove I oughta want you."

"To prove nothing," he said. "Just because it might be fun. Like I told you—"

"First make some death together, then make some sex," she finished for him.

Just to keep her talking and make her feel increasingly at ease with him, he said, "Does he live in an apartment or a house?"

"Why's it matter?"

"Lots more ways to get into a house, and neighbors aren't as close."

"It's a house," she said.

"Why do you want him dead?"

"He wanted me, I didn't want him, and he felt he could take what he wanted anyway."

"Couldn't have been easy taking anything from you."

Her eyes were colder than ever. "The bastard had to have stitches in his face when it was over."

"But he still got what he wanted?"

"He was bigger than me."

She turned away from him and gazed at the road ahead.

A breeze had risen from the west, and the fog no longer eddied lazily through the night. It churned across the highway like smoke billowing off a vast fire, as if the entire coastline was ablaze, whole cities incinerated and the ruins smouldering.

Vassago kept glancing at her profile, wishing that he could go with her to El Toro and see how deep in blood she would wade for vengeance. Then he would have liked to convince her to come with him to his hideaway and give herself, of her own free will, to his collection. Whether she knew it or not, she wanted death. She would be grateful for the sweet pain that would be her ticket to damnation. Pale skin almost luminescent against her black clothes, filled with hatred so intense that it made her darkly radiant, she would be an incomparable vision as she walked to her destiny among Vassago's collection and accepted the killing blow, a willing sacrifice for his repatriation to Hell.

He knew, however, that she would not accede to his fantasy and die for him even if death was what she wanted. She would die only for herself, when she eventually concluded that termination was her deepest desire.

The moment she began to realize what he really wanted from her, she would lash out at him. She would be harder to control— and would do more damage—than Neon. He preferred to take each new acquisition to his museum of death while she was still alive, extracting the life from her beneath the malevolent gaze of the funhouse Lucifer. But he knew that he did not have that luxury with Lisa. She would not be easy to subdue, even with a sudden unexpected blow. And once he had lost the advantage of surprise, she would be a fierce adversary.

He was not concerned about being hurt. Nothing, including the prospect of pain, could frighten him. Indeed, each blow she landed, each cut she opened in him, would be an exquisite thrill, pure pleasure.

The problem was, she might be strong enough to get away from him, and he could not risk her escape. He wasn't worried that she would report him to the cops. She existed in a subculture that was suspicious and scornful of the police, seething with hatred for them. If she slipped out of his grasp, however, he would lose the chance to add her to his collection. And he was convinced that her tremendous perverse energy would be the final offering that would win him readmission to Hell.

"You feeling anything yet?" she asked, still looking ahead at the fog, into which they barreled at a dangerous speed.

"A little," he said.

"I don't feel anything." She opened her purse again and began rummaging through it, taking stock of what other pills and capsules she possessed. "We need some kind of booster to help the crap kick in good."

While Lisa was distracted by her search for the right chemical to enhance the PCP, Vassago drove with his left hand and reached under his seat with his right to get the revolver that he had taken off Morton Redlow. She looked up just as he thrust the muzzle against her left side. If she knew what was happening, she showed no surprise. He fired two shots, killing her instantly.

Hatch cleaned up the spilled Pepsi with paper towels. By the time he stepped to the kitchen sink to wash his hands, he was still shaking but not as badly as he had been.

Terror, which had been briefly all-consuming, made some room for curiosity. He hesitantly touched the rim of the stainless-steel sink and then the faucet, as if they might dissolve beneath his hand. He struggled to understand how a dream could continue after he had awakened. The only explanation, which he could not accept, was insanity.

He turned on the water, adjusted hot and cold, pumped some liquid soap out of the container, began to lather his hands, and looked up at the window above the sink, which faced onto the rear yard. The yard was gone. A highway lay in its place. The kitchen window had become a windshield. Swaddled in fog and only partially revealed by two headlight beams, the pavement rolled toward him as if the house was racing over it at sixty miles an hour. He sensed a presence beside him where there should have been nothing but the double ovens. When he turned his head he saw the blonde clawing in her purse. He realized that something was in his hand, firmer than mere lather, and he looked down at a revolver—

—the kitchen snapped completely out of existence. He was in a car, rocketing along a foggy highway, pushing the muzzle of the revolver into the blonde's side. With horror, as she looked up at him, he felt his finger squeeze the trigger once, twice. She was punched sideways by the dual impact as the ear-shattering crash of the shots slammed through the car.

Vassago could not have anticipated what happened next.

The gun must have been loaded with magnum cartridges, for the two shots ripped through the blonde more violently than he expected and slammed her into the passenger door. Either her door was not properly shut or one of the rounds punched all the way through her, damaging the latch, because the door flew open. Wind rushed into the Pontiac, shrieking like a living beast, and Lisa was snatched out into the night.

He jammed on the brakes and looked at the rearview mirror. As the car began to fishtail, he saw the blonde's body tumbling along the pavement behind him.

He intended to stop, throw the car into reverse, and go back for her, but even at that dead hour of the morning, other traffic shared the freeway. He saw two sets of headlights maybe half a mile behind him, bright smudges in the mist but clarifying by the second. Those drivers would encounter the body before he could reach it and scoop it into the Pontiac.

Taking his foot off the brake and accelerating, he swung the car hard to the left, across two lanes, then whipped it back to the right, forcing the door to slam shut. It rattled in its frame but didn't pop open again. The latch must be at least partially effective.

Although visibility had declined to about a hundred feet, he put the Pontiac up to eighty, bulleting blindly into the churning fog. Two exits later, he left the freeway and rapidly slowed down. On surface streets he made his way out of the area as swiftly as possible, obeying speed limits because any cop who stopped him would surely notice the blood splashed across the upholstery and glass of the passenger door.

In the rearview mirror, Hatch saw the body tumbling along the pavement, vanishing into the fog. Then for a brief moment he saw his own reflection from the bridge of his nose to his eyebrows. He was wearing sunglasses even though driving at night. No. *He* wasn't wearing them. The driver of the car was wearing them, and the reflection at which he stared was not his own. Although he seemed to be the driver, he realized that he was not, because even the dim glimpse he got of the eyes behind the tinted lenses was sufficient to convince him that they were peculiar, troubled, and utterly different from his own eyes. Then—

—he was standing at the kitchen sink again, breathing hard and making choking sounds of revulsion. Beyond the window lay only the backyard, blanketed by night and fog.

"Hatch?"

Startled, he turned.

Lindsey was standing in the doorway, in her bathrobe. "Is something wrong?"

Wiping his soapy hands on his sweatshirt, he tried to speak, but terror had rendered him mute.

She hurried to him. "Hatch?"

He held her tightly and was glad for her embrace, which at last squeezed the words from him. "I shot her, she flew out of the car, Jesus God Almighty, bounced along the highway like a rag doll!"

7

At Hatch's request, Lindsey brewed a pot of coffee. The familiarity of the delicious aroma was an antidote to the strangeness of the night. More than anything else, that smell restored a sense of normalcy that helped settle Hatch's nerves. They drank the coffee at the breakfast table at one end of the kitchen.

Hatch insisted on closing the Levolor blind over the nearby window. He said, "I have the feeling . . . something's out there . . . and I don't want it looking in at us." He could not explain what he meant by "something."

When Hatch had recounted everything that had happened to him since waking from the nightmare of the icy blonde, the switchblade, and the mutilated eye, Lindsey had only one explanation to offer. "No matter how it seemed at the time, you must not have been fully awake when you got out of bed. You were sleepwalking. You didn't really wake up until I stepped into the kitchen and called your name."

"I've never been a sleepwalker," he said.

She tried to make light of his objection. "Never too late to take up a new affliction."

"I don't buy it."

"Then what's your explanation?"

"I don't have one."

"So sleepwalking," she said.

He stared down into the white porcelain cup that he clasped in both hands, as if he were a Gypsy trying to foresee the future in the patterns of light on the surface of the black brew. "Have you ever dreamed you were someone else?"

"I suppose so," she said.

He looked hard at her. "No supposing. Have you ever seen a dream through the eyes of a stranger? A specific dream you can tell me about?"

"Well . . . no. But I'm sure I must've, at one time. I just don't remember. Dreams are smoke, after all. They fade so fast. Who remembers them for long?"

"I'll remember this one for the rest of my life," he said.

Although they returned to bed, neither of them could get to sleep again. Maybe it was partly the coffee. She thought he had wanted the coffee precisely because he hoped that it would prevent sleep, sparing him a return to the nightmare. Well, it had worked.

They both were lying on their backs, staring at the ceiling.

At first he had been unwilling to turn off the bedside lamp, though he had revealed his reluctance only in the hesitancy with which he clicked the switch. He was almost like a child who was old enough to know real fears from false ones but not quite old enough to escape all of the latter, certain that some monster lurked under the bed but ashamed to say as much.

Now, with the lamp off and with only the indirect glow of distant streetlamps piercing the windows between the halves of the drapes, his anxiety had infected her. She found it easy to imagine that some shadows on the ceiling moved, bat-lizard-spider forms of singular stealth and malevolent purpose.

They talked softly, on and off, about nothing special. They both knew what they wanted to talk about, but they were afraid of it. Unlike the creepy-crawlies on the ceiling and things that lived under children's beds, it was a real fear. Brain damage.

Since waking up in the hospital, reanimated, Hatch had been having bad dreams of unnerving power. He didn't have them every night. His sleep might even be undisturbed for as long as three or four nights in a row. But he was having them more frequently, week by week, and the intensity was increasing.

They were not always the same dreams, as he described them, but they contained similar elements. Violence. Horrific images of naked, rotting bodies contorted into peculiar positions. Always, the dreams unfolded from the point of view of a stranger, the same mysterious figure, as if Hatch were a spirit in possession of the man but unable to control him, along for the ride. Routinely the nightmares began or ended—or began *and* ended—in the same setting: an assemblage of unusual buildings and other queer structures that resisted identification, all of it unlighted and seen most often as a series of baffling silhouettes against a night sky. He also saw cavernous rooms and mazes of concrete corridors that were somehow revealed in spite of having no windows or artificial lighting. The location was, he said, familiar to him, but recognition remained elusive, for he never saw enough to be able to identify it.

Until tonight, they had tried to convince themselves that his affliction would be short-lived. Hatch was full of positive thoughts, as usual. Bad dreams were not remarkable. Everyone had them. They were often caused by stress. Alleviate the stress, and the nightmares went away.

But they were not fading. And now they had taken a new and deeply disturbing turn: sleepwalking.

Or perhaps he was beginning, while awake, to hallucinate the same images that troubled his sleep.

Shortly before dawn, Hatch reached out for her beneath the sheets and took her hand, held it tight. "I'll be all right. It's nothing, really. Just a dream."

"First thing in the morning, you should call Nyebern," she said, her heart sinking like a stone in a pond. "We haven't been straight with him. He told you to let him know immediately if there were any symptoms—"

"This isn't really a symptom," he said, trying to put the best face on it.

"Physical *or* mental symptoms," she said, afraid for him—and for herself if something *was* wrong with him.

"I had all the tests, most of them twice. They gave me a clean bill of health. No brain damage."

"Then you've nothing to worry about, do you? No reason to delay seeing Nyebern."

"If there'd been brain damage, it would've showed up right away. It's not a residual thing, doesn't kick in on a delay."

They were silent for a while.

She could no longer imagine that creepy-crawlies moved through the shadows on the ceiling. False fears had evaporated the moment he had spoken the name of the biggest real fear that they faced.

At last she said, "What about Regina?"

He considered her question for a while. Then: "I think we should go ahead with it, fill out the papers—assuming she wants to come with us, of course."

"And if . . . you've got a problem? And it gets worse?"

"It'll take a few days to make the arrangements and be able to bring her home. By then we'll have the results of the physical, the tests. I'm sure I'll be fine."

"You're too relaxed about this."

"Stress kills."

"If Nyebern finds something seriously wrong . . .?"

"Then we'll ask the orphanage for a postponement if we have to. The thing is, if we tell them I'm having problems that don't allow me to go ahead with the papers tomorrow, they might have second thoughts about our suitability. We might be rejected and never have a chance with Regina."

The day had been so perfect, from their meeting in Salvatore Gujilio's office to their lovemaking before the fire and again in the massive old Chinese sleigh bed. The future had looked so bright, the worst behind them. She was stunned at how suddenly they had taken another nasty plunge.

She said, "God, Hatch, I love you."

In the darkness he moved close to her and took her in his arms. Until long after dawn, they just held each other, saying nothing because, for the moment, everything had been said.

Later, after they showered and dressed, they went downstairs and had more coffee at the breakfast table. Mornings, they always listened to the radio, an all-news station. That was how they heard about Lisa Blaine, the blonde who had been shot twice and thrown from a moving car on the San Diego Freeway the previous night—at precisely the time that Hatch, standing in the kitchen, had a vision of the trigger being pulled and the body tumbling along the pavement in the wake of the car.

8

For reasons he could not understand, Hatch was compelled to see the section of the freeway where the dead woman had been found. "Maybe something will click," was all the explanation he could offer.

He drove their new red Mitsubishi. They went north on the coast highway, then east on a series of surface streets to the South Coast Plaza Shopping Mall, where they entered the San Diego Freeway heading south. He wanted to come upon the site of the murder from the same direction in which the killer had been traveling the previous night.

By nine-fifteen, rush-hour traffic should have abated, but all of the lanes were still clogged. They made halting progress south-ward in a haze of exhaust fumes, from which the car air-condition-ing spared them.

The marine layer that surged in from the Pacific during the night had burned off. Trees stirred in a spring breeze, and birds swooped in giddy arcs across the cloudless, piercingly blue sky. The day did not seem like one in which anyone would have reason to think of death.

They passed the MacArthur Boulevard exit, then Jamboree, and with every turn of the wheels, Hatch felt the muscles growing tenser in his neck and shoulders. He was overcome by the uncanny feeling that he actually had followed this route last night, when fog had obscured the airport, hotels, office buildings, and the brown hills in the distance, though in fact he had been at home.

"They were going to El Toro," he said, which was a detail he had not remembered until now. Or perhaps he had only now perceived it by the grace of some sixth sense.

"Maybe that's where she lived—or where he lives."

Frowning, Hatch said, "I don't think so."

As they crept forward through the snarled traffic, he began to recall not just details of the dream but the *feeling* of it, the edgy atmosphere of pending violence.

His hands slipped on the steering wheel. They were clammy. He blotted them on his shirt.

"I think in some ways," he said, "the blonde was almost as dangerous as I . . . as he was. . . ."

"What do you mean?"

"I don't know. It's just the feeling I had then."

Sunshine glimmered on—and glinted off—the multitude of vehicles that churned both north and south in two great rivers of steel and chrome and glass. Outside, the temperature was hovering around eighty degrees. But Hatch was cold.

As a sign notified them of the upcoming Culver Boulevard exit, Hatch leaned forward slightly. He let go of the steering wheel with his right hand and reached under his seat. "It was here that he went for the gun . . . pulled it out . . . she was looking in her purse for something. . . ."

He would not have been too surprised if he had found a gun under his seat, for he still had a frighteningly clear recollection of how fluidly the dream and reality had mingled, separated, and mingled again last night. Why not now, even in daylight? He let out a hiss of relief when he found that the space beneath his seat was empty.

"Cops," Lindsey said.

Hatch was so caught up in the re-creation of the events in the nightmare that he didn't immediately realize what Lindsey was talking about. Then he saw black-and-whites and other police vehicles parked along the interstate.

Bent forward, intently studying the dusty ground before them, uniformed officers were walking the shoulder of the highway and picking through the dry grass beyond it. They were evidently conducting an expanded search for evidence to discover anything else that might have fallen out of the killer's car before, with, or after the blonde.

He noticed that every one of the cops was wearing sunglasses, as were he and Lindsey. The day was eye-stingingly bright.

But the killer had been wearing sunglasses, too, when he had looked in the rearview mirror. Why would he have been wearing them in the dark in dense fog, for God's sake?

Shades at night in bad weather was more than just affectation or eccentricity. It was weird.

Hatch still had the imaginary gun in his hand, withdrawn from under the seat. But because they were moving so much slower than the killer had been driving, they had not yet reached the spot at which the revolver had been fired.

Traffic was creeping bumper-to-bumper not because the rush hour was heavier than usual but because motorists were slowing to stare at the police. It was what the radio traffic reporters called "gawkers' block."

"He was really barreling along," Hatch said.

"In heavy fog."

"And sunglasses."

"Stupid," Lindsey said.

"No. This guy's smart."

"Sounds stupid to me."

"Fearless." Hatch tried to settle back into the skin of the man with whom he had shared a body in the nightmare. It wasn't easy. Something about the killer was totally alien and firmly resisted analysis. "He's extremely cold . . . cold and dark inside . . . he doesn't think like you or me. . . ." Hatch struggled to find words to convey what the killer had felt like. "Dirty." He shook his head. "I don't mean he was unwashed, nothing like that. It's more as if . . . well, as if he was contaminated." He sighed and gave up. "Anyway, he's utterly fearless. Nothing scares him. He believes that nothing can hurt him. But in his case that's not the same as recklessness. Because . . . somehow he's right."

"What're you saying—that he's invulnerable?"

"No. Not exactly. But nothing you could do to him . . . would matter to him."

Lindsey hugged herself. "You make him sound . . . inhuman."

At the moment the police search for evidence was concentrated in the quarter of a mile just south of the Culver Boulevard exit. When Hatch got past that activity, traffic began to move faster.

The imaginary gun in his right hand seemed to take on greater substance. He could almost feel the cold steel against his palm.

When he pointed the phantom revolver at Lindsey and glanced

at her, she winced. He saw her clearly, but he could also see, in memory, the face of the blonde as she had looked up from her purse with too little reaction time even to show surprise.

"Here, right here, two shots, fast as I . . . as he could pull the trigger," Hatch said, shuddering because the memory of violence was far easier to recapture than were the mood and malign spirit of the gunman. "Big holes in her." He could see it so clearly. "Jesus, it was awful." He was really into it. "The way she tore open. And the sound like thunder, the end of the world." The bitter taste of stomach acid rose in his throat. "She was thrown back by the impact, against the door, instantly dead, but the door flew open. He wasn't expecting it to fly open. He wanted her, she was part of his collection now, but then she was gone, out into the night, gone, rolling like a piece of litter along the blacktop."

Caught up in the dream memory, he rammed his foot down on the brake pedal, as the killer had done.

"Hatch, no!"

A car, then another, then a third, swerved around them in flashes of chrome and sun-silvered glass, horns blaring, narrowly avoiding a collision.

Shaking himself out of the memory, Hatch accelerated again, back into the traffic flow. He was aware of people staring at him from other cars.

He didn't care about their scrutiny, for he had picked up the trail as if he were a bloodhound. It was not actually a scent that he followed. It was an indefinable something that led him on, maybe psychic vibrations, a disturbance in the ether made by the killer's passage just as a shark's fin would carve a trough in the surface of the sea, although the ether had not repaired itself with the alacrity of water.

"He considered going back for her, knew it was hopeless, so he drove on," Hatch said, aware that his voice had become low and slightly raspy, as if he were recounting secrets that were painful to reveal.

"Then I walked into the kitchen, and you were making an odd choking-gasping sound," Lindsey said. "Gripping the edge of the counter tight enough to crack the granite. I thought you were having a heart attack—"

"Drove very fast," Hatch said, accelerating only slightly himself, "seventy, eighty, even faster, anxious to get away before the traffic behind him encountered the body."

Realizing that he was not merely speculating on what the killer had done, Lindsey said, "You're remembering more than you dreamed, past the point when I came into the kitchen and woke you."

"Not remembering," he said huskily.

"Then what?"

"Sensing . . ."

"Now?"

"Yes."

"How?"

"Somehow." He simply could not explain it better than that. "Somehow," he whispered, and he followed the ribbon of pavement across that largely flat expanse of land, which seemed to darken in spite of the bright morning sun, as if the killer cast a shadow vastly larger than himself, a shadow that lingered behind him even hours after he had gone. "Eighty . . . eighty-five . . . almost ninety miles an hour . . . able to see only a hundred feet ahead." If any traffic had been there in the fog, the killer would have crashed into it with cataclysmic force. "He didn't take the first exit, wanted to get farther away than that . . . kept going . . . going. . . ."

He almost didn't slow down in time to make the exit for State Route 133, which became the canyon road into Laguna Beach. At the last moment he hit the brakes too hard and whipped the wheel to the right. The Mitsubishi slid as they departed the interstate, but he decreased speed and immediately regained full control.

"He got off here?" Lindsey asked.

"Yes."

Hatch followed the new road to the right.

"Did he go into Laguna?"

"I . . . don't think so."

He braked to a complete halt at a crossroads marked by a stop sign. He pulled onto the shoulder. Open country lay ahead, hills dressed in crisp brown grass. If he went straight through the crossroads, he'd be heading into Laguna Canyon, where developers had not yet managed to raze the wilderness and erect more tract homes. Miles of brushland and scattered oaks flanked the canyon route all the way into Laguna Beach. The killer also might have turned left or right. Hatch looked in each direction, searching for . . . for whatever invisible signs had guided him that far.

After a moment, Lindsey said, "You don't know where he went from here?"

"Hideaway."

"Huh?"

Hatch blinked, not sure why he had chosen that word. "He went back to his hideaway . . . into the ground. . . ."

"Ground?" Lindsey asked. With puzzlement she surveyed the sere hills.

". . . into the darkness . . ."

"You mean he went underground somewhere?"

". . . cool, cool silence . . ."

Hatch sat for a while, staring at the crossroads as a few cars came and went. He had reached the end of the trail. The killer was not there; he knew that much, but he did not know where the man had gone. Nothing more came to him—except, strangely, the sweet chocolate taste of Oreo cookies, as intense as if he had just bitten into one.

9

At The Cottage in Laguna Beach, they had a late breakfast of homefries, eggs, bacon, and buttered toast. Since he had died and been resuscitated, Hatch didn't worry about things like his cholesterol count or the long-term effects of passive inhalation of other people's cigarette smoke. He supposed the day would come when little risks would seem big again, whereupon he would return to a diet high in fruits and vegetables, scowl at smokers who blew their filth his way, and open a bottle of fine wine with a mixture of delight and a grim awareness of the health consequences of consuming alcohol. At the moment he was appreciating life too much to worry unduly about losing it again—which was why he was determined not to let the dreams and the death of the blonde push him off the deep end.

Food had a natural tranquilizing effect. Each bite of egg yolk soothed his nerves.

"Okay," Lindsey said, going at her breakfast somewhat less heartily than Hatch did, "let's suppose there was brain damage of some sort, after all. But minor. So minor it never showed up on any of the tests. Not bad enough to cause paralysis or speech problems or anything like that. In fact, by an incredible stroke of luck, a one in a billion chance, this brain damage had a freak effect that was actually beneficial. It could've made a few new connections in the cerebral tissues, and left you psychic."

"Bull."

"Why?"

"I'm not psychic."

"Then what do you call it?"

"Even if I was psychic, I wouldn't say it was beneficial."

Because the breakfast rush had passed, the restaurant was not too busy. The nearest tables to theirs were vacant. They could discuss the morning's events without fear of being overheard, but Hatch kept glancing around self-consciously anyway.

Immediately following his reanimation, the media had swarmed to Orange County General Hospital, and in the days after Hatch's release, reporters had virtually camped on his doorstep at home. After all, he had been dead longer than any man alive, which made him eligible for considerably more than the fifteen minutes of fame that Andy Warhol had said would eventually be every person's fate in celebrity-obsessed America. He'd done nothing to earn his fame. He didn't want it. He hadn't fought his way out of death; Lindsey, Nyebern, and the resuscitation team had dragged him back. He was a private person, content with just the quiet respect of the better antique dealers who knew his shop and traded with him sometimes. In fact, if the only respect he had was Lindsey's, if he was famous only in her eyes and only for being a good husband, that would be enough for him. By steadfastly refusing to talk to the press, he had finally convinced them to leave him alone and chase after whatever newly born two-headed goat—or its equivalent—was available to fill newspaper space or a minute of the airwaves between deodorant commercials.

Now, if he revealed that he had come back from the dead with some strange power to connect with the mind of a psycho killer, swarms of newspeople would descend on him again. He could not tolerate even the prospect of it. He would find it easier to endure a plague of killer bees or a hive of Hare Krishna solicitors with collection cups and eyes glazed by spiritual transcendence.

"If it's not some psychic ability," Lindsey persisted, "then what *is* it?"

"I don't know."

"That's not good enough."

"It could pass, never happen again. It could be a fluke."

"You don't believe that."

"Well . . . I want to believe it."

"We have to deal with this."

"Why?"

"We have to try to understand it."

"Why?"

"Don't 'why' me like a five-year-old child."

"Why?"

"Be serious, Hatch. A woman's dead. She may not be the first. She may not be the last."

He put his fork on his half-empty plate, and swallowed some orange juice to wash down the homefries. "Okay, all right, it's like a psychic vision, yeah, just the way they show it in the movies. But it's more than that. Creepier."

He closed his eyes, trying to think of an analogy. When he had it, he opened his eyes and looked around the restaurant again to be sure no new diners had entered and sat near them.

He looked regretfully at his plate. His eggs were getting cold. He sighed.

"You know," he said, "how they say identical twins, separated at birth and raised a thousand miles apart by utterly different adopted families, will still grow up to live similar lives?"

"Sure, I've heard of that. So?"

"Even raised apart, with totally different backgrounds, they'll choose similar careers, achieve the same income levels, marry women who resemble each other, even give their kids the same names. It's uncanny. And even if they don't know they're twins, even if each of them was told he was an only child when he was adopted, they'll sense each other out there, across the miles, even if they don't know who or what they're sensing. They have a bond that no one can explain, not even geneticists."

"So how does this apply to you?"

He hesitated, then picked up his fork. He wanted to eat instead of talk. Eating was safe. But she wouldn't let him get away with that. His eggs were congealing. His tranquilizers. He put the fork down again.

"Sometimes," he said, "I see through this guy's eyes when I'm sleeping, and now sometimes I can even feel him out there when I'm awake, and it's like the psychic crap in movies, yeah. But I also feel this . . . this bond with him that I really *can't* explain or describe to you, no matter how much you prod me about it."

"You're not saying you think he's your twin or something?"

"No, not at all. I think he's a lot younger than me, maybe only twenty or twenty-one. And no blood relation. But it's that kind of bond, that mystical twin crap, as if this guy and I share something, have some fundamental quality in common."

"Like what?"

"I don't know. I wish I did." He paused. He decided to be entirely truthful. "Or maybe I don't."

Later, after the waitress had cleared away their empty dishes and brought them strong black coffee, Hatch said, "There's no way I'm going to go to the cops and offer to help them, if that's what you're thinking."

"There is a duty here—"

"I don't know anything that could help them anyway."

She blew on her hot coffee. "You know he was driving a Pontiac."

"I don't even think it was his."

"Whose then?"

"Stolen, maybe."

"That was something else you sensed?"

"Yeah. But I don't know what he looks like, his name, where he lives, anything useful."

"What if something like that comes to you? What if you see something that could help the cops?"

"Then I'll call it in anonymously."

"They'll take the information more seriously if you give it to them in person."

He felt violated by the intrusion of this psychotic stranger into his life. That violation made him angry, and he feared his anger more than he feared the stranger, or the supernatural aspect of the situation, or the prospect of brain damage. He dreaded being driven by some extremity to discover that his father's hot temper was within him, too, waiting to be tapped.

"It's a homicide case," he said. "They take *every* tip seriously in a murder investigation, even if it's anonymous. I'm not going to let them make headlines out of me again."

From the restaurant they went across town to Harrison's Antiques, where Lindsey had an art studio on part of the top floor in addition to the one at home. When she painted, a regular change of environment contributed to fresher work.

In the car, with the sun-spangled ocean visible between some of the buildings to their right, Lindsey pressed the point that she had nagged him about over breakfast, because she knew that Hatch's only serious character flaw was a tendency to be too easy-going. Jimmy's death was the only bad thing in his life that he had never been able to rationalize, minimalize, and put out of mind. And even with that, he had tried to suppress it rather than face up to his grief, which is why his grief had a chance to grow. Given time, and not much of it, he'd begin to downplay the importance of what had just happened to him.

She said, "You've still got to see Nyebern."

"I suppose so."

"Definitely."

"If there's brain damage, if that's where this psychic stuff comes from, you said yourself it was *benevolent* brain damage."

"But maybe it's degenerative, maybe it'll get worse."

"I really don't think so," he said. "I feel fine otherwise."

"You're no doctor."

"All right," he said. He braked for the traffic light at the crossing to the public beach in the heart of town. "I'll call him. But we have to see Gujilio later this afternoon."

"You can still squeeze in Nyebern if he has time for you."

Hatch's father had been a tyrant, quick-tempered, sharp-tongued, with a penchant for subduing his wife and disciplining his son by the application of regular doses of verbal abuse in the form of nasty mockery, cutting sarcasm, or just plain threats. Anything at all could set Hatch's father off, or nothing at all, because secretly he cherished irritation and actively sought new sources of it. He was a man who believed he was not destined to be happy—and he insured that his destiny was fulfilled by making himself and everyone around him miserable.

Perhaps afraid that the potential for a murderously bad temper was within him, too, or only because he'd had enough tumult in his life, Hatch had consciously striven to make himself as mellow as his father was high-strung, as sweetly tolerant as his father was narrow-minded, as greathearted as his father was unforgiving, as determined to roll with all of life's punches as his father was determined to punch back at even imaginary blows. As a result, he was the nicest man Lindsey had ever known, the nicest by light-years or by whatever measure niceness was calculated: bunches, bucketsful, gobs. Sometimes, however, Hatch turned away from an unpleasantness that had to be dealt with, rather than risk getting in touch with any negative emotion that was remotely reminiscent of his old man's paranoia and anger.

The light changed from red to green, but three young women in bikinis were in the crosswalk, laden with beach gear and heading for the ocean. Hatch didn't just wait for them. He watched them with a smile of appreciation for the way they filled out their suits.

"I take it back," Lindsey said.

"What?"

"I was just thinking what a nice guy you are, too nice, but obviously you're a piece of lecherous scum."

"Nice scum, though."

"I'll call Nyebern as soon as we get to the shop," Lindsey said.

He drove up the hill through the main part of town, past the old Laguna Hotel. "Okay. But I'm sure as hell not going to tell him I'm suddenly psychic. He's a good man, but he won't be able to sit on that kind of news. The next thing I know, my face'll be all over the cover of the *National Enquirer*. Besides, I'm not psychic, not exactly. I don't know what the hell I am—aside from lecherous scum."

"So what'll you tell him?"

"Just enough about the dreams so he'll realize how troubling they are and how strange, so he'll order whatever tests I ought to have. Good enough?"

"I guess it'll have to be."

In the tomb-deep blackness of his hideaway, curled naked upon the stained and lumpy mattress, fast asleep, Vassago saw sunlight, sand, the sea, and three bikinied girls beyond the windshield of a red car.

He was dreaming and knew he dreamed, which was a peculiar sensation. He rolled with it.

He saw, as well, the dark-haired and dark-eyed woman about whom he had dreamed yesterday, when she had been behind the wheel of that same car. She had appeared in other dreams, once in a wheelchair, when she had been laughing and weeping at the same time.

He found her more interesting than the scantily clad beach bunnies because she was unusually vital. Radiant. Through the unknown man driving the car, Vassago somehow knew that the woman had once considered embracing death, had hesitated on the edge of either active or passive self-destruction, and had rejected an early grave—

. . . water, he sensed a watery vault, cold and suffocating, narrowly escaped . . .

—whereafter she had been more full of life, energetic, and vivid than ever before. She had cheated death. Denied the devil. Vassago hated her for that, because it was in the service of death that he had found meaning to his own existence.

He tried to reach out and touch her through the body of the man driving the car. Failed. It was only a dream. Dreams could not be controlled. If he could have touched her, he would have made her regret that she had turned away from the comparatively painless death by drowning that could have been hers.

FIVE

1

When she moved in with the Harrisons, Regina almost thought she had died and gone to Heaven, except she had her own bathroom, and she didn't believe anyone had his own bathroom up in Heaven because in Heaven no one needed a bathroom. They were not all permanently constipated in Heaven or anything like that, and they certainly didn't just do their business out in public, for God's sake (sorry, God), because no one in his right mind would want to go to Heaven if it was the kind of place where you had to watch where you stepped. It was just that in Heaven all the concerns of earthly existence passed away. You didn't even have a body in Heaven; you were probably just a sphere of mental energy, sort of like a balloon full of golden glowing gas, drifting around among the angels, singing the praises of God—which was pretty weird when you thought about it, all those glowing and singing balloons, but the most you'd ever have to do in the way of waste elimination was maybe vent a little gas now and then, which wouldn't even smell bad, probably like the sweet incense in church, or perfume.

That first day in the Harrisons' house, late Monday afternoon, the twenty-ninth of April, she would remember forever, because they were so nice. They didn't even mention the real reason why they gave her a choice between a bedroom on the second floor and a den on the first floor that could be converted into a bedroom.

183

"One thing in its favor," Mr. Harrison said about the den, "is the view. Better than the view from the upstairs room."

He led Regina to the big windows that looked out on a rose garden ringed by a border of huge ferns. The view *was* pretty.

Mrs. Harrison said, "And you'd have all these bookshelves, which you might want to fill up gradually with your own collection, since you're a book lover."

Actually, without ever hinting at it, their concern was that she might find the stairs troublesome. But she didn't mind stairs so much. In fact she liked stairs, she loved stairs, she ate stairs for breakfast. In the orphanage, they had put her on the first floor, until she was eight years old and realized she'd been given ground-level accommodations because of her clunky leg brace and deformed right hand, whereupon she immediately demanded to be moved to the third floor. The nuns would not hear of it, so she threw a tantrum, but the nuns knew how to deal with that, so she tried withering scorn, but the nuns could not be withered, so she went on a hunger strike, and finally the nuns surrendered to her demand on a trial basis. She'd lived on the third floor for more than two years, and she had never used the elevator. When she chose the second-floor bedroom in the Harrisons' house, without having seen it, neither of them tried to talk her out of it, or wondered aloud if she were "up" to it, or even blinked. She loved them for that.

The house was gorgeous—cream walls, white woodwork, modern furniture mixed with antiques, Chinese bowls and vases, everything just so. When they took her on a tour, Regina actually felt as dangerously clumsy as she had claimed to be in the meeting in Mr. Gujilio's office. She moved with exaggerated care, afraid that she would knock over one precious item and kick off a chain reaction that would spread across the entire room, then through a doorway into the next room and from there throughout the house, one beautiful treasure tipping into the next like dominoes in a world-championship toppling contest, two-hundred-year-old porcelains exploding, antique furniture reduced to match sticks, until they were left standing in mounds of worthless rubble, coated with the dust of what had been a *fortune* in interior design.

She was so absolutely certain it was going to happen that she wracked her mind urgently, room by room, for something winning to say when catastrophe struck, after the last exquisite crystal candy dish had crashed off the last disintegrating table that had once been the property of the First King of France. "Oops," did not seem appropriate, and neither did "Jesus Christ!" because they thought they had adopted a good Catholic girl not a foul-mouthed heathen (sorry, God), and neither did "somebody pushed me," because that was a lie, and lying bought you a ticket to Hell, though she suspected she was going to wind up in Hell anyway, considering how she couldn't stop thinking the Lord's name in vain and using vulgarities. No balloon full of glowing golden gas for her.

Throughout the house, the walls were adorned with art, and Regina noted that the most wonderful pieces all had the same signature at the bottom right corner: Lindsey Sparling. Even as much of a screwup as she was, she was smart enough to figure that the name Lindsey was no coincidence and that Sparling must be Mrs. Harrison's maiden name. They were the strangest and most beautiful paintings Regina had ever seen, some of them so bright and full of good feeling that you had to smile, some of them dark and brooding. She wanted to spend a long time in front of each of them, sort of soaking them up, but she was afraid Mr. and Mrs. Harrison would think she was a brownnosing phony, pretending interest as a way of apologizing for the wisecracks she had made in Mr. Gujilio's office about paintings on velvet.

Somehow she got through the entire house without destroying anything, and the last room was hers. It was bigger than any room at the orphanage, and she didn't have to share it with anyone. The windows were covered with white plantation shutters. Furnishings included a corner desk and chair, a bookcase, an armchair with footstool, nightstands with matching lamps—and an amazing bed.

"It's from about 1850," Mrs. Harrison said, as Regina let her hand glide slowly over the beautiful bed.

"English," Mr. Harrison said. "Mahogany with hand-painted decoration under several coats of lacquer."

On the footboard, side rails, and headboard, the dark-red and dark-yellow roses and emerald-green leaves seemed alive, not bright against the deeply colored wood but so lustrous and dewy-looking that she was sure she would be able to smell them if she put her nose to their petals.

Mrs. Harrison said, "It might seem a little *old* for a young girl, a little stuffy—"

"Yes, of course," Mr. Harrison said, "we can send it over to the store, sell it, let you choose something you'd like, something modern. This was just furnished as a guest room."

"No," Regina said hastily. "I like it, I really do. Could I keep it, I mean even though it's so expensive?"

"It's not that expensive," Mr. Harrison said, "and of course you can keep anything you want."

"Or get rid of anything you want," Mrs. Harrison said.

"Except us, of course," Mr. Harrison said.

"That's right," Mrs. Harrison said, "I'm afraid we come with the house."

Regina's heart was pounding so hard she could barely get her breath. Happiness. And fear. Everything was so wonderful—but surely it couldn't last. Nothing so good could last very long.

Sliding, mirrored doors covered one wall of the bedroom, and Mrs. Harrison showed Regina a closet behind the mirrors. The hugest closet in the world. Maybe you needed a closet that size if you were a movie star, or if you were one of those men she had read about, who liked to dress up in women's clothes sometimes, 'cause then you'd need both a girl's and boy's wardrobe. But it was much bigger than she needed; it would hold ten times the clothes that she possessed.

With some embarrassment, she looked at the two cardboard suitcases she had brought with her from St. Thomas's. They held everything she owned in the world. For the first time in her life, she realized she was poor. Which was peculiar, really, not to have understood her poverty before, since she was an orphan who had inherited nothing. Well, nothing other than a bum leg and a twisted right hand with two fingers missing.

As if reading Regina's mind, Mrs. Harrison said, "Let's go shopping."

They went to South Coast Plaza Mall. They bought her too many clothes, books, anything she wanted. Regina worried that they were overspending and would have to eat beans for a year to balance their budget—she didn't like beans—but they failed to pick up on her hints about the virtues of frugality. Finally she had to stop them by pretending that her weak leg was bothering her.

From the mall they went to dinner at an Italian restaurant. She had eaten out twice before, but only at a fast-food place, where the owner treated all the kids at the orphanage to burgers and fries. This was a *real* restaurant, and there was so much to absorb that she could hardly eat, keep up her end of the table conversation, *and* enjoy the place all at the same time. The chairs weren't made out of hard plastic, and neither were the knives and forks. The plates weren't either paper or Styrofoam, and drinks came in actual glasses, which must mean that the customers in real restaurants were not as clumsy as those in fast-food places and could be trusted with breakable things. The waitresses weren't teenagers, and they brought your food to you instead of handing it across a counter by the cash register. And they didn't make you pay for it until *after* you'd eaten it!

Later, back at the Harrison house, after Regina unpacked her things, brushed her teeth, put on pajamas, took off her leg brace, and got into bed, both the Harrisons came in to say goodnight. Mr. Harrison sat on the edge of her bed and told her that everything might seem strange at first, even unsettling, but that soon enough she would feel at home, then he kissed her on the forehead and said, "Sweet dreams, princess." Mrs. Harrison was next, and she sat on the edge of the bed, too. She talked for a while about all the things they would do together in the days ahead. Then she kissed Regina on the cheek, said, "Goodnight, honey," and turned off the overhead light as she went out the door into the hall.

Regina had never before been kissed goodnight, so she had not known how to respond. Some of the nuns were huggers; they liked to give you an affectionate squeeze now and then, but none of them was a smoocher. For as far back as Regina could remember, a flicker of the dorm lights was the signal to be in bed within fifteen minutes, and when the lights went out, each kid was responsible for getting tucked in himself. Now she had been tucked in twice and kissed goodnight twice, all in the same evening, and she had been too surprised to kiss either of them in return, which she now realized she should have done.

"You're such a screwup, Reg," she said aloud.

Lying in her magnificent bed, with the painted roses twining around her in the darkness, Regina could imagine the conversation they were having, right that minute, in their own bedroom:

Did she kiss you goodnight?

No, did she kiss you?

No. Maybe she's a cold fish.

Maybe she's a psycho demon child.

Yeah, like that kid in The Omen.

You know what I'm worried about?

She'll stab us to death in our sleep.

Let's hide all the kitchen knives.

Better hide the power tools, too.

You still have the gun in the nightstand?

Yeah, but a gun will never stop her.

Thank God, we have a crucifix.

We'll sleep in shifts.

Send her back to the orphanage tomorrow.

"Such a screwup," Regina said. "Shit." She sighed. "Sorry, God." Then she folded her hands in prayer and said softly, "Dear God, if you'll convince the Harrisons to give me one more chance, I'll never say 'shit' again, and I'll be a better person." That didn't seem like a good enough bargain from God's point of view, so she threw in other inducements: "I'll continue to keep an A average in school, I'll never again put Jell-O in the holy water font, and I'll give serious thought to becoming a nun." Still not good enough. "And I'll eat beans." That ought to do it. God was probably proud of beans. After all, He'd made all kinds of them. Her refusal to eat green or wax or Lima or navy or any other kind of beans had no doubt been noted in Heaven, where they had her down in the Big Book of Insults to God—*Regina, currently age ten, thinks God pulled a real boner when He created beans.* She yawned. She felt better now about her chances with the Harrisons and about her relationship with God, though she didn't feel better about the change in her diet. Anyway, she slept.

2

While Lindsey was washing her face, scrubbing her teeth, and brushing her hair in the master bathroom, Hatch sat in bed with the newspaper. He read the science page first, because it contained the real news these days. Then he skimmed the entertainment section and read his favorite comic strips before turning, at last, to the A section where the latest exploits of politicians were as terrifying and darkly amusing as usual. On page three he saw the story about Bill Cooper, the beer deliveryman whose truck they had found crosswise on the mountain road that fateful, snowy night in March.

Within a couple of days of being resuscitated, Hatch had heard that the trucker had been charged with driving under the influence and that the percentage of alcohol in his blood had been more than twice that required for a conviction under the law. George Glover, Hatch's personal attorney, had asked him if he wanted to press a civil suit against Cooper or the company for which he worked, but Hatch was not by nature litigious. Besides, he dreaded becoming bogged down in the dull and thorny world of lawyers and courtrooms. He was alive. That was all that mattered. A drunk-driving charge would be brought against the trucker without Hatch's involvement, and he was satisfied to let the system handle it.

He had received two pieces of correspondence from William Cooper, the first just four days after his reanimation. It was an apparently sincere, if long-winded and obsequious, apology seeking personal absolution, which was delivered to the hospital where Hatch was undergoing physical therapy. "Sue me if you want,"

Cooper wrote, "I deserve it. I'd give you everything if you wanted it, though I don't got much, I'm no rich man. But no matter whether you sue me or if not, I most sincerely hope you'll find it in your generous heart to forgive me one ways or another. Except for the genius of Dr. Nyebern and his wonderful people, you'd be dead for sure, and I'd carry it on my conscience all the rest of my days." He rambled on in that fashion for four pages of tightly spaced, cramped, and at times inscrutable handwriting.

Hatch had responded with a short note, assuring Cooper that he did not intend to sue him and that he harbored no animosity toward him. He also had urged the man to seek counseling for alcohol abuse if he had not already done so.

A few weeks later, when Hatch was living at home again and back at work, after the media storm had swept over him, a second letter had arrived from Cooper. Incredibly, he was seeking Hatch's help to get his truck-driving job back, from which he had been fired subsequent to the charges that the police had filed against him. "I been chased down for driving drunk twice before, it's true," Cooper wrote, "but both them times, I was in my car, not the truck, on my own time, not during work hours. Now my job is gone, plus they're fixing to take away my license, which'll make life hard. I mean, for one thing, how am I going to get a new job without a license? Now what I figure is, from your kind answer to my first letter, you proved yourself a fine Christian gentleman, so if you was to speak up on my behalf, it would be a big help. After all, you didn't wind up dead, and in fact you got a lot of publicity out of the whole thing, which must've helped your antique business a considerable amount."

Astonished and uncharacteristically furious, Hatch had filed the letter without answering it. In fact he quickly put it out of his mind, because he was scared by how angry he grew whenever he contemplated it.

Now, according to the brief story on page three of the paper, based on a single technical error in police procedures, Cooper's attorney had won a dismissal of all charges against him. The article included a three-sentence summary of the accident and a silly reference to Hatch as "holding the current record for being

dead the longest time prior to a successful resuscitation," as if he
had arranged the entire ordeal with the hope of winning a place in
the next edition of the *Guinness Book of World Records*.

Other revelations in the piece made Hatch curse out loud and
sit up straight in bed, culminating with the news that Cooper was
going to sue his employer for wrongful termination and expected
to get his old job back or, failing that, a substantial financial
settlement. "I have suffered considerable humiliation at the hands
of my former employer, subsequent to which I developed a serious
stress-related health condition," Cooper had told reporters, obviously disgorging an attorney-written statement that he had memo-
rized. "Yet even Mr. Harrison has written to tell me that he holds
me blameless for the events of that night."

Anger propelled Hatch off the bed and onto his feet. His face
felt flushed, and he was shaking uncontrollably.

Ludicrous. The drunken bastard was trying to get his job back
by using Hatch's compassionate note as an endorsement, which
required a complete misrepresentation of what Hatch had actually
written. It was deceptive. It was unconscionable.

"Of all the fucking nerve!" Hatch said fiercely between clenched
teeth.

Dropping most of the newspaper at his feet, crumpling the page
with the story in his right hand, he hurried out of the bedroom and
descended the stairs two at a time. In the den, he threw the paper
on the desk, banged open a sliding closet door, and jerked out the
top drawer on a three-drawer filing cabinet.

He had saved Cooper's handwritten letters, and although they
were not on printed stationery, he knew the trucker had included
not only a return address but a phone number on both pieces of
correspondence. He was so disturbed, he flicked past the correct
file folder—labeled MISCELLANEOUS BUSINESS—cursed softly but
fluently when he couldn't find it, then searched backward and
pulled it out. As he pawed through the contents, other letters
slipped out of the folder and clattered to the floor at his feet.

Cooper's second letter had a telephone number carefully hand-
printed at the top. Hatch put the disarranged file folder on the
cabinet and hurried to the phone on the desk. His hand was

shaking so badly that he couldn't read the number, so he put the letter on the blotter, in the cone of light from the brass desk lamp.

He punched William Cooper's number, intent on telling him off. The line was busy.

He jammed his thumb down on the disconnect button, got the dial tone, and tried again. Still busy.

"Sonofabitch!" He slammed down the receiver, but snatched it up again because there was nothing else he could do to let off steam. He tried the number a third time, using the redial button. It was still busy, of course, because no more than half a minute had passed since the first time he had tried it. He smashed the handset into the cradle so hard he might have broken the phone.

On one level he was startled by the savagery of the act, the childishness of it. But that part of him was not in control, and the mere awareness that he was over the top did not help him regain a grip on himself.

"Hatch?"

He looked up in surprise at the sound of his name and saw Lindsey, in her bathrobe, standing in the doorway between the den and the foyer.

Frowning, she said, "What's wrong?"

"What's wrong?" he asked, his fury growing irrationally, as if she were somehow in league with Cooper, as if she were only pretending to be unaware of this latest turn of events. "I'll tell you what's wrong. They let this Cooper bastard off the hook! The son of a bitch kills me, runs me off the goddamned road and *kills* me, then slips off the hook and has the nerve to try to use the letter I wrote him to get his job back!" He snatched up the crumpled newspaper and shook it at her, almost accusingly, as if she knew what was in it. "Get his job back—so he can run someone else off the fucking road and kill *them!*"

Looking worried and confused, Lindsey stepped into the den. "They let him off the hook? How?"

"A technicality. Isn't that cute? A cop misspells a word on the citation or something, and the guy walks!"

"Honey, calm down—"

"Calm down? Calm *down?*" He shook the crumpled newspaper

again. "You know what else it says here? The jerk sold his story
to that sleazy tabloid, the one that kept chasing after me, and I
wouldn't have anything to do with them. So now this drunken son
of a bitch sells them the story about"—he was spraying spittle he
was so angry; he flattened out the newspaper, found the article,
read from it—"about 'his emotional ordeal and his role in the
rescue that saved Mr. Harrison's life.' What role did he have in my
rescue? Except he used his CB to call for help after we went off the
road, which we wouldn't have done if he hadn't been there in the
first place! He's not only keeping his driver's license and probably
going to get his job back, but he's making money off the whole
damn thing! If I could get my hands on the bastard, I'd kill him,
I swear I would!"

"You don't mean that," she said, looking shocked.

"You better believe I do! The irresponsible, greedy bastard. I'd
like to kick him in the head a few times to knock some sense into
him, pitch *him* into that freezing river—"

"Honey, lower your voice—"

"Why the hell should I lower my voice in my own—"

"You'll wake Regina."

It was not the mention of the girl that jolted him out of his blind
rage, but the sight of himself in the mirrored closet door beside
Lindsey. Actually, he didn't see himself at all. For an instant he
saw a young man with thick black hair falling across his forehead,
wearing sunglasses, dressed all in black. He knew he was looking
at the killer, but the killer seemed to be *him*. At that moment they
were one and the same. That aberrant thought—and the young
man's image—passed in a second or two, leaving Hatch staring at
his familiar reflection.

Stunned less by the hallucination than by that momentary confusion of identity, Hatch gazed into the mirror and was appalled
as much by what he saw now as by the brief glimpse of the killer.
He looked apoplectic. His hair was disarranged. His face was red
and contorted with rage, and his eyes were . . . wild. He reminded
himself of his father, which was unthinkable, intolerable.

He could not remember the last time he had been that angry. In
fact he had *never* been in a comparable rage. Until now, he'd

thought he was incapable of that kind of outburst or of the intense anger that could lead to it.

"I . . . I don't know what happened."

He dropped the crumpled page of the newspaper. It struck his desk and fell to the floor with a crisp rustling noise that wrought an inexplicably vivid picture in his mind—

dry brown leaves tumbling in a breeze along the cracked pavement in a crumbling, abandoned amusement park

—and for just a moment he was *there,* with weeds sprouting up around him from cracks in the blacktop, dead leaves whirling past, the moon glaring down through the elaborate open-beam supports of a roller-coaster track. Then he was in his office again, leaning weakly against his desk.

"Hatch?"

He blinked at her, unable to speak.

"What's wrong?" she asked, moving quickly to him. She touched his arm tentatively, as if she thought he might shatter from the contact—or perhaps as if she expected him to respond to her touch with a blow struck in anger.

He put his arms around her, and hugged her tightly. "Lindsey, I'm sorry. I don't know what happened, what got into me."

"It's all right."

"No, it isn't. I was so . . . so *furious.*"

"You were just angry, that's all."

"I'm sorry," he repeated miserably.

Even if it had appeared to her to be nothing but anger, he knew that it had been more than that, something strange, a terrible rage. White hot. Psychotic. He had felt an edge beneath him, as if he were teetering on the brink of a precipice, with only his heels planted on solid ground.

To Vassago's eyes, the monument of Lucifer cast a shadow even in absolute darkness, but he could still see and enjoy the cadavers in their postures of degradation. He was enraptured by the organic collage that he had created, by the sight of the humbled forms and the stench that arose from them. His hearing was not remotely as acute as his night vision, but he did not believe that he was entirely imagining the soft, wet sounds of decomposition to which he swayed as a music lover might sway to strains of Beethoven.

When he was suddenly overcome by anger, he was not sure why. It was a quiet sort of rage at first, curiously unfocused. He opened himself to it, enjoyed it, fed it to make it grow.

A vision of a newspaper flashed through his mind. He could not see it clearly, but something on the page was the cause of his anger. He squinted as if narrowing his eyes would help him see the words.

The vision passed, but the anger remained. He nurtured it the way a happy man might consciously force a laugh beyond its natural span just because the sound of laughter buoyed him. Words blurted from him, "Of all the fucking nerve!"

He had no idea where the exclamation had come from, just as he had no idea why he had said the name "Lindsey" out loud in that lounge in Newport Beach, several weeks ago, when these weird experiences had begun.

He was so abruptly energized by anger that he turned away from his collection and stalked across the enormous chamber, up the ramp down which the gargoyle gondolas had once plunged, and out into the night, where the moon forced him to put on his sunglasses again. He could not stand still. He had to move, move. He walked the abandoned midway, not sure who or what he was looking for, curious about what would happen next.

Disjointed images flashed through his mind, none remaining long enough to allow contemplation: the newspaper, a book-lined den, a filing cabinet, a hand-written letter, a telephone. . . . He walked faster and faster, pivoting suddenly onto new avenues or into narrower passageways between the decaying buildings, in a fruitless search for a connection that would link him more clearly with the source of the pictures that appeared and swiftly faded from his mind.

As he passed the roller coaster, cold moonlight fell through the maze of supporting crossbeams and glinted off the track in such a way as to make those twin ribbons of steel look like rails of ice. When he lifted his gaze to stare at the monolithic—and suddenly mysterious—structure, an angry exclamation burst from him: "Pitch *him* into that freezing river!"

A woman said, *Honey, lower your voice.*

Though he knew that her voice had arisen from within him, as an auditory adjunct to the fragmentary visions, Vassago turned in search of her anyway. She was *there*. In a bathrobe. Standing just this side of a doorway that had no right to be where it was, with no walls surrounding it. To the left of the doorway, to the right of it, and above it, there was only the night. The silent amusement park. But beyond the doorway, past the woman who stood in it, was what appeared to be the entrance foyer of a house, a small table with a vase of flowers, a staircase curving up to a second floor.

She was the woman he had thus far seen only in his dreams, first in a wheelchair and most recently in a red automobile on a sun-splashed highway. As he took a step toward her, she said, *You'll wake Regina.*

He halted, not because he was afraid of waking Regina, who-ever the hell she was, and not because he still didn't want to get his hands on the woman, which he did—she was so *vital*—but because he became aware of a full-length mirror to the left of the Twilight-Zone door, a mirror floating impossibly in the night air. It was filled with his reflection, except that it was not him but a man he had never seen before, his size but maybe twice his age, lean and fit, his face contorted in rage.

The look of rage gave way to one of shock and disgust, and both Vassago and the man in the vision turned from the mirror to the woman in the doorway. "Lindsey, I'm sorry," Vassago said.

Lindsey. The name he had spoken three times at that lounge in Newport Beach.

Until now, he had not linked it to this woman who, nameless, had appeared so often in his recent dreams.

"Lindsey," Vassago repeated.

He was speaking of his own volition this time, not repeating what the man in the mirror was saying, and that seemed to shatter the vision. The mirror and the reflection in it flew apart in a billion shards, as did the doorway and the dark-eyed woman.

As the hushed and moon-washed park reclaimed the night, Vassago reached out with one hand toward the spot where the woman had stood. "Lindsey." He longed to touch her. So alive, she was. "Lindsey." He wanted to cut her open and enfold her beating heart in both hands, until its metronomic pumping slowed . . . slowed . . . slowed to a full stop. He wanted to be holding her heart when life retreated from it and death took possession.

As swiftly as the flood of rage had poured into Hatch, it drained out of him. He balled up the pages of the newspaper and threw them in the waste can beside the desk, without glancing again at the story about the truck driver. Cooper was pathetic, a self-destructive loser who would bring his own punishment down upon himself sooner or later; and it would be worse than anything that Hatch would have done to him.

Lindsey gathered the letters that were scattered on the floor in front of the filing cabinet. She returned them to the file folder labeled MISCELLANEOUS BUSINESS.

The letter from Cooper was on the desk beside the telephone. When Hatch picked it up, he looked at the hand-written address at the top, above the telephone number, and a ghost of his anger returned. But it was a pale spirit of the real thing, and in a moment it vanished like a revenant. He took the letter to Lindsey and put it in the file folder, which she reinserted into the cabinet.

Standing in moonglare and night breeze, in the shadow of the roller coaster, Vassago waited for additional visions.

He was intrigued by what had transpired, though not surprised. He had traveled Beyond. He knew another world existed, separated from this one by the flimsiest of curtains. Therefore, events of a supernatural nature did not astonish him.

Just when he began to think that the enigmatic episode had

reached a conclusion, one more vision flickered through his mind. He saw a single page of a hand-written letter. White, lined paper. Blue ink. At the top was a name. William X. Cooper. And an address in the city of Tustin.

"Pitch *him* into that freezing river," Vassago muttered, and knew somehow that William Cooper was the object of the un-focused anger that had overcome him when he was with his collection in the funhouse, and which later seemed to link him with the man he had seen in the mirror. It was an anger he had embraced and amplified because he wanted to understand whose anger it was and why he could feel it, but also because anger was the yeast in the bread of violence, and violence was the staple of his diet.

From the roller coaster he went directly to the subterranean garage. Two cars waited there.

Morton Redlow's Pontiac was parked in the farthest corner, in the deepest shadows. Vassago had not used it since last Thursday night, when he had killed Redlow and later the blonde. Though he believed the fog had provided adequate cover, he was concerned that the Pontiac might have been glimpsed by witnesses who had seen the woman tumble from it on the freeway.

He longed to return to the land of endless night and eternal damnation, to be once more among his own kind, but he did not want to be gunned down by police until his collection was finished. If his offering was incomplete when he died, he believed that he would be deemed as yet unfit for Hell and would be pulled back into the world of the living to start another collection.

The second car was a pearl-gray Honda that had belonged to a woman named Renata Desseux, whom he had clubbed on the back of the head in a shopping-mall parking lot on Saturday night, two nights after the fiasco with the blonde. She, instead of the neo-punker named Lisa, had become the latest addition to his collection.

He had removed the license plates from the Honda, tossed them in the trunk, and later replaced them with plates stolen off an old Ford on the outskirts of Santa Ana. Besides, Hondas were so ubiquitous that he felt safe and anonymous in this one. He drove off the park grounds and out of the county's largely unpopulated eastern hills toward the panorama of golden light that filled the lowlands as far south and as far north as he could see, from the hills to the ocean.

Urban sprawl.

Civilization.

Hunting grounds.

The very immensity of southern California—thousands of square miles, tens of millions of people, even excluding Ventura County to the north and San Diego County to the south—was Vassago's ally in his determination to acquire the pieces of his collection without arousing the interest of the police. Three of his victims had been taken from different communities in Los Angeles County, two from Riverside, the rest from Orange County, spread over many months. Among the hundreds of missing persons reported during that time, his few acquisitions would not affect the statistics enough to alarm the public or alert the authorities.

He was also abetted by the fact that these last years of the century and the millennium were an age of inconstancy. Many people changed jobs, neighbors, friends, and marriages with little or no concern for continuity in life. As a result, there were fewer people to notice or care when any one person vanished, fewer to harass authorities into a meaningful response. And more often than not, those who disappeared were later discovered in changed circumstances of their own invention. A young executive might trade the grind of corporate life for a job as a blackjack dealer in Vegas or Reno, and a young mother—disillusioned with the demands of an infant and an infantile husband—might end up dealing cards or serving drinks or dancing topless in those same cities, leaving on the spur of the moment, blowing off their past lives as if a standard middle-class existence was as much a cause for shame as a criminal background. Others were found deep in the arms of various addictions, living in cheap rat-infested hotels that rented rooms by the week to the glassy-eyed legions of the counterculture. Because it was California, many missing persons eventually turned up in religious communes in Marin County or in Oregon, worshipping some new god or new manifestation of an old god or even just some shrewd-eyed man who said he *was* God.

It was a new age, disdaining tradition. It provided for whatever lifestyle one wished to pursue. Even one like Vassago's.

If he had left bodies behind, similarities in the victims and methods of murder would have linked them. The police would have realized that one perpetrator of unique strength and cunning was on the prowl, and they would have established a special task force to find him.

But the only bodies he had not taken to the Hell below the funhouse were those of the blonde and the private detective. No pattern would be deduced from just those two corpses, for they had died in radically different ways. Besides, Morton Redlow might not be found for weeks yet.

The only links between Redlow and the neo-punker were the detective's revolver, with which the woman had been shot, and his car, out of which she had fallen. The car was safely hidden in the farthest corner of the long-abandoned park garage. The gun was in the Styrofoam cooler with the Oreo cookies and other snacks, at the bottom of the elevator shaft more than two floors below the funhouse. He did not intend to use it again.

He was unarmed when, after driving far north into the county, he arrived at the address he had seen on the hand-written letter in the vision. William X. Cooper, whoever the hell he was and if he actually existed, lived in an attractive garden-apartment complex called Palm Court. The name of the place and the street number were carved in a decorative wooden sign, floodlit from the front and backed by the promised palms.

Vassago drove past Palm Court, turned right at the corner, and parked two blocks away. He didn't want anyone to remember the Honda sitting in front of the building. He didn't flat-out intend to kill this Cooper, just talk to him, ask him some questions, especially about the dark-haired, dark-eyed bitch named Lindsey. But he was walking into a situation he did not understand, and he needed to take every precaution. Besides, the truth was, these days he killed most of the people to whom he bothered to talk any length of time.

After closing the file drawer and turning off the lamp in the den, Hatch and Lindsey stopped at Regina's room to make sure she was all right, moving quietly to the side of her bed. The hall light, falling through her door, revealed that the girl was sound asleep. The small knuckles of one fisted hand were against her chin. She was breathing evenly through slightly parted lips. If she dreamed, her dreams must have been pleasant.

Hatch felt his heart pinch as he looked at her, for she seemed so desperately young. He found it hard to believe that he had ever been as young as Regina was just then, for youth was innocence. Having been raised under the hateful and oppressive hand of his father, he had surrendered innocence at an early age in return for an intuitive grasp of aberrant psychology that had permitted him to survive in a home where anger and brutal "discipline" were the rewards for innocent mistakes and misunderstandings. He knew that Regina could not be as tender as she looked, for life had given her reasons of her own to develop thick skin and an armored heart.

Tough as they might be, however, they were both vulnerable, child and man. In fact, at that moment Hatch felt more vulnerable than the girl. If given a choice between her infirmities—the game leg, the twisted and incomplete hand—and whatever damage had been done to some deep region of his brain, he would have opted for her physical impairments without hesitation. After recent experiences, including the inexplicable escalation of his anger into blind rage, Hatch did not feel entirely in control of himself. And from the time he had been a small boy, with the terrifying example of his father to shape his fears, he had feared nothing half as much as being out of control.

I will not fail you, he promised the sleeping child.

He looked at Lindsey, to whom he owed his lives, both of them, before and after dying. Silently he made her the same promise: I will not fail you.

He wondered if they were promises he could keep.

Later, in their own room, with the lights out, as they lay on their separate halves of the bed, Lindsey said, "The rest of the test results should be back to Dr. Nyebern tomorrow."

Hatch had spent most of Saturday at the hospital, giving blood and urine samples, submitting to the prying of X-ray and sonogram machines. At one point he had been hooked up to more electrodes than the creature that Dr. Frankenstein, in those old movies, had energized from kites sent aloft in a lightning storm.

He said, "When I spoke to him today, he told me everything was looking good. I'm sure the rest of the tests will all come in negative, too. Whatever's happening to me, it has nothing to do with any mental or physical damage from the accident or from being . . . dead. I'm healthy, I'm okay."

"Oh, God, I hope so."

"I'm just fine."

"Do you really think so?"

"Yes, I really think so, I really do." He wondered how he could lie to her so smoothly. Maybe because the lie was not meant to hurt or harm, merely to soothe her so she could get some sleep.

"I love you," she said.

"I love you, too."

In a couple of minutes—shortly before midnight, according to the digital clock at bedside—she was asleep, snoring softly.

Hatch was unable to sleep, worrying about what he might learn of his future—or lack of it—tomorrow. He suspected that Dr. Nyebern would be gray-faced and grim, bearing somber news of some meaningful shadow detected in one lobe of Hatch's brain or another, a patch of dead cells, lesion, cyst, or tumor. Something deadly. Inoperable. And certain to get worse.

His confidence had been increasing slowly ever since he had gotten past the events of Thursday night and Friday morning, when he had dreamed of the blonde's murder and, later, had actually followed the trail of the killer to the Route 133 off-ramp from the San Diego Freeway. The weekend had been uneventful. The day just past, enlivened and uplifted by Regina's arrival, had been delightful. Then he had seen the newspaper piece about Cooper, and had lost control.

He hadn't told Lindsey about the stranger's reflection that he had seen in the den mirror. This time he was unable to pretend that he might have been sleepwalking, half awake, half dreaming. He had been wide awake, which meant the image in the mirror was an hallucination of one kind or another. A healthy, undamaged brain didn't hallucinate. He hadn't shared that terror with her because he knew, with the receipt of the test results tomorrow, there would be fear enough to go around.

Unable to sleep, he began to think about the newspaper story again, even though he didn't want to chew on it any more. He tried to direct his thoughts away from William Cooper, but he returned to the subject the way he might have obsessively probed at a sore tooth with his tongue. It almost seemed as if he were being *forced* to think about the truck driver, as if a giant mental magnet was pulling his attention inexorably in that direction. Soon, to his dismay, anger rose in him again. Worse, almost at once, the anger exploded into fury and a hunger for violence so intense that he had to fist his hands at his sides and clench his teeth and struggle to keep from letting loose a primal cry of rage.

From the banks of mailboxes in the breezeway at the main entrance to the garden apartments, Vassago learned that William Cooper was in apartment twenty-eight. He followed the breezeway into the courtyard, which was filled with palms and ficuses and ferns and too many landscape lights to please him, and he climbed an exterior staircase to the covered balcony that served the second-floor units of the two-story complex.

No one was in sight. Palm Court was silent, peaceful.

Though it was a few minutes past midnight, lights were on in the Cooper apartment. Vassago could hear a television turned low.

The window to the right of the door was covered with Levolor blinds. The slats were not tightly closed. Vassago could see a kitchen illuminated only by the low-wattage bulb in the range hood.

To the left of the door a larger window looked onto the balcony and courtyard from the apartment living room. The drapes were not drawn all the way shut. Through the gap, a man could be seen slumped in a big recliner with his feet up in front of the television. His head was tilted to one side, his face toward the window, and he appeared to be asleep. A glass containing an inch of golden liquid stood beside a half-empty bottle of Jack Daniel's on a small table next to the recliner. A bag of cheese puffs had been knocked off the table, and some of the bright orange contents had scattered across the bile-green carpet.

Vassago scanned the balcony to the left, right, and on the other side of the courtyard. Still deserted.

He tried to slide open Cooper's living-room window, but it was either corroded or locked. He moved to the right again, toward the kitchen window, but he stopped at the door on the way and, without any real hope, tried it. The door was unlocked. He pushed it open, went inside—and locked it behind him.

The man in the recliner, probably Cooper, did not stir as Vassago quietly pulled the drapes all the way shut across the big living-room window. No one else, passing on the balcony, would be able to look inside.

Already assured that the kitchen, dining area, and living room were deserted, Vassago moved catlike through the bathroom and two bedrooms (one without furniture, used primarily for storage) that comprised the rest of the apartment. The man in the recliner was alone.

On the dresser in the bedroom, Vassago spotted a wallet and a ring of keys. In the wallet he found fifty-eight dollars, which he took, and a driver's license in the name of William X. Cooper. The photograph on the license was of the man in the living room, a few years younger and, of course, not in a drunken stupor.

He returned to the living room with the intention of waking Cooper and having an informative little chat with him. Who is Lindsey? Where does she live?

But as he approached the recliner, a current of anger shot through him, too sudden and causeless to be his own, as if he were a human radio that received other people's emotions. And what he was receiving was the same anger that had suddenly struck him while he had been with his collection in the funhouse hardly an hour ago. As before, he opened himself to it, amplified the current with his own singular rage, wondering if he would receive visions, as he had on that previous occasion. But this time, as he stood looking down on William Cooper, the anger flared too abruptly into insensate fury, and he lost control. From the table beside the recliner, he grabbed the Jack Daniel's by the neck of the bottle.

Lying rigid in his bed, hands fisted so tightly that even his blunt fingernails were gouging painfully into his palms, Hatch had the crazy feeling that his mind had been invaded. His flicker of anger had been like opening a door just a hairline crack but wide enough for something on the other side to get a grip and tear it off its hinges. He felt something unnameable storming into him, a force without form or features, defined only by its hatred and rage. Its fury was that of the hurricane, the typhoon, beyond mere human dimensions, and he knew that he was too small a vessel to contain all of the anger that was pumping into him. He felt as if he would explode, shatter as if he were not a man but a crystal figurine.

The half-full bottle of Jack Daniel's whacked the side of the sleeping man's head with such impact that it was almost as loud as a shotgun blast. Whiskey and sharp fragments of glass showered up, rained down, splattered and clinked against the television set, the other furniture, and the walls. The air was filled with the velvety aroma of corn-mash bourbon, but underlying it was the scent of blood, for the gashed and battered side of Cooper's face was bleeding copiously.

The man was no longer merely sleeping. He had been hammered into a deeper level of unconsciousness.

Vassago was left with just the neck of the bottle in his hand. It terminated in three sharp spikes of glass that dripped bourbon and made him think of snake fangs glistening with venom. Shifting his grip, he raised the weapon above his head and brought it down, letting out a fierce hiss of rage, and the glass serpent bit deep into William Cooper's face.

The volcanic wrath that erupted into Hatch was unlike anything he had ever experienced before, far beyond any rage that his father had ever achieved. Indeed, it was nothing he could have generated within himself for the same reason that one could not manufacture sulfuric acid in a paper cauldron: the vessel would be dissolved by the substance it was required to contain. A high-pressure lava flow of anger gushed into him, so hot that he wanted to scream, so white-hot that he had no time to scream. Consciousness was burned away, and he fell into a mercifully dreamless darkness where there was neither anger nor terror.

Vassago realized that he was shouting with wordless, savage glee. After a dozen or twenty blows, the glass weapon had utterly disintegrated. He finally, reluctantly dropped the short fragment of the bottle neck still in his white-knuckled grip. Snarling, he threw himself against the Naugahyde recliner, tipping it over and rolling the dead man onto the bile-green carpet. He picked up the end table and pitched it into the television set, where Humphrey Bogart was sitting in a military courtroom, rolling a couple of ball bearings in his leathery hand, talking about strawberries. The screen imploded, and Bogart was transformed into a shower of yellow sparks, the sight of which ignited new fires of destructive frenzy in Vassago. He kicked over a coffee table, tore two K Mart prints off the walls and smashed the glass out of the frames, swept a collection of cheap ceramic knickknacks off the mantel. He would have liked nothing better than to have continued from one end of the apartment to the other, pulling all the dishes out of the kitchen cabinets and smashing them, reducing all the glassware to bright shards, seizing the food in the refrigerator and heaving it against the walls, hammering one piece of furniture against another until everything was broken and splintered, but he was halted by the sound of a siren, distant now, rapidly drawing nearer, the meaning of it penetrating even through the mist of blood frenzy that clouded his thoughts. He headed for the door, then swung away from it, realizing that people might have come out into the courtyard or might be watching from their windows. He ran out of the living room, back the short hall, to the window in the master bedroom, where he pulled aside the drapes and looked onto the roof over the building-long carport. An alleyway, bordered by a block wall, lay beyond. He twisted open the latch on the double-hung window, shoved up the bottom half, squeezed through, dropped onto the roof of the long carport, rolled to the edge, fell to the pavement, and landed on his feet as if he were a cat. He lost his sunglasses, scooped them up, put them on again. He sprinted left, toward the back of the property, with the siren louder now, much louder, very close. When he came to the next flank of the eight-foot-high concrete-block wall that ringed the property, he swiftly clambered over it with the agility of a spider skittering up any porous surface, and then he was over, into another alleyway serving carports along the back of another apartment complex, and so he ran from serviceway to serviceway, picking a route through the maze by sheer instinct, and came out on the street where he had parked, half a block from the pearl-gray Honda. He got in the car, started the engine, and drove away from there as sedately as he could manage, sweating and breathing so hard that he steamed up the windows. Reveling in the fragrant mélange of bourbon, blood, and perspiration, he was tremendously excited, so profoundly *satisfied* by the violence he had unleashed that he pounded the steering wheel and let out peals of laughter that had a shrieky edge.

For a while he drove randomly from one street to another with no idea where he was headed. After his laughter faded, when his heart stopped racing, he gradually oriented himself and struck out south and east, in the general direction of his hideaway.

If William Cooper could have provided any connection to the

woman named Lindsey, that lead was now closed to Vassago forever. He wasn't worried. He didn't know what was happening to him, why Cooper or Lindsey or the man in the mirror had been brought to his attention by these supernatural means. But he knew that if he only trusted in his dark god, everything would eventually be made clear to him.

He was beginning to wonder if Hell had let him go willingly, returning him to the land of the living in order to use him to deal with certain people whom the god of darkness wanted dead. Perhaps he'd not been stolen from Hell, after all, but had been *sent* back to life on a mission of destruction that was only slowly becoming comprehensible. If that were the case, he was pleased to make himself the instrument of the dark and powerful divinity whose company he longed to rejoin, and he anxiously awaited whatever task he might be assigned next.

Toward dawn, after several hours in a deep slumber of almost deathlike perfection, Hatch woke and did not know where he was. For a moment he drifted in confusion, then washed up on the shore of memory: the bedroom, Lindsey breathing softly in her sleep beside him, the ash-gray first light of morning like a fine silver dust on the windowpanes.

When he recalled the inexplicable and inhuman fit of rage that had slammed through him with paralytic force, Hatch stiffened with fear. He tried to remember where that spiraling anger had led, in what act of violence it had culminated, but his mind was blank. It seemed to him that he had simply passed out, as if that unnaturally intense fury had overloaded the circuits in his brain and blown a fuse or two.

Passed out—or blacked out? There was a fateful difference between the two. Passed out, he might have been in bed all night, exhausted, as still as a stone on the floor of the sea. But if he *blacked* out, remaining conscious but unaware of what he was doing, in a psychotic fugue, God alone knew what he might have done.

Suddenly he sensed that Lindsey was in grave danger.

Heart hammering against the cage of his ribs, he sat up in bed and looked at her. The dawn light at the window was too soft to reveal her clearly. She was only a shadowy shape against the sheets.

He reached for the switch on the bedside lamp, but then hesitated. He was afraid of what he might see.

I would never hurt Lindsey, never, he thought desperately.

But he remembered all too well that, for a moment last night, he had not been entirely himself. His anger at Cooper had seemed to open a door within him, letting in a monster from some vast darkness beyond.

Trembling, he finally clicked the switch. In the lamplight he saw that Lindsey was untouched, as fair as ever, sleeping with a peaceful smile.

Greatly relieved, he switched off the lamp—and thought of Regina. The engine of anxiety revved up again.

Ridiculous. He would no sooner harm Regina than Lindsey. She was a defenseless child.

He could not stop shaking, wondering.

He slipped out of bed without disturbing his wife. He picked up his bathrobe from the back of the armchair, pulled it on, and quietly left the room.

Barefoot, he entered the hall, where a pair of skylights admitted large pieces of the morning, and followed it to Regina's room. He moved swiftly at first, then more slowly, weighed down by dread as heavy as a pair of iron boots.

He had a mental image of the flower-painted mahogany bed splashed with blood, the sheets sodden and red. For some reason, he had the crazy notion that he would find the child with fragments of glass in her ravaged face. The weird specificity of that image convinced him that he had, indeed, done something unthinkable after he had blacked out.

When he eased open the door and looked into the girl's room, she was sleeping as peacefully as Lindsey, in the same posture he had seen her in last night, when he and Lindsey had checked on her before going to bed. No blood. No broken glass.

Swallowing hard, he pulled the door shut and returned along

the hall as far as the first skylight. He stood in the fall of dim morning light, looking up through the tinted glass at a sky of indeterminate hue, as if an explanation would suddenly be writ large across the heavens.

No explanation came to him. He remained confused and anxious.

At least Lindsey and Regina were fine, untouched by whatever presence he had connected with last night.

He was reminded of an old vampire movie he had once seen, in which a wizened priest had warned a young woman that the undead could enter her house only if she invited them—but that they were cunning and persuasive, capable of inducing even the wary to issue that mortal invitation.

Somehow a bond existed between Hatch and the psychotic who had killed the young blond punker named Lisa. By failing to repress his anger at William Cooper, he had strengthened that bond. His anger was the key that opened the door. When he indulged in anger, he was issuing an invitation just like the one against which the priest in that movie had warned the young woman. He could not explain how he knew this to be true, but he *did* know it, all right, knew it in his bones. He just wished to God he *understood* it.

He felt lost.

Small and powerless and afraid.

And although Lindsey and Regina had come through the night unharmed, he sensed more strongly than ever that they were in great danger. Growing greater by the day. By the hour.

3

Before dawn, the thirtieth of April, Vassago bathed outdoors with bottled water and liquid soap. By the first light of day, he had safely ensconced in the deepest part of his hideaway. Lying on his mattress, staring up the elevator shaft, he treated himself to Oreos and warm root beer, then to a couple of snack-size bags of Reese's Pieces.

Murder was always enormously satisfying. Tremendous internal pressures were released with the strike of a killing blow. More important, each murder was an act of rebellion against all things holy, against commandments and laws and rules and the irritatingly prissy systems of manners employed by human beings to support the fiction that life was precious and endowed with meaning. Life was cheap and pointless. Nothing mattered but sensation and the swift gratification of all desires, which only the strong and free really understood. After every killing, Vassago felt as liberated as the wind and mightier than any steel machine.

Until one special, glorious night in his twelfth year, he had been one of the enslaved masses, dumbly plodding through life according to the rules of so-called civilization, though they made no sense to him. He pretended to love his mother, father, sister, and a host of relatives, though he felt nothing more for them than he did for strangers encountered on the street. As a child, when he was old enough to begin thinking about such things, he wondered if something was wrong with him, a crucial element missing from his makeup. As he listened to himself playing the game of love, employing strategies of false affection and shameless flattery, he was amazed at how convincing others found him, for he could hear the insincerity in his voice, could feel the fraudulence in every gesture, and was acutely aware of the deceit behind his every loving smile. Then one day he suddenly heard the deception in their voices and saw it in their faces, and he realized that none of *them* had ever experienced love, either, or any of the nobler sentiments toward which a civilized person was supposed to aspire—selflessness, courage, piety, humility, and all the rest of that dreary catechism. *They* were all playing the game, too. Later he came to the conclusion that most of them, even the adults, had never enjoyed his degree of insight, and remained unaware that other people were exactly like them. Each person thought he was unique, that something was missing in him, and that he must play the game well or be uncovered and ostracized as something less than human. God had tried to create a world of love, had failed, and had commanded His creations to pretend to the perfection with which He had been unable to imbue them. Perceiving that stunning truth, Vassago had taken his first step toward freedom. Then one summer night when he was twelve, he finally understood that in order to be really free, totally free, he had to act upon his understanding, begin to live differently from the herd of humanity, with his own pleasure as the only consideration. He had to be willing to exercise the power over others which he possessed by virtue of his insight into the true nature of the world. That night he learned that the ability to kill without compunction was the purest form of power, and that the exercise of power was the greatest pleasure of them all. . . .

In those days, before he died and came back from the dead and chose the name of the demon prince Vassago, the name to which he had answered and under which he had lived was Jeremy. His best friend had been Tod Ledderbeck, the son of Dr. Sam Ledderbeck, a gynecologist whom Jeremy called the "crack quack" when he wanted to rag Tod.

In the morning of that early June day, Mrs. Ledderbeck had taken Jeremy and Tod to Fantasy World, the lavish amusement park that, against all expectations, had begun to give Disneyland a run for its money. It was in the hills, a few miles east of San Juan Capistrano, somewhat out of the way—just as Magic Mountain had been a bit isolated before the suburbs north of Los Angeles had spread around it, and just as Disneyland had seemed to be in the middle of nowhere when first constructed on farmland near the obscure town of Anaheim. It was built with Japanese money, which worried some people who believed the Japanese were going to own the whole country some day, and there were rumors of Mafia money being involved, which only made it more mysterious and appealing. But finally what mattered was that the atmosphere of the place was cool, the rides radical, and the junk food almost deliriously junky. Fantasy World was where Tod wanted to spend his twelfth birthday, in the company of his best friend, free of parental control from morning until ten o'clock at night, and Tod usually got what he wanted because he was a good kid; everyone liked him; he knew exactly how to play the game.

Mrs. Ledderbeck left them off at the front gate and shouted after them as they raced away from the car: "I'll pick you up right here at ten o'clock! Right here at ten o'clock sharp!"

After paying for their tickets and getting onto the grounds of the park, Tod said, "What do you wanna do first?"

"I don't know. What do you wanna do first?"

"Ride the Scorpion?"

"Yeah!"

"Yeah!"

Bang, they were off, hurrying toward the north end of the park where the track for the Scorpion—"The Roller Coaster with a Sting!" the TV ads all proclaimed—rose in sweet undulant terror against the clear blue sky. The park was not crowded yet, and they didn't need to snake between cow-slow herds of people. Their tennis shoes pounded noisily on the blacktop, and each slap of rubber against pavement was a shout of freedom. They rode the Scorpion, yelling and screaming as it plummeted and whipped and turned upside down and plummeted again, and when the ride ended, they ran directly to the boarding ramp and did it once more.

Then, as now, Jeremy had loved speed. The stomach-flopping sharp turns and plunges of amusement-park rides had been a childish substitute for the violence he had unknowingly craved. After two rides on the Scorpion, with so many speeding-swooping-looping-twisting delights ahead, Jeremy was in a terrific mood.

But Tod tainted the day as they were coming down the exit ramp from their second trip on the roller coaster. He threw one arm around Jeremy's shoulders and said, "Man, this is gonna be for sure the greatest birthday anybody's ever had, just you and me."

The camaraderie, like all camaraderie, was totally fake. Deception. Fraud. Jeremy hated all that phoney-baloney crap, but Tod was full of it. Best friends. Blood brothers. You and me against the world.

Jeremy wasn't sure what rubbed him the rawest: that Tod jived him all the time about being good buddies and seemed to think that Jeremy was taken in by the con—or that sometimes Tod seemed dumb enough to be suckered by his *own* con. Recently, Jeremy had begun to suspect that some people played the game of life so well, they didn't realize it was a game. They deceived even themselves with all their talk of friendship, love, and compassion. Tod was looking more and more like one of *those* hopeless jerks.

Being best friends was just a way to get a guy to do things for you that he wouldn't do for anyone else in a thousand years. Friendship was also a mutual defense arrangement, a way of joining forces against the mobs of your fellow citizens who would just as soon smash your face and take whatever they wanted from you. Everyone knew that's all friendship was, but no one ever talked truthfully about it, least of all Tod.

Later, on their way from the Haunted House to an attraction called Swamp Creature, they stopped at a stand selling blocks of ice cream dipped in chocolate and rolled in crushed nuts. They sat on plastic chairs at a plastic table, under a red umbrella, against a backdrop of acacias and manmade waterfalls, chomping down, and everything was fine at first, but then Tod had to spoil it.

"It's great coming to the park without grownups, isn't it?" Tod said with his mouth full. "You can eat ice cream before lunch, like this. Hell, you can eat it for lunch, too, if you want, and after lunch, and nobody's there to whine at you about spoiling your appetite or getting sick."

"It's great," Jeremy agreed.

"Let's sit here and eat ice cream till we puke."

"Sounds good to me. But let's not waste it."

"Huh?"

Jeremy said, "Let's be sure, when we puke, we just don't spew on the ground. Let's be sure we puke *on* somebody."

"Yeah!" Tod said, getting the drift right away, "on somebody who deserves it, who's really pukeworthy."

"Like those girls," Jeremy said, indicating a pair of pretty teenagers who were passing by. They wore white shorts and bright summery blouses, and they were so sure that they were cute, you wanted to puke on them even if you hadn't eaten anything and all you could manage was the dry heaves.

"Or those old farts," Tod said, pointing to an elderly couple buying ice cream nearby.

"No, not them," Jeremy said. "They already *look* like they've been puked on."

Tod thought that was so hilarious, he choked on his ice cream. In some ways Tod was all right.

"Funny about this ice cream," he said when he stopped choking.

Jeremy bit: "What's funny about it?"

"I know the ice cream is made from milk, which comes from cows. And they make chocolate out of cocoa beans. But whose nuts do they crush to sprinkle over it all?"

Yeah, for sure, old Tod was all right in some ways.

But just when they were laughing the loudest, feeling good, he leaned across the table, swatted Jeremy lightly alongside the head, and said, "You and me, Jer, we're gonna be *tight* forever, friends till they feed us to the worms. Right?"

He really believed it. He had conned himself. He was so stupidly sincere that he made Jeremy want to puke on *him*.

Instead, Jeremy said, "What're you gonna do next, try to kiss me on the lips?"

Grinning, not picking up on the impatience and hostility aimed at him, Tod said, "Up your grandma's ass."

"Up *your* grandma's ass."

"My grandma doesn't have an ass."

"Yeah? Then what's she sit on?"

"Your face."

They kept ragging each other all the way to Swamp Creature. The attraction was hokey, not well done, but good for a lot of jokes because of that. For a while, Tod was just wild and fun to be around.

Later, however, after they came out of Space Battle, Tod started referring to them as "the two best rocket jockeys in the universe," which half embarrassed Jeremy because it was so stupid and juvenile. It also irritated him because it was just another way of saying "we're buddies, blood brothers, pals." They'd get on the Scorpion, and just as it pulled out of the station, Tod would say, "This is nothing, this is just a Sunday drive to the two best rocket jockeys in the universe." Or they'd be on their way into World of the Giants, and Tod would throw his arm around Jeremy's shoulder and say, "The two best rocket jockeys in the universe can handle a fucking giant, can't we, bro?"

Jeremy wanted to say, *Look, you jerk, the only reason we're friends is because your old man and mine are sort of in the same kind of work, so we got thrown together. I hate this arm-around-the-shoulders shit, so just knock it off, let's have some laughs and be happy with that. Okay?*

But he did not say anything of the sort because, of course, good players in life never admitted that they knew it was all just a game. If you let the other players see you didn't care about the rules and regulations, they wouldn't let you play. Go to Jail. Go directly to Jail. Don't pass Go. Don't have any fun.

By seven o'clock that evening, after they had eaten enough junk food to produce radically interesting vomit if they really did decide to puke on anyone, Jeremy was so tired of the rocket jockey crap and so irritated by Tod's friendship rap, that he couldn't wait for ten o'clock to roll around and Mrs. Ledderbeck to pull up to the gate in her station wagon.

They were on the Millipede, blasting through one of the pitch-black sections of the ride, when Tod made one too many references to the two best rocket jockeys in the universe, and Jeremy decided to kill him. The instant the thought flashed through his mind, he knew he had to murder his "best friend." It felt so *right*. If life was a game with a zillion-page book of rules, it wasn't going to be a whole hell of a lot of fun—unless you found ways to break the rules and still be allowed to play. *Any* game was a bore if you played by the rules—Monopoly, 500 rummy, baseball. But if you stole bases, filched cards without getting caught, or changed the numbers on the dice when the other guy was distracted, a dull game could be a kick. And in the game of life, getting away with murder was the biggest kick of all.

When the Millipede shrieked to a halt at the debarkation platform, Jeremy said, "Let's do it again."

"Sure," Tod said.

They hurried along the exit corridor, in a rush to get outside and
into line again. The park had filled up during the day, and the wait
to board any ride was now at least twenty minutes.

When they came out of the Millipede pavillion, the sky was
black in the east, deep blue overhead, and orange in the west.
Twilight came sooner and lasted longer at Fantasy World than in
the western part of the county, because between the park and the
distant sea rose ranks of high, sun-swallowing hills. Those ridges
were now black silhouettes against the orange heavens, like Hal-
loween decorations out of season.

Fantasy World had taken on a new, manic quality with the
approach of night. Christmas-style lights outlined the rides and
buildings. White twinkle lights lent a festive sparkle to all the trees,
while a pair of unsynchronized spotlights swooped back and forth
across the snow-covered peak of the manmade Big Foot Mountain. On every side neon glowed in all the hues that neon offered,
and out on Mars Island, bursts of brightly colored laser beams
shot randomly into the darkening sky as if fending off a spaceship
attack. Scented with popcorn and roasted peanuts, a warm breeze
snapped garlands of pennants overhead. Music of every period
and type leaked out of the pavilions, and rock-'n'-roll boomed
from the open-air dance floor at the south end of the park, and
from somewhere else came the bouncy strains of Big Band swing.
People laughed and chattered excitedly, and on the thrill rides they
were screaming, screaming.

"Daredevil this time," Jeremy said as he and Tod sprinted to the
end of the Millipede boarding line.

"Yeah," Tod said, "daredevil!"

The Millipede was essentially an indoor roller coaster, like
Space Mountain at Disneyland, except instead of shooting up and
down and around one huge room, it whipped through a long series
of tunnels, some lit and some not. The lap bar, meant to restrain
the riders, was tight enough to be safe, but if a kid was slim and

agile, he could contort himself in such way as to squeeze out from under it, scramble over it, and stand in the leg well. Then he could lean against the lap bar and grip it behind his back—or hook his arms around it—riding daredevil.

It was a stupid and dangerous thing to do, which Jeremy and Tod realized. But they had done it a couple of times anyway, not only on the Millipede but on other rides in other parks. Riding daredevil pumped up the excitement level at least a thousand percent, especially in pitch-dark tunnels where it was impossible to see what was coming next.

"Rocket jockeys!" Tod said when they were halfway through the line. He insisted on giving Jeremy a low five and then a high five, though they looked like a couple of asshole kids. "No rocket jockey is afraid of daredeviling the Millipede, right?"

"Right," Jeremy said as they inched through the main doors and entered the pavilion. Shrill screams echoed to them from the riders on the cars that shot away into the tunnel ahead.

According to legend (as kid-created legends went at every amusement park with a similar ride), a boy had been killed riding daredevil on the Millipede because he'd been too tall. The ceiling of the tunnel was high in all lighted stretches, but they said it dropped low at one spot in a darkened passage—maybe because air-conditioning pipes passed through at that point, maybe because the engineers made the contractor put in another support that hadn't been planned for, maybe because the architect was a no-brain. Anyway, this tall kid, standing up, smacked his head into the low part of the ceiling, never even saw it coming. It instantly pulverized his face, decapitated him. All the unsuspecting bozos riding behind him were splattered with blood and brains and broken teeth.

Jeremy didn't believe it for a minute. Fantasy World hadn't been built by guys with horse turds for brains. They had to have figured kids would find a way to get out from under the lap bars, because nothing was entirely kid-proof, and they would have kept the ceiling high all the way through. Legend also had it that the low overhang was still somewhere in one of the dark sections of the tunnel, with bloodstains and flecks of dried brains on it, which was total cow flop.

For anybody riding daredevil, standing up, the real danger was that he would fall out of the car when it whipped around a sharp turn or accelerated unexpectedly. Jeremy figured there were six or eight particularly radical curves on the Millipede course where Tod Ledderbeck might easily topple out of the car with only minimal assistance.

The line moved slowly forward.

Jeremy was not impatient or afraid. As they drew closer to the boarding gates, he became more excited but also more confident. His hands were not trembling. He had no butterflies in his belly. He just wanted to *do* it.

The boarding chamber for the ride was constructed to resemble a cavern with immense stalactites and stalagmites. Strange bright-eyed creatures swam in the murky depths of eerie pools, and albino mutant crabs prowled the shores, reaching up with huge wicked claws toward the people on the boarding platform, snapping at them but not quite long-armed enough to snare any dinner.

Each train had six cars, and each car carried two people. The cars were painted like segments of a Millipede; the first had a big insect head with moving jaws and multifaceted black eyes, not a cartoon but a really fierce monster face; the one at the back boasted a curved stinger that looked more like part of a scorpion than the ass-end of a Millipede. Two trains were boarding at any one time, the second behind the first, and they shot off into the tunnel with only a few seconds between them because the whole operation was computer-controlled, eliminating any danger that one train would crash into the back of another.

Jeremy and Tod were among the twelve customers that the attendant sent to the first train.

Tod wanted the front car, but they didn't get it. That was the best position from which to ride daredevil because everything would happen to them first: every plunge into darkness, every squirt of cold steam from the wall vents, every explosion through swinging doors into whirling lights. Besides, part of the fun of riding daredevil was showing off, and the front car provided a perfect platform for exhibitionism, with the occupants of the last five cars as a captive audience in the lighted stretches.

With the first car claimed, they raced for the sixth. Being the last to experience every plunge and twist of the track was next-best to being first, because the squeals of the riders ahead of you raised your adrenaline level and expectations. Something about being securely in the middle of the train just didn't go with daredevil riding.

The lap bars descended automatically when all twelve people were aboard. An attendant came along the platform, visually inspecting to be sure all of the restraints had locked into place.

Jeremy was relieved they had not gotten the front car, where they would have had ten witnesses behind them. In the tomb-dark confines of the unlit sections of tunnel, he wouldn't be able to see his own hand an inch in front of his face, so it wasn't likely that anyone would be able to see him push Tod out of the car. But this was a big-time violation of the rules, and he didn't want to take any chances. Now, potential witnesses were all safely in front of them, staring straight ahead; in fact they could not easily glance back, since every seat had a high back to prevent whiplash.

When the attendant finished checking the lap bars, he turned and signaled the operator, who was seated at an instrument panel on a rock formation to the right of the tunnel entrance.

"Here we go," Tod said.

"Here we go," Jeremy agreed.

"Rocket jockeys!" Tod shouted.

Jeremy gritted his teeth.

"Rocket jockeys!" Tod repeated.

What the hell. One more time wouldn't hurt. Jeremy yelled: "Rocket jockeys!"

The train did not pull away from the boarding station with the jerky uncertainty of most roller coasters. A tremendous blast of compressed air shot it forward at high speed, like a bullet out of a barrel, with a *whoosh!* that almost hurt the ears. They were pinned against their seats as they flashed past the operator and into the black mouth of the tunnel.

Total darkness.

He was only twelve then. He had not died. He had not been to Hell. He had not come back. He was as blind in darkness as anyone else, as Tod.

Then they slammed through swinging doors and up a long incline of well-lit track, moving fast at first but gradually slowing to a crawl. On both sides they were menaced by pale white slugs as big as men, which reared up and shrieked at them through round mouths full of teeth that whirled like the blades in a garbage disposal. The ascent was six or seven stories, at a steep angle, and other mechanical monsters gibbered, hooted, snarled, and squealed at the train; all of them were pale and slimy, with either glowing eyes or blind black eyes, the kind of critters you might think would live miles below the surface of the earth—if you didn't know *any* science at all.

That initial slope was where daredevils had to take their stand. Though a couple of other inclines marked the course of the Millipede, no other section of the track provided a sufficiently extended period of calm in which to execute a safe escape from the lap bar.

Jeremy contorted himself, wriggling up against the back of the seat, inching over the lap bar, but at first Tod did not move. "Come on, dickhead, you've gotta be in position before we get to the top."

Tod looked troubled. "If they catch us, they'll kick us out of the park."

"They won't catch us."

At the far end of the ride, the train would coast along a final stretch of dark tunnel, giving riders a chance to calm down. In those last few seconds, before they returned to the fake cavern from which they had started, it was just possible for a kid to scramble back over the lap bar and shoehorn himself into his seat. Jeremy knew he could do it; he was not worried about getting caught. Tod didn't have to worry about getting under the lap bar

221

again, either, because by then Tod would be dead; he wouldn't have to worry about anything ever.

"I don't want to be kicked out for daredeviling," Tod said as the train approached the halfway point on the long, long initial incline. "It's been a neat day, and we still have a couple hours before Mom comes for us."

Mutant albino rats chattered at them from the fake rock ledges on both sides as Jeremy said, "Okay, so be a dorkless wonder." He continued to extricate himself from the lap bar.

"I'm no dorkless wonder," Tod said defensively.

"Sure, sure."

"I'm not."

"Maybe when school starts again in September, you'll be able to get into the Young Homemakers Club, learn how to cook, knit nice little doilies, do flower arranging."

"You're a jerkoff, you know that?"

"Ooooooooooo, you've broken my heart now," Jeremy said as he extracted both of his legs from the well under the lap bar and crouched on the seat. "You girls sure know how to hurt a guy's feelings."

"Creepazoid."

The train strained up the slope with the hard clicking and clattering so specific to roller coasters that the sound alone could make the heart pump faster and the stomach flutter.

Jeremy scrambled over the lap bar and stood in the well in front of it, facing forward. He looked over his shoulder at Tod, who sat scowling behind the restraint. He didn't care that much if Tod joined him or not. He had already decided to kill the boy, and if he didn't have a chance to do it at Fantasy World on Tod's twelfth birthday, he would do it somewhere else, sooner or later. Just thinking about doing it was a lot of fun. Like that song said in the television commercial where the Heinz ketchup was so thick it took what seemed like hours coming out of the bottle: *An-tic-i-paaa-aa-tion.* Having to wait a few days or even weeks to get another good chance to kill Tod would only make the killing that much more fun. So he didn't rag Tod any more, just looked at him scornfully. *An-tic-i-paaa-aa-tion.*

"I'm not afraid," Tod insisted.

"Yeah."

"I just don't want to spoil the day."

"Sure."

"Creepazoid," Tod said again.

Jeremy said, "Rocket jockey, my ass."

That insult had a powerful effect. Tod was so sold on his own friendship con that he could actually be stung by the implication that he didn't know how a real friend was supposed to behave. The expression on his broad and open face revealed not only a world of hurt but a surprising desperation that startled Jeremy. Maybe Tod *did* understand what life was all about, that it was nothing but a brutal game with every player concentrated on the purely selfish goal of coming out a winner, and maybe old Tod was rattled by that, scared by it, and was holding on to one last hope, to the idea of friendship. If the game could be played with a partner or two, if it was really everyone else in the world against your own little team, that was tolerable, better than everyone in the world against just *you*. Tod Ledderbeck and his good buddy Jeremy against the rest of humanity was even sort of romantic and adventurous, but Tod Ledderbeck alone obviously made his bowels quiver.

Sitting behind the lap bar, Tod first looked stricken, then resolute. Indecision gave way to action, and Tod moved fast, wriggling furiously against the restraint.

"Come on, come on," Jeremy urged. "We're almost to the top."

Tod eeled over the lap bar, into the leg well where Jeremy stood. He caught his foot in that restraining mechanism, and almost fell out of the car.

Jeremy grabbed him, hauled him back. *This* was not the place for Tod to take a fall. They weren't moving fast enough. At most he'd suffer a couple of bruises.

Then they were side by side, their feet planted wide on the floor of the car, leaning back against the restraint from under which they had escaped, arms behind them, hands locked on the lap bar, grinning at each other, as the train reached the top of the incline. It slammed through swinging doors into the next stretch of light-

223

less tunnel. The track remained flat just long enough to crank up the riders' tension a couple of notches. *An-tic-i-paaa-aa-tion.* When Jeremy could not hold his breath any longer, the front car tipped over the brink, and the people up there screamed in the darkness. Then in rapid succession the second and third and fourth and fifth cars—

"Rocket jockeys!" Jeremy and Tod shouted in unison.

—and the final car of the train followed the others into a steep plunge, building speed by the second. Wind whooshed past them and whipped their hair out behind their heads. Then came a swooping turn to the right when it was least expected, a little upgrade to toss the stomach, another turn to the right, the track tilting so the cars were tipped onto their sides, faster, faster, then a straightaway and another incline, using their speed to go higher than ever, slowing toward the top, slowing, slowing. *An-tic-i-paaa-aa-tion.* They went over the edge and down, down, down, waaaaaaaaaay down so hard and fast that Jeremy felt as if his stomach had fallen out of him, leaving a hole in the middle of his body. He knew what was coming, but he was left breathless by it nonetheless. The train did a loop-de-loop, turning upside down. He pressed his feet tight to the floor and gripped the lap bar behind him as if he were trying to fuse his flesh with the steel, because it felt as if he would fall out, straight down onto the section of the track that had led them into the loop, to crack his skull open on the rails below. He knew centripetal force would hold him in place even though he was standing up where he didn't belong, but what he knew was of no consequence: *what you* felt *always carried a lot more weight than what you* knew, *emotion mattered more than intellect.* Then they were out of the loop, banging through another pair of swinging doors onto a second lighted incline, using their tremendous speed to build height for the next series of plunges and sharp turns.

Jeremy looked at Tod.

The old rocket jockey was a little green.

"No more loops," Tod shouted above the clatter of the train wheels. "The worst is behind us."

Jeremy exploded with laughter. He thought: *The worst is still ahead for you, dickhead. And for me the best is yet to come. An-tic-i-paaa-aa-tion.*

Tod laughed, too, but certainly for different reasons.

At the top of the second incline, the rattling cars pushed through a third set of swinging doors, returning to a grave-dark world that thrilled Jeremy because he knew Tod Ledderbeck had just seen the last light of his life. The train snapped left and right, swooped up and plummeted down, rolled onto its side in a series of corkscrew turns.

Through it all Jeremy could feel Tod beside him. Their bare arms brushed together, and their shoulders bumped as they swayed with the movement of the train. Every contact sent a current of intense pleasure through Jeremy, made the hairs stand up on his arms and on the back of his neck, pebbled his skin with gooseflesh. He knew that he possessed the ultimate power over the other boy, the power of life and death, and he was different from the other gutless wonders of the world because he wasn't afraid to *use* the power.

He waited for a section of track near the end of the ride, where he knew the undulant motion would provide the greatest degree of instability for daredevil riders. By then Tod would be feeling confident—*the worst is behind us*—and easier to catch by surprise. The approach to the killing ground was announced by one of the most unusual tricks in the ride, a three-hundred-and-sixty-degree turn at high speed, with the cars on their sides all the way around. When they finished that circle and leveled out once more, they would immediately enter a series of six hills, all low but packed close together, so the train would move like an inchworm on drugs, pulling itself up-down-up-down-up-down-up-down toward the last set of swinging doors, which would admit them to the cavernous boarding and disembarkation chamber where they had begun.

The train began to tilt.

They entered the three-hundred-and-sixty-degree turn.

The train was on its side.

Tod tried to remain rigid, but he sagged a little against Jeremy, who was on the inside of the car when it curved to the right. The old rocket jockey was whooping like an air-raid siren, doing his best to hype himself and get the most out of the ride, now that the worst was behind them.

An-tic-i-paa-aa-tion.

Jeremy estimated they were a third of the way around the circle. . . . halfway around . . . two-thirds. . . .

The track leveled out. The train stopped fighting gravity.

With a suddenness that almost took Jeremy's breath away, the train hit the first of the six hills and shot upward.

He let go of the lap bar with his right hand, the one farthest from Tod.

The train swooped down.

He made a fist of his right hand.

And almost as soon as the train dropped, it swooped upward again toward the crown of the second hill.

Jeremy swung his fist in a roundhouse blow, trusting instinct to find Tod's face.

The train dropped.

His fist hit home, smashing Tod hard in the face, and he felt the boy's nose split.

The train shot upward again, with Tod screaming, though no one would hear anything special about it among the screams of all the other passengers.

Just for a split second, Tod would probably think he'd smacked into the overhang where, in legend, a boy had been decapitated. He would let go of the lap bar in panic. At least that was what Jeremy hoped, so as soon as he hit the old rocket jockey, when the train started to drop down the third hill, Jeremy let go of the lap bar, too, and threw himself against his best friend, grabbing him, lifting and shoving, hard as he could. He felt Tod trying to get a fistful of his hair, but he shook his head furiously and shoved harder, took a kick on the hip—

—the train shot up the fourth hill—

—Tod went over the edge, out into the darkness, away from the car, as if he had dropped into deep space. Jeremy started to topple with him, grabbed frantically for the lap bar in the seamless blackness, found it, held on—

—down, the train swooped down the fourth hill—

—Jeremy thought he heard one last scream from Tod and then a solid *thunk!* as he hit the tunnel wall and bounced back onto the tracks in the wake of the train, although it might have been imagination—

—up, the train shot up the fifth hill with a rollicking motion that made Jeremy want to whoop his cookies—

—Tod was either dead back there in the darkness or stunned, half-conscious, trying to get to his feet—

—down the fifth hill, and Jeremy was whipped back and forth, almost lost his grip on the bar, then was soaring again, up the sixth and final hill—

—and if he wasn't dead back there, Tod was maybe just beginning to realize that another train was coming—

—down, down the sixth hill and onto the last straightaway.

As soon as he knew he was on stable ground, Jeremy scrambled back across the restraint bar and wriggled under it, first his left leg, then his right leg.

The last set of doors was rushing toward them in the dark. Beyond would be light, the main cavern, and attendants who would see that he had been daredevil riding.

He squirmed frantically to pass his hips through the gap between the back of the seat and the lap bar. Not too difficult, really. It was easier to slip under the bar than it had been to get out from beneath its protective grip.

They hit the swinging doors—*wham!*—and coasted at a steadily declining speed toward the disembarkation platform, a hundred feet this side of the gates through which they had entered the roller coaster. People were jammed on the boarding platform, and a lot of them were looking back at the train as it came out of the tunnel mouth. For a moment Jeremy expected them to point at him and cry, "Murderer!"

Just as the train coasted up to the disembarkation gates and came to a full stop, red emergency lights blinked on all over the cavern, showing the way to the exits. A computerized alarm voice

227

echoed through speakers set high in the fake rock formations: *"The Millipede has been brought to an emergency stop. All riders please remain in your seats—"*

As the lap bar released automatically at the end of the ride, Jeremy stood on the seat, grabbed a handrail, and pulled himself onto the disembarkation platform.

"—all riders please remain in your seats until attendants arrive to lead you out of the tunnels—"

The uniformed attendants on the platforms were looking to one another for guidance, wondering what had happened.

"—all riders remain in your seats—"

From the platform, Jeremy looked back toward the tunnel out of which his own train had just entered the cavern. He saw another train pushing through the swinging doors.

"—all other guests please proceed in an orderly fashion to the nearest exit—"

The oncoming train was no longer moving fast or smoothly. It shuddered and tried to jump the track.

With a jolt, Jeremy saw what was jamming the foremost wheels and forcing the front car to rise off the rails. Other people on the platform must have seen it, too, because suddenly they started to scream, not the we-sure-are-having-a-damned-fine-time screams that could be heard all over the carnival, but screams of horror and revulsion.

"—all riders remain in your seats—"

The train rocked and spasmed to a complete stop far short of the disembarkation platform. Something was dangling from the fierce mouth of the insect head that protruded from the front of the first car, snared in the jagged mandibles. It was the rest of the old rocket jockey, a nice bite-size piece for a monster bug the size of that one.

"—all other guests please proceed in an orderly fashion to the nearest exit—"

"Don't look, son," an attendant said compassionately, turning Jeremy away from the gruesome spectacle. "For God's sake, get out of here."

The shocked attendants had recovered enough to begin to direct the waiting crowd toward exit doors marked with glowing red signs. Realizing that he was bursting with excitement, grinning like a fool, and too overcome with joy to successfully play the bereaved best friend of the deceased, Jeremy joined the exodus, which was conducted in a panicky rush, with some pushing and shoving.

In the night air, where Christmasy lights continued to twinkle and the laser beams shot into the black sky and rainbows of neon rippled on every side, where thousands of customers continued their pursuit of pleasure without the slightest awareness that Death walked among them, Jeremy sprinted away from the Millipede. Dodging through the crowds, narrowly avoiding one collision after another, he had no idea where he was going. He just kept on the move until he was far from the torn body of Tod Ledderbeck.

He finally stopped at the manmade lake, across which a few Hovercraft buzzed with travelers bound to and from Mars Island. He felt as if he were on Mars himself, or some other alien planet where the gravity was less than that on earth. He was buoyant, ready to float up, up, and away.

He sat on a concrete bench to anchor himself, with his back to the lake, facing a flower-bordered promenade along which passed an endless parade of people, and he surrendered to the giddy laughter that insistently bubbled in him like Pepsi in a shaken bottle. It gushed out, such effervescent giggles in such long spouts that he had to hug himself and lean back on the bench to avoid falling off. People glanced at him, and one couple stopped to ask if he was lost. His laughter was so intense that he was choking with it, tears streaming down his face. They thought he was crying, a twelve-year-old ninny who had gotten separated from his family and was too much of a pussy to handle it. Their incomprehension only made him laugh harder.

When the laughter passed, he sat forward on the bench, staring at his sneakered feet, working on the line of crap he would give Mrs. Ledderbeck when she came to collect him and Tod at ten o'clock—assuming park officials didn't identify the body and get in touch with her before that. It was eight o'clock. "He wanted to ride daredevil," Jeremy mumbled to his sneakers, "and I tried to talk him out of it, but he wouldn't listen, he called me a dickhead when I wouldn't go with him. I'm sorry, Mrs. Ledderbeck, Doctor Ledderbeck, but he talked that way sometimes. He thought it made him sound cool." Good enough so far, but he needed more of a tremor in his voice: "I wouldn't ride daredevil, so he went on the Millipede by himself. I waited at the exit, and when all those people came running out, talking about a body all torn and bloody, I knew who it had to be and I . . . and I . . . just sort of, you know, snapped. I just snapped." The boarding attendants wouldn't remember whether Tod had gotten on the ride by himself or with another boy; they dealt with thousands of passengers a day, so they weren't going to recall who was alone or who was with whom. "I'm so sorry, Mrs. Ledderbeck, I should've been able to talk him out of it. I should've stayed with him and stopped him somehow. I feel so stupid, so . . . so helpless. How could I let him get on the Millipede? What kind of best friend am I?"

Not bad. It needed a little work, and he would have to be careful not to overdramatize it. Tears, a breaking voice. But no wild sobs, no thrashing around.

He was sure he could pull it off.

He was a Master of the Game now.

As soon as he felt confident about his story, he realized he was hungry. Starving. He was literally shaking with hunger. He went to a refreshment stand and bought a hot dog with the works—onions, relish, chili, mustard, ketchup—and wolfed it down. He chased it with Orange Crush. Still shaking. He had an ice cream sandwich made with chocolate-chip oatmeal cookies for the "bread."

His visible shaking stopped, but he still trembled inside. Not with fear. It was a delicious shiver, like the flutter in the belly that he'd experienced during the past year whenever he looked at a girl and thought of being with her, but indescribably better than that. And it was a little like the thrilling shiver that caressed his spine when he slipped past the safety railing and stood on the very edge of a sandy cliff in Laguna Beach Park, looking down at the waves crashing on the rocks and feeling the earth crumble slowly under the toes of his shoes, working its way back to mid-sole . . . waiting, waiting, wondering if the treacherous ground would abruptly give way and drop him to the rocks far below before he would have time to leap backward and grab the safety railing, but still waiting . . . waiting.

But this thrill was better than all of those combined. It was growing by the minute rather than diminishing, a sensuous inner heat which the murder of Tod had not quenched but fueled.

His dark desire became an urgent need.

He prowled the park, seeking satisfaction.

He was a little surprised that Fantasy World continued to turn as if nothing had happened in the Millipede. He had expected the whole operation to close down, not just that one ride. Now he realized money was more important than mourning one dead customer. And if those who'd seen Tod's battered body had spread the story to others, it was probably discounted as a rehash of the legend. The level of frivolity in the park had not noticeably declined.

Once he dared to pass the Millipede, although he stayed at a distance because he still did not trust himself to be able to conceal his excitement over his achievement and his delight in the new status that he had attained. Master of the Game. Chains were looped from stanchion to stanchion in front of the pavilion, to block anyone attempting to gain access. A CLOSED FOR REPAIRS sign was on the entrance door. Not for repairs to old Tod. The rocket jockey was beyond repair. No ambulance was in sight, which they might have *thought* they needed, and no hearse was anywhere to be seen. No police, either. Weird.

Then he remembered a TV story about the world under Fantasy World: catacombs of service tunnels, storage rooms, security and ride-computer control centers, just like at Disneyland. To avoid disturbing the paying customers and drawing the attention of the morbidly curious, they were probably using the tunnels now to bring in the cops and corpse-pokers from the coroner's office.

The shivers within Jeremy increased. The desire. The need.

231

He was a Master of the Game. No one could touch him.

Might as well give the cops and corpse-pokers more to do, keep them entertained.

He kept moving, seeking, alert for opportunity. He found it where he least expected it, when he stopped at a men's restroom to take a leak.

A guy, about thirty, was at one of the sinks, checking himself out in the mirror, combing his thick blond hair, which glistened with Vitalis. He had arranged an array of personal objects on the ledge under the mirror: wallet, car keys, a tiny aerosol bottle of Binaca breath freshener, a half-empty pack of Dentyne (this guy had a bad-breath fixation), and a cigarette lighter.

The lighter was what immediately caught Jeremy's attention. It was not just a plastic Bic butane disposable, but one of those steel models, shaped like a miniature slice of bread, with a hinged top that flipped back to reveal a striker wheel and a wick. The way the overhead fluorescent gleamed on the smooth curves of that lighter, it seemed to be a supernatural object, full of its own eerie radiance, a beacon for Jeremy's eyes alone.

He hesitated a moment, then went to one of the urinals. When he finished and zipped up, the blond guy was still at the sink, primping himself.

Jeremy always washed his hands after using a bathroom because that was what polite people did. It was one of the rules that a good player followed.

He went to the sink beside the primper. As he lathered his hands with liquid soap from the pump dispenser, he could not take his eyes off the lighter on the shelf inches away. He told himself he should avert his gaze. The guy would realize he was thinking about snatching the damn thing. But its sleek silvery contours held him rapt. Staring at it as he rinsed the lather from his hands, he imagined that he could hear the crisp crackle of all-consuming flames.

Returning his wallet to his hip pocket but leaving the other objects on the ledge, the guy turned away from the sink and went to one of the urinals. As Jeremy was about to reach for the lighter, a father and his teenage son entered. They could have screwed everything up, but they went into two of the stalls and closed the doors. Jeremy knew that was a sign. Do it, the sign said. Take it, go, do it, do it. Jeremy glanced at the man at the urinal, plucked the lighter off the shelf, turned and walked out without drying his hands. No one ran after him.

Clutching the lighter tightly in his right hand, he prowled the park, searching for the perfect kindling. The desire in him was so intense that his shivers spread outward from his crotch and belly and spine, appearing once more in his hands, and in his legs, too, which sometimes were rubbery with excitement.

Need . . .

Finishing the last of the Reese's Pieces, Vassago neatly rolled the empty bag into a tight tube, tied the tube in a knot to make the smallest possible object of it, and dropped it into a plastic garbage bag that was just to the left of the iceless Styrofoam cooler. Neatness was one of the rules in the world of the living.

He enjoyed losing himself in the memory of that special night, eight years ago, when he had been twelve and had changed forever, but he was tired now and wanted to sleep. Maybe he would dream of the woman named Lindsey. Maybe he would have another vision that would lead him to someone connected with her, for somehow she seemed to be part of his destiny; he was being drawn toward her by forces he could not entirely understand but which he respected. Next time, he would not make the mistake he had made with Cooper. He would not let the need overwhelm him. He would ask questions first. When he had received all the answers, and only then, he would free the beautiful blood and, with it, another soul to join the infinite throngs beyond this hateful world.

4

Tuesday morning, Lindsey stayed home to get some work done in her studio while Hatch took Regina to school on his way to a meeting with an executor of an estate in North Tustin who was seeking bids on a collection of antique Wedgwood urns and vases. After lunch he had an appointment with Dr. Nyebern to learn the results of the tests he had undergone on Saturday. By the time he picked up Regina and returned home late in the afternoon, Lindsey figured to have finished the canvas she had been working on for the past month.

That was the plan, anyway, but all the fates and evil elves—and her own psychology—conspired to prevent the fulfillment of it. First of all the coffee maker went on the fritz. Lindsey had to tinker with the machine for an hour to find and fix the problem. She was a good tinkerer, and fortunately the brewer was fixable. She could not face the day without a blast of caffeine to jump-start her heart. She knew coffee was bad for her, but so was battery acid and cyanide, and she didn't drink either one of those, which showed she had more than her share of self-control when it came to destructive dietary habits; hell, she was an absolute rock!

By the time she got up to her second-floor studio with a mug and a full thermos besides, the light coming through the north-facing windows was perfect for her purposes. She had everything she needed. She had her paints, brushes, and palette knives. She had her supply cabinet. She had her adjustable stool and her easel and her stereo system with stacks of Garth Brooks, Glenn Miller, and Van Halen CDs, which somehow seemed the right mix of background music for a painter whose style was a combination of neoclassicism and surrealism. The only things she didn't have were an interest in the work at hand and the ability to concentrate.

She was repeatedly diverted by a glossy black spider that was exploring the upper right-hand corner of the window nearest to her. She didn't like spiders, but she was loath to kill them anyway. Later, she would have to capture it in a jar to release it outside. It crept upside down across the window header to the left-hand corner, immediately lost interest in that territory, and returned to the right-hand corner, where it quivered and flexed its long legs and seemed to be taking pleasure from some quality of that particular niche that was apprehensible only to spiders.

Lindsey turned to her painting again. Nearly complete, it was one of her best, lacking only a few refining touches.

But she hesitated to open paints and pick up a brush because she was every bit as devoted a worrier as she was an artist. She was anxious about Hatch's health, of course—both his physical and mental health. She was apprehensive, too, about the strange man who had killed the blonde, and about the eerie connection between that savage predator and her Hatch.

The spider crept down the side of the window frame to the right-hand corner of the sill. After using whatever arachnid senses it possessed, it rejected that nook, as well, and returned once more to the *upper* right-hand corner.

Like most people Lindsey considered psychics to be good subjects for spooky movies but charlatans in real life. Yet she had been quick to suggest clairvoyance as an explanation for what had been happening to Hatch. She had pressed the theory more insistently when he had declared that he was not psychic.

Now, turning away from the spider and staring frustratedly at the unfinished canvas before her, she realized why she had become such an earnest advocate of the reality of psychic power in the car on Friday, when they had followed the killer's trail to the head of Laguna Canyon Road. If Hatch had become psychic, eventually he would begin to receive impressions from all sorts of people, and his link to this murderer would not be unique. But if he was *not* psychic, if the bond between him and this monster was more profound and infinitely stranger than random clairvoyant reception, as he insisted that it was, then they were hip-deep into the unknown. And the unknown was a hell of a lot scarier than something you could describe and define.

Besides, if the link between them was more mysterious and intimate than psychic reception, the consequences for Hatch might be psychologically disastrous. What mental trauma might result from being even briefly inside the mind of a ruthless killer? Was the link between them a source of contamination, as any such intimate *biological* link would have been? If so, perhaps the virus of madness could creep across the ether and infect Hatch.

No. Ridiculous. Not her husband. He was reliable, levelheaded, mellow, as sane a human being as any who walked the earth.

The spider had taken possession of the upper right-hand corner of the window. It began to spin a web.

Lindsey remembered Hatch's anger last night when he had seen the story about Cooper in the newspaper. The hardness of rage in his face. The unsettling fevered look in his eyes. She had never seen Hatch like that. His father, yes, but never him. Though she knew he worried that he might have some of his father in him, she had never seen evidence of it before. And maybe she had not seen evidence of it last night, either. What she had seen might be some of the rage of the killer leaking back into Hatch along the link that existed between them—

No. She had nothing to fear from Hatch. He was a good man, the best she had ever met. He was such a deep well of goodness that all the madness of the blond girl's killer could be dropped into him, and he would dilute it until it was without effect.

A glistening, silky filament spewed from the spider's abdomen as the arachnid industriously claimed the corner of the window for its lair. Lindsey opened a drawer in her equipment cabinet and took out a small magnifying glass, which she used to observe the spinner more closely. Its spindly legs were prickled with hundreds of fine hairs that could not be seen without the assistance of the lens. Its horrid, multifaceted eyes looked everywhere at once, and its ragged maw worked continuously as if in anticipation of the first living fly to become stuck in the trap that it was weaving.

Although she understood that it was a part of nature as surely as she was, and therefore not evil, the thing nevertheless revolted Lindsey. It was a part of nature that she preferred not to dwell upon: the part that had to do with hunting and killing, with things that fed eagerly on the living. She put the magnifying glass on the windowsill and went downstairs to get a jar from the kitchen pantry. She wanted to capture the spider and get it out of her house before it was any more securely settled.

Reaching the foot of the stairs, she glanced at the window beside the front door and saw the postman's car. She collected the mail from the box at the curb: a few bills, the usual minimum of two mail-order catalogues, and the latest issue of *Arts American.*

She was in the mood to seize any excuse not to work, which was unusual for her, because she loved her work. Quite forgetting that she had come downstairs in the first place for a jar in which to transport the spider, she took the mail back up to her studio and settled down in the old armchair in the corner with a fresh mug of coffee and *Arts American.*

She spotted the article about herself as soon as she glanced at the table of contents. She was surprised. The magazine had covered her work before, but she had always known in advance that articles were forthcoming. Usually the writer had at least a few questions for her, even if he was not doing a straight interview.

Then she saw the byline and winced. S. Steven Honell. She knew before reading the first word that she was the target of a hatchet job.

Honell was a well-reviewed writer of fiction who, from time to time, also wrote about art. He was in his sixties and had never married. A phlegmatic fellow, he had decided as a young man to forego the comforts of a wife and family in the interest of his writing. To write well, he said, one ought to possess a monk's preference for solitude. In isolation, one was forced to confront oneself more directly and honestly than possible in the hustle-bustle of the peopled world, and through oneself also confront the nature of every human heart. He had lived in splendid isolation first in northern California, then in New Mexico. Most recently he had settled at the eastern edge of the developed part of Orange County at the end of Silverado Canyon, which was part of a series of brush-covered hills and ravines spotted with numerous California live oaks and less numerous rustic cabins.

In September of the previous year, Lindsey and Hatch had gone to a restaurant at the civilized end of Silverado Canyon, which served strong drinks and good steaks. They had eaten at one of the tables in the taproom, which was paneled in knotty pine with limestone columns supporting the roof. An inebriated white-haired man, sitting at the bar, was holding forth on literature, art, and politics. His opinions were strongly held and expressed in caustic language. From the affectionate tolerance the curmudgeon received from the bartender and patrons on the other bar stools, Lindsey guessed he was a regular customer and a local character who told only half as many tales as were told about him.

Then Lindsey recognized him. S. Steven Honell. She had read and liked some of his writing. She'd admired his selfless devotion to his art; for she could not have sacrificed love, marriage, and children for her painting, even though the exploration of her creative talent was as important to her as having enough food to eat and water to drink. Listening to Honell, she wished that she and Hatch had gone somewhere else for dinner because she would never again be able to read the author's work without remembering some of the vicious statements he made about the writings and personalities of his contemporaries in letters. With each drink, he grew more bitter, more scathing, more indulgent of his own darkest instincts, and markedly more garrulous. Liquor revealed the gabby fool hidden inside the legend of taciturnity; anyone wanting to shut him up would have needed a horse veterinarian's hypodermic full of Demerol or a .357 Magnum. Lindsey ate faster, deciding to skip dessert and depart Honell's company as swiftly as possible.

Then he recognized her. He kept glancing over his shoulder at her, blinking his rheumy eyes. Finally he unsteadily approached their table. "Excuse me, are you Lindsey Sparling, the artist?" She had known that he sometimes wrote about American art, but she had not imagined he would know her work or her face. "Yes, I am," she said, hoping he would not say that he liked her work and that he would not tell her who he was. "I like your work very much," he said. "I won't bother you to say more." But just as she relaxed and thanked him, he told her his name, and she was obligated to say that she liked his work, too, which she did, though now she saw it in a light different from that in which it had previously appeared to her. He seemed less like a man who had sacrificed family love for his art than like a man incapable of giving that love. In isolation he might have found a greater power to create; but he had also found more time to admire himself and contemplate the infinite number of ways in which he was superior to the ruck of his fellow men. She tried not to let her distaste show, spoke only glowingly of his novels, but he seemed to sense her disapproval. He quickly terminated the encounter and returned to the bar.

He never looked her way again during the night. And he no longer held forth to the assembled drinkers about anything, his attention directed largely at the contents of his glass.

Now, sitting in the armchair in her studio, holding the copy of *Arts American,* and staring at Honell's byline, she felt her stomach curdle. She had seen the great man in his cups, when he had uncloaked more of his true self than it was his nature to reveal. Worse, she was a person of some accomplishment, who moved in circles that might bring her into contact with people Honell also knew. He saw her as a threat. One way of neutralizing her was to undertake a well-written, if unfair, article criticizing her body of work; thereafter, he could claim that any tales she told about him were motivated by spite, of questionable truthfulness. She knew what to expect from him in the *Arts American* piece, and Honell did not surprise her. Never before had she read criticism so vicious yet so cunningly crafted to spare the critic accusations of personal animosity.

When she finished, she closed the magazine and put it down gently on the small table beside her chair. She didn't want to pitch it across the room because she knew that reaction would have pleased Honell if he had been present to see it.

Then she said, "To hell with it," picked up the magazine, and threw it across the room with all the force she could muster. It slapped hard against the wall and clattered to the floor.

Her work was important to her. Intellect, emotion, talent, and craft went into it, and even on those occasions when a painting did not turn out as well as she had hoped, no creation ever came easily. Anguish always was a part of it. And more self-revelation than seemed prudent. Exhilaration and despair in equal measure. A critic had every right to dislike an artist if his judgment was based on thoughtful consideration and an understanding of what the artist was trying to achieve. But *this* was not genuine criticism. This was sick invective. Bile. Her work was important to her, and he had shit on it.

Filled with the energy of anger, she got up and paced. She knew that by surrendering to anger she was letting Honell win; this was the response he had hoped to extract from her with his dental-pliers criticism. But she couldn't help it.

She wished Hatch was there, so she could share her fury with him. He had a calming effect greater than a fifth of bourbon.

Her angry pacing brought her eventually to the window where by now the fat black spider had constructed an elaborate web in the upper right-hand corner. Realizing that she had forgotten to get a jar from the pantry, Lindsey picked up the magnifying glass and examined the silken filigree of the eight-legged fisherman's net, which glimmered with a pastel mother-of-pearl iridescence. The trap was so delicate, so alluring. But the living loom that spun it was the very essence of all predators, strong for its size and sleek and quick. Its bulbous body glistened like a drop of thick black blood, and its rending mandibles worked the air in anticipation of the flesh of prey not yet snared.

The spider and Steven Honell were of a kind, utterly alien to her and beyond understanding regardless of how long she observed them. Both spun their webs in silence and isolation. Both had brought their viciousness into her house uninvited, one through words in a magazine and the other through a tiny crack in a window frame or door jamb. Both were poisonous, vile.

She put down the magnifying glass. She could do nothing about Honell, but at least she could deal with the spider. She snatched two Kleenex from a box atop her supply cabinet, and in one swift movement she swept up the spinner and its web, crushing both.

She threw the wad of tissues in the waste can.

Though she usually captured a spider when possible and kindly returned it to the outdoors, she had no compunction about the way she had dealt with this one. Indeed, if Honell had been present at that moment, when his hateful attack was still so fresh in her mind, she might have been tempted to deal with him in some manner as quick and violent as the treatment she had accorded the spider.

She returned to her stool, regarded the unfinished canvas, and was suddenly certain what refinements it required. She opened tubes of paint and set out her brushes. That wasn't the first time she had been motivated by an unjust blow or a puerile insult, and she wondered how many artists of all kinds had produced their best work with the determination to rub it in the faces of the naysayers who had tried to undercut or belittle them.

When Lindsey had been at work on the painting for ten or fifteen minutes, she was stricken by an unsettling thought which brought her back to the worries that had preoccupied her before the arrival of the mail and *Arts American.* Honell and the spider were not the only creatures who had invaded her home uninvited. The unknown killer in sunglasses also had invaded it, in a way, by feedback through the mysterious link between him and Hatch. And what if he was as aware of Hatch as Hatch was of him? He might find a way to track Hatch down and invade their home for real, with the intention of doing far more harm than either the spider or Honell could ever accomplish.

5

Previously, Hatch had visited Jonas Nyebern in his office at Orange County General, but that Tuesday his appointment was at the medical building off Jamboree Road, where the physician operated his private practice.

The waiting room was remarkable, not for its short-nap gray carpet and standard-issue furniture, but for the artwork on its walls. Hatch was surprised and impressed by a collection of high-quality antique oil paintings portraying religious scenes of a Catholic nature: the passion of St. Jude, the Crucifixion, the Holy Mother, the Annunciation, the Resurrection, and much more.

The most curious thing was not that the collection was worth considerable money. After all, Nyebern was an extremely successful cardiovascular surgeon who came from a family of more than average resources. But it was odd that a member of the medical profession, which had taken an increasingly agnostic public posture throughout the last few decades, should choose religious art of any kind for his office walls, let alone such obvious denominational art that might offend non-Catholics or nonbelievers.

When the nurse escorted Hatch out of the waiting room, he discovered the collection continued along the hallways serving the entire suite. He found it peculiar to see a fine oil of Jesus' agony in Gethsemane hung to the left of a stainless-steel and white-enamel scale, and beside a chart listing ideal weight according to height, age, and sex.

After weighing in and having his blood pressure and pulse taken, he waited for Nyebern in a small private room, sitting on the end of an examination table that was covered by a continuous roll of sanitary paper. On one wall hung an eye chart and an exquisite depiction of the Ascension in which the artist's skill with light was so great that the scene became three-dimensional and the figures therein seemed almost alive.

Nyebern kept him waiting only a minute or two, and entered with a broad smile. As they shook hands, the physician said, "I won't draw out the suspense, Hatch. The tests all came in negative. You've got a clean bill of health."

Those words were not as welcome as they ought to have been. Hatch had been hoping for some finding that would point the way to an understanding of his nightmares and his mystical connection with the man who had killed the blond punker. But the verdict did not in the least surprise him. He had suspected that the answers he sought were not going to be that easy to find.

"So your nightmares are only that," Nyebern said, "and nothing more—just nightmares."

Hatch had not told him about the vision of the gunshot blonde who had later been found dead, for real, on the freeway. As he had made clear to Lindsey, he was not going to set himself up to become a headline again, at least not unless he saw enough of the killer to identify him to the police, more than he'd glimpsed in the mirror last night, in which case he would have no choice but to face the media spotlight.

"No cranial pressure," Nyebern said, "no chemicoelectrical imbalance, no sign of a shift in the location of the pineal gland—which can sometimes lead to severe nightmares and even waking hallucinations . . ." He went over the tests one by one, methodical as usual.

As he listened, Hatch realized that he always remembered the physician as being older than he actually was. Jonas Nyebern had a grayness about him, and a gravity, that left the impression of advanced age. Tall and lanky, he hunched his shoulders and stooped slightly to de-emphasize his height, resulting in a posture more like that of an elderly man than of someone his true age, which was fifty. At times there was about him, as well, an air of sadness, as if he had known great tragedy.

When he finished going over the tests, Nyebern looked up and smiled again. It was a warm smile, but that air of sadness clung to him in spite of it. "The problem isn't physical, Hatch."

"Is it possible you could have missed something?"

"Possible, I suppose, but very unlikely. We—"

"An extremely minor piece of brain damage, a few hundred cells, might not show up on your tests yet have a serious effect."

"As I said, very unlikely. I think we can safely assume that this is strictly an emotional problem, a perfectly understandable consequence of the trauma you've been through. Let's try a little standard therapy."

"Psychotherapy?"

"Do you have a problem with that?"

"No."

Except, Hatch thought, it won't work. This isn't an emotional problem. This is real.

"I know a good man, first-rate, you'll like him," Nyebern said, taking a pen from the breast pocket of his white smock and writing the name of the psychotherapist on the blank top sheet of a prescription pad. "I'll discuss your case with him and tell him you'll be calling. Is that all right?"

"Yeah. Sure. That's fine."

He wished he could tell Nyebern the whole story. But then he would *definitely* sound as if he needed therapy. Reluctantly he faced the realization that neither a medical doctor nor a psychotherapist could help him. His ailment was too strange to respond to standard treatments of any kind. Maybe what he needed was a witch doctor. Or an exorcist. He *did* almost feel as if the black-clad killer in sunglasses was a demon testing his defenses to determine whether to attempt possessing him.

They chatted a couple of minutes about things non-medical.

Then as Hatch was getting up to go, he pointed to the painting of the Ascension. "Beautiful piece."

"Thank you. It is exceptional, isn't it?"

"Italian."

"That's right."

"Early eighteenth century?"

"Right again," Nyebern said. "You know religious art?"

"Not all that well. But I think the whole collection is Italian from the same period."

"That it is. Another piece, maybe two, and I'll call it complete."

"Odd to see it here," Hatch said, stepping closer to the painting beside the eye chart.

"Yes, I know what you mean," Nybern said, "but I don't have enough wall space for all this at home. There, I'm putting together a collection of *modern* religious art."

"Is there any?"

"Not much. Religious subject matter isn't fashionable these days among the really talented artists. The bulk of it is done by hacks. But here and there . . . someone with genuine talent is seeking enlightenment along the old paths, painting these subjects with a contemporary eye. I'll move the modern collection here when I finish this one and dispose of it."

Hatch turned away from the painting and regarded the doctor with professional interest. "You're planning to sell?"

"Oh, no," the physician said, returning his pen to his breast pocket. His hand, with the long elegant fingers that one expected of a surgeon, lingered at the pocket, as if he were pledging the truth of what he was saying. "I'll donate it. This will be the sixth collection of religious art I've put together over the past twenty years, then given away."

Because he could roughly estimate the value of the artwork he had seen on the walls of the medical suite, Hatch was astonished by the degree of philanthropy indicated by Nyebern's simple statement. "Who's the fortunate recipient?"

"Well, usually a Catholic university, but on two occasions another Church institution," Nyebern said.

The surgeon was staring at the depiction of the Ascension, a distant gaze in his eyes, as if he were seeing something beyond the painting, beyond the wall on which it hung, and beyond the farthest horizon. His hand still lingered over his breast pocket.

"Very generous of you," Hatch said.

"It's not an act of generosity." Nyebern's faraway voice now matched the look in his eyes. "It's an act of atonement."

That statement begged for a question in response, although Hatch felt that asking it was an intrusion of the physician's privacy. "Atonement for what?"

Still staring at the painting, Nyebern said, "I never talk about it."

"I don't mean to pry. I just thought—"

"Maybe it would do me good to talk about it. Do you think it might?"

Hatch did not answer—partly because he didn't believe the doctor was actually listening to him anyway.

"Atonement," Nyebern said again. "At first . . . atonement for being the son of my father. Later . . . for being the father of my son."

Hatch didn't see how either thing could be a sin, but he waited, certain that the physician would explain. He was beginning to feel like that party-goer in the old Coleridge poem, waylaid by the distraught Ancient Mariner who had a tale of terror that he was driven to impart to others lest, by keeping it to himself, he lose what little sanity he still retained.

Gazing unblinking at the painting, Nyebern said, "When I was only seven, my father suffered a psychotic breakdown. He shot and killed my mother and my brother. He wounded my sister and me, left us for dead, then killed himself."

"Jesus, I'm sorry," Hatch said, and he thought of his own

245

father's bottomless well of anger. "I'm very sorry, Doctor." But he still did not understand the failure or sin for which Nyebern felt the need to atone.

"Certain psychoses may sometimes have a genetic cause. When I saw signs of sociopathic behavior in my son, even at an early age, I should have known what was coming, should've prevented it somehow. But I couldn't face the truth. Too painful. Then two years ago, when he was eighteen, he stabbed his sister to death—"

Hatch shuddered.

"—then his mother," Nyebern said.

Hatch started to put a hand on the doctor's arm, then pulled back when he sensed that Nyebern's pain could never be eased and that his wound was beyond healing by any medication as simple as consolation. Although he was speaking of an intensely personal tragedy, the physician plainly was not seeking sympathy or the intimacy of friendship from Hatch. Suddenly he seemed almost frighteningly self-contained. He was talking about the tragedy because the time had come to take it out of his personal darkness to examine it again, and he would have spoken of it to anyone who had been in that place at that time instead of Hatch—or perhaps to the empty air itself if no one at all had been present.

"And when they were dead," Nyebern said, "Jeremy took the same knife into the garage, a butcher knife, secured it by the handle in the vise on my workbench, stood on a stool, and fell forward, impaling himself on the blade. He bled to death."

The physician's right hand was still at his breast pocket, but he no longer seemed like a man pledging the truth of what he said. Instead, he reminded Hatch of a painting of Christ with the Sacred Heart revealed, the slender hand of divine grace pointing to that symbol of sacrifice and promise of eternity.

At last Nyebern looked away from the Ascension and met Hatch's eyes. "Some say evil is just the consequences of our actions, no more than a result of our will. But I believe it's that—and much more. I believe evil is a very real force, an energy quite apart from us, a presence in the world. Is that what you believe, Hatch?"

"Yes," Hatch said at once, and somewhat to his surprise.

Nyebern looked down at the prescription pad in his left hand.

He took his right hand away from his breast pocket, tore the top sheet off the pad, and gave it to Hatch. "His name's Foster. Dr. Gabriel Foster. I'm sure he'll be able to help you."

"Thanks," Hatch said numbly.

Nyebern opened the door of the examination room and gestured for Hatch to precede him.

In the hallway, the physician said, "Hatch?"

Hatch stopped and looked back at him.

"Sorry," Nyebern said.

"For what?"

"For explaining why I donate the paintings."

Hatch nodded. "Well, I asked, didn't I?"

"But I could have been much briefer."

"Oh?"

"I could have just said—maybe I think the only way for me to get into Heaven is to buy my way."

Outside, in the sun-splashed parking lot, Hatch sat in his car for a long time, watching a wasp that hovered over the red hood as if it thought it had found an enormous rose.

The conversation in Nyebern's office had seemed strangely like a dream, and Hatch felt as if he were still rising out of sleep. He sensed that the tragedy of Jonas Nyebern's death-haunted life had a direct bearing on his own current problems, but although he reached for the connection, he could not grasp it.

The wasp swayed to the left, to the right, but faced steadily toward the windshield as though it could see him in the car and was mysteriously drawn to him. Repeatedly, it darted at the glass, bounced off, and resumed its hovering. Tap, hover, tap, hover, tap-tap, hover. It was a very determined wasp. He wondered if it was one of those species that possessed a single stinger that broke off in the target, resulting in the subsequent death of the wasp. Tap, hover, tap, hover, tap-tap-tap. If it was one of those species, did it fully understand what reward it would earn by its persistence? Tap, hover, tap-tap-tap.

◆◆

After seeing the last patient of the day, a follow-up visit with an engaging thirty-year-old woman on whom he had performed an aortal graft last March, Jonas Nyebern entered his private office at the back of the medical suite and closed the door. He went behind the desk, sat down, and looked in his wallet for a slip of paper on which was written a telephone number that he chose not to include on his Rolodex. He found it, pulled the phone close, and punched in the seven numbers.

Following the third ring, an answering machine picked up as it had on his previous calls yesterday and earlier that morning: *"This is Morton Redlow. I'm not in the office right now. After the beep, please leave a message and a number where you can be reached, and I will get back to you as soon as possible."*

Jonas waited for the signal, then spoke softly. "Mr. Redlow, this is Dr. Nyebern. I know I've left other messages, but I was under the impression that I would receive a report from you last Friday. Certainly by the weekend at the latest. Please call me as soon as possible. Thank you."

He hung up.

He wondered if he had reason to worry.

He wondered if he had any reason *not* to worry.

6

Regina sat at her desk in Sister Mary Margaret's French class, weary of the smell of chalk dust and annoyed by the hardness of the plastic seat under her butt, learning how to say, *Hello, I am an American. Can you direct me to the nearest church where I might attend Sunday Mass?*

Très boring.

She was still a fifth-grade student at St. Thomas's Elementary School, because continued attendance was a strict condition of her adoption. (Trial adoption. Nothing final yet. Could blow up. The Harrisons could decide they preferred raising parakeets to children, give her back, get a bird. Please, God, make sure they realize that in Your divine wisdom You designed birds so they poop a lot. Make sure they know what a mess it'll be keeping the cage clean.) When she graduated from St. Thomas's Elementary, she would move on to St. Thomas's High School, because St. Thomas's had its fingers in everything. In addition to the children's care home and the two schools, it had a day-care center and a thrift shop. The parish was like a conglomerate, and Father Jiminez was sort of a big executive like Donald Trump, except Father Jiminez didn't run around with bimbos or own gambling casinos. The bingo parlor hardly counted. (Dear God, that stuff about birds pooping a lot—that was in no way meant as a criticism. I'm sure You had Your reasons for making birds poop a lot, all over everything, and like the mystery of the Holy Trinity, it's just one of those things we ordinary humans can't ever quite understand. No offense meant.) Anyway, she didn't mind going to St. Thomas's School, because both the nuns and the lay teachers pushed you hard, and you ended up learning a lot, and she loved to learn.

By the last class on that Tuesday afternoon, however, she was full up with learning, and if Sister Mary Margaret called on her to say anything in French, she would probably confuse the word for church with the word for sewer, which she had done once before, much to the delight of the other kids and to her own mortification. (Dear God, please remember that I made myself say the Rosary as penance for that boner, just to prove I didn't mean anything by it, it was only a mistake.) When the dismissal bell rang, she was the first out of her seat and the first out of the classroom door, even though most of the kids at St. Thomas's School did not come from St. Thomas's Home and were not disabled in any way.

All the way to her locker and all the way from her locker to the front exit, she wondered if Mr. Harrison would really be waiting for her, as he had promised. She imagined herself standing on the sidewalk with kids swarming around her, unable to spot his car, the crowd gradually diminishing until she stood alone, and still no sign of his car, and her waiting as the sun set and the moon rose and her wristwatch ticked toward midnight, and in the morning when the kids returned for another day of school, she'd just go back inside with them and not tell anyone the Harrisons didn't want her any more.

He was there. In the red car. In a line of cars driven by other kids' parents. He leaned across the seat to open the door for her as she approached.

When she got in with her book bag and closed the door, he said, "Hard day?"

"Yeah," she said, suddenly shy when shyness had never been one of her major problems. She was having trouble getting the hang of this family thing. She was afraid maybe she'd never get it.

He said, "Those nuns."

"Yeah," she agreed.

"They're tough."

"Tough."

"Tough as nails, those nuns."

"Nails," she said, nodding agreement, wondering if she would ever be able to speak more than one-word sentences again.

As he pulled away from the curb, he said, "I'll bet you could put any nun in the ring with any heavyweight champion in the whole history of boxing—I don't care if it was even Muhammad Ali— and she'd knock him out in the first round."

Regina couldn't help grinning at him.

"Sure," he said. "Only Superman could survive a fight with a real hardcase nun. Batman? Fooie! Even your *average* nun could mop up the floor with Batman—or make soup out of the whole gang of Teenage Mutant Ninja Turtles."

"They mean well," she said, which was three words, at least, but sounded goofy. She might be better off not talking at all; she just didn't have any experience at this father-kid stuff.

"Nuns?" he said. "Well, of course, they mean well. If they didn't mean well, they wouldn't be nuns. They'd be maybe Mafia hitmen, international terrorists, United States Congressmen."

He did not speed home like a busy man with lots to do, but like somebody out for a leisurely drive. She had not been in a car with him enough to know if that was how he always drove, but she suspected maybe he was loafing along a little slower than he usually did, so they could have more time together, just the two of them. That was sweet. It made her throat a little tight and her eyes watery. Oh, terrific. A pile of cow flop could've carried on a better conversation than she was managing, so now she was going to burst into tears, which would really cement the relationship. Surely every adoptive parent desperately hoped to receive a mute, emotionally unstable girl with physical problems—right? It was all the rage, don't you know. Well, if she did cry, her treacherous sinuses would kick in, and the old snot-faucet would start gushing, which would surely make her even *more* appealing. He'd give up the idea of a leisurely drive, and head for home at such tremendous speed that he'd have to stand on the brakes a mile from the house to avoid shooting straight through the back of the garage. (Please, God, help me here. You'll notice I thought "cow flop" not "cow shit," so I deserve a little mercy.)

They chatted about this and that. Actually, for a while he chatted and she pretty much just grunted like she was a subhuman out on a pass from the zoo. But eventually she realized, to her surprise, that she was talking in complete sentences, had been doing so for a couple of miles, and was at ease with him.

He asked her what she wanted to be when she grew up, and she just about bent his ear clear off explaining that some people actually made a living writing the kinds of books she liked to read and that she had been composing her own stories for a year or two. Lame stuff, she admitted, but she would get better at it. She was very bright for ten, older than her years, but she couldn't expect actually to have a career going until she was eighteen, maybe sixteen if she was lucky. When had Mr. Christopher Pike started publishing? Seventeen? Eighteen? Maybe he'd been as old as twenty, but certainly no older, so that's what she would shoot for—being the next Mr. Christopher Pike by the time she was twenty. She had an entire notebook full of story ideas. Quite a few of those ideas were good even when you crossed out the embarrassingly childish ones like the story about the intelligent pig from space that she had been so hot about for a while but now saw was hopelessly dumb. She was still talking about writing books when they pulled into the driveway of the house in Laguna Niguel, and he actually seemed interested.

She figured she might get the hang of this family thing yet.

Vassago dreamed of fire. The click of the cigarette-lighter cover being flipped open in the dark. The dry rasp of the striker wheel scraping against the flint. A spark. A young girl's white summer dress flowering into flames. The Haunted House ablaze. Screams as the calculatedly spooky darkness dissolved under licking tongues of orange light. Tod Ledderbeck was dead in the cavern of the Millipede, and now the house of plastic skeletons and rubber ghouls was abruptly filled with real terror and pungent death.

He had dreamed of that fire previously, countless times since the night of Tod's twelfth birthday. It always provided the most beautiful of all the chimeras and phantasms that passed behind his eyes in sleep.

But on this occasion, strange faces and images appeared in the flames. The red car again. A solemnly beautiful, auburn-haired child with large gray eyes that seemed too old for her face. A small hand, cruelly bent, with fingers missing. A name, which had come to him once before, echoed through the leaping flames and melting shadows in the Haunted House. *Regina . . . Regina . . . Regina.*

The visit to Dr. Nyebern's office had depressed Hatch, both because the tests had revealed nothing that shed any light on his strange experiences and because of the glimpse he had gotten into the physician's own troubled life. But Regina was a medicine for melancholy if ever there had been one. She had all the enthusiasm of a child her age; life had not beaten her down one inch.

On the way from the car to the front door of the house, she moved more swiftly and easily than when she had entered Salvatore Gujilio's office, but the leg brace did give her a measured and solemn gate. A bright yellow and blue butterfly accompanied her every step, fluttering gaily a few inches from her head, as if it knew that her spirit was very like itself, beautiful and buoyant.

She said solemnly, "Thank you for picking me up, Mr. Harrison."

"You're welcome, I'm sure," he said with equal gravity.

They would have to do something about this "Mr. Harrison" business before the day was out. He sensed that her formality was partly a fear of getting too close—and then being rejected as she had been during the trial phase of her first adoption. But it was also a fear of saying or doing the wrong thing and unwittingly destroying her own prospects for happiness.

At the front door, he said, "Either Lindsey or I will be at the school for you every day—unless you've got a driver's license and would just rather come and go on your own."

She looked up at Hatch. The butterfly was describing circles in the air above her head, as if it were a living crown or halo. She said, "You're teasing me, aren't you?"

"Well, yes, I'm afraid I am."

She blushed and looked away from him, as if she was not sure if being teased was a good or bad thing. He could almost hear her inner thoughts: *Is he teasing me because he thinks I'm cute or because he thinks I'm hopelessly stupid,* or something pretty close to that.

Throughout the drive home from school, Hatch had seen that Regina suffered from her share of self-doubt, which she thought she concealed but which, when it struck, was evident in her lovely, wonderfully expressive face. Each time he sensed a crack in the kid's self-confidence, he wanted to put his arms around her, hug her tight, and reassure her—which would be exactly the wrong thing to do because she would be appalled to realize that her moments of inner turmoil were so obvious to him. She prided herself on being tough, resilient, and self-sufficient. She projected that image as armor against the world.

"I hope you don't mind some teasing," he said as he inserted the key in the door. "That's the way I am. I could check myself into a Teasers Anonymous program, shake the habit, but it's a tough outfit. They beat you with rubber hoses and make you eat Lima beans."

When enough time passed, when she felt she was loved and part of a family, her self-confidence would be as unshakable as she wanted it to be now. In the meantime, the best thing he could do for her was pretend that he saw her exactly as she wished to be seen—and quietly, patiently help her finish becoming the poised and assured person she hoped to be.

As he opened the door and they went inside, Regina said, "I used to hate Lima beans, all kinds of beans, but I made a deal with God. If he gives me . . . something I 'specially want, I'll eat every kind of bean there is for the rest of my life without ever complaining."

In the foyer, closing the door behind them, Hatch said, "That's quite an offer. God ought to be impressed."

"I sure hope so," she said.

And in Vassago's dream, Regina moved in sunlight, one leg embraced in steel, a butterfly attending her as it might a flower. A house flanked by palm trees. A door. She looked up at Vassago, and her eyes revealed a soul of tremendous vitality and a heart so vulnerable that the beat of his own was quickened even in sleep.

They found Lindsey upstairs, in the extra bedroom that served as her at-home studio. The easel was angled away from the door, so Hatch couldn't see the painting. Lindsey's blouse was half in and half out of her jeans, her hair was in disarray, a smear of rust-red paint marked her left cheek, and she had a look that Hatch knew from experience meant she was in the final fever of work on a piece that was turning out to be everything she had hoped.

"Hi, honey," Lindsey said to Regina. "How was school?"

Regina was flustered, as she always seemed to be, by any term of endearment. "Well, school is school, you know."

"Well, you must like it. I know you get good grades."

Regina shrugged off the compliment and looked embarrassed.

Repressing the urge to hug the kid, Hatch said to Lindsey, "She's going to be a writer when she grows up."

"Really?" Lindsey said. "That's exciting. I knew you loved books, but I didn't realize you wanted to write them."

"Neither did I," the girl said, and suddenly she was in gear and off, her initial awkwardness with Lindsey past, words pouring out of her as she crossed the room and went behind the easel to have a look at the work in progress, "until just last Christmas, when my gift under the tree at the home was six paperbacks. Not books for a ten-year-old, either, but the real stuff, because I read at a tenth-grade level, which is *fifteen* years old. I'm what they call precocious. Anyway, those books made the best gift ever, and I thought it'd be neat if someday a girl like me at the home got *my* books under the tree and felt the way I felt, not that I'll ever be as good a writer as Mr. Daniel Pinkwater or Mr. Christopher Pike. Jeez, I mean, they're right up there with Shakespeare and Judy Blume. But I've got good stories to tell, and they're not all that intelligent-pig-from-space crap. Sorry. I mean poop. I mean junk. Intelligent-pig-from-space junk. They're not all like that."

Lindsey never showed Hatch—or anyone else—a canvas in progress, withholding even a glimpse of it until the final brush stroke had been applied. Though she was evidently near completion of the current painting, she was still working on it, and Hatch was surprised that she didn't even twitch when Regina went around to the front of the easel to have a look. He decided that no kid, just because she had a cute nose and some freckles, was going to be accorded a privilege he was denied, so he also walked boldly around the easel to take a peek.

It was a stunning piece of work. The background was a field of stars, and superimposed over it was the transparent face of an ethereally beautiful young boy. Not just any boy. Their Jimmy. When he was alive she had painted him a few times, but never since his death—until now. It was an idealized Jimmy of such perfection that his face might have been that of an angel. His loving eyes were turned upward, toward a warm light that rained down upon him from beyond the top of the canvas, and his expression was more profound than joy. Rapture. In the foreground, as the focus of the work, floated a black rose, not transparent like the face, rendered in such sensuous detail that Hatch could almost feel the velvety texture of each plush petal. The green skin of the stem was moist with a cool dew, and the thorns were portrayed with such piercingly sharp points that he half believed they would prick like real thorns if touched. A single drop of blood glistened on one of the black petals. Somehow Lindsey had imbued the floating rose with an aura of preternatural power, so it drew the eye, demanded attention, almost mesmeric in its effect. Yet the boy did not look down at the rose; he gazed up at the radiant object only he could see, the implication being that, as powerful as the rose might be, it was of no interest whatsoever when compared to the source of the light above.

From the day of Jimmy's death until Hatch's resuscitation, Lindsey had refused to take solace from any god who would create a world with death in it. He recalled a priest suggesting prayer as a route to acceptance and psychological healing, and Lindsey's response had been cold and dismissive: *Prayer never works. Expect no miracles, Father. The dead stay dead, and the living only wait to join them.* Something had changed in her now. The black rose in the painting was death. Yet it had no power over Jimmy. He had gone beyond death, and it meant nothing to him. He was rising above it. And by being able to conceive of the painting and bring it off so flawlessly, Lindsey had found a way to say goodbye to the boy at last, goodbye without regrets, goodbye without bitterness, goodbye with love and with a startling new acceptance of the need for belief in something more than a life that ended always in a cold, black hole in the ground.

"It's so beautiful," Regina said with genuine awe. "Scary in a way, I don't know why . . . scary . . . but so beautiful."

Hatch looked up from the painting, met Lindsey's eyes, tried to say something, but could not speak. Since his resuscitation, there had been a rebirth of Lindsey's heart as well as his own, and they had confronted the mistake they had made by losing five years to grief. But on some fundamental level, they had not accepted that life could ever be as sweet as it had been before that one small death; they had not really let Jimmy go. Now, meeting Lindsey's eyes, he knew that she had finally embraced hope again without reservation. The full weight of his little boy's death fell upon Hatch as it had not in years, because if Lindsey could make peace with God, he must do so as well. He tried to speak again, could not, looked again at the painting, realized he was going to cry, and left the room.

He didn't know where he was going. Without quite remembering taking any step along the route, he went downstairs, into the den that they had offered to Regina as a bedroom, opened the French doors, and stepped into the rose garden at the side of the house.

In the warm, late-afternoon sun, the roses were red, white, yellow, pink, and the shade of peach skins, some only buds and some as big as saucers, but not one of them black. The air was full of their enchanting fragrance.

With the taste of salt in the corners of his mouth, he reached out with both hands toward the nearest rose-laden bush, intending to touch the flowers, but his hands stopped short of them. With his arms thus forming a cradle, he suddenly could feel a weight draped across them. In reality, nothing was in his arms, but the burden he felt was no mystery; he remembered, as if it had been an hour ago, how the body of his cancer-wasted son had felt.

In the final moments before death's hateful visitation, he had pulled the wires and tubes from Jim, had lifted him off the sweat-soaked hospital bed, and had sat in a chair by the window, holding him close and murmuring to him until the pale, parted lips drew no more breath. Until his own death, Hatch would remember precisely the weight of the wasted boy in his arms, the sharpness of bones with so little flesh left to pad them, the awful dry heat pouring off skin translucent with sickness, the heart-rending fragility.

He felt all that now, in his empty arms, there in the rose garden.

257

When he looked up at the summer sky, he said, "Why?" as if there were Someone to answer. "He was so small," Hatch said. "He was so damned small."

As he spoke, the burden was heavier than it had ever been in that hospital room, a thousand tons in his empty arms, maybe because he still didn't want to free himself of it as much as he thought he did. But then a strange thing happened—the weight in his arms slowly diminished, and the invisible body of his son seemed to float out of his embrace, as if the flesh had been transmuted entirely to spirit at long last, as if Jim had no need of comforting or consolation any more.

Hatch lowered his arms.

Maybe from now on the bittersweet memory of a child lost would be only the sweet memory of a child loved. And maybe, henceforth, it would not be a memory so heavy that it oppressed the heart.

He stood among the roses.

The day was warm. The late-afternoon light was golden.

The sky was perfectly clear—and utterly mysterious.

Regina asked if she could have some of Lindsey's paintings in her room, and she sounded sincere. They chose three. Together they hammered in picture hooks and hung the paintings where she wanted them—along with a foot-tall crucifix she had brought from her room at the orphanage.

As they worked, Lindsey said, "How about dinner at a really super pizza parlor I know?"

"Yeah!" the girl said enthusiastically. "I love pizza."

"They make it with a nice thick crust, lots of cheese."

"Pepperoni?"

"Cut thin, but lots of it."

"Sausage?"

"Sure, why not. Though you're sure this isn't getting to be a pretty revolting pizza for a vegetarian like you?"

Regina blushed. "Oh, that. I was such a little shit that day. Oh, Jeez, sorry. I mean, such a smartass. I mean, such a jerk."

"That's okay," Lindsey said. "We all behave like jerks now and then."

"You don't. Mr. Harrison doesn't."

"Oh, just wait." Standing on a stepstool in front of the wall opposite the bed, Lindsey pounded in a nail for a picture hook. Regina was holding the painting for her. As she took it from the girl to hang it, Lindsey said, "Listen, will you do me a favor at dinner tonight?"

"Favor? Sure?"

"I know it's still awkward for you, this new arrangement. You don't really feel at home and probably won't for a long time—"

"Oh, it's very nice here," the girl protested.

Lindsey slipped the wire over the picture hook and adjusted the painting until it hung straight. Then she sat down on the stepstool, which just about brought her and the girl eye to eye. She took hold of both of Regina's hands, the normal one and the different one. "You're right—it's very nice here. But you and I both know that's not the same as *home.* I wasn't going to push you on this. I was going to let you take your time, but . . . Even if it seems a little premature to you, do you think tonight at dinner you could stop calling us Mr. and Mrs. Harrison? Especially Hatch. It would be very important to him, just now, if you could at least call him Hatch."

The girl lowered her eyes to their interlocked hands. "Well, I guess . . . sure . . . that would be okay."

"And you know what? I realize this is asking more than it's fair to ask yet, before you really know him that well. But do you know what would be the best thing in the world for him right now?"

The girl was still staring at their hands. "What?"

"If somehow you could find it in your heart to call him Dad. Don't say yes or no just now. Think about it. But it would be a wonderful thing for you to do for him, for reasons I don't have time to explain right here. And I promise you this, Regina—he is a good man. He will do anything for you, put his life on the line for you if it ever came to that, and never ask for anything. He'd be upset if he knew I was even asking you for this. But all I'm asking, really, is for you to think about it."

After a long silence, the girl looked up from their linked hands and nodded. "Okay. I'll think about it."

"Thank you, Regina." She got up from the stepstool. "Now let's hang that last painting."

Lindsey measured, penciled a spot on the wall, and nailed in a picture hook.

When Regina handed over the painting, she said, "It's just that all my life . . . there's never been anyone I called Mom or Dad. It's a very new thing."

Lindsey smiled. "I understand, honey. I really do. And so will Hatch if it takes time."

In the blazing Haunted House, as the cries for help and the screams of agony swelled louder, a strange object appeared in the firelight. A single rose. A black rose. It floated as if an unseen magician was levitating it. Vassago had never encountered anything more beautiful in the world of the living, in the world of the dead, or in the realm of dreams. It shimmered before him, its petals so smooth and soft that they seemed to have been cut from swatches of the night sky unspoiled by stars. The thorns were exquisitely sharp, needles of glass. The green stem had the oiled sheen of a serpent's skin. One petal held a single drop of blood.

The rose faded from his dream, but later it returned—and with it the woman named Lindsey and the auburn-haired girl with the soft-gray eyes. Vassago yearned to possess all three: the black rose, the woman, and the girl with the gray eyes.

After Hatch freshened up for dinner, while Lindsey finished getting ready in the bathroom, he sat alone on the edge of their bed and read the article by S. Steven Honell in *Arts American.* He could shrug off virtually any insult to himself, but if someone slammed Lindsey, he always reacted with anger. He couldn't even deal well with reviews of her work that *she* thought had made valid criticisms. Reading Honell's vicious, snide, and ultimately stupid diatribe dismissing her entire career as "wasted energy," Hatch grew angrier by the sentence.

As had happened the previous night, his anger erupted into fiery rage with volcanic abruptness. The muscles in his jaws clenched so hard, his teeth ached. The magazine began to shake because his hands were trembling with fury. His vision blurred slightly, as if he were looking at everything through shimmering waves of heat, and he had to blink and squint to make the fuzzy-edged words on the page resolve into readable print.

As when he had been lying in bed last night, he felt as if his anger opened a door and as if something entered him through it, a foul spirit that knew only rage and hate. Or maybe it had been with him all along but sleeping, and his anger had roused it. He was not alone inside his own head. He was aware of another presence, like a spider crawling through the narrow space between the inside of his skull and the surface of his brain.

He tried to put the magazine aside and calm down. But he kept reading because he was not in full possession of himself.

Vassago moved through the Haunted House, untroubled by the hungry fire, because he had planned an escape route. Sometimes he was twelve years old, and sometimes he was twenty. But always his path was lit by human torches, some of whom had collapsed into silent melting heaps upon the smoking floor, some of whom exploded into flames even as he passed them.

In the dream he was carrying a magazine, folded open to an article that angered him and seemed imperative he read. The edges of the pages curled in the heat and threatened to catch fire. Names leaped at him from the pages. Lindsey. Lindsey Sparling. Now he had a last name for her. He felt an urge to toss the magazine aside, slow his breathing, calm down. Instead he stoked his anger, let a sweet flood of rage overwhelm him, and told himself that he must know more. The edges of the magazine pages curled in the heat. Honell. Another name. Steven Honell. Bits of burning debris fell on the article. Steven S. Honell. No. The S first. S. Steven Honell. The paper caught fire. Honell. A writer. A barroom. Silverado Canyon. In his hands, the magazine burst into flames that flashed into his face—

He shed sleep like a fired bullet shedding its brass jacket, and sat up in his dark hideaway. Wide awake. Excited. He knew enough now to find the woman.

One moment rage like a fire swept through Hatch, and the next moment it was extinguished. His jaws relaxed, his tense shoulders sagged, and his hands unclenched so suddenly that he dropped the magazine on the floor between his feet.

He continued to sit on the edge of the bed for a while, stunned and confused. He looked toward the bathroom door, relieved that Lindsey had not walked in on him while he had been . . . Been what? In his trance? Possessed?

He smelled something peculiar, out of place. Smoke.

He looked at the issue of *Arts American* on the floor between his feet. Hesitantly, he picked it up. It was still folded open to Honell's article about Lindsey. Although no visible vapors rose from the magazine, the paper exuded the heavy smell of smoke. The odors of burning wood, paper, tar, plastics . . . and something worse. The edges of the paper were yellow-brown and crisp, as if they had been exposed to almost enough heat to induce spontaneous combustion.

7

When the knock came at the door, Honell was sitting in a rocking chair by the fireplace. He was drinking Chivas Regal and reading one of his own novels, *Miss Culvert,* which he had written twenty-five years ago when he was only thirty.

He re-read each of his nine books once a year because he was in perpetual competition with himself, striving to improve as he grew old instead of settling quietly into senescence the way most writers did. Constant betterment was a formidable challenge because he had been *awfully* good at an early age. Every time he re-read himself, he was surprised to discover that his body of work was considerably more impressive than he remembered it.

Miss Culvert was a fictional treatment of his mother's self-absorbed life in the respectable upper-middle-class society of a downstate Illinois town, an indictment of the self-satisfied and stiflingly bland "culture" of the Midwest. He had really captured the essence of the bitch. Oh, how he had captured her. Reading *Miss Culvert,* he was reminded of the hurt and horror with which his mother had received the novel on first publication, and he decided that as soon as he had finished the book, he would take down the sequel, *Mrs. Towers,* which dealt with her marriage to his father, her widowhood, and her second marriage. He remained convinced that the sequel was what had killed her. Officially, it was a heart attack. But cardiac infarction had to be triggered by something, and the timing was satisfyingly concurrent with the release of *Mrs. Towers* and the media attention it received.

When the unexpected caller knocked, a pang of resentment shot through Honell. His face puckered sourly. He preferred the company of his own characters to that of anyone who might conceivably come visiting, uninvited. Or invited, for that matter. All of the people in his books were carefully refined, clarified, whereas people in real life were unfailingly . . . well, fuzzy, murky, pointlessly complex.

He glanced at the clock on the mantel. Ten past nine o'clock.

The knock sounded again. More insistent this time. It was probably a neighbor, which was a dismaying thought because his neighbors were all fools.

He considered not answering. But in these rural canyons, the locals thought of themselves as "neighborly," never as the pests they actually were, and if he didn't respond to the knocking, they would circle the house, peeping in windows, out of a country-folk concern for his welfare. God, he hated them. He tolerated them only because he hated the people in the cities even more, and *loathed* suburbanites.

He put down his Chivas and the book, pushed up from the rocking chair, and went to the door with the intention of giving a fierce dressing-down to whoever was out there on the porch. With his command of language, he could mortify anyone in about one minute flat, and have them running for cover in two minutes. The pleasure of meting out humiliation would almost compensate for the interruption.

When he pulled the curtain back from the glass panes in the front door, he was surprised to see that his visitor was not one of the neighbors—in fact, not anyone he recognized. The boy was no more than twenty, pale as the wings of the snowflake moths that batted against the porch light. He was dressed entirely in black and wore sunglasses.

Honell was unconcerned about the caller's intentions. The canyon was less than an hour from the most heavily populated parts of Orange County, but it was nonetheless remote by virtue of its forbidding geography and the poor condition of the roads. Crime was no problem, because criminals were generally attracted to more populous areas where the pickings were more plentiful. Besides, most of the people living in the cabins thereabouts had nothing worth stealing.

He found the pale young man intriguing.

"What do you want?" he asked without opening the door.

"Mr. Honell?"

"That's right."

"S. Steven Honell?"

"Are you going to make a torture of this?"

"Sir, excuse me, but are you the writer?"

College student. That's what he had to be.

A decade ago—well, nearly two—Honell had been besieged by college English majors who wanted to apprentice under him or just worship at his feet. They were an inconstant crowd, however, on the lookout for the latest trend, with no genuine appreciation for high literary art.

Hell, these days, most of them couldn't even read; they were college students in name only. The institutions through which they matriculated were little more than day-care centers for the terminally immature, and they were no more likely to study than to fly to Mars by flapping their arms.

"Yes, I'm the writer. What of it?"

"Sir, I'm a great admirer of your books."

"Listened to them on audiotape, have you?"

"Sir? No, I've read them, all of them."

The audiotapes, licensed by his publisher without his consent, were abridged by two-thirds. Travesties.

"Ah. Read them in comic-book format, have you?" Honell said sourly, though to the best of his knowledge the sacrilege of comic-book adaptation had not yet been perpetrated.

"Sir, I'm sorry to intrude like this. It really took a lot of time for me to work up the courage to come see you. Tonight I finally had the guts, and I knew if I delayed I'd never get up the nerve again. I am in awe of your writing, sir, and if you could spare me the time, just a little time, to answer a few questions, I'd be most grateful."

A little conversation with an intelligent young man might, in fact, have more charm than re-reading *Miss Culvert*. A long time had passed since the last such visitor, who had come to the eyrie in which Honell had then been living above Santa Fe. After only a brief hesitation, he opened the door.

"Come in, then, and we'll see if you really understand the complexities of what you've read."

The young man stepped across the threshold, and Honell turned away, heading back toward the rocking chair and the Chivas.

"This is very kind of you, sir," the visitor said as he closed the door.

"Kindness is a quality of the weak and stupid, young man. I've other motivations." As he reached his chair, he turned and said,

"Take off those sunglasses. Sunglasses at night is the worst kind of Hollywood affectation, not the sign of a serious person."

"I'm sorry, sir, but they're not an affectation. It's just that this world is so much more painfully bright than Hell—which I'm sure you'll eventually discover."

Hatch had no appetite for dinner. He only wanted to sit alone with the inexplicably heat-curled issue of *Arts American* and stare at it until, by God, he *forced* himself to understand exactly what was happening to him. He was a man of reason. He could not easily embrace supernatural explanations. He was not in the antiques business by accident; he had a need to surround himself with things that contributed to an atmosphere of order and stability.

But kids also hungered for stability, which included regular mealtimes, so they went to dinner at a pizza parlor, after which they caught a movie at the theater complex next door. It was a comedy. Though the film couldn't make Hatch forget the strange problems plaguing him, the frequent sound of Regina's musical giggle did somewhat soothe his abraded nerves.

Later, at home, after he had tucked the girl in bed, kissed her forehead, wished her sweet dreams, and turned off the light, she said, "Goodnight . . . Dad."

He was in her doorway, stepping into the hall, when the word "dad" stopped him. He turned and looked back at her.

"Goodnight," he said, deciding to receive her gift as casually as she had given it, for fear that if he made a big deal about it, she would call him Mr. Harrison forever. But his heart soared.

In the bedroom, where Lindsey was undressing, he said, "She called me Dad."

"Who did?"

"Be serious, who do you think?"

"How much did you pay her?"

"You're just jealous 'cause she hasn't called you Mom yet."

"She will. She's not so afraid any more."

"Of you?"

"Of taking a chance."

Before getting undressed for bed, Hatch went downstairs to check the telephone answering machine in the kitchen. Funny, after all that had happened to him and considering the problems he still had to sort out, the mere fact that the girl had called him Dad was enough to quicken his step and lift his spirits. He descended the stairs two at a time.

The answering machine was on the counter to the left of the refrigerator, below the cork memo board. He was hoping to have a response from the estate executor to whom he had given a bid for the Wedgwood collection that morning. The window on the machine showed three messages. The first was from Glenda Dockridge, his right hand at the antique shop. The second was from Simpson Smith, a friend and antique dealer on Melrose Place in Los Angeles. The third was from Janice Dimes, a friend of Lindsey's. All three were reporting the same news: *Hatch, Lindsey, Hatch and Lindsey, have you seen the paper, have you read the paper, have you heard the news about Cooper, about that guy who ran you off the road, about Bill Cooper, he's dead, he was killed, he was killed last night.*

Hatch felt as if a refrigerant, instead of blood, pumped through his veins.

Last evening he had raged about Cooper getting off scot-free, and had wished him dead. No, wait. He'd said he wanted to hurt him, make him pay, pitch *him* in that icy river, but he hadn't actually wanted Cooper dead. And so what if he *had* wanted him dead? He had not actually killed the man. He was not at fault for what had happened.

Punching the button to erase the messages, he thought: The cops will want to talk to me sooner or later.

Then he wondered why he was worried about the police. Maybe the murderer was already in custody, in which case no suspicion would fall upon him. But why should he come under suspicion anyway? He had done nothing. *Nothing.* Why was guilt creeping through him like the Millipede inching up a long tunnel?

Millipede?

The utterly enigmatic nature of that image chilled him. He couldn't reference the source of it. As if it wasn't his own thought but something he had . . . *received.*

He hurried upstairs.

Lindsey was lying on her back in bed, adjusting the covers around her.

The newspaper was on his nightstand, where she always put it. He snatched it up and quickly scanned the front page.

"Hatch?" she said. "What's wrong?"

"Cooper's dead."

"What?"

"The guy driving the beer truck. William Cooper. Murdered."

She threw back the covers and sat on the edge of the bed.

He found the story on page three. He sat beside Lindsey, and they read the article together.

According to the newspaper, police were interested in talking to a young man in his early twenties, with pale skin and dark hair. A neighbor had glimpsed him fleeing down the alleyway behind the Palm Court apartments. He might have been wearing sunglasses. At night.

"He's the same damned one who killed the blonde," Hatch said fearfully. "The sunglasses in the rearview mirror. And now he's picking up on my thoughts. He's acting out *my* anger, murdering people that I'd like to see punished."

"That doesn't make sense. It can't be."

"It is." He felt sick. He looked at his hands, as if he might actually find the truck driver's blood on them. "My God, I sent him after Cooper."

He was so appalled, so psychologically oppressed by a sense of responsibility for what had happened, that he wanted desperately to wash his hands, scrub them until they were raw. When he tried to get up, his legs were too weak to support him, and he had to sit right down again.

Lindsey was baffled and horrified, but she did not react to the news story as strongly as Hatch did.

Then he told her about the reflection of the black-clad young man in sunglasses, which he had seen in the mirrored door in place of his own image, last night in the den when he had been ranting about Cooper. He told her, as well, how he lay in bed after she was asleep, brooding about Cooper, and how his anger suddenly exploded into artery-popping rage. He spoke of the sense he'd had of being invaded and overwhelmed, ending in the blackout. And for a kicker, he recounted how his anger had escalated unreasonably as he had read the piece in *Arts American* earlier this evening, and he took the magazine out of his nightstand to show her the inexplicably scorched pages.

By the time Hatch finished, Lindsey's anxiety matched his, but dismay at his secretiveness seemed greater than anything else she was feeling. "Why'd you hide all of this from me?"

"I didn't want to worry you," he said, knowing how feeble it sounded.

"We've never hidden anything from each other before. We've always shared everything. Everything."

"I'm sorry, Lindsey. I just . . . it's just that . . . these last couple months . . . the nightmares of rotting bodies, violence, fire, . . . and the last few days, all this *weirdness*. . . ."

"From now on," she said, "there'll be no secrets."

"I only wanted to spare you—"

"No secrets," she insisted.

"Okay. No secrets."

"And you're not responsible for what happened to Cooper. Even if there is some kind of link between you and this killer, and even if that's why Cooper became a target, it's not your fault. You didn't *know* that being angry at Cooper was equivalent to a death sentence. You couldn't have done anything to prevent it."

Hatch looked at the heat-seared magazine in her hands, and a shudder of dread passed through him. "But it'll be my fault if I don't try to save Honell."

Frowning, she said, "What do you mean?"

"If my anger somehow focused this guy on Cooper, why wouldn't it also focus him on Honell?"

269

Honell woke to a world of pain. The difference was, this time he was on the receiving end of it—and it was physical rather than emotional pain. His crotch ached from the kick he'd taken. A blow to his throat had left his esophagus feeling like broken glass. His headache was excruciating. His wrists and ankles burned, and at first he could not understand why; then he realized he was tied to the four posts of something, probably his bed, and the ropes were chafing his skin.

He could not see much, partly because his vision was blurred by tears but also because his contact lenses had been knocked out in the attack. He knew he had been assaulted, but for a moment he could not recall the identity of his assailant.

Then the young man's face loomed over him, blurred at first like the surface of the moon through an unadjusted telescope. The boy bent closer, closer, and his face came into focus, handsome and pale, framed by thick black hair. He was not smiling in the tradition of movie psychotics, as Honell expected he would be. He was not scowling, either, or even frowning. He was expressionless— except, perhaps, for a subtle hint of that solemn professional curiosity with which an entomologist might study some new mutant variation of a familiar species of insect.

"I'm sorry for this discourteous treatment, sir, after you were kind enough to welcome me into your home. But I'm rather in a hurry and couldn't take the time to discover what I need to know through ordinary conversation."

"Whatever you want," Honell said placatingly. He was shocked to hear how drastically his mellifluous voice, always a reliable tool for seduction and expressive instrument of scorn, had changed. It was raspy, marked by a wet gurgle, thoroughly disgusting.

"I would like to know who Lindsey Sparling is," the young man said dispassionately, "and where I can find her."

Hatch was surprised to find Honell's number in the telephone book. Of course, the author's name was not as familiar to the average citizen as it had been during his brief glory years, when he had published *Miss Culvert* and *Mrs. Towers*. Honell didn't need to be worried about privacy these days; evidently the public gave him more of it than he desired.

While Hatch called the number, Lindsey paced the length of the bedroom and back. She had made her position clear: she didn't think Honell would interpret Hatch's warning as anything other than a cheap threat.

Hatch agreed with her. But he had to try.

He was spared the humiliation and frustration of listening to Honell's reaction, however, because no one answered the phone out there in the far canyons of the desert night. He let it ring twenty times.

He was about to hang up, when a series of images snapped through his mind with a sound like short-circuiting electrical wires: a disarranged bed quilt; a bleeding, rope-encircled wrist; a pair of frightened, bloodshot, myopic eyes . . . and in the eyes, the twin reflections of a dark face looming close, distinguished only by a pair of sunglasses.

Hatch slammed down the phone and backed away from it as if the receiver had turned into a rattlesnake in his hand. "It's happening now."

The ringing phone fell silent.

Vassago stared at it, but the ringing did not resume.

He returned his attention to the man who was tied spread-eagle to the brass posts of the bed. "So Lindsey Harrison is the married name?"

"Yes," the old guy croaked.

"Now what I most urgently need, sir, is an address."

The public telephone was outside of a convenience store in a shopping center just two miles from the Harrison house. It was protected from the elements by a Plexiglas hood and surrounded by a curved sound shield. Hatch would have preferred the greater privacy of a real booth, but those were hard to find these days, a luxury of less cost-conscious times.

He parked at the end of the center, at too great a distance for anyone in the glass-fronted convenience store to notice—and perhaps recall—his license number.

He walked through a cool, blustery wind to the telephone. The center's Indian laurels were infested with thrips, and drifts of dead, tightly curled leaves blew along the pavement at Hatch's feet. They made a dry, scuttling sound. In the urine-yellow glow of the parking-lot lights, they almost looked like hordes of insects, queerly mutated locusts perhaps, swarming toward their subterranean hive.

The convenience store was not busy, and everything else in the shopping center was closed. He hunched his shoulders and head into the pay phone sound shield, convinced he wouldn't be overheard.

He did not want to call the police from home, because he knew they had equipment that printed out every caller's number at their end. If they found Honell dead, Hatch didn't want to become their prime suspect. And if his concern for Honell's safety proved to be unfounded, he didn't want to be on record with the police as some kind of nutcase or hysteric.

Even as he punched in the number with one bent knuckle and held the handset with a Kleenex to avoid leaving prints, he was uncertain what to say. He knew what he could *not* say: *Hi, I was dead eighty minutes, then brought back to life, and now I have this crude but at times effective telepathic connection to a psychotic killer, and I think I should warn you he's about to strike again.* He could not imagine the authorities taking him any more seriously than they would take a guy who wore a pyramid-shaped aluminum-foil hat to protect his brain from sinister radiation and who bothered them with complaints about evil, mind-warping extraterrestrials next door.

He had decided to call the Orange County Sheriff's Department rather than any particular city's police agency, because the crimes committed by the man in sunglasses fell in several jurisdictions.

When the sheriff's operator answered, Hatch talked fast, talked over her when she began to interrupt, because he knew they could trace him to a pay phone given enough time. "The man who killed the blonde and dumped her on the freeway last week is the same guy who killed William Cooper last night, and tonight he's going to murder Steven Honell, the writer, if you don't give him protection quick, and I mean right now. Honell lives in Silverado Canyon, I don't know the address, but he's probably in your jurisdiction, and he's a dead man if you don't move now."

He hung up, turned away from the phone, and headed for his car, jamming the Kleenex into his pants pocket. He felt less relieved than he had expected to, and more of a fool than seemed reasonable.

On his way back to the car, he was walking into the wind. All the laurel leaves, sucked dry by thrips, were now blown toward him instead of with him. They hissed against the blacktop and crunched under his shoes.

He knew that the trip had been a waste and that his effort to help Honell had been ineffective. The sheriff's department would probably treat it like just another crank call.

When he got home, he parked in the driveway, afraid that the clatter of the garage door would wake Regina. His scalp prickled when he got out of the car. He stood for a minute, surveying the shadows along the house, around the shrubbery, under the trees. Nothing.

Lindsey was pouring a cup of coffee for him when he walked into the kitchen.

He took it, sipped gratefully at the hot brew. Suddenly he was colder than he had been while standing out in the night chill.

"What do you think?" she asked worriedly. "Did they take you seriously?"

"Pissing in the wind," he said.

Vassago was still driving the pearl-gray Honda belonging to Renata Desseux, the woman he had overpowered in the mall parking lot on Saturday night and later added to his collection. It was a fine car and handled well on the twisting roads as he drove down the canyon from Honell's place, heading for more populated areas of Orange County.

As he rounded a particularly sharp curve, a patrol car from the sheriff's department swept past him, heading up the canyon. Its siren was not blaring, but its emergency beacons splashed red and blue light on the shale banks and on the gnarled branches of the overhanging trees.

He divided his attention between the winding road ahead and the dwindling taillights of the patrol car in his rearview mirror, until it rounded another bend upslope and vanished. He was sure the cop was speeding to Honell's. The unanswered, interminably ringing telephone, which had interrupted his interrogation of the author, was the trigger that had set the sheriff's department in motion, but he could not figure how or why.

Vassago did not drive faster. At the end of Silverado Canyon, he turned south on Santiago Canyon Road and maintained the legal speed limit as any good citizen was expected to do.

8

In bed in the dark, Hatch felt his world crumbling around him. He was going to be left with dust.

Happiness with Lindsey and Regina was within his grasp. Or was that an illusion? Were they infinitely beyond his reach?

He wished for an insight that would give him a new perspective on these apparently supernatural events. Until he could understand the nature of the evil that had entered his life, he could not fight it.

Dr. Nyebern's voice spoke softly in his mind: *I believe evil is a very real force, an energy quite apart from us, a presence in the world.*

He thought he could smell a lingering trace of smoke from the heat-browned pages of *Arts American.* He had put the magazine in the desk in the den downstairs, in the drawer with a lock. He had added the small key to the ring he carried.

He had never locked anything in the desk before. He was not sure why he had done so this time. Protecting evidence, he'd told himself. But evidence of what? The singed pages of the magazine proved nothing to anyone about anything.

No. That was not precisely true. The existence of the magazine proved, to him if to no one else, that he wasn't merely imagining and hallucinating everything that was happening to him. What he had locked away, for his own peace of mind, was indeed evidence. Evidence of his sanity.

Beside him, Lindsey was also awake, either uninterested in sleep or unable to find a way into it. She said, "What if this killer . . ."

Hatch waited. He didn't need to ask her to finish the thought, for he knew what she was going to say. After a moment she said just what he expected:

"What if this killer is aware of you as much as you're aware of him? What if he comes after you . . . us . . . Regina?"

"Tomorrow we're going to start taking precautions."

"What precautions?"

"Guns, for one thing."

"Maybe this isn't something we can handle ourselves."

"We don't have any choice."

"Maybe we need police protection."

"Somehow I don't think they'll commit a lot of manpower to protect a guy just because he claims to have a supernatural bond with a psychotic killer."

The wind that had harried laurel leaves across the shopping-center parking lot now found a loose brace on a section of rain gutter and worried it. Metal creaked softly against metal.

Hatch said, "I went somewhere when I died, right?"

"What do you mean?"

"Purgatory, Heaven, Hell—those are the basic possibilities for a Catholic, if what we say we believe turns out to be true."

"Well . . . you've always said you had no near-death experience."

275

"I didn't. I can't remember anything from . . . the Other Side. But that doesn't mean I wasn't there."

"What's your point?"

"Maybe this killer isn't an ordinary man."

"You're losing me, Hatch."

"Maybe I brought something back with me."

"Back with you?"

"From wherever I was while I was dead."

"Something?"

Darkness had its advantages. The superstitious primitive within could speak of things that would seem too foolish to voice in a well-lighted place.

He said, "A spirit. An entity."

She said nothing.

"My passage in and out of death might have opened a door somehow," he said, "and let something through."

"Something," she said again, but with no note of inquiry in her voice, as there had been before. He sensed that she knew what he meant—and did not like the theory.

"And now it's loose in the world. Which explains its link to me—and why it might kill people who anger me."

She was silent awhile. Then: "If something was brought back, it's evidently pure evil. What—are you saying that when you died, you went to Hell and this killer piggy-backed with you from there?"

"Maybe. I'm no saint, no matter what you think. After all, I've got at least Cooper's blood on my hands."

"That happened after you died and were brought back. Besides, you don't share in the guilt for that."

"It was my anger that targeted him, my anger—"

"Bullshit," Lindsey said sharply. "You're the best man I've ever known. If housing in the afterlife includes a Heaven and Hell, you've earned the apartment with a better view."

His thoughts were so dark, he was surprised that he could smile. He reached under the sheets, found her hand, and held it gratefully. "I love you, too."

"Think up another theory if you want to keep me awake and interested."

"Let's just make a little adjustment to the theory we already have. What if there's an afterlife, but it isn't ordered like anything theologians have ever described. It wouldn't have to be *either* Heaven or Hell that I came back from. Just another place, stranger than here, different, with unknown dangers."

"I don't like that much better."

"If I'm going to deal with this thing, I have to find a way to explain it. I can't fight back if I don't even know where to throw my punches."

"There's got to be a more logical explanation," she said.

"That's what I tell myself. But when I try to find it, I keep coming back to the illogical."

The rain gutter creaked. The wind soughed under the eaves and called down the flue of the master-bedroom fireplace.

He wondered if Honell was able to hear the wind wherever he was—and whether it was the wind of this world or the next.

Vassago parked directly in front of Harrison's Antiques at the south end of Laguna Beach. The shop occupied an entire Art Deco building. The big display windows were unlighted as Tuesday passed through midnight, becoming Wednesday.

Steven Honell had been unable to tell him where the Harrisons lived, and a quick check of the telephone book turned up no listed number for them. The writer had known only the name of their business and its approximate location on Pacific Coast Highway.

Their home address was sure to be on file somewhere in the store's office. Getting it might be difficult. A decal on each of the big Plexiglas windows and another on the front door warned that the premises were fitted with a burglar alarm and protected by a security company.

He had come back from Hell with the ability to see in the dark, animal-quick reflexes, a lack of inhibitions that left him capable of any act or atrocity, and a fearlessness that made him every bit as formidable an adversary as a robot might have been. But he could not walk through walls, or transform himself from flesh into vapor into flesh again, or fly, or perform any of the other feats that were within the powers of a true demon. Until he had earned his way back into Hell either by acquiring a perfect collection in his museum of the dead or by killing those he had been sent here to destroy, he possessed only the minor powers of the demon demimonde, which were insufficient to defeat a burglar alarm.

He drove away from the store.

In the heart of town, he found a telephone booth beside a service station. Despite the hour, the station was still pumping gasoline, and the outdoor lighting was so bright that Vassago was forced to squint behind his sunglasses.

Swooping around the lamps, moths with inch-long wings cast shadows as large as ravens on the pavement.

The floor of the telephone booth was littered with cigarette butts. Ants teamed over the corpse of a beetle.

Someone had taped a hand-lettered OUT OF ORDER notice to the coin box, but Vassago didn't care because he didn't intend to call anyone. He was only interested in the phone book, which was secured to the frame of the booth by a sturdy chain.

He checked "Antiques" in the Yellow Pages. Laguna Beach had a lot of businesses under that heading; it was a regular shoppers' paradise. He studied their space ads. Some had institutional names like International Antiques, but others were named after their owners, as was Harrison's Antiques.

A few used both first *and* last names, and some of the space ads also included the full names of the proprietors because, in that business, personal reputation could be a drawing card. Robert O. Loffman Antiques in the Yellow Pages cross-referenced neatly with a Robert O. Loffman in the white pages, providing Vassago with a street address, which he committed to memory.

On his way back to the Honda, he saw a bat swoop out of the night. It arced down through the blue-white glare from the service-station lights, snatching a fat moth from the air in mid-flight, then vanished back up into the darkness from which it had come. Neither predator nor prey made a sound.

Loffman was seventy years old, but in his best dreams he was eighteen again, spry and limber, strong and happy. They were never sex dreams, no bosomy young women parting their smooth thighs in welcome. They weren't power dreams, either, no running or jumping or leaping off cliffs into wild adventures. The action was always mundane: a leisurely walk along a beach at twilight, barefoot, the feel of damp sand between his toes, the froth on the incoming waves sparkling with reflections of the dazzling purple-red sunset; or just sitting on the grass in the shadow of a date palm on a summer afternoon, watching a hummingbird sip nectar from the bright blooms in a bed of flowers. The mere fact that he was young again seemed miracle enough to sustain a dream and keep it interesting.

At the moment he was eighteen, lying on a big bench swing on the front porch of the Santa Ana house in which he had been born and raised. He was just swinging gently and peeling an apple that he intended to eat, nothing more, but it was a wonderful dream, rich with scents and textures, more erotic than if he had imagined himself in a harem of undressed beauties.

"Wake up, Mr. Loffman."

He tried to ignore the voice because he wanted to be alone on that porch. He kept his eyes on the curled length of peel that he was paring from the apple.

"Come on, you old sleepyhead."

He was trying to strip the apple in one continuous ribbon of peel.

"Did you take a sleeping pill or what?"

To Loffman's regret, the front porch, the swing, the apple and paring knife dissolved into darkness. His bedroom.

He struggled awake and realized an intruder was present. A barely visible, spectral figure stood beside the bed.

279

Although he'd never been the victim of a crime and lived in as safe a neighborhood as existed these days, age had saddled Loffman with feelings of vulnerability. He had started keeping a loaded pistol next to the lamp at his bedside. He reached for it now, his heart pounding hard as he groped along the cool marble surface of the 18th-century French ormolu chest that served as his nightstand. The gun was gone.

"I'm sorry, sir," the intruder said. "I didn't mean to scare you. Please calm down. If it's the pistol you're after, I saw it as soon as I came in. I have it now."

The stranger could not have seen the gun without turning on the light, and the light would have awakened Loffman sooner. He was sure of that, so he kept groping for the weapon.

From out of the darkness, something cold and blunt probed against his throat. He twitched away from it, but the coldness followed him, pressing insistently, as if the specter tormenting him could see him clearly in the gloom. He froze when he realized what the coldness was. The muzzle of the pistol. Against his Adam's apple. It slid slowly upward, under his chin.

"If I pulled the trigger, sir, your brains would be all over the headboard. But I do not need to hurt you, sir. Pain is quite unnecessary as long as you cooperate. I only want you to answer one important question for me."

If Robert Loffman actually had been eighteen, as in his best dreams, he could not have valued the remainder of his time on earth more highly than he did at seventy, in spite of having far less of it to lose now. He was prepared to hold onto life with all the tenacity of a burrowing tick. He would answer any question, perform any deed to save himself, regardless of the cost to his pride and dignity. He tried to convey all of that to the phantom who held the pistol under his chin, but it seemed to him that he produced a gabble of words and sounds that, in sum, had no meaning whatsoever.

"Yes, sir," the intruder said, "I understand, and I appreciate your attitude. Now correct me if I am wrong, but I suppose the antique business, being relatively small when compared to others, is a tight community here in Laguna. You all know each other, see each other socially, you're friends."

Antique business? Loffman was tempted to believe that he was still asleep and that his dream had become an absurd nightmare. Why would anyone break into his house in the dead of night to talk about the antique business at gunpoint?

"We know each other, some of us are good friends, of course, but some bastards in this business are thieves," Loffman said. He was babbling, unable to stop, hopeful that his obvious fear would testify to his truthfulness, whether this was nightmare or reality. "They're nothing more than crooks with cash registers, and you aren't friends with that kind if you have any self-respect at all."

"Do you know Mr. Harrison of Harrison's Antiques?"

"Oh, yes, very well, I know him quite well, he's a reputable dealer, totally trustworthy, a nice man."

"Have you been to his house?"

"His house? Yes, certainly, on three or four occasions, and he's been here to mine."

"Then you must have the answer to that important question I mentioned, sir. Can you give me Mr. Harrison's address and clear directions to it?"

Loffman sagged with relief upon realizing that he would be able to provide the intruder with the desired information. Only fleetingly, he considered that he might be putting Harrison in great jeopardy. But maybe it was a nightmare, after all, and revelation of the information would not matter. He repeated the address and directions several times, at the intruder's request.

"Thank you, sir. You've been most helpful. Like I said, causing you any pain is quite unnecessary. But I'm going to hurt you anyway, because I enjoy it so much."

So it *was* a nightmare after all.

Vassago drove past the Harrison house in Laguna Niguel. Then he circled the block and drove past it again.

The house was a powerful attractant, similar in style to all of the other houses on the street but so different from them in some indescribable but fundamental way that it might as well have been an isolated structure rising out of a featureless plain. Its windows were dark, and the landscape lighting had evidently been turned off by a timer, but it could not have been more of a beacon to Vassago if light had blazed from every window.

As he drove slowly past the house a second time, he felt its immense gravity pulling him. His immutable destiny involved this place and the vital woman who lived within.

Nothing he saw suggested a trap. A red car was parked in the driveway instead of in the garage, but he couldn't see anything ominous about that. Nevertheless, he decided to circle the block a third time to give the house another thorough looking over.

As he turned the corner, a lone silvery moth darted through his headlight beams, refracting them and briefly glowing like an ember from a great fire. He remembered the bat that had swooped into the service-station lights to snatch the hapless moth out of the air, eating it alive.

Long after midnight, Hatch had finally dozed off. His sleep was a deep mine, where veins of dreams flowed like bright ribbons of minerals through the otherwise dark walls. None of the dreams was pleasant, but none of them was grotesque enough to wake him.

Currently he saw himself standing at the bottom of a ravine with ramparts so steep they could not be climbed. Even if the slopes had risen at an angle that allowed ascent, they would not have been scaleable because they were composed of a curious, loose white shale that crumbled and shifted treacherously. The shale radiated a soft calcimine glow, which was the only light, for the sky far above was black and moonless, deep but starless. Hatch moved restlessly from one end of the long narrow ravine to the other, then back again, filled with apprehension but unsure of the cause of it.

Then he realized two things that made the fine hairs tingle on the back of his neck. The white shale was not composed of rock and the shells of millions of ancient sea creatures; it was made of human skeletons, splintered and compacted but recognizable here and there, where the articulated bones of two fingers survived compression or where what seemed a small animal's burrow proved to be the empty eye socket in a skull. He became aware, as well, that the sky was not empty, that something circled in it, so black that it blended with the heavens, its leathery wings working silently. He could not see it, but he could feel its gaze, and he sensed a hunger in it that could never be satisfied.

In his troubled sleep, Hatch turned and murmured anxious, wordless sounds into his pillow.

Vassago checked the car clock. Even without its confirming numbers, he knew instinctively that dawn was less than an hour away.

He no longer could be sure he had enough time to get into the house, kill the husband, and take the woman back to his hideaway before sunrise. He could not risk getting caught in the open in daylight. Though he would not shrivel up and turn to dust like the living dead in the movies, nothing as dramatic as that, his eyes were so sensitive that his glasses would not provide adequate protection from full sunlight. Dawn would render him nearly blind, dramatically affecting his ability to drive and bringing him to the attention of any policeman who happened to spot his weaving, halting progress. In that debilitated condition, he might have difficulty dealing with the cop.

More important, he might lose the woman. After appearing so often in his dreams, she had become an object of intense desire. Before, he had seen acquisitions of such quality that he had been convinced they would complete his collection and earn him immediate readmission to the savage world of eternal darkness and hatred to which he belonged—and he had been wrong. But none of those others had appeared to him in dreams. *This* woman was the true jewel in the crown for which he had been seeking. He must avoid taking possession of her prematurely, only to lose her before he could draw the life from her at the base of the giant Lucifer and wrench her cooling corpse into whatever configuration seemed most symbolic of her sins and weaknesses.

As he cruised past the house for the third time, he considered leaving immediately for his hideaway and returning here as soon as the sun had set the following evening. But that plan had no appeal. Being so close to her excited him, and he was loath to be separated from her again. He felt the tidal pull of her in his blood.

He needed a place to hide that was near her. Perhaps a secret corner in her own house. A niche in which she was unlikely to look during the long, bright, hostile hours of the day.

He parked the Honda two blocks from their house and returned on foot along the tree-flanked sidewalk. The tall, green-patinated streetlamps had angled arms at the top that directed their light onto the roadway, and only a ghost of their glow reached past the sidewalk onto the front lawns of the silent houses. Confident that neighbors were still sleeping and unlikely to see him prowling through shadow-hung shrubbery around the perimeter of the house, he searched quietly for an unlocked door, an unlatched window. He had no luck until he came to the window on the back wall of the garage.

Regina was awakened by a scraping noise, a dull *thump-thump* and a soft protracted squeak. Still unaccustomed to her new home, she always woke in confusion, not sure where she was, certain only that she was not in her room at the orphanage. She fumbled for the bedside lamp, clicked it on, and squinted at the glare for a second before orienting herself and realizing the noises that had bumped her out of sleep had been *sneaky* sounds. They had stopped when she had snapped on the light. Which seemed even sneakier.

She clicked the light off and listened in the darkness, which was now filled with aureoles of color because the lamp had worked like a camera flashbulb on her eyes, temporarily stealing her night vision. Though the sounds did not resume, she believed they had come from the backyard.

Her bed was comfortable. The room almost seemed to be scented with the perfume of the painted flowers. Encircled by those roses, she felt safer than she had ever felt before.

Although she didn't want to get up, she was also aware that the Harrisons were having problems of some kind, and she wondered if these sneaky sounds in the middle of the night somehow might be related to that. Yesterday during the drive from school, as well as last night during dinner and after the movie, she had sensed a tension in them that they were trying to conceal from her. Even though she knew herself to be a screwup around whom anyone would have a right to feel nervous, she was sure that she was not the cause of their edginess. Before going to sleep, she had prayed that their troubles, if they had any, would prove to be minor and would be dealt with soon, and she had reminded God of her selfless pledge to eat beans of all varieties.

If there was any possibility the sneaky noises were related to the Harrisons' uneasy state of mind, Regina supposed she had an obligation to check it out. She looked up and back at the crucifix above her bed, and sighed. You couldn't rely on Jesus and Mary for everything. They were busy people. They had a universe to run. God helped those who helped themselves.

She slipped out from under the covers, stood, and made her way to the window, leaning against furniture and then the wall. She was not wearing her leg brace, and she needed the support.

The window looked onto the small backyard behind the garage, the area from which the suspicious noises had seemed to come. Night-shadows from the house, trees, and shrubs were unrelieved by moonlight. The longer Regina stared, the less she could make out, as if the darkness were a sponge soaking up her ability to see. It became easy to believe that *every* impenetrable pocket of gloom was alive and watchful.

The garage window had been unlocked but difficult to open. The hinges at the top were corroded, and the frame was paint-sealed to the jamb in places. Vassago made more noise than he intended, but he didn't think he had been loud enough to draw the attention of anyone in the house. Then just as the paint cracked and the hinges moved to grant him access, a light had appeared in another window on the second floor.

He had backed away from the garage at once, even though the light went off again even as he moved. He had taken cover in a stand of six-foot eugenia bushes near the property fence.

From there he saw her appear at the obsidian window, more visible to him, perhaps, than she would have been if she had left the lamp on. It was the girl he had seen in dreams a couple of times, most recently with Lindsey Harrison. They had faced each other across a levitated black rose with one drop of blood glistening on a velvet petal.

Regina.

He stared at her in disbelief, then with growing excitement. Earlier in the night, he had asked Steven Honell if the Harrisons had a daughter, but the author had told him that he knew only of a son who had died years ago.

Separated from Vassago by nothing but the night air and one pane of glass, the girl seemed to float above him as if she were a vision. In reality she was, if anything, lovelier than she had been in his dreams. She was so exceptionally vital, so full of life, that he would not have been surprised if she could walk the night as confidently as he did, though for a reason different from his; she seemed to have within her all the light she needed to illuminate her path through any darkness. He drew back farther into the eugenias, convinced that she possessed the power to see him as clearly as he saw her.

A trellis covered the wall immediately below her window. A lush trumpet vine with purple flowers grew up the sturdy lattice to the windowsill, and then around one side almost to the eaves. She was like some princess locked in a tower, pining for a prince to climb up the vine and rescue her. The tower that served as her prison was life itself, and the prince for whom she waited was Death, and that from which she longed to be rescued was the curse of existence.

Vassago said softly, "I am here for you," but he did not move from his hiding place.

After a couple of minutes, she turned away from the window. Vanished. A void lay behind the glass where she had stood.

He ached for her return, one more brief look at her.

Regina.

He waited five minutes, then another five. But she did not come to the window again.

At last, aware that dawn was closer than ever, he crept to the back of the garage once more. Because he had already freed it, the window swung out silently this time. The opening was tight, but he eeled through with only the softest scrape of clothes against wood.

Lindsey dozed in half-hour and hour naps throughout the night, but her sleep was not restful. Each time she woke, she was sticky with perspiration, even though the house was cool. Beside her, Hatch issued murmured protests in his sleep.

Toward dawn she heard noise in the hall and rose up from her pillows to listen. After a moment she identified the sound of the toilet flushing in the guest bathroom. Regina.

She settled back on her pillows, oddly soothed by the fading sound of the toilet. It seemed like such a mundane—not to say ridiculous—thing from which to take solace. But a long time had passed without a child under her roof. It felt good and right to hear the girl engaged in ordinary domestic business; it made the night seem less hostile. In spite of their current problems, the promise of happiness might be more real than it had been in years.

In bed again, Regina wondered why God had given people bowels and bladders. Was that really the best possible design, or was He a little bit of a comedian?

She remembered getting up at three o'clock in the morning at the orphanage, needing to pee, encountering a nun on the way to the bathroom down the hall, and asking the good sister that very question. The nun, Sister Sarafina, had not been startled at all. Regina had been too young then to know how to startle a nun; that took years of thinking and practice. Sister Sarafina had responded without pause, suggesting that perhaps God wanted to give people a reason to get up in the middle of the night so they would have another opportunity to think of Him and be grateful for the life He had granted them. Regina had smiled and nodded, but she had figured Sister Sarafina was either too tired to think straight or a little dim-witted. God had too much class to want His children thinking about Him all the time while they were sitting on the pot.

Satisfied from her visit to the bathroom, she snuggled down in the covers of her painted mahogany bed and tried to think of an explanation better than the one the nun had given her years ago. No more curious noises arose from the backyard, and even before the vague light of dawn touched the windowpanes, she was asleep again.

High, decorative windows were set in the big sectional doors, admitting just enough light from the streetlamps out front to reveal to Vassago, without his sunglasses, that only one car, a black Chevy, was parked in the three-car garage. A quick inspection of that space did not reveal any hiding place where he might conceal himself from the Harrisons and be beyond the reach of sunlight until the next nightfall.

Then he saw the cord dangling from the ceiling over one of the empty parking stalls. He slipped his hand through the loop and pulled downward gently, less gently, then less gently still, but always steadily and smoothly, until the trapdoor swung open. It was well oiled and soundless.

When the door was all the way open, Vassago slowly unfolded the three sections of the wooden ladder that were fixed to the back of it. He took plenty of time, more concerned with silence than with speed.

He climbed into the garage attic. No doubt there were vents in the eaves, but at the moment the place appeared to be sealed tight.

With his sensitive eyes, he could see a finished floor, lots of cardboard boxes, and a few small items of furniture stored under dropcloths. No windows. Above him, the underside of rough roofing boards were visible between open rafters. At two points in the long rectangular chamber, light fixtures dangled from the peaked ceiling; he did not turn on either of them.

Cautiously, quietly, as if he were an actor in a slow-motion film, he stretched out on his belly on the attic floor, reached down through the hole, and pulled up the folding ladder, section by section. Slowly, silently, he secured it to the back of the trapdoor. He eased the door into place again with no sound but the soft *spang* of the big spring that held it shut, closing himself off from the three-car garage below.

He pulled a few of the dropcloths off the furniture. They were relatively dust free. He folded them to make a nest among the boxes and then settled down to await the passage of the day.

Regina. Lindsey. I am with you.

SIX

1

Lindsey drove Regina to school Wednesday morning. When she got back to the house in Laguna Niguel, Hatch was at the kitchen table, cleaning and oiling the pair of Browning 9mm pistols that he had acquired for home security.

He had purchased the guns five years ago, shortly after Jimmy's cancer had been diagnosed as terminal. He had professed a sudden concern about the crime rate, though it never had been—and was not then—particularly high in their part of Orange County. Lindsey had known, but had never said, that he was not afraid of burglars but of the disease that was stealing his son from him; and because he was helpless to fight off the cancer, he secretly longed for an enemy who *could* be dispatched with a pistol.

The Brownings had never been used anywhere but on a firing range. He had insisted that Lindsey learn to shoot alongside him. But neither of them had even taken target practice in a year or two.

"Do you really think that's wise?" she asked, indicating the pistols.

He was tight-lipped. "Yes."

"Maybe we should call the police."

"We've already discussed why we can't."

"Still, it might be worth a try."

"They won't help us. Can't."

She knew he was right. They had no proof that they were in danger.

"Besides," he said, keeping his eyes on the pistol as he worked a tubular brush in and out of the barrel, "when I first started cleaning these, I turned on the TV to have some company. Morning news."

The small set, on a pull-out swivel shelf in the end-most of the kitchen cabinets, was off now.

Lindsey didn't ask him what had been on the news. She was afraid that she would be sorry to hear it—and was convinced that she already knew what he would tell her.

Finally looking up from the pistol, Hatch said, "They found Steven Honell last night. Tied to the four corners of his bed and beaten to death with a fireplace poker."

At first Lindsey was too shocked to move. Then she was too weak to continue standing. She pulled a chair out from the table and settled into it.

For a while yesterday, she had hated Steven Honell as much as she had ever hated anyone in her life. More. Now she felt no animosity for him whatsoever. Just pity. He had been an insecure man, concealing his insecurity from himself behind a pretense of contemptuous superiority. He had been petty and vicious, perhaps worse, but now he was dead; and death was too great a punishment for his faults.

She folded her arms on the table and put her head down on them. She could not cry for Honell, for she had liked nothing about him—except his talent. If the extinguishing of his talent was not enough to bring tears, it did at least cast a pall of despair over her.

"Sooner or later," Hatch said, "the son of a bitch is going to come after me."

Lindsey lifted her head even though it felt as if it weighed a thousand pounds. "But why?"

"I don't know. Maybe we'll never know why, never understand it. But somehow he and I are linked, and eventually he'll come."

"Let the cops handle him," she said, painfully aware that there was no help for them from the authorities but stubbornly unwilling to let go of that hope.

"Cops can't find him," Hatch said grimly. "He's smoke."

"He won't come," she said, willing it to be true.

"Maybe not tomorrow. Maybe not next week or even next month. But as sure as the sun rises every morning, he'll come. And we'll be ready for him."

"Will we?" she wondered.

"Very ready."

"Remember what you said last night."

He looked up from the pistol again and met her eyes. "What?"

"That maybe he's not just an ordinary man, that he might have hitchhiked back with you from . . . somewhere else."

"I thought you dismissed that theory."

"I did. I can't believe it. But do you? Really?"

Instead of answering, he resumed cleaning the Browning.

She said, "If you believe it, even half believe it, put any credence in it at all—then what good is a gun?"

He didn't reply.

"How can bullets stop an evil spirit?" she pressed, feeling as if her memory of waking up and taking Regina to school was just part of a continuing dream, as if she was not caught in a real-life dilemma but in a nightmare. "How can something from beyond the grave be stopped with just a gun?"

"It's all I have," he said.

Like many doctors, Jonas Nyebern did not maintain office hours or perform surgery on Wednesday. However, he never spent the afternoon golfing, sailing, or playing cards at the country club. He used Wednesdays to catch up on paperwork, or to write research papers and case studies related to the Resuscitation Medicine Project at Orange County General.

That first Wednesday in May, he planned to spend eight or ten busy hours in the study of his house on Spyglass Hill, where he had lived for almost two years, since the loss of his family. He hoped to finish writing a paper that he was going to deliver at a conference in San Francisco on the eighth of May.

The big windows in the teak-paneled room looked out on Corona Del Mar and Newport Beach below. Across twenty-six miles of gray water veined with green and blue, the dark palisades of Santa Catalina Island rose against the sky, but they were unable to make the vast Pacific Ocean seem any less immense or less humbling than if they had not been there.

He did not bother to draw the drapes because the panorama never distracted him. He had bought the property because he had hoped that the luxuries of the house and the magnificence of the view would make life seem beautiful and worth living in spite of great tragedy. But only his work had managed to do that for him, and so he always went directly to it with no more than a glance out of the windows.

That morning, he could not concentrate on the white words against the blue background on his computer screen. His thoughts were not pulled toward Pacific vistas, however, but toward his son, Jeremy.

On that overcast spring day two years ago, when he had come home to find Marion and Stephanie stabbed so often and so brutally that they were beyond revival, when he had found an unconscious Jeremy impaled on the vise-held knife in the garage and rapidly bleeding to death, Jonas had not blamed an unknown madman or burglars caught by surprise in the act. He had known at once that the murderer was the teenage boy slumped against the workbench with his life drizzling onto the concrete floor. Something had been wrong with Jeremy—*missing* in him—all his life, a difference that had become more marked and frightening as the years passed, though Jonas had tried for so long to convince himself the boy's attitudes and actions were manifestations of ordinary rebelliousness. But the madness of Jonas's father, having skipped one generation, had appeared again in Jeremy's corrupted genes.

The boy survived the extraction of the knife and the frantic ambulance ride to Orange County General, which was only minutes away. But he died on the stretcher as they were wheeling him along a hospital corridor.

Jonas had recently convinced the hospital to establish a special resuscitation team. Instead of using the bypass machine to warm the dead boy's blood, they employed it to recirculate *cooled* blood into his body, hastening to lower his body temperature drastically to delay cell deterioration and brain damage until surgery could be performed. The air conditioner was set all the way down at fifty, bags of crushed ice were packed along the sides of the patient, and Jonas personally opened the knife wound to search for—and re-pair—the damage that would foil reanimation.

He might have known at the time why he wanted so desperately to save Jeremy, but afterwards he was never able to understand his motivations fully, clearly.

Because he was my son, Jonas sometimes thought, and was therefore my responsibility.

But what parental responsibility did he owe to the slaughterer of his daughter and wife?

I saved him to ask him *why,* to pry from him an explanation, Jonas told himself at other times.

But he knew there was no answer that would make sense. Nei-ther philosophers nor psychologists—not even the murderers themselves—had ever, in all of history, been able to provide an adequate explanation for a single act of monstrous sociopathic violence.

The only cogent answer, really, was that the human species was imperfect, stained, and carried within itself the seeds of its own destruction. The Church would call it the legacy of the Serpent, dating back to the Garden and the Fall. Scientists would refer to the mysteries of genetics, biochemistry, the fundamental actions of nucleotides. Maybe they were both talking about the same stain, merely describing it in different terms. To Jonas it seemed that this answer, whether provided by scientists or theologians, was always unsatisfying in precisely the same way and to the same degree, for it suggested no solution, prescribed no preventative. Except faith in God or in the potential of science.

Regardless of his reasons for taking the action he did, Jonas

had saved Jeremy. The boy had been dead for thirty-one minutes, not an absolute record even in those days, because the
young girl in Utah had already been reanimated after being in
the arms of Death for sixty-six minutes. But she'd been severely
hypothermic, while Jeremy had died warm, which made the feat
a record of one kind, anyway. Actually, revival after thirty-one
minutes of warm death was as miraculous as revival after eighty
minutes of cold death. His own son and Hatch Harrison were
Jonas's most amazing successes to date—if the first one qualified
as a success.

For ten months Jeremy lay in a coma, feeding intravenously but
able to breathe on his own and otherwise in need of no life-support
machines. Early in that period, he was moved from the hospital to
a high-quality nursing home.

During those months, Jonas could have petitioned a court to
have the boy removed from the intravenous feed. But Jeremy would
have perished from starvation or dehydration, and sometimes even
a comatose patient might suffer pain from such a cruel death,
depending on the depth of his stupor. Jonas was not prepared to be
the cause of that pain. More insidiously, on a level so deep that even
he did not realize it until much later, he suffered from the egotistic
notion that he still might extract from the boy—supposing the boy
ever woke—an explanation of sociopathic behavior that had eluded
all other seekers in the history of mankind. Perhaps he thought he
would have greater insight owing to his unique experience with the
madness of his father and his son, orphaned and wounded by the
first, widowed by the second. In any event he paid the nursing-home
bills. And every Sunday afternoon, he sat at his son's bedside,
staring at the pale, placid face in which he could see so much of
himself.

After ten months, Jeremy regained consciousness. Brain damage had left him aphasic, without the power to speak or read. He
had not known his name or how he had gotten to be where he was.
He reacted to his face in the mirror as if it were that of a stranger,
and he did not recognize his father. When the police came to
question him, he exhibited neither guilt nor comprehension. He
had awakened as a dullard, his intellectual capacity severely re-

duced from what it had been, his attention span short, easily confused.

With gestures, he complained vigorously of severe eye pain and sensitivity to bright light. An ophthalmological examination revealed a curious—indeed, inexplicable—degeneration of the irises. The contractile membrane seemed to have been partially eaten away. The sphincter pupillae—the muscle causing the iris to contract, thereby shrinking the pupil and admitting less light to the eye—had all but atrophied. Also, the dilator pupillae had shrunk, pulling the iris wide open. And the connection between the dilator muscle and oculomotor nerve was fused, leaving the eye virtually no ability to reduce the amount of incoming light. The condition was without precedent and degenerative in nature, making surgical correction impossible. The boy was provided with heavily tinted, wraparound sunglasses. Even then he preferred to pass daylight hours only in rooms where metal blinds or heavy drapes could close off the windows.

Incredibly, Jeremy became a favorite of the staff at the rehabilitation hospital to which he was transferred a few days after awakening at the nursing home. They were inclined to feel sorry for him because of his eye affliction, and because he was such a good-looking boy who had fallen so low. In addition, he now had the sweet temperament of a shy child, a result of his IQ loss, and there was no sign whatsoever of his former arrogance, cool calculation, and smouldering hostility.

For over four months he walked the halls, helped the nurses with simple tasks, struggled with a speech therapist to little effect, stared out the windows at the night for hours at a time, ate well enough to put flesh on his bones, and exercised in the gym during the evening with most of the lights off. His wasted body was rebuilt, and his straw-dry hair regained its luster.

Almost ten months ago, when Jonas was beginning to wonder where Jeremy could be placed when he was no longer able to benefit from physical or occupational therapy, the boy had disappeared. Although he had shown no previous inclination to roam beyond the grounds of the rehabilitation hospital, he walked out unnoticed one night, and never came back.

Jonas had assumed the police would be quick to track the boy. But they had been interested in him only as a missing person, not as a suspected murderer. If he had regained all of his faculties, they would have considered him both a threat and a fugitive from justice, but his continued—and apparently permanent—mental disabilities were a kind of immunity. Jeremy was no longer the same person that he had been when the crimes were committed; with his diminished intellectual capacity, inability to speak, and beguilingly simple personality, no jury would ever convict.

A missing-person investigation was no investigation at all. Police manpower had to be directed against immediate and serious crimes.

Though the cops believed that the boy had probably wandered away, fallen into the hands of the wrong people, and already been exploited and killed, Jonas knew his son was alive. And in his heart he knew that what was loose in the world was not a smiling dullard but a cunning, dangerous, and exceedingly sick young man.

They had all been deceived.

He could not prove that Jeremy's retardation was an act, but in his heart he knew that he had allowed himself to be fooled. He had accepted the new Jeremy because, when it came right down to it, he could not bear the anguish of having to confront the Jeremy who had killed Marion and Stephanie. The most damning proof of his own complicity in Jeremy's fraud was the fact that he had not requested a CAT scan to determine the precise nature of the brain damage. At the time he told himself the fact of the damage was the only thing that mattered, not its precise etiology, an incredible reaction for any physician but not so incredible for a father who was unwilling to come face-to-face with the monster inside his son.

And now the monster was set free. He had no proof, but he knew. Jeremy was out there somewhere. The old Jeremy.

For ten months, through a series of three detective agencies, he had sought his son, because he shared in the moral, though not the legal, responsibility for any crimes the boy committed. The first two agencies had gotten nowhere, eventually concluding that their inability to pick up a trail meant no trail existed. The boy, they reported, was most likely dead.

The third, Morton Redlow, was a one-man shop. Though not as glitzy as the bigger agencies, Redlow possessed a bulldog determination that encouraged Jonas to believe progress would be made. And last week, Redlow had hinted that he was onto something, that he would have concrete news by the weekend.

The detective had not been heard from since. He had failed to respond to messages left on his phone machine.

Now, turning away from his computer and the conference paper he was unable to work on, Jonas picked up the telephone and tried the detective again. He got the recording. But he could no longer leave his name and number, because the incoming tape on Redlow's machine was already full of messages. It cut him off.

Jonas had a bad feeling about the detective.

He put down the phone, got up from the desk, and went to the window. His spirits were so low, he doubted they could be lifted any more by anything as simple as a magnificent view, but he was willing to try. Each new day was filled with so much more dread than the day before it, he needed all the help he could get just to be able to sleep at night and rise in the morning.

Reflections of the morning sun rippled in silver filaments through the incoming waves, as if the sea were a great piece of rippling blue-gray fabric with interwoven metallic threads.

He told himself that Redlow was only a few days late with his report, less than a week, nothing to be worried about. The failure to return answering-machine messages might only mean the detective was ill or preoccupied with a personal crisis.

But he knew. Redlow had found Jeremy and, in spite of every warning from Jonas, had underestimated the boy.

A yacht with white sails was making its way south along the coast. Large white birds kited in the sky behind the ship, diving into the sea and out again, no doubt snaring fish with each plunge. Graceful and free, the birds were a beautiful sight, though not to the fish, of course. Not to the fish.

Lindsey went to her studio between the master bedroom and the room beside Regina's. She moved her high stool from the easel to the drawing board, opened her sketch pad, and started to plan her next painting.

She felt that it was important to focus on her work, not only because the making of art could soothe the soul as surely as the appreciation of it, but because sticking to everyday routine was the only way she could try to push back the forces of irrationality that seemed to be surging like black floodwaters into their lives. Nothing could really go too far wrong—could it?—if she just kept painting, drinking her usual black coffee, eating three meals a day, washing dishes when they needed washed, brushing her teeth at night, showering and rolling on her deodorant in the morning. How could some homicidal creature from Beyond intrude into an *orderly* life? Surely ghouls and ghosts, goblins and monsters, had no power over those who were properly groomed, deodorized, fluoridated, dressed, fed, employed, and motivated.

That was what she wanted to believe. But when she tried to sketch, she couldn't quiet the tremors in her hands.

Honell was dead.

Cooper was dead.

She kept looking at the window, expecting to see that the spider had returned. But there was no scurrying black form or the lacework of a new web. Just glass. Treetops and blue sky beyond.

After a while Hatch stopped in. He hugged her from behind, and kissed her cheek.

But he was in a solemn rather than romantic mood. He had one of the Brownings with him. He put the pistol on the top of her supply cabinet. "Keep this with you if you leave the room. He's not going to come around during the day. I know that. I feel it. Like he's a vampire or something, for God's sake. But it still doesn't hurt to be careful, especially when you're here alone."

She was dubious, but she said, "All right."

"I'm going out for a while. Do a little shopping."

"For what?" She turned on her stool, facing him more directly.

"We don't have enough ammunition for the guns."

"Both have full clips."

"Besides, I want to get a shotgun."

"Hatch! Even if he comes, and he probably won't, it's not going to be a war. A man breaks into your house, it's a matter of a shot or two, not a pitched battle."

Standing before her, he was stone-faced and adamant. "The right shotgun is the best of all home-defensive weapons. You don't have to be a good shot. The spread gets him. I know just which one I want. It's a short-barreled, pistol-grip with—"

She put one hand flat against his chest in a "stop" gesture. "You're scaring the crap out of me."

"Good. If we're scared, we're likely to be more alert, less careless."

"If you really think there's danger, then we shouldn't have Regina here."

"We can't send her back to St. Thomas's," he said at once, as if he had already considered that.

"Only until this is resolved."

"No." He shook his head. "Regina's too sensitive, you know that, too fragile, too quick to interpret everything as rejection. We might not be able to make her understand—and then she might not give us a second chance."

"I'm sure she—"

"Besides, we'd have to tell the orphanage something. If we concocted some lie—and I can't imagine what it would be—they'd know we were flimflamming them. They'd wonder why. Pretty soon they'd start second-guessing their approval of us. And if we told them the truth, started jabbering about psychic visions and telepathic bonds with psycho killers, they'd write us off as a couple of nuts, never give her back to us."

He *had* thought it out.

Lindsey knew what he said was true.

He kissed her lightly again. "I'll be back in an hour. Two at most."

When he had gone, she stared at the gun for a while.

Then she turned angrily away from it and picked up her pencil. She tore off a page from the big drawing tablet. The new page was blank. White and clean. It stayed that way.

Nervously chewing her lip, she looked at the window. No web. No spider. Just the glass pane. Treetops and blue skies beyond.

She had never realized until now that a pristine blue sky could be ominous.

The two screened vents in the garage attic were provided for ventilation. The overhanging roof and the density of the screen mesh did not allow much penetration by the sun, but some wan light entered with the vague currents of cool morning air.

Vassago was untroubled by the light, in part because his nest was formed by piles of boxes and furniture that spared him a direct view of the vents. The air smelled of dry wood, aging cardboard.

He was having difficulty getting to sleep, so he tried to relax by imagining what a fine fire might be fueled by the contents of the garage attic. His rich imagination made it easy to envision sheets of red flames, spirals of orange and yellow, and the sharp pop of sap bubbles exploding in burning rafters. Cardboard and packing paper and combustible memorabilia disappeared in silent rising curtains of smoke, with a papery crackling like the manic applause of millions in some dark and distant theater. Though the conflagration was in his mind, he had to squint his eyes against the phantom light.

Yet the fantasy of fire did not entertain him—perhaps because the attic would be filled merely with burning *things,* mere lifeless objects. Where was the fun in that?

Eighteen had burned to death—or been trampled—in the Haunted House on the night that Tod Ledderbeck had perished in the cavern of the Millipede. *There* had been a fire.

He had escaped all suspicion in the rocket jockey's death and the disaster at the Haunted House, but he'd been shaken by the repercussions of his night of games. The deaths at Fantasy World were at the top of the news for at least two weeks, and were the primary topic of conversation around school for maybe a month. The park closed temporarily, reopened to poor business, closed again for refurbishing, reopened to continued low attendance, and eventually succumbed two years later to all of the bad publicity and to a welter of lawsuits. A few thousand people lost their jobs. And Mrs. Ledderbeck had a nervous breakdown, though Jeremy figured it was part of her act, pretending she had actually loved Tod, the same crappy hypocrisy he saw in everyone.

But other, more personal repercussions were what shook Jeremy. In the immediate aftermath, toward morning of the long sleepless night that followed his adventures at Fantasy World, he realized he had been out of control. Not when he killed Tod. He knew that was right and good, a Master of the Game proving his mastery. But from the moment he had tipped Tod out of the Millipede, he had been drunk on power, banging around the park in a state of mind similar to what he imagined he'd have been like after chugging a six-pack or two. He had been swacked, plastered, crocked, totally wasted, polluted, stinko with power, for he had taken unto himself the role of Death and become the one whom all men feared. The experience was not only inebriating: it was addictive; he wanted to repeat it the next day, and the day after that, and every day for the rest of his life. He wanted to set someone afire again, and he wanted to know what it felt like to take a life with a sharp blade, with a gun, with a hammer, with his bare hands. That night he had achieved an early puberty, erect with fantasies of death, orgasmic at the contemplation of murders yet to be committed. Shocked by that first sexual spasm and the fluid that escaped him, he finally understood, toward dawn, that a Master of the Game not only had to be able to kill without fear but had to *control* the powerful desire to kill again that was generated by killing once.

Getting away with murder proved his superiority to all the other players, but he could not continue to get away with it if he were out of control, berserk, like one of those guys you saw on the news who opened up with a semiautomatic weapon on a crowd at a shopping mall. That was not a Master. That was a fool and a loser. A Master must pick and choose, select his targets with great care, and eliminate them with style.

Now, lying in the garage attic on a pile of folded dropcloths, he thought that a Master must be like a spider. Choose his killing ground. Weave his web. Settle down, pull in his long legs, make a small and insignificant thing of himself . . . and wait.

Plenty of spiders shared the attic with him. Even in the gloom they were visible to his exquisitely sensitive eyes. Some of them were admirably industrious. Others were alive but as cunningly still as death. He felt an affinity for them. His little brothers.

The gun shop was a fortress. A sign near the front door warned that the premises were guarded by multi-system silent alarms and also, at night, by attack dogs. Steel bars were welded over the windows. Hatch noticed the door was at least three inches thick, wood but probably with a steel core, and that the three hinges on the inside appeared to have been designed for use on a bathysphere to withstand thousands of tons of pressure deep under the sea. Though much weapons-associated merchandise was on open shelves, the rifles, shotguns, and handguns were in locked glass cases or securely chained in open wall racks. Video cameras had been installed near the ceiling in each of the four corners of the long main room, all behind thick sheets of bulletproof glass.

The shop was better protected than a bank. Hatch wondered if he was living in a time when weaponry had more appeal to thieves than did money itself.

The four clerks were pleasant men with easy camaraderie among themselves and a folksy manner with customers. They wore straight-hemmed shirts outside their pants. Maybe they prized comfort. Or maybe each was carrying a handgun in a holster underneath his shirt, tucked into in the small of his back.

Hatch bought a Mossberg short-barreled, pistol-grip, pump-action 12-gauge shotgun.

"The perfect weapon for home-defense," the clerk told him. "You have this, you don't really need anything else."

Hatch supposed that he should be grateful he was living in an age when the government promised to protect and defend its citizens from threats even so small as radon in the cellar and the ultimate environmental consequences of the extinction of the one-eyed, blue-tailed gnat. In a less civilized era—say the turn of the century—he no doubt would have required an armory containing hundreds of weapons, a ton of explosives, and a chain-mail vest to wear when answering the door.

He decided irony was a bitter form of humor and not to his taste. At least not in his current mood.

He filled out the requisite federal and state forms, paid with a credit card, and left with the Mossberg, a cleaning kit, and boxes of ammunition for the Brownings as well as the shotgun. Behind him, the shop door fell shut with a heavy thud, as if he were exiting a vault.

After putting his purchases in the trunk of the Mitsubishi, he got behind the wheel, started the engine—and froze with his hand on the gearshift. Beyond the windshield, the small parking lot had vanished. The gun shop was no longer there.

As if a mighty sorcerer had cast an evil spell, the sunny day had disappeared. Hatch was in a long, eerily lighted tunnel. He glanced out the side windows, turned to check the back, but the illusion or hallucination—whatever the hell it might be—enwrapped him, as realistic in its detail as the parking lot had been.

When he faced forward, he was confronted by a long slope in the center of which was a narrow-gauge railroad track. Suddenly the car began to move as if it were a train pulling up that hill.

Hatch jammed his foot down on the brake pedal. No effect.

He closed his eyes, counted to ten, listening to his heart pound harder by the second and unsuccessfully willing himself to relax. When he opened his eyes, the tunnel was still there.

He switched the car engine off. He heard it die. The car continued to move.

The silence that followed the cessation of the engine noise was brief. A new sound arose: *clackety-clack, clackety-clack, clackety-clack.*

An inhuman shriek erupted to the left, and from the corner of his eye, Hatch detected threatening movement. He snapped his head toward it. To his astonishment he saw an utterly alien figure, a pale white slug as big as a man. It reared up and shrieked at him through a round mouth full of teeth that whirled like the sharp blades in a garbage disposal. An identical beast shrieked from a niche in the tunnel wall to his right, and more of them ahead, and beyond them other monsters of other forms, gibbering, hooting, snarling, squealing as he passed them.

In spite of his disorientation and terror, he realized that the grotesqueries along the tunnel walls were mechanical beasts, not real. And as that understanding sank in, he finally recognized the familiar sound. *Clackety-clack, clackety-clack.* He was on an indoor roller coaster, yet in his car, moving with decreasing speed toward the high point, with a precipitous fall ahead.

He did not argue with himself that this couldn't be happening, did not try to shake himself awake or back to his senses. He was past denial. He understood that he did not have to *believe* in this experience to insure its continuation; it would progress whether he believed in it or not, so he might as well grit his teeth and get through it.

Being past denial didn't mean, however, that he was past fear. He was scared shitless.

Briefly he considered opening the car door and getting out. Maybe that would break the spell. But he didn't try it because he was afraid that when he stepped out he would not be in the parking lot in front of the gun shop but in the tunnel, and that the car would continue uphill without him. Losing contact with his little red Mitsubishi might be like slamming a door on reality, consigning himself forever to the vision, with no way out, no way back.

The car passed the last mechanical monster. It reached the crest of the inclined track. Pushed through a pair of swinging doors. Into darkness. The doors fell shut behind. The car crept forward.

Forward. Forward. Abruptly it dropped as if into a bottomless pit.

Hatch cried out, and with his cry the darkness vanished. The sunny spring day made a welcome reappearance. The parking lot. The gun shop.

His hands were locked so tightly around the steering wheel that they ached.

Throughout the morning, Vassago was awake more than asleep. But when he dozed, he was back in the Millipede again, on that night of glory.

In the days and weeks following the deaths at Fantasy World, he had without doubt proved himself a Master by exerting iron control over his compulsive desire to kill. Merely the memory of having killed was sufficient to release the periodic pressure that built in him. Hundreds of times, he relived the sensuous details of each death, temporarily quenching his hot need. And the knowledge that he would kill again, any time he could do so without arousing suspicion, was an additional restraint on self-indulgence.

He did not kill anyone else for two years. Then, when he was fourteen, he drowned another boy at summer camp. The kid was smaller and weaker, but he put up a good fight. When he was found floating facedown in the pond, it was the talk of the camp for the rest of that month. Water could be as thrilling as fire.

When he was sixteen and had a driver's license, he wasted two transients, both hitchhikers, one in October, the other a couple of days before Thanksgiving. The guy in November was just a college kid going home for the holiday. But the other one was something else, a predator who thought he had stumbled across a foolish and naive high-school boy who would provide him with some thrills of his own. Jeremy had used knives on both of them.

At seventeen, when he discovered Satanism, he couldn't read enough about it, surprised to find that his secret philosophy had been codified and embraced by clandestine cults. Oh, there were relatively benign forms, propagated by gutless wimps who were just looking for a way to play at wickedness, an excuse for hedonism. But real believers existed, as well, committed to the truth that God had failed to create people in His image, that the bulk of humanity was equivalent to a herd of cattle, that selfishness was admirable, that pleasure was the only worthwhile goal, and that the greatest pleasure was the brutal exercise of power over others.

The ultimate expression of power, one privately published volume had assured him, was to destroy those who had spawned you, thereby breaking the bonds of family "love." The book said that one must as violently as possible reject the whole hypocrisy of rules, laws, and noble sentiments by which other men pretended to live. Taking that advice to heart was what had earned him a place in Hell—from which his father had pulled him back.

But he would soon be there again. A few more deaths, two in particular, would earn him repatriation to the land of darkness and the damned.

The attic grew warmer as the day progressed.

A few fat flies buzzed back and forth through his shadowy retreat, and some of them settled down forever on one or another of the alluring but sticky webs that spanned the junctions of the rafters. *Then* the spiders moved.

In the warm, closed space, Vassago's dozing became a deeper sleep with more intense dreams. Fire and water, blade and bullet.

Crouching at the corner of the garage, Hatch reached between two azaleas and flipped open the cover on the landscape-lighting control box. He adjusted the timer to prevent the pathway and shrubbery lights from blinking off at midnight. Now they would stay on until sunrise.

He closed the metal box, stood, and looked around at the quiet, well-groomed street. All was harmony. Every house had a tile roof in shades of tan and sand and peach, not the more stark orange-red tiles of many older California homes. The stucco walls were cream-colored or within a narrow range of coordinated pastels specified by the "Covenants, Conventions & Restrictions" that came with the grant deed and mortgage. Lawns were green and recently mown, flower beds were well tended, and trees were neatly trimmed. It was difficult to believe that unspeakable violence could ever intrude from the outer world into such an orderly, upwardly mobile community, and *inconceivable* that anything supernatural could stalk those streets. The neighborhood's normalcy was so solid that it seemed like encircling stone ramparts crowned with battlements.

Not for the first time, he thought that Lindsey and Regina might be perfectly safe there—but for him. If madness had invaded this fortress of normalcy, he had opened the door to it. Maybe he was mad himself; maybe his weird experiences were nothing as grand as psychic visions, merely the hallucinations of an insane mind. He would bet everything he owned on his sanity—though he also could not dismiss the slim possibility that he would lose the bet. In any event, whether or not he was insane, he was the conduit for whatever violence might rain down on them, and perhaps they would be better off if they went away for the duration, put some distance between themselves and him until this crazy business was settled.

Sending them away seemed wise and responsible—except that a small voice deep inside him spoke against that option. He had a terrible hunch—or was it more than a hunch?—that the killer would not be coming after him but after Lindsey and Regina. If they went away somewhere, just Lindsey and the girl, that homicidal monster would follow them, leaving Hatch to wait alone for a showdown that would never happen.

All right, then they had to stick together. Like a family. Rise or fall as one.

Before leaving to pick Regina up at school, he slowly circled the house, looking for lapses in their defenses. The only one he found was an unlocked window at the back of the garage. The latch had been loose for a long time, and he had been meaning to fix it. He got some tools from one of the garage cabinets and worked on the mechanism until the bolt seated securely in the catch.

As he'd told Lindsey earlier, he didn't think the man in his visions would come as soon as tonight, probably not even this week, maybe not for a month or longer, but he *would* come eventually. Even if that unwelcome visit was days or weeks away, it felt good to be prepared.

2

Vassago woke.

Without opening his eyes, he knew that night was coming. He could feel the oppressive sun rolling off the world and slipping over the edge of the horizon. When he did open his eyes, the last fading light coming through the attic vents confirmed that the waters of the night were on the rise.

Hatch found that it was not exactly easy to conduct a normal domestic life while waiting to be stricken by a terrifying, maybe even bloody, vision so powerful it would blank out reality for its duration. It was hard to sit in your pleasant dining room, smile, enjoy the pasta and Parmesan bread, make with the light banter, and tease a giggle from the young lady with the solemn gray eyes—when you kept thinking of the loaded shotgun secreted in the corner behind the Coromandel screen or the handgun in the adjacent kitchen atop the refrigerator, above the line of sight of a small girl's eyes.

He wondered how the man in black would enter when he came. At night, for one thing. He only came out at night. They didn't have to worry about him going after Regina at school. But would he boldly ring the bell or knock smartly on the door, while they were still up and around with all the lights on, hoping to catch them off-guard at a civilized hour when they might assume it was a neighbor come to call? Or would he wait until they were asleep, lights off, and try to slip through their defenses to take them unaware?

Hatch wished they had an alarm system, as they did at the store. When they sold the old house and moved into the new place following Jimmy's death, they should have called Brinks right away. Valuable antiques graced every room. But for the longest time after Jimmy had been taken from them, it hadn't seemed to matter if anything—or everything—else was taken as well.

Throughout dinner, Lindsey was a trooper. She ate a mound of rigatoni as if she had an appetite, which was something Hatch could not manage, and she filled his frequent worried silences with natural-sounding patter, doing her best to preserve the feeling of an ordinary night at home.

Regina was sufficiently observant to know something was wrong. And though she was tough enough to handle nearly any-thing, she was also infected with seemingly chronic self-doubt that would probably lead her to interpret their uneasiness as dissatis-faction with her.

Earlier Hatch and Lindsey had discussed what they might be able to tell the girl about the situation they faced, without alarm-ing her more than was necessary. The answer seemed to be: noth-ing. She had been with them only two days. She didn't know them well enough to have this crazy stuff thrown at her. She'd hear about Hatch's bad dreams, his waking hallucinations, the heat-browned magazine, the murders, all of it, and figure she had been entrusted to a couple of lunatics.

Anyway the kid didn't really need to be warned at this stage. They could look out for her; it was what they were sworn to do.

Hatch found it difficult to believe that just three days ago the problem of his repetitive nightmares had not seemed significant enough to delay a trial adoption. But Honell and Cooper had not been dead then, and supernatural forces seemed only the material of popcorn movies and *National Enquirer* stories.

Halfway through dinner he heard a noise in the kitchen. A click and scrape. Lindsey and Regina were engaged in an intense con-versation about whether Nancy Drew, girl detective of countless books, was a "dorkette," which was Regina's view, or whether she was a smart and savvy girl for her times but just old-fashioned when you looked at her from a more modern viewpoint. Either they were too engrossed in their debate to hear the noise in the kitchen—or there had been no noise, and he had imagined it.

"Excuse me," he said, getting up from the table, "I'll be right back."

He pushed through the swinging door into the large kitchen and looked around suspiciously. The only movement in the deserted room was a faint ribbon of steam still unraveling from the crack between the tilted lid and the pot of hot spaghetti sauce that stood on a ceramic pad on the counter beside the stove.

Something thumped softly in the L-shaped family room, which opened off the kitchen. He could see part of that room from where he stood but not all of it. He stepped silently across the kitchen and through the archway, taking the Browning 9mm off the top of the refrigerator as he went.

The family room was also deserted. But he was sure that he had not imagined that second noise. He stood for a moment, looking around in bafflement.

His skin prickled, and he whirled toward the short hallway that led from the family room to the foyer inside the front door. Nothing. He was alone. So why did he feel as if someone was holding an ice cube against the back of his neck?

He moved cautiously into the hallway until he came to the coat closet. The door was closed. Directly across the hall was the powder room. That door was also shut. He felt drawn toward the foyer, and his inclination was to trust his hunch and move on, but he didn't want to put either of those closed doors at his back.

When he jerked open the closet door, he saw at once that no one was in there. He felt stupid with the gun thrust out in front of him and pointing at nothing but a couple of coats on hangers, playing a movie cop or something. Better hope it wasn't the final reel. Sometimes, when the story required it, they killed off the good guy in the end.

He checked the powder room, found it also empty, and continued into the foyer. The uncanny feeling was still with him but not as strong as before. The foyer was deserted. He glanced at the stairs, but no one was on them.

He looked in the living room. No one. He could see a corner of the dining-room table through the archway at the end of the living room. Although he could hear Lindsey and Regina still discussing Nancy Drew, he couldn't see them.

He checked the den, which was also off the entrance foyer. And the closet in the den. And the kneehole space under the desk.

Back in the foyer, he tried the front door. It was locked, as it should have been.

No good. If he was this jumpy already, what in the name of God was he going to be like in another day or week? Lindsey would have to pry him off the ceiling just to give him his morning coffee each day.

Nevertheless, reversing the route he had just taken through the house, he stopped in the family room to try the sliding glass doors that served the patio and backyard. They were locked, with the burglar-foiling bar inserted properly in the floor track.

In the kitchen once more, he tried the door to the garage. It was unlocked, and again he felt as if spiders were crawling on his scalp.

He eased the door open. The garage was dark. He fumbled for the switch, clicked the lights on. Banks of big fluorescent tubes dropped a flood of harsh light straight down the width and breadth of the room, virtually eliminating shadows, revealing nothing out of the ordinary.

Stepping over the threshold, he let the door ease shut behind him. He cautiously walked the length of the room with the large roll-up sectional doors on his right, the backs of the two cars on his left. The middle stall was empty.

His rubber-soled Rockports made no sound. He expected to surprise someone crouched along the far side of one of the cars, but no one was sheltering behind either of them.

At the end of the garage, when he was past the Chevy, he abruptly dropped to the floor and looked under the car. He could see all the way across the room, beneath the Mitsubishi, as well. No one was hiding under either vehicle. As best as he could tell, considering that the tires provided blind spots, no one appeared to be circling the cars to keep out of his sight.

He got up and turned to a regular door in the end wall. It served the side yard and had a thumb-turn dead-bolt lock, which was engaged. No one could get in that way.

Returning to the kitchen door, he stayed to the back of the garage. He tried only the two storage cabinets that had tall doors and were large enough to provide a hiding place for a grown man. Neither was occupied.

He checked the window latch he had repaired earlier in the day. It was secure, the bolt seated snugly in the vertically mounted hasp.

Again, he felt foolish. Like a grown man engaged in a boy's game, fancying himself a movie hero.

How fast would he have reacted if someone *had* been hiding in one of those tall cabinets and had flung himself outward when the door opened? Or what if he had dropped to the floor to look under the Chevy, and *right there* had been the man in black, face-to-face with him, inches away?

He was glad he hadn't been required to learn the answer to either of those unnerving questions. But at least, having asked them, he no longer felt foolish, because indeed the man in black might have been there.

Sooner or later the bastard *would* be there. Hatch was no less certain than ever about the inevitability of a confrontation. Call it a hunch, call it a premonition, call it Christmas turkey if you liked, but he knew that he could trust the small warning voice within him.

As he was passing the front of the Mitsubishi, he saw what appeared to be a dent on the hood. He stopped, sure that it must be a trick of light, the shadow of the pull-cord that hung from the ceiling trap. It was directly over the hood. He swatted the dangling cord, but the mark on the car didn't leap and dance as it would have done if it had been just the cord shadow.

Leaning over the grille, he touched the smooth sheet metal and felt the depression, shallow but as big as his hand. He sighed heavily. The car was still new, and already it needed a session in the body shop. Take a brand new car to the mall, and an hour after it's out of the showroom, some damn fool would park beside it and slam open his door into yours. It never failed.

He hadn't noticed the dent either when he had come home this afternoon from the gun shop or when he'd brought Regina back from school. Maybe it wasn't as visible from inside the car, behind the steering wheel; maybe you had to be out in front, looking at it from the right angle. It sure seemed big enough to be seen from anywhere.

He was trying to figure how it could have happened—somebody must have been passing by and dropped something on the car—when he saw the footprint. It was in a gossamer coating of beige dust on the red paint, the sole and part of the heel of a walking shoe probably not much different from the ones he was wearing. Someone had stood on or walked across the hood of the Mitsubishi.

It must have happened outside St. Thomas's School, because it was the kind of thing a kid might do, showing off to friends. Having allowed too much time for bad traffic, Hatch had arrived at St. Tom's twenty minutes before classes let out. Rather than wait in the car, he'd gone for a walk to work off some excess nervous energy. Probably, some wiseass and his buddies from the adjacent high school—the footprint was too big to belong to a smaller kid—sneaked out a little ahead of the final bell, and were showing off for each other as they raced away from the school, maybe leaping and clambering over obstacles instead of going around them, as if they'd escaped from a prison with the bloodhounds close on their—

"Hatch?"

Startled out of his train of thought just when it seemed to be leading somewhere, he spun around toward the voice as if it did not sound familiar to him, which of course it did.

Lindsey stood in the doorway between the garage and kitchen. She looked at the gun in his hand, met his eyes. "What's wrong?"

"Thought I heard something."

"And?"

"Nothing." She had startled him so much that he had forgotten the footprint and dent on the car hood. As he followed her into the kitchen, he said, "This door was open. I locked it earlier."

"Oh, Regina left one of her books in the car when she came home from school. She went out just before dinner to get it."

"You should have made sure she locked up."

"It's only the door to the garage," Lindsey said, heading toward the dining room.

He put a hand on her shoulder to stop her, turned her around. "It's a point of vulnerability," he said with perhaps more anxiety than such a minor breach of security warranted.

"Aren't the outer garage doors locked?"

"Yes, and this one should be locked, too."

"But as many times as we go back and forth from the kitchen"—they had a second refrigerator in the garage—"it's just convenient to leave the door unlocked. We've always left it un-locked."

"We don't any more," he said firmly.

They were face-to-face, and she studied him worriedly. He knew she thought he was walking a fine line between prudent precau-tions and a sort of quiet hysteria, even treading the wrong way over that line sometimes. On the other hand, *she* hadn't had the benefit of his nightmares and visions.

Perhaps the same thought crossed Lindsey's mind, for she nod-ded and said, "Okay. I'm sorry. You're right."

He leaned back into the garage and turned off the lights. He closed the door, engaged the deadbolt—and felt no safer, really.

She had started toward the dining room again. She glanced back as he followed her, indicating the pistol in his hand. "Going to bring that to the table?"

Deciding he had come down a little heavy on her, he shook his head and bugged his eyes out, trying to make a Christopher Lloyd face and lighten the moment: "I think some of my rigatoni are still alive. I don't like to eat them till they're dead."

"Well, you've got the shotgun behind the Coromandel screen for that," she reminded him.

"You're right!" He put the pistol on top of the refrigerator again. "And if that doesn't work, I can always take them out in the driveway and run them over with the car!"

She pushed open the swinging door, and Hatch followed her into the dining room.

Regina looked up and said, "Your food's getting cold."

Still making like Christopher Lloyd, Hatch said, "Then we'll get some sweaters and mittens for them!"

Regina giggled. Hatch *adored* the way she giggled.

After the dinner dishes were done, Regina went to her room to study. "Big history test tomorrow," she said.

Lindsey returned to her studio to try to get some work done. When she sat down at her drawing board, she saw the second Browning 9mm. It was still atop the low art-supply cabinet, where Hatch had put it earlier in the day.

She scowled at it. She didn't necessarily disapprove of guns themselves, but this one was more than merely a handgun. It was a symbol of their powerlessness in the face of the amorphous threat that hung over them. Keeping a gun ever within reach seemed an admission that they were desperate and couldn't control their own destiny. The sight of a snake coiled on the cabinet could not have carved a deeper scowl on her face.

She didn't want Regina walking in and seeing it.

She pulled open the first drawer of the cabinet and shoved aside some gum erasers and pencils to make room for the weapon. The Browning barely fit in that shallow space. Closing the drawer, she felt better.

During the long morning and afternoon, she had accomplished nothing. She had made lots of false starts with sketches that went nowhere. She was not even close to being ready to prepare a canvas.

Masonite, actually. She worked on Masonite, as did most artists these days, but she still thought of each rectangle as a canvas, as though she were the reincarnation of an artist from another age and could not shake her old way of thinking. Also, she painted in acrylics rather than oils. Masonite did not deteriorate over time the way canvas did, and acrylics retained their true colors far better than oil-based paints.

Of course if she didn't *do* something soon, it wouldn't matter if she used acrylics or cat's piss. She couldn't call herself an artist in the first place if she couldn't come up with an idea that excited her and a composition that did the idea justice. Picking up a thick charcoal pencil, she leaned over the sketch pad that was open on the drawing board in front of her. She tried to knock inspiration off its perch and get its lazy butt flying again.

After no more than a minute, her gaze floated off the page, up and up, until she was staring at the window. No interesting sight waited to distract her tonight, no treetops gracefully swaying in a breeze or even a patch of cerulean sky. The night beyond the pane was featureless.

The black backdrop transformed the window glass into a mirror in which she saw herself looking over the top of the drawing board. Because it was not a true mirror, her reflection was transparent, ghostly, as if she had died and come back to haunt the last place she had ever known on earth.

That was an unsettling thought, so she returned her attention to the blank page of the drawing tablet in front of her.

After Lindsey and Regina went upstairs, Hatch walked from room to room on the ground floor, checking windows and doors to be sure they were secured. He had inspected the locks before. Doing it again was pointless. He did it anyway.

When he reached the pair of sliding glass doors in the family room, he switched on the outdoor patio lights to augment the low landscape lighting. The backyard was now bright enough for him to see most of it—although someone could have been crouched among the shrubs along the rear fence. He stood at the doors, waiting for one of the shadows along the perimeter of the property to shift.

Maybe he was wrong. Maybe the guy would never come after them. In which case, in a month or two or three, Hatch would most likely be certifiably mad from the tension of waiting. He almost thought it would be better if the creep came now and got it over with.

He moved on to the breakfast nook and examined those windows. They were still locked.

Regina returned to her bedroom and prepared her corner desk for homework. She put her books to one side of the blotter, pens and felt-tip Hi-Liter to the other side, and her notebook in the middle, everything squared-up and neat.

As she got her desk set up, she worried about the Harrisons. Something was wrong with them.

Well, not wrong in the sense that they were thieves or enemy spies or counterfeiters or murderers or child-eating cannibals. For a while she'd had an idea for a novel in which this absolute screwup girl is adopted by a couple who *are* child-eating cannibals, and she finds a pile of child bones in the basement, and a recipe file in the kitchen with cards that say things like LITTLE GIRL KABOB and GIRL SOUP, with instructions like "INGREDIENTS: one tender young girl, unsalted; one onion, chopped; one pound carrots, diced. . . ." In the story the girl goes to the authorities, but they will not believe her because she's widely known as a screwup and a teller of tall tales. Well, that was fiction, and this was real life, and the Harrisons seemed perfectly happy eating pizza and pasta and hamburgers.

She clicked on the fluorescent desk lamp.

Though there was nothing wrong with the Harrisons themselves, they definitely had problems, because they were tense and trying hard to hide it. Maybe they weren't able to make their mortgage payments, and the bank was going to take the house, and all three of them would have to move back into her old room at the orphanage. Maybe they had discovered that Mrs. Harrison had a sister she'd never heard about before, an evil twin like all those people on television shows were always discovering they had. Or maybe they owed money to the Mafia and couldn't pay it and were going to get their legs broken.

Regina withdrew a dictionary from the bookshelves and put it on the desk.

If they had a bad problem, Regina hoped it was the Mafia thing, because she could handle that pretty well. The Harrisons' legs would get better eventually, and they'd learn an important lesson about not borrowing money from loansharks. Meanwhile, she could take care of them, make sure they got their medicine, check their temperatures now and then, bring them dishes of ice cream with a little animal cookie stuck in the top of each one, and even empty their bedpans (Gross!) if it came to that. She knew a lot about nursing, having been on the receiving end of so much of it at various times over the years. (Dear God, if their big problem is *me,* could I have a miracle here and get the problem changed to the Mafia, so they'll keep me and we'll be happy? In exchange for the miracle, I'd even be willing to have my legs broken, too. At least talk it over with the guys at the Mafia and see what they say.)

When the desk was fully prepared for homework, Regina decided that she needed to be dressed more comfortably in order to study. Having changed out of her parochial-school uniform when she had gotten home, she was wearing gray corduroy pants and a lime-green, long-sleeve cotton sweater. Pajamas and a robe were much better for studying. Besides, her leg brace was making her itch in a couple of places, and she wanted to take it off for the day.

When she slid open the mirrored closet door, she was face-to-face with a crouching man dressed all in black and wearing sunglasses.

3

On yet one more tour of the downstairs, Hatch decided to turn off the lamps and chandeliers as he went. With the landscape and exterior house lights all ablaze but the interior dark, he would be able to see a prowler without being seen himself.

He concluded the patrol in the unlighted den, which he had decided to make his primary guard station. Sitting at the big desk in the gloom, he could look through the double doors into the front foyer and cover the foot of the stairs to the second floor. If anyone tried to enter through a den window or the French doors to the rose garden, he would know at once. If the intruder breached their security in another room, Hatch would nail the guy when he tried to go upstairs, because the spill of second-floor hall light illuminated the steps. He couldn't be everywhere at once, and the den seemed to be the most strategic position.

He put both the shotgun and the handgun on top of the desk, within easy reach. He couldn't see them well without the lights on, but he could grab either of them in an instant if anything happened. He practiced a few times, sitting in his swivel chair and facing the foyer, then abruptly reaching out to grab the Browning, this time the Mossberg 12-gauge, Browning, Browning, Mossberg, Browning, Mossberg, Mossberg. Every time, maybe because his reactions were heightened by adrenaline, his right hand swooped through darkness and with precise accuracy came to rest upon the handgrip of the Browning or the stock of the Mossberg, whichever was wanted.

He took no satisfaction in his preparedness, because he knew he could not remain vigilant twenty-four hours a day, seven days a week. He had to sleep and eat. He had not gone to the shop today, and he could take off a few days more, but he couldn't leave everything to Glenda and Lew indefinitely; sooner or later he would have to go to work.

Realistically, even with breaks to eat and sleep, he would cease to be an effective watchman long before he needed to return to work. Sustaining a high degree of mental and physical alertness was a draining enterprise. In time he'd have to consider hiring a guard or two from a private security firm, and he didn't know how much that would cost. More important, he didn't know how reliable a hired guard would be.

He doubted he would ever have to make that decision, because the bastard was going to come soon, maybe tonight. On a primitive level, a vague impression of the man's intentions flowed to Hatch along whatever mystical bond they shared. It was like a child's words spoken into a tin can and conveyed along a string to another tin can, where they were reproduced as dim fuzzy sounds, most of the coherency lost due to the poor quality of the conductive material but the essential tone still perceptible. The current message on the psychic string could not be heard in any detail, but the primary meaning was clear: *Coming . . . I'm coming . . . I'm coming . . .*

Probably after midnight. Hatch sensed that their encounter would take place between that dead hour and dawn. It was now exactly 7:46 by his watch.

He withdrew his ring of car and house keys from his pocket, found the desk key that he had added earlier, opened the locked drawer, and took out the heat-darkened, smoke-scented issue of *Arts American,* letting the keys dangle in the lock. He held the magazine in both hands in the dark, hoping the feel of it would, like a talisman, amplify his magical vision and allow him to see precisely when, where, and how the killer would arrive.

Mingled odors of fire and destruction—some so bitterly pungent that they were nauseating, others merely ashy—rose from the crisp pages.

Vassago clicked off the fluorescent desk lamp. He crossed the girl's room to the door, where he also switched off the ceiling light.

He put his hand on the doorknob but hesitated, reluctant to leave the child behind him. She was so exquisite, so vital. He *knew* the moment he had pulled her into his arms that she was the caliber of acquisition that would complete his collection and win him the eternal reward he sought.

Stifling her cry and cutting off her breathing with one gloved hand, he had swept her into the closet and crushed her against him with his strong arms. He had held her so fiercely that she could barely squirm and couldn't kick against anything to draw attention to her plight.

When she had passed out in his arms, he had been almost in a swoon and had been overcome by the urge to kill her right there. In her closet. Among the soft piles of clothes that had fallen off the hangers above them. The scent of freshly laundered cotton and spray starch. The warm fragrance of wool. And girl. He wanted to wring her neck and feel her life energy pass through his powerful hands, into him, and through him to the land of the dead.

He had taken so long to shake off that overpowering desire that he almost *had* killed her. She fell silent and still. By the time he unclamped his hand from her nose and mouth, he thought he had smothered her. But when he put his ear to her parted lips, he could hear and feel faint exhalations. A hand against her chest rewarded him with the solid thud of her slow, strong heartbeat.

Now, looking back at the child, Vassago repressed the need to kill by promising himself that he would have satisfaction long before dawn. Meanwhile, he must be a Master. Exercise control.

Control.

He opened the door and studied the second-floor hallway beyond the girl's room. Deserted. A chandelier was aglow at the far end, at the head of the stairs, in front of the entrance to the master bedroom, producing too much light for his comfort if he had not had his sunglasses. He still needed to squint.

He must butcher neither the child nor the mother until he had both of them in the museum of the dead, where he had killed all the others who were part of his collection. He knew now why he had been drawn to Lindsey and Regina. Mother and daughter. Bitch and mini-bitch. To regain his place in Hell, he was expected to commit the same act that had won him damnation in the first place: the murder of a mother and her daughter. As his own mother and sister were not available to be killed again, Lindsey and Regina had been selected.

Standing in the open doorway, he listened to the house. It was silent.

He knew the artist was not the girl's birth mother. Earlier, when the Harrisons were in the dining room and he slipped into the house from the garage, he'd had time to poke around in Regina's room. He'd found mementoes with the orphanage name on them, for the most part cheaply printed drama programs handed out at holiday plays in which the girl had held minor roles. Nevertheless, he had been drawn to her and Lindsey, and his own master apparently judged them to be suitable sacrifices.

The house was so still that he would have to move as quietly as a cat. He could manage that.

He glanced back at the girl on the bed, able to see her better in the darkness than he could see most of the details of the too-bright hallway. She was still unconscious, one of her own scarves wadded in her mouth and another tied around her head to keep the gag in place. Strong lengths of cord, which he had untied from around storage boxes in the garage attic, tightly bound her wrists and ankles.

Control.

Leaving Regina's door open behind him, he eased along the hallway, staying close to the wall, where the plywood sub-flooring under the thick carpet was least likely to creak.

He knew the layout. He had cautiously explored the second floor while the Harrisons had been finishing dinner.

Beside the girl's room was a guest bedroom. It was dark now. He crept on toward Lindsey's studio.

Because the main hallway chandelier was directly ahead of him, his shadow fell in his wake, which was fortunate. Otherwise, if the woman happened to be looking toward the hall, she would have been warned of his approach.

He inched to the studio door and stopped.

Standing with his back flat to the wall, eyes straight ahead, he could see between the balusters under the handrail of the open staircase, to the foyer below. As far as he could tell, no lights were on downstairs.

He wondered where the husband had gone. The tall doors to the master bedroom were open, but no lights were on in there. He could hear small noises coming from within the woman's studio, so he figured she was at work. If the husband was with her, surely they would have exchanged a few words, at least, during the time Vassago had been making his way along the hall.

He hoped the husband had gone out on an errand. He had no particular need to kill the man. And any confrontation would be dangerous.

From his jacket pocket, he withdrew the supple leather sap, filled with lead shot, that he had appropriated last week from Morton Redlow, the detective. It was an extremely effective-looking blackjack. It felt good in his hand. In the pearl-gray Honda, two blocks away, a handgun was tucked under the driver's seat, and Vassago almost wished he had brought it. He had taken it from the antique dealer, Robert Loffman, in Laguna Beach a couple of hours before dawn that morning.

But he didn't want to shoot the woman and the girl. Even if he just wounded and disabled them, they might bleed to death before he got them back to his hideaway and down into the museum of death, to the altar where his offerings were arranged. And if he used a gun to remove the husband, he could risk only one shot, maybe two. Too much gunfire was bound to be heard by neighbors and the source located. In that quiet community, once gunfire was identified, cops would be crawling over the place in two minutes.

The sap was better. He hefted it in his right hand, getting the feel of it.

With great care, he leaned across the doorjamb. Tilted his head. Peeked into the studio.

She sat on the stool, her back to the door. He recognized her even from behind. His heart galloped almost as fast as when the girl had struggled and passed out in his arms. Lindsey was at the drawing board, charcoal pencil in her right hand. Busy, busy, busy. Pencil making a soft snaky hiss as it worked against the paper.

No matter how determined she was to keep her attention firmly on the problem of the blank sheet of drawing paper, Lindsey looked up repeatedly at the window. Her creative block crumbled only when she surrendered and began to *draw* the window. The uncurtained frame. Darkness beyond the glass. Her face like the countenance of a ghost engaged in a haunting. When she added the spider web in the upper right-hand corner, the concept jelled, and suddenly she became excited. She thought she might title it *The Web of Life and Death,* and use a surreal series of symbolic items to knit the theme into every corner of the canvas. Not canvas, Masonite. In fact, just paper now, only a sketch, but worth pursuing.

She repositioned the drawing tablet on the board, setting it higher. Now she could just raise her eyes slightly from the page to look over the top of the board at the window, and didn't have to keep raising and lowering her head.

More elements than just her face, the window, and the web would be required to give the painting depth and interest. As she worked she considered and rejected a score of additional images.

Then an image appeared almost magically in the glass above her own reflection: the face that Hatch had described from nightmares. Pale. A shock of dark hair. The sunglasses.

For an instant she thought it was a supernatural event, an apparition in the glass. Even as her breath caught in her throat, however, she realized that she was seeing a reflection like her own and that the killer in Hatch's dreams was in their house, leaning around the doorway to look at her. She repressed an impulse to scream. As soon as he realized she had seen him, she would lose what little advantage she had, and he would be all over her, slashing at her, pounding on her, finishing her off before Hatch even got upstairs. Instead, she sighed loudly and shook her head as if displeased with what she was getting down on the drawing paper.

Hatch might already be dead.

She slowly put down her charcoal pencil, letting her fingers rest on it as if she might decide to pick it up again and go on.

If Hatch wasn't dead, how else could this bastard have gotten to the second floor? No. She couldn't think about Hatch being dead, or she would be dead herself, and then Regina. Dear God, Regina.

She reached toward the top drawer of the supply cabinet at her side, and a shiver went through her as she touched the cold chrome handle.

Reflecting the door behind her, the window showed the killer not just leaning around the jamb now, but stepping boldly into the open doorway. He paused arrogantly to stare at her, evidently relishing the moment. He was unnaturally quiet. If she had not seen his image in the glass, she would have had no awareness whatsoever of his presence.

She pulled open the drawer, felt the gun under her hand.

Behind her, he crossed the threshold.

She drew the pistol out of the drawer and swung around on her stool in one motion, bringing the heavy weapon up, clasping it in both hands, pointing it at him. She would not have been entirely surprised if he had not been there, and if her first impression of him only as an apparition in the windowpane had turned out to be correct. But he was there, all right, one step inside the door when she drew down on him with the Browning.

She said, "Don't move, you son of a bitch."

Whether he thought he saw weakness in her or whether he just didn't give a damn if she shot him or not, he backed out of the doorway and into the hall even as she swung toward him and told him not to move.

"Stop, damn it!"

He was gone. Lindsey would have shot him without hesitation, without moral compunction, but he moved so incredibly fast, like a cat springing for safety, that all she would have gotten was a piece of the doorjamb.

Shouting for Hatch, she was off the high stool and leaping for the door even as the last of the killer—a black shoe, his left foot—vanished out of the door frame. But she brought herself up short, realizing he might not have gone anywhere, might be waiting just to the side of the door, expecting her to come through in a panic, then step in behind her and pound her across the back of the head or push her into the stair railing and over and out and down onto the foyer floor. Regina. She couldn't delay. He might be going after Regina. A hesitation of only a second, then she crashed through her fear and through the open door, all this time shouting Hatch's name.

Looking to her right as she came into the hall, she saw the guy going for Regina's door, also open, at the far end. The room was dark beyond when there ought to have been lights, Regina studying. She didn't have time to stop and aim. Almost squeezed the trigger. Wanted to pump out bullets in the hope that one of them would nail the bastard. But Regina's room was so dark, and the girl could be anywhere. Lindsey was afraid that she would miss the killer and blow away the girl, bullets flying through the open doorway. So she held her fire and went after the guy, screaming Regina's name now instead of Hatch's.

He disappeared into the girl's room and threw the door shut behind him, a hell of a slam that shook the house. Lindsey hit that barrier a second later, bounced off it. Locked. She heard Hatch shouting her name—thank God, he was alive, he was alive—but she didn't stop or turn around to see where he was. She stepped back and kicked the door hard, then kicked it again. It was only a privacy latch, flimsy, it ought to pop open easily, but didn't.

She was going to kick it again, but the killer spoke to her through the door. His voice was raised but not a shout, menacing but cool, no panic in it, no fear, just businesslike and a little loud, terrifyingly smooth and calm: "Get away from the door, or I'll kill the little bitch."

Just before Lindsey began to shout his name, Hatch was sitting at the desk in the den, lights off, holding *Arts American* in both hands. A vision hit him with an electric sound, the crackle of a current jumping an arc, as if the magazine were a live power cable that he had gripped in his bare hands.

He saw Lindsey from behind, sitting on the high stool in her office, at the drawing board, working on a sketch. Then she was not Lindsey any more. Suddenly she was another woman, taller, also seen from behind but not on the stool, in an armchair in a different room in a strange house. She was knitting. A bright skein of yarn slowly unraveled from a retaining bowl on the small table beside her chair. Hatch thought of her as "mother," though she was nothing whatsoever like his mother. He looked down at his right hand, in which he held a knife, immense, already wet with blood. He approached her chair. She was unaware of him. As Hatch, he wanted to cry out and warn her. But as the user of the knife, through whose eyes he was seeing everything, he wanted only to savage her, tear the life out of her, and thereby complete the task that would free him. He stepped to the back of her armchair. She hadn't heard him yet. He raised the knife high. He struck. She screamed. He struck. She tried to get out of the chair. He moved around her, and from his point of view it was like a swooping shot in a movie meant to convey flight, the smooth glide of a bird or bat. He pushed her back into the chair, struck. She raised her hands to protect herself. He struck. He struck. And now, as if it was all a loop of film, he was behind her again, standing in the doorway, except she wasn't "mother" any more, she was Lindsey again, sitting at the drawing board in her upstairs studio, reaching to the top drawer of her supply cabinet and pulling it open. His gaze rose from her to the window. He saw himself—pale face, dark hair, sunglasses—and knew she had seen him. She spun around on the stool, a pistol coming up, the muzzle aimed straight at his chest—

"Hatch!"

His name, echoing through the house, shattered the link. He shot up from the desk chair, shuddering, and the magazine fell out of his hands.

"Hatch!"

Reaching out in the darkness, he unerringly found the handgrip of the Browning, and raced out of the den. As he crossed the foyer and climbed the stairs two at a time, looking up as he went, trying to see what was happening, he heard Lindsey stop shouting his name and start screaming "Regina!" Not the girl, Jesus, please, not the girl. Reaching the top of the stairs, he thought for an instant that the slamming door was a shot. But the sound was too distinct to be mistaken for gunfire, and as he looked back the hall he saw Lindsey bounce off the door to Regina's room with another crash. As he ran to join her, she kicked the door, kicked again, and then she stumbled back from it as he reached her.

"Lemme try," he said, pushing past her.

"No! He said back off or he'll kill her."

For a couple of seconds, Hatch stared at the door, literally shaking with frustration. Then he took hold of the knob, tried to turn it slowly. But it was locked, so he put the muzzle of the pistol against the base of the knob plate.

"Hatch," Lindsey said plaintively, "he'll kill her."

He thought of the young blonde taking two bullets in the chest, flying backward out of the car onto the freeway, tumbling, tumbling along the pavement into the fog. And the mother suffering the massive blade of the butcher knife as she dropped her knitting and struggled desperately for her life.

He said, "He'll kill her anyway, turn your face away," and he pulled the trigger.

Wood and thin metal dissolved into splinters. He grabbed the brass knob, it came off in his hand, and he threw it aside. When he shoved on the door, it creaked inward an inch but no farther. The cheap lock had disintegrated. But the shank on which the knob had been seated was still bristling from the wood, and something must have been wedged under the other knob on the inside. He pushed on the shank with the palm of his hand, but that didn't provide enough force to move it; whatever was wedged against the other side—most likely the girl's desk chair—was exerting upward pressure, thereby holding the shank in place.

Hatch gripped the Browning by its barrel and used the butt as a hammer. Cursing, he pounded the shank, driving it inch by inch back through the door.

Just as the shank flew free and clattered to the floor inside, a vivid series of images flooded through Hatch's mind, temporarily washing away the upstairs hall. They were all from the killer's eyes: a weird angle, looking up at the side of a house, this house, the wall outside Regina's bedroom. The open window. Below the sill, a tangle of trumpet-vine runners. A hornlike flower in his face. Latticework under his hands, splinters digging into his skin. Clutching with one hand, searching with the other for a new place to grip, one foot dangling in space, a weight bearing down hard over his shoulder. Then a creaking, a splitting sound. A sudden sense of perilous looseness in the geometric web to which he clung—

Hatch was snapped back to reality by a brief, loud noise from beyond the door: clattering and splintering wood, nails popping loose with tortured screeches, scraping, a crash.

Then a new wave of psychic images and sensations flushed through him. Falling. Backward and out into the night. Not far, hitting the ground, a brief flash of pain. Rolling once on the grass. Beside him, a small huddled form, lying still. Scuttling to it, seeing the face. Regina. Eyes closed. A scarf tied across her mouth—

"Regina!" Lindsey cried.

When reality clicked into place once again, Hatch was already slamming his shoulder against the bedroom door. The brace on the other side fell away. The door shuddered open. He went inside, slapping the wall with one hand until he found the light switch. In the sudden glare, he stepped over the fallen desk chair and swung the Browning right, then left. The room was deserted, which he already knew from his vision.

At the open window he looked out at the collapsed trellis and tangled vines on the lawn below. There was no sign of the man in sunglasses or of Regina.

"Shit!" Hatch hurried back across the room, grabbing Lindsey, turning her around, pushing her through the door, into the hall, toward the head of the stairs. "You take the front, I'll take the back, he's got her, stop him, go, go." She didn't resist, picked up at once on what he was saying, and flew down the steps with him at her heels. "Shoot him, bring him down, aim for the legs, can't worry about hitting Regina, he's getting away!"

In the foyer Lindsey reached the front door even as Hatch was coming off the bottom step and turning toward the short hallway.

He dashed into the family room, then into the kitchen, peering out the back windows of the house as he ran past them. The lawn and patios were well lighted, but he didn't see anyone out there.

He tore open the door between the kitchen and the garage, stepped through, switched on the lights. He raced across the three stalls, behind the cars, to the exterior door at the far end even before the last of the fluorescent tubes had stopped flickering and come all the way on.

He disengaged the dead-bolt lock, stepped out into the narrow side yard, and glanced to his right. No killer. No Regina. The front of the house lay in that direction, the street, more houses facing theirs from the other side. That was part of the territory Lindsey already was covering.

His heart knocked so hard, it seemed to drive each breath out of his lungs before he could get it all the way in.

She's only ten, only ten.

He turned left and ran along the side of the house, around the corner of the garage, into the backyard, where the fallen trellis and trumpet vines lay in a heap.

So small, a little thing. God, please.

Afraid of stepping on a nail and disabling himself, he skirted the debris and searched frantically along the perimeter of the property, plunging recklessly into the shrubbery, probing behind the tall eugenias.

No one was in the backyard.

He reached the side of the property farthest from the garage, almost slipped and fell as he skidded around the corner, but kept his balance. He thrust the Browning out in front of him with both hands, covering the walkway between the house and the fence. No one there, either.

He'd heard nothing from out front, certainly no gunfire, which meant Lindsey must be having no better luck than he was. If the killer had not gone that way, the only other thing he could have done was scale the fence on one side or another, escaping into someone else's property.

Turning away from the front of the house, Hatch surveyed the seven-foot-high fence that encircled the backyard, separating it from the abutting yards of the houses to the east, west, and south. Developers and Realtors called it a fence in southern California, although it was actually a wall, concrete blocks reinforced with steel and covered with stucco, capped with bricks, painted to match the houses. Most neighborhoods had them, guarantors of privacy at swimming pools or barbecues. Good fences make good neighbors, make strangers for neighbors—and make it damn easy for an intruder to scramble over a single barrier and vanish from one part of the maze into another.

Hatch was on an emotional wire-walk across a chasm of despair, his balance sustained only by the hope that the killer couldn't move fast with Regina in his arms or over his shoulder. He looked east, west, south, frozen by indecision.

Finally he started toward the back wall, which was on their southern flank. He halted, gasping and bending forward, when the mysterious connection between him and the man in sunglasses was re-established.

Again Hatch saw through the other man's eyes, and in spite of the sunglasses the night seemed more like late twilight. He was in a car, behind the steering wheel, leaning across the console to adjust the unconscious girl in the passenger seat as if she were a mannequin. Her wrists were lashed together in her lap, and she was held in place by the safety harness. After arranging her auburn hair to cover the scarf that crossed the back of her head, he pushed her against the door, so she slumped with her face turned away from the side window. People in passing cars would not be able to see the gag in her mouth. She appeared to be sleeping. Indeed she was so pale and still, he suddenly wondered if she was dead. No point in taking her to his hideaway if she was already dead. Might as well open the door and push her out, dump the little bitch right there. He put his hand against her cheek. Her skin was wonderfully smooth but seemed cool. Pressing his fingertips to her throat, he detected her heartbeat in a carotid artery, thumping strongly, so strongly. She was so *alive,* even more vital than she had seemed in the vision with the butterfly flitting around her head. He had never before made an acquisition of such value, and he was grateful to all the powers of Hell for giving her to him. He thrilled at the prospect of reaching deep within and clasping that strong young heart as it twitched and thudded into final stillness, all the while staring into her beautiful gray eyes to watch life pass out of her and death enter—

Hatch's cry of rage, anguish, and terror broke the psychic connection. He was in his backyard again, holding his right hand up in front of his face, staring at it in horror, as if Regina's blood already stained his trembling fingers.

He turned away from the back fence, and sprinted along the east side of the house, toward the front.

But for his own hard breathing, all was quiet. Evidently some of the neighbors weren't home. Others hadn't heard anything, or at least not enough to bring them outside.

The serenity of the community made him want to scream with frustration. Even as his own world was falling apart, however, he realized the appearance of normality was exactly that—merely an *appearance,* not a reality. God knew what might be happening behind the walls of some of those houses, horrors equal to the one that had overcome him and Lindsey and Regina, perpetrated not by an intruder but by one member of a family upon another. The human species possessed a knack for creating monsters, and the beasts themselves often had a talent for hiding away behind convincing masks of sanity.

When Hatch reached the front lawn, Lindsey was nowhere to be seen. He hurried to the walkway, through the open door—and discovered her in the den, where she was standing beside the desk, making a phone call.

"You find her?" she asked.

"No. What're you doing?"

"Calling the police."

Taking the receiver out of her hand, dropping it onto the phone, he said, "By the time they get here, listen to our story, and start to *do* something, he'll be gone, he'll have Regina so far away they'll never find her—until they stumble across her body someday."

"But we need help—"

Snatching the shotgun off the desk and pushing it into her

334

hands, he said, "We're going to follow the bastard. He's got her in a car. A Honda, I think."

"You have a license number?"

"No."

"Did you see if—"

"I didn't actually *see* anything," he said, jerking open the desk drawer, plucking out the box of 12-gauge ammunition, handing that to her as well, desperately aware of the seconds ticking away. "I'm connecting with him, it flickers in and out, but I think the link is good enough, strong enough." He pulled his ring of keys from the desk lock, in which he had left them dangling when he had taken the magazine from the drawer. "We can stay on his ass if we don't let him get too far ahead of us." Hurrying into the foyer, he said, "But we have to *move.*"

"Hatch, wait!"

He stopped and swiveled to face her as she followed him out of the den.

She said, "You go, follow them if you think you can, and I'll stay here to talk to the cops, get them started—"

Shaking his head, he said, "No. I need you to drive. These . . . these visions are like being punched, I sort of black out, I'm disoriented while it's happening. There's no way I won't run the car right off the damn road. Put the shotgun and the shells in the Mitsubishi." Climbing the stairs two at a time, he shouted back to her: "And get flashlights."

"Why?"

"I don't know, but we'll need them."

He was lying. He had been somewhat surprised to hear himself ask for flashlights, but he knew his subconscious was driving him at the moment, and he had a hunch why flashlights were going to be essential. In his nightmares over the past couple of months, he had often moved through cavernous rooms and a maze of concrete corridors that were somehow revealed in spite of having no windows or artificial lighting. One tunnel in particular, sloping down into perfect blackness, into something unknown, filled him with such dread that his heart swelled and pounded as if it would burst. *That* was why they needed flashlights—because they were going where he had previously been only in dreams or in visions, into the heart of the nightmare.

He was all the way upstairs and entering Regina's room before he realized that he didn't know why he had gone there. Stopping just inside the threshold, he looked down at the broken doorknob and the overturned desk chair, then at the closet where clothes had fallen off the hangers and were lying in a pile, then at the open window where the night breeze had begun to stir the draperies.

Something . . . something important. Right here, right now, in this room, something he needed.

But what?

He switched the Browning to his left hand, wiped the damp palm of his right hand against his jeans. By now the son of a bitch in the sunglasses had started the car and was on his way out of the neighborhood with Regina, probably on Crown Valley Parkway already. Every second counted.

Although he was beginning to wonder if he had flown upstairs in a panic rather than because there was anything he really needed, Hatch decided to trust the compulsion a little further. He went to the corner desk and let his gaze travel over the books, pencils, and a notebook. The bookcase next to the desk. One of Lindsey's paintings on the wall beside it.

Come on, come on. Something he needed . . . needed as badly as the flashlights, as badly as the shotgun and the box of shells. Something.

He turned, saw the crucifix, and went straight for it. He scrambled onto Regina's bed and wrenched the cross from the wall behind it.

Off the bed and on the floor again, heading out of the room and along the hall toward the stairs, he gripped the icon tightly, fisted his right hand around it. He realized he was holding it as if it were not an object of religious symbolism and veneration but a weapon, a hatchet or cleaver.

By the time he got to the garage, the big sectional door was rolling up. Lindsey had started the car.

When Hatch got in the passenger's side, Lindsey looked at the crucifix. "What's that for?"

336

"We'll need it."

Backing out of the garage, she said, "Need it for what?"

"I don't know."

As the car rolled into the street, she looked at Hatch curiously. "A crucifix?"

"I don't know, but maybe it'll be useful. When I linked with him he was . . . he felt thankful to all the powers of Hell, that's how it went through his mind, thankful to all the powers of Hell for giving Regina to him." He pointed left. "That way."

Fear had aged Lindsey a few years in the past ten minutes. Now the lines in her face grew deeper still as she threw the car in gear and turned left. "Hatch, what are we dealing with here, one of those Satanists, those crazies, guys in these cults you read about in the paper, when they catch one of them, they find severed heads in the refrigerator, bones buried under the front porch?"

"Yeah, maybe, something like that." At the intersection he said, "Left here. Maybe something like that . . . but worse, I think."

"We can't handle this, Hatch."

"The hell we can't," he said sharply. "There's no time for anybody else to handle it. If we don't, Regina's dead."

They came to an intersection with Crown Valley Parkway, which was a wide four- to six-lane boulevard with a garden strip and trees planted down the center. The hour was not yet late, and the parkway was busy, though not crowded.

"Which way?" Lindsey asked.

Hatch put his Browning on the floor. He did not let go of the crucifix. He held it in both hands. He looked left and right, left and right, waiting for a feeling, a sign, something. The headlights of passing cars washed over them but brought no revelations.

"Hatch?" Lindsey said worriedly.

Left and right, left and right. Nothing. Jesus.

Hatch thought about Regina. Auburn hair. Gray eyes. Her right hand curled and twisted like a claw, a gift from God. No, not from God. Not this time. Can't blame them all on God. She might have been right: a gift from her parents, drug-users' legacy.

A car pulled up behind them, waiting to get out onto the main street.

The way she walked, determined to minimize the limp. The way she never concealed her deformed hand, neither ashamed nor proud of it, just accepting. Going to be a writer. Intelligent pigs from outer space.

The driver waiting behind them blew his horn.

"Hatch?"

Regina, so small under the weight of the world, yet always standing straight, her head never bowed. Made a deal with God. In return for something precious to her, a promise to eat beans. And Hatch knew what the precious thing was, though she had never said it, knew it was a family, a chance to escape the orphanage.

The other driver blew his horn again.

Lindsey was shaking. She started to cry.

A chance. Just a chance. All the girl wanted. Not to be alone any more. A chance to sleep in a bed painted with flowers. A chance to love, be loved, grow up. The small curled hand. The small sweet smile. *Goodnight . . . Dad.*

The driver behind them blew his horn insistently.

"Right," Hatch said abruptly. "Go right."

With a sob of relief, Lindsey turned right onto the parkway. She drove faster than she usually did, changing lanes as traffic required, crossing the south-county flatlands toward the distant foothills and the night-shrouded mountains in the east.

At first Hatch was not sure that he had done more than guess at what direction to take. But soon conviction came to him. The boulevard led east between endless tracts of houses that speckled the hills with lights as if they were thousands of memorial flames on the tiers of immense votive-candle racks, and with each mile he sensed more strongly that he and Lindsey were following in the wake of the beast.

Because he had agreed there would be no more secrets between them, because he thought she should know—and could handle—a full understanding of the extremity of Regina's circumstances, Hatch said, "What he wants to do is hold her beating heart in his bare hand for its last few beats, feel the life go out of it."

"Oh, God."

"She's still alive. She has a chance. There's hope."

He believed what he said was true, had to believe it or go mad. But he was troubled by the memory of having said those same things so often in the weeks before cancer had finally finished with Jimmy.

Part III

DOWN AMONG THE DEAD

Death is no fearsome mystery.
He is well known to thee and me.
He hath no secrets he can keep
to trouble any good man's sleep.

◆

Turn not thy face from Death away.
Care not he takes our breath away.
Fear him not, he's not thy master,
rushing at thee faster, faster.
Not thy master but servant to
the Maker of thee, what or Who
created Death, created thee
—and is the only mystery.

THE BOOK OF COUNTED SORROWS

SEVEN

1

Jonas Nyebern and Kari Dovell sat in armchairs before the big windows in the darkened living room of his house on Spyglass Hill, looking at the millions of lights that glimmered across Orange and Los Angeles counties. The night was relatively clear, and they could see as far as Long Beach Harbor to the north. Civilization sprawled like a luminescent fungus, devouring all.

A bottle of Robert Mondavi chenin blanc was in an ice bucket on the floor between their chairs. It was their second bottle. They had not eaten dinner yet. He was talking too much.

They had been seeing each other socially once or twice a week for more than a month. They had not gone to bed together, and he didn't think they ever would. She was still desirable, with that odd combination of grace and awkwardness that sometimes reminded him of an exotic long-legged crane, even if the side of her that was a serious and dedicated physician could never quite let the woman in her have full rein. However, he doubted she even expected physical intimacy. In any case, he didn't believe he was capable of it. He was a haunted man; too many ghosts waited to bedevil him if happiness came within his reach. What each of them got from the relationship was a friendly ear, patience, and genuine sympathy without maudlin excess.

That evening he talked about Jeremy, which was not a subject conducive to romance even if there had been any prospect of it. Mostly he worried over the signs of Jeremy's congenital madness that he'd failed to realize—or admit—were signs.

Even as a child Jeremy had been unusually quiet, invariably preferring solitude to anyone's company. That was explained away as simple shyness. From the earliest age he seemed to have no interest in toys, which was written off to his indisputably high intelligence and a too-serious nature. But now all those untouched model airplanes and games and balls and elaborate Erector sets were disquieting indications that his interior fantasy life had been richer than any entertainment that could be provided by Tonka, Mattel, or Lionel.

"He was never able to receive a hug without stiffening a little," Jonas remembered. "When he returned a kiss for a kiss, he always planted his lips on the air instead of your cheek."

"Lots of kids have difficulty being demonstrative," Kari insisted. She lifted the wine bottle from the ice, leaned out, and refilled the glass he held. "It would seem like just another aspect of his shyness. Shyness and self-effacement aren't faults, and you couldn't be expected to see them that way."

"But it wasn't self-effacement," he said miserably. "It was an inability to feel, to care."

"You can't keep beating yourself up like this, Jonas."

"What if Marion and Stephanie weren't even the first?"

"They must have been."

"But what if they weren't?"

"A teenage boy might be a killer, but he's not going to have the sophistication to get away with murder for any length of time."

"What if he's killed someone since he slipped away from the rehab hospital?"

"He's probably been victimized himself, Jonas."

"No. He's not the victim type."

"He's probably dead."

"He's out there somewhere. Because of me."

Jonas stared at the vast panorama of lights. Civilization lay in all its glimmering wonder, all its blazing glory, all its bright terror.

As they approached the San Diego Freeway, Interstate 405, Hatch said, "South. He's gone south."

Lindsey flipped on the turn signal and caught the entrance ramp just in time.

At first she had glanced at Hatch whenever she could take her eyes off the road, expecting him to tell her what he was seeing or receiving from the man they were trailing. But after a while she focused on the highway whether she needed to or not, because he was sharing nothing with her. She suspected his silence simply meant he was seeing very little, that the link between him and the killer was either weak or flickering on and off. She didn't press him to include her, because she was afraid that if she distracted him, the bond might be broken altogether—and Regina lost.

Hatch continued to hold the crucifix. Even from the corner of her eye, Lindsey could see how the fingertips of his left hand ceaselessly traced the contours of the cast-metal figure suffering upon the faux dogwood cross. His gaze seemed to be turned inward, as if he were virtually unaware of the night and the car in which he traveled.

Lindsey realized that her life had become as surreal as any of her paintings. Supernatural experiences were juxtaposed with the familiar mundane world. Disparate elements filled the composition: crucifixes and guns, psychic visions and flashlights.

In her paintings, she used surrealism to elucidate a theme, provide insight. In real life, each intrusion of the surreal only further confused and mystified her.

Hatch shuddered and leaned forward as far as the safety harness would allow, as if he had seen something fantastic and frightening cross the highway, though she knew he was not actually looking at the blacktop ahead. He slumped back into his seat. "He's taken the Ortega Highway exit. East. The same exit's coming up for us in a couple of miles. East on the Ortega Highway."

Sometimes the headlights of oncoming cars forced him to squint in spite of the protection provided by his heavily tinted glasses.

As he drove, Vassago periodically glanced at the unconscious girl in the seat beside him, facing him. Her chin rested on her breast. Though her head was tipped down and auburn hair hung over one side of her face, he could see her lips pulled back by the scarf that held in the gag, the tilt of her pixie nose, all of one closed eyelid and most of the other—such long lashes—and part of her smooth brow. His imagination played with all the possible ways he might disfigure her to produce the most effective offering.

She was perfect for his purposes. With her beauty compromised by her leg and deformed hand, she was already a symbol of God's fallibility. A trophy, indeed, for his collection.

He was disappointed that he had failed to get the mother, but he had not given up hope of acquiring her. He was toying with the idea of not killing the child tonight. If he kept her alive for only a few days, he might have an opportunity to make another bid for Lindsey. If he had them together, able to work on them at the same time, he could present their corpses as a mocking version of Michelangelo's *Pietà,* or dismember them and stitch them together in a highly imaginative obscene collage.

He was waiting for guidance, another vision, before deciding what to do.

As he took the Ortega Highway off-ramp and turned east, he recalled how Lindsey, at the drawing board in her studio, had reminded him of his mother at her knitting on the afternoon when he had killed her. Having disposed of his sister and mother with the same knife in the same hour, he had known in his heart that he had paved the way to Hell, had been so convinced that he had taken the final step and impaled himself.

A privately published book had described for him that route to damnation. Titled *The Hidden,* it was the work of a condemned murderer named Thomas Nicene who had killed his own mother and a brother, and then committed suicide. His carefully planned descent into the Pit had been foiled by a paramedic team with too much dedication and a little luck. Nicene was revived, healed, imprisoned, put on trial, convicted of murder, and sentenced to death. Rule-playing society had made it clear that the power of death, even the right to choose one's own, was not ever to be given to an individual.

While awaiting execution, Thomas Nicene had committed to paper the visions of Hell that he had experienced during the time that he had been on the edge of this life, before the paramedics denied him eternity. His writings had been smuggled out of prison to fellow believers who could print and distribute them. Nicene's book was filled with powerful, convincing images of darkness and cold, not the heat of classic hells, but visions of a kingdom of vast spaces, chilling emptiness. Peering through Death's door and the door of Hell beyond, Thomas had seen titanic powers at work on mysterious structures. Demons of colossal size and strength strode through night mists across lightless continents on unknown missions, each clothed in black with a flowing cape and upon its head a shining black helmet with a flared rim. He had seen dark seas crashing on black shores under starless and moonless skies that gave the feeling of a subterranean world. Enormous ships, windowless and mysterious, were driven through the tenebrous waves by powerful engines that produced a noise like the anguished screams of multitudes.

When he had read Nicene's words, Jeremy had known they were truer than any ever inked upon a page, and he had determined to follow the great man's example. Marion and Stephanie became his tickets to the exotic and enormously attractive netherworld where he belonged. He had punched those tickets with a butcher knife and delivered himself to that dark kingdom, encountering precisely what Nicene promised. He had never imagined that his own escape from the hateful world of the living would be undone not by paramedics but by his own father.

He would soon earn repatriation to the damned.

Glancing at the girl again, Vassago remembered how she had

felt when she shuddered and collapsed limply in his fierce embrace. A shiver of delicious anticipation whidded through him.

He had considered killing his father to learn if that act would win him back his citizenship in Hades. But he was wary of his old man. Jonas Nyebern was a life-giver and seemed to shine with an inner light that Vassago found forbidding. His earliest memories of his father were wrapped up in images of Christ and angels and the Holy Mother and miracles, scenes from the paintings that Jonas collected and with which their home had always been decorated. And only two years ago, his father had resurrected him in the manner of Jesus raising cold Lazarus. Consequently, he thought of Jonas not merely as the enemy but as a figure of power, an embodiment of those bright forces that were opposed to the will of Hell. His father was no doubt protected, untouchable, living in the loathsome grace of that *other* deity.

His hopes, then, were pinned on the woman and the girl. One acquisition made, the other pending.

He drove east past endless tracts of houses that had sprung up in the six years since Fantasy World had been abandoned, and he was grateful that the spawning multitudes of life-loving hypocrites had not pressed to the very perimeter of his special hideaway, which still lay miles beyond the last of the new communities. As the peopled hills passed by, as the land grew steadily less hospitable though still inhabited, Vassago drove more slowly than he would have done any other night.

He was waiting for a vision that would tell him if he should kill the child upon arrival at the park or wait until the mother was his, as well.

Turning his head to look at her once more, he discovered she was watching him. Her eyes shone with the reflected light from the instrument panel. He could see that her fear was great.

"Poor baby," he said. "Don't be afraid. Okay? Don't be afraid. We're just going to an amusement park, that's all. You know, like Disneyland, like Magic Mountain?"

If he was unable to acquire the mother, perhaps he should look for another child about the same size as Regina, a particularly pretty one with four strong, healthy limbs. He could then remake this girl with the arm, hand, and leg of the other, as if to say that he, a mere twenty-year-old expatriate of Hell, could do a better job than the Creator. That would make a fine addition to his collection, a singular work of art.

He listened to the contained thunder of the engine. The hum of the tires on the pavement. The soft whistle of wind at the windows.

Waiting for an epiphany. Waiting for guidance. Waiting to be told what he should do. Waiting, waiting, a vision to behold.

Even before they reached the Ortega Highway off-ramp, Hatch received a flurry of images stranger than anything he had seen before. None lasted longer than a few seconds, as if he were watching a film with no narrative structure. Dark seas crashing on black shores under starless and moonless skies. Enormous ships, windowless and mysterious, driven through the tenebrous waves by powerful engines that produced a noise like the anguished screams of multitudes. Colossal demonic figures, a hundred feet tall, striding alien landscapes, black capes flowing behind them, heads encased in black helmets as shiny as glass. Titanic, half-glimpsed machines at work on monumental structures of such odd design that purpose and function could not even be guessed.

Sometimes Hatch saw that hideous landscape in chillingly vivid detail, but sometimes he saw only descriptions of it in words on the printed pages of a book. If it existed, it must be on some far world, for it was not of this earth. But he was never sure if he was receiving pictures of a real place or one that was merely imagined. At times it seemed as vividly depicted as any street in Laguna but at other times seemed tissue-paper thin.

Jonas returned to the living room with the box of items he had saved from Jeremy's room, and put it down beside his armchair. He withdrew from the box a small, shoddily printed volume titled

The Hidden and gave it to Kari, who examined it as if he had handed her an object encrusted with filth.

"You're right to wrinkle your nose at it," he said, picking up his glass of wine and moving to the large window. "It's nonsense. Sick and twisted but nonsense. The author was a convicted killer who claimed to have seen Hell. His description isn't like anything in Dante, let me tell you. Oh, it possesses a certain romance, undeniable power. In fact, if you were a psychotic young man with delusions of grandeur and a bent for violence, with the unnaturally high testosterone levels that usually accompany a mental condition like that, then the Hell he describes would be your ultimate wet dream of power. You would swoon over it. You might not be able to get it out of your mind. You might *long* for it, do anything to be a part of it, achieve damnation."

Kari put the book down and wiped her fingertips on the sleeve of her blouse. "This author, Thomas Nicene—you said he killed his mother."

"Yes. Mother and brother. Set the example." Jonas knew he had already drunk too much. He took another long sip of his wine anyway. Turning from the night view, he said, "And you know what makes it all so absurd, pathetically absurd? If you read that damn book, which I did afterward, trying to understand, and if you're not psychotic and disposed to believe it, you'll see right away that Nicene isn't reporting what he saw in Hell. He's taking his inspiration from a source as stupidly obvious as it is stupidly ridiculous. Kari, his Hell is nothing more than the Evil Empire in the *Star Wars* movies, somewhat changed, expanded upon, filmed through the lens of religious myth, but still *Star Wars.*" A bitter laugh escaped him. He chased it with more wine. "His demons are nothing more than hundred-foot-tall versions of Darth Vader, for God's sake. Read his description of Satan and then go look at whichever film Jabba the Hut was a part of. Old Jabba the Hut is a ringer for Satan, if you believe this lunatic." One more glass of chenin blanc, one more glass. "Marion and Stephanie died—" A sip. Too long a sip. Half the glass gone. "—died so Jeremy could get into Hell and have great, dark, antiheroic adventures in a fucking Darth Vader costume."

He had offended or unsettled her, probably both. That had not been his intention, and he regretted it. He wasn't sure what his intention had been. Maybe just to unburden himself. He had never done so before, and he didn't know why he'd chosen to do so tonight—except that Morton Redlow's disappearance had scared him more than anything since the day he had found the bodies of his wife and daughter.

Instead of pouring more wine for herself, Kari rose from her armchair. "I think we should get something to eat."

"Not hungry," he said, and heard the slur of the inebriate in his voice. "Well, maybe we should have something."

"We could go out somewhere," she said, taking the wine glass from his hand and putting it on the nearest end table. Her face was quite lovely in the ambient light that came through the view windows, the golden radiance from the web of cities below. "Or call for pizza."

"How about steaks? I've got some filets in the freezer."

"That'll take too long."

"Sure won't. Just thaw 'em out in the microwave, throw 'em on the grill. There's a big Gaggenau grill in the kitchen."

"Well, if that's what you'd like."

He met her eyes. Her gaze was as clear, penetrating, and forthright as ever, but Jonas saw a greater tenderness in her eyes than before. He supposed it was the same concern she had for her young patients, part of what made her a first-rate pediatrician. Maybe that tenderness had always been there for him, too, and he had just not seen it until now. Or perhaps this was the first time she realized how desperately he needed nurturing.

"Thank you, Kari."

"For what?"

"For being you," he said. He put his arm around her shoulders as he walked her to the kitchen.

Mixed with the visions of gargantuan machines and dark seas and colossal demonic figures, Hatch received an array of images of other types. Choiring angels. The Holy Mother in prayer. Christ with the Apostles at the Last Supper, Christ in Gethsemane, Christ in agony upon the cross, Christ ascending.

He recognized them as paintings Jonas Nyebern might have collected at one time or another. They were different periods and styles from those he had seen in the physician's office, but in the same spirit. A connection was made, a braiding of wires in his subconscious, but he didn't understand what it meant yet.

And more visions: the Ortega Highway. Glimpses of the nightscapes unrolling on both sides of an eastward-bound car. Instruments on a dashboard. Oncoming headlights that sometimes made him squint. And suddenly Regina. Regina in the backsplash of yellow light from that same instrument panel. Eyes closed. Head tipped forward. Something wadded in her mouth and held in place by a scarf.

She opens her eyes.

Looking into Regina's terrified eyes, Hatch broke from the visions like an underwater swimmer breaking for air. "She's alive!"

He looked at Lindsey, who shifted her gaze from the highway to him. "But you never said she wasn't."

Until then he did not realize how little faith he'd had in the girl's continued existence.

Before he could take heart from the sight of her gray eyes gleaming in the yellow dashboard light of the killer's car, Hatch was hit by new clairvoyant visions that pummeled him as hard as a series of blows from real fists:

Contorted figures loomed out of murky shadows. Human forms in bizarre positions. He saw a woman as withered and dry as tumbleweed, another in a repugnant state of putrefaction, a mummified face of indeterminate sex, a bloated green-black hand raised in horrid supplication. The collection. His collection. He saw Regina's face again, eyes open, revealed in the dashboard lights. So many ways to disfigure, to mutilate, to mock God's work. Regina. *Poor baby. Don't be afraid. Okay? Don't be afraid. We're only going to an amusement park. You know, like Disneyland, like Magic Mountain?* How nicely will she fit in my collection. Corpses as performance art, held in place by wires, rebar, blocks of wood. He saw frozen screams, silent forever. Skeletal jaws held open in eternal cries for mercy. The precious collection. Regina, sweet baby, pretty baby, such an exquisite acquisition.

Hatch came out of his trance, clawing wildly at his safety harness, for it felt like binding wires, ropes, and cords. He tore at the straps as a panicked victim of premature burial might rip at his enwrapping shrouds. He realized that he was shouting, too, and sucking breath as if in fear of suffocation, letting it out at once in great explosive exhalations. He heard Lindsey saying his name, understood that he was terrifying her, but could not cease thrashing or crying out for long seconds, until he had found the release on the safety harness and cast it off.

With that, he was fully back in the Mitsubishi, contact with the madman broken for the moment, the horror of the collection diminished though not forgotten, not in the least forgotten. He turned to Lindsey, remembering her fortitude in the icy waters of that mountain river the night that she had saved him. She would need all of that strength and more tonight.

"Fantasy World," he said urgently, "where they had the fire years ago, abandoned now, that's where he's going. Jesus Christ, Lindsey, drive like you've never driven in your life, put the pedal to the floor, the son of a bitch, the crazy rotten son of a bitch is taking her down among the dead!"

And they were flying. Though she could have no idea what he meant, they were suddenly flying eastward faster than was safe on that highway, through the last clusters of closely spaced lights, out of civilization into ever darker realms.

While Kari searched the refrigerator in the kitchen for the makings of a salad, Jonas went to the garage to liberate a couple of steaks from the chest-style freezer. The garage vents brought in the coolish night air, which he found refreshing. He stood for a moment just inside the door from the house, taking slow deep breaths to clear his head a little.

He had no appetite for anything except perhaps more wine, but he did not want Kari to see him drunk. Besides, though he had no surgery scheduled for the following day, he never knew what emergency might require the skills of the resuscitation team, and he felt a responsibility to those potential patients.

In his darkest hours, he sometimes considered leaving the field of resuscitation medicine to concentrate on cardiovascular surgery. When he saw a reanimated patient return to a useful life of work and family and service, he knew a reward sweeter than most other men could ever know. But in the moment of crisis, when the candidate for resuscitation lay on the table, Jonas rarely knew anything about him, which meant he might sometimes bring evil back into the world once the world had shed it. That was more than a moral dilemma to him; it was a crushing weight upon his conscience. Thus far, being a religious man—though with his share of doubts—he had trusted in God to guide him. He had decided that God had given him his brain and his skills to use, and it was not his place to out-guess God and withhold his services from any patient.

Jeremy, of course, was an unsettling new factor in the equation. If he had brought Jeremy back, and if Jeremy had killed innocent people . . . It did not bear thinking about.

The cool air no longer seemed refreshing. It seeped into the hollows of his spine.

Okay, dinner. Two steaks. Filet mignon. Lightly grilled, with a little Worcestershire sauce. Salads with no dressing but a squirt of lemon and a sprinkle of black pepper. Maybe he *did* have an appetite. He didn't eat much red meat; it was a rare treat. He was a heart surgeon, after all, and saw firsthand the gruesome effects of a high-fat diet.

He went to the freezer in the corner. He pushed the latch-release and put up the lid.

Within lay Morton Redlow, late of the Redlow Detective Agency, pale and gray as if carved from marble but not yet obscured by a layer of frost. A smear of blood had frozen into a brittle crust on his face, and there was a terrible vacancy where his nose had been. His eyes were open. Forever.

Jonas did not recoil. As a surgeon, he was equally familiar with the horrors and wonders of biology, and he was not easily repulsed. Something in him withered when he saw Redlow. Something in him died. His heart turned as cold as that of the detective before him. In some fundamental way, he knew that he was finished as a man. He didn't trust God any more. Not any more. What God? But he was not nauseated or forced to turn away in disgust.

He saw the folded note clutched in Redlow's stiff right hand. The dead man let go of it easily, for his fingers had contracted during the freezing process, shrinking away from the paper around which the killer had pressed them.

Numbly, he unfolded the letter and immediately recognized his son's neat penmanship. The post-coma aphasia had been faked. His retardation was an immensely clever ruse.

The note said, *Dear Daddy: For a proper burial, they'll need to know where to find his nose. Look up his back end. He stuck it in my business, so I stuck it in his. If he'd had any manners, I would have treated him better. I'm sorry, sir, if this behavior distresses you.*

Lindsey drove with utmost urgency, pushing the Mitsubishi to its limits, finding every planning flaw in a highway not always designed for speed. There was little traffic as they moved deeper into the east, which stacked the odds in their favor when once she crossed the center line in the middle of a too-tight turn.

Having snapped on his safety harness again, Hatch used the car phone to get Jonas Nyebern's office number from information, then to call the number itself, which was answered at once by a physician's-service operator. She took his message, which baffled her. Although the operator seemed sincere in her promise to pass it on to the doctor, Hatch was not confident that his definition of "immediately" and hers were materially the same.

He saw all the connections so clearly now, but he knew he could not have seen them sooner. Jonas's question in the office on Monday took on a new significance: Did Hatch, he asked, believe that evil was only the result of the acts of men, or did he think that evil was a real force, a presence that walked the world? The story Jonas had told of losing wife and daughter to a homicidal, psychopathic son, and the son himself to suicide, connected now to the vision of the woman knitting. The father's collections. And the son's. The Satanic aspects to the visions were what one might expect from a bad son in mindless rebellion against a father to whom religion was a center post of life. And finally—he and Jeremy Nyebern shared one obvious link, miraculous resurrection at the hands of the same man.

"But how does that explain anything?" Lindsey demanded, when he told her only a little more than he had told the physician's-service operator.

"I don't know."

He couldn't think about anything except what he had seen in those last visions, less than half of which he understood. The part he *had* comprehended, the nature of Jeremy's collection, filled him with fear for Regina.

Without having seen the collection as Hatch had seen it, Lindsey was fixated, instead, on the mystery of the link, which was somewhat explained—yet not explained at all—by learning the identity of the killer in sunglasses. "What about the visions? How do they fit the damned composition?" she insisted, trying to make sense of the supernatural in perhaps not too different a way from that in which she made sense of the world by reducing it to ordered images on Masonite.

"I don't know," he said.

"The link that's letting you follow him—"

"I don't know."

She took a turn too wide. The car went off the pavement, onto the gravel shoulder. The back end slid, gravel spraying out from beneath the tires and rattling against the undercarriage. The guardrail flashed close, too close, and the car was shaken by the hard bang-bang-bang of sheet metal taking a beating. She seemed to bring it back under control by a sheer effort of will, biting her lower lip so hard it appeared as if she would draw blood.

Although Hatch was aware of Lindsey and the car and the

reckless pace they were keeping along that sometimes dangerously curved highway, he could not turn his mind from the outrage he had seen in the vision. The longer he thought about Regina being added to that grisly collection, the more his fear was augmented by anger. It was the hot, uncontainable anger he had seen so often in his father, but directed now against something deserving of hatred, against a target worthy of such seething rage.

As he approached the entrance road to the abandoned park, Vassago glanced away from the now lonely highway, to the girl who was bound and gagged in the other seat. Even in that poor light he could see that she had been straining at her bonds. Her wrists were chafed and beginning to bleed. Little Regina had hopes of breaking free, striking out or escaping, though her situation was so clearly hopeless. Such vitality. She thrilled him.

The child was so special that he might not need the mother at all, if he could think of a way to place her in his collection that would result in a piece of art with all the power of the various mother-daughter tableaux that he had already conceived.

He had been unconcerned with speed. Now, after he turned off the highway onto the park's long approach road, he accelerated, eager to return to the museum of the dead with the hope that the atmosphere there would inspire him.

Years ago, the four-lane entrance had been bordered by lush flowers, shrubbery, and groupings of palms. The trees and larger shrubs had been dug up, potted, and hauled away ages ago by agents of the creditors. The flowers had died and turned to dust when the landscape watering system had been shut off.

Southern California was a desert, transformed by the hand of man, and when the hand of man moved on, the desert reclaimed its rightful territory. So much for the genius of humanity, God's imperfect creatures. The pavement had cracked and hoved from years of inattention, and in places it had begun to vanish under drifts of sandy soil. His headlights revealed tumbleweed and scraps of other desert brush, already brown hardly six weeks after the end of the rainy season, chased westward by a night wind that came out of the parched hills.

When he reached the tollbooths he slowed down. They stretched across all four lanes. They had been left standing as a barrier to easy exploration of the shuttered park, linked and closed off by chains so heavy that simple bolt cutters could not sever them. Now the bays, once overseen by attendants, were filled with tangled brush that the wind had put there and trash deposited by vandals. He pulled around the booths, bouncing over a low curb and traveling on the sun-hardened soil of the planting beds where lush tropical landscaping would once have blocked the way, then back to the pavement when he had bypassed the barrier.

At the end of the entrance road, he switched off his headlights. He didn't need them, and he was at last beyond the notice of any highway patrolmen who might pull him over for driving without lights. His eyes immediately felt more comfortable, and now if his pursuers drew too close, they would not be able to follow him by sight alone.

He angled across the immense and eerily empty parking lot. He was heading toward a service road at the southwest corner of the inner fence that circumscribed the grounds of the park proper.

As the Honda jolted over the pot-holed blacktop, Vassago ransacked his imagination, which was a busy abattoir of psychotic industry, seeking solutions for the artistic problems presented by the child. He conceived and rejected concept after concept. The image must stir him. Excite him. If it was really art, he would know it; he would be moved.

As Vassago lovingly envisioned tortures for Regina, he became aware of that other strange presence in the night and its singular rage. Suddenly he was plunged into another psychic vision, a flurry of familiar elements, with one crucial new addition: he got a glimpse of Lindsey behind the wheel of a car . . . a car phone in a man's trembling hand . . . and then the object that instantly resolved his artistic dilemma . . . a crucifix. The nailed and tortured body of Christ in its famous posture of noble self-sacrifice.

He blinked away that image, glanced at the petrified girl in the car with him, blinked her away as well, and in his imagination saw the two combined—girl and cruciform. He would use Regina to mock the Crucifixion. Yes, lovely, perfect. But not raised upon a cross of dogwood. Instead, she must be executed upon the segmented belly of the Serpent, under the bosom of the thirty-foot Lucifer in the deepest regions of the funhouse, crucified and her sacred heart revealed, as backdrop to the rest of his collection. Such a cruel and stunning use of her negated the need to include her mother, for in such a pose she would alone be his crowning achievement.

Hatch was frantically trying to contact the Orange County Sheriff's Department on the cellular car phone, which was having transmission problems, when he felt the intrusion of another mind. He "saw" images of Regina disfigured in a multitude of ways, and he began to shake with rage. Then he was struck by a vision of a crucifixion; it was so powerful, vivid, and monstrous that it almost rendered him unconscious as effectively as a skull-cracking blow from a hard-swung hammer.

He urged Lindsey to drive faster, without explaining what he had seen. He couldn't speak of it.

The terror was amplified by Hatch's perfect understanding of the statement Jeremy intended to make by the perpetration of the outrage. Was God in error to have made His Only Begotten Child a man? Should Christ have been a woman? Were not women those who had suffered the most and therefore served as the greatest symbol of self-sacrifice, grace, and transcendence? God had granted women a special sensitivity, a talent for understanding and tenderness, for caring and nurturing—then had dumped them into a world of savage violence in which their singular qualities made them easy targets for the cruel and depraved.

Horror enough existed in that truth, but a greater horror, for Hatch, lay in the discovery that anyone as insane as Jeremy Nyebern could have such a complex insight. If a homicidal sociopath could perceive such a truth and grasp its theological implications, then creation itself must be an asylum. For surely, if the universe were a rational place, no madman would be able to understand any portion of it.

Lindsey reached the approach road to Fantasy World and took the turn so fast and sharp that the Mitsubishi slid sideways and felt, for a moment, as if it would roll. But it remained upright. She pulled hard on the wheel, brought it around, tramped on the accelerator.

Not Regina. No way was Jeremy going to be permitted to realize his decadent vision with that lamb of innocence. Hatch was prepared to die to prevent it.

Fear and fury flooded him in equal torrents. The plastic casing of the cellular-phone handset creaked in his right fist as though the pressure of his grip would crack it as easily as if it had been an eggshell.

Tollbooths appeared ahead. Lindsey braked indecisively, then seemed to notice the tire tracks through the drifting, sandy earth at the same time Hatch saw them. She whipped the car to the right, and it bounced over the concrete border of what had once been a flower bed.

He had to rein in his rage, not succumb to it as his father had always done, for if he didn't remain in control of himself, Regina was as good as dead. He tried to place the emergency 911 call again. Tried to hold fast to his reason. He must not descend to the level of the walking filth through whose eyes he had seen the bound wrists and frightened eyes of his child.

The surge of rage pouring back across the telepathic wire excited Vassago, pumped up his own hatred, and convinced him that he must not wait until both the woman and the child were within his grasp. Even the prospect of the single crucifixion brought him such a richness of loathing and revulsion that he knew his artistic concept was of sufficient power. Once realized through the flesh of the gray-eyed girl, his art would reopen the doors of Hell to him.

He had to stop the Honda at the entrance to the service road, which appeared to be blocked by a padlocked gate. He had broken the massive padlock long ago. It only hung through the hasp with the appearance of effectiveness. He got out of the car, opened the gate, drove through, got out again and closed it.

Behind the wheel once more, he decided not to leave the Honda in the underground garage or go to the museum of the dead through the catacombs. No time. God's slow but persistent paladins were closing in on him. He had so much to do, so much, in so few precious minutes. It wasn't fair. He needed time. Every artist needed *time*. To save a few minutes, he was going to have to drive along the wide pedestrian walkways, between the rotting and empty pavilions, and park in front of the funhouse, take the girl across the dry lagoon and in by way of the gondola doors, through the tunnel with the chain-drive track still in the concrete floor and down into Hell by that more direct route.

While Hatch was on the phone with the sheriff's department, Lindsey drove into the parking lot. The tall lamp poles shed no light. Vistas of empty blacktop faded away in every direction. Straight ahead a few hundred yards stood the once glittery but now dark and decaying castle through which the paying customers had entered Fantasy World. She saw no sign of Jeremy Nyebern's car, and not enough dust on the acres of unprotected, windswept pavement to track him by his tire prints.

She drove as close to the castle as she could get, halted by a long row of ticket booths and crowd-control stanchions of poured concrete. They looked like massive barricades erected on a heavily defended beach to prevent enemy tanks from being put ashore.

When Hatch slammed down the handset, Lindsey was not sure what to make of his end of the conversation, which had alternated between pleading and angry insistence. She didn't know whether the cops were coming or not, but her sense of urgency was so great, she didn't want to take time to ask him about it. She just wanted to move, move. She threw the car into park the moment it braked to a full stop, didn't even bother to switch off the engine or the headlights. She liked the headlights, a little something against the cloying night. She flung open her door, ready to go in on foot. But he shook his head, no, and picked up his Browning from the floor at his feet.

"What?" she demanded.

"He went in by car somehow, somewhere. I think I'll find the creep quicker if we stay on his trail, go in the way he went in, let myself open to this bond between us. Besides, the place is so damned huge, we'll get around it faster in a car."

She got behind the wheel again, popped the Mitsubishi into gear, and said, *"Where?"*

He hesitated only a second, perhaps a fraction of a second, but it seemed that any number of small helpless girls could have been slaughtered in that interlude before he said, "Left, go left, along the fence."

2

Vassago parked the car by the lagoon, cut the engine, got out, and went around to the girl's side. Opening her door, he said, "Here we are, angel. An amusement park, just like I promised you. Isn't it fun? Aren't you amused?"

He swung her around on her seat to bring her legs out of the car. He took his switchblade from his jacket pocket, snapped the well-honed knife out of the handle, and showed it to her.

Even with the thinnest crescent moon, and although her eyes were not as sensitive as his, she saw the blade. He saw her see it, and he was thrilled by the quickening of terror in her face and eyes.

"I'm going to free your legs so you can walk," he told her, turning the blade slowly, slowly, so a quicksilver glimmer trickled liquidly along the cutting edge. "If you're stupid enough to kick me, if you think you can catch my head maybe and knock me silly long enough to get away, then *you're* silly, angel. It won't work, and then I'll have to cut you to teach you a lesson. Do you hear me, precious? Do you understand?"

She emitted a muffled sound through the wadded scarf in her mouth, and the tone of it was an acknowledgement of his power.

"Good," he said. "Good girl. So wise. You'll make a fine Jesus, won't you? A really fine little Jesus."

He cut the cords binding her ankles, then helped her out of the car. She was unsteady, probably because her muscles had cramped during the trip, but he did not intend to let her dawdle. Seizing her by one arm, leaving her wrists bound in front of her and the gag in place, he pulled her around the front of the car to the retaining wall of the funhouse lagoon.

The retaining wall was two feet high on the outside, twice that on the inside where the water once had been. He helped Regina over it, onto the dry concrete floor of the broad lagoon. She hated to let him touch her, even though he still wore gloves, because she could feel his coldness through the gloves, or thought she could, his coldness and damp skin, which made her want to scream. She knew already that she couldn't scream, not with the gag filling her mouth. If she tried to scream she only choked on it and had trouble breathing, so she had to let him help her over the wall. Even when he didn't touch her bare hand with his gloved one, even when he gripped her arm and there was also her sweater between them, the contact made her belly quiver so badly that she thought she was going to vomit, but she fought that urge because, with the gag in her mouth, she would choke to death on her own regurgitation.

Through ten years of adversity, Regina had developed lots of tricks to get her through bad times. There was the think-of-something-worse trick, where she endured by imagining what more terrible circumstances might befall her than those in which she actually found herself. Like thinking of eating dead mice dipped in chocolate when she felt sorry for herself about having to eat lime Jell-O with peaches. Like thinking about being blind on top of her other disabilities. After the awful shock of being rejected during her first trial adoption with the Dotterfields, she had often spent hours with her eyes closed to show herself what she *might* have suffered if her eyes had been as faulty as her right arm. But the think-of-something-worse trick wasn't working now because she couldn't think of anything worse than being where she was, with this stranger dressed all in black and wearing sunglasses at night, calling her "baby" and "precious." None of her other tricks were working, either.

As he pulled her impatiently across the lagoon, she dragged her right leg as if she could not move fast. She needed to slow him down to gain time to think, to find some new trick.

But she was just a kid, and tricks didn't come that easy, not even to a smart kid like her, not even to a kid who had spent ten years devising so many clever tricks to make everyone think that she could take care of herself, that she was tough, that she would never cry. But her trick bag was finally empty, and she was more afraid than she had ever been.

He dragged her past big boats like the gondolas in Venice of which she had seen pictures, but these had dragon prows from Viking ships. With the stranger pulling impatiently on her arm, she limped past a fearful snarling serpent's head bigger than she was.

Dead leaves and moldering papers had blown down into the empty pool. In the nocturnal breeze, which occasionally gusted heartily, that trash eddied around them with the hiss-splash of a ghost sea.

"Come on, precious one," he said in his honey-smooth but unkind voice, "I want you to walk to your Golgotha just as He did. Don't you think that's fitting? Is that so much to ask? Hmmm? I'm not also insisting that you carry your own cross, am I? What do you say, precious, will you *move your ass?*"

She was scared, with no fine tricks left to hide the fact, no tricks left to hold back her tears, either. She began to shake and cry, and her right leg grew weak for real, so she could hardly remain standing let alone move as fast as he demanded.

In the past, she would have turned to God at a moment like this, would have talked to Him, talked and talked, because no one had talked to God more often or more bluntly than she had done from

the time she was just little. But she had been talking to God in the
car, and she had not heard Him listening. Over the years, all their
conversations had been one-sided, yes, but she had always heard
Him listening, at least, a hint of His great slow steady breathing.
But now she knew He couldn't be listening because if He was
there, hearing how desperate she was, He would not have failed to
answer her this time. He was gone, and she didn't know where,
and she was alone as she had never been.

When she was so overcome by tears and weakness that she
could not walk at all, the stranger scooped her up. He was very
strong. She was unable to resist, but she didn't hold on to him,
either. She just curled her arms against her chest, made small fists
of her hands, and pulled away within herself.

"Let me carry my little Jesus," he said, "my sweet little lamb,
it will be my privilege to carry you." There was no warmth in his
voice in spite of the way he was talking. Only hatred and scorn.
She knew that tone, had heard it before. No matter how hard you
tried to fit in and be everybody's friend, some kids hated you if you
were too different, and in their voices you heard this same thing,
and shrank from it.

He carried her through the open, broken, rotting doors into a
darkness that made her feel so small.

Lindsey didn't even bother getting out of the car to see if the gate
could be opened. When Hatch pointed the way, she jammed the
accelerator to the floor. The car bucked, shot forward. They
crashed onto the grounds of the park, demolishing the gate and
sustaining more damage to their already battered car, including
one shattered headlight.

At Hatch's direction, she followed a service loop around half
the park. On the left was a high fence covered with the gnarled and
bristling remnants of a vine that once might have concealed the
chainlink entirely but had died when the irrigation system had
been shut off. On the right were the backs of rides that had been
too permanently constructed to be dismantled easily. There were

also buildings fronted by fantastic facades held up by angled supports that could be seen from behind.

Leaving the service road, they drove between two structures and onto what had once been a winding promenade along which crowds had moved throughout the park. The largest Ferris wheel she had ever seen, savaged by wind and sun and years of neglect, rose in the night like the bones of a leviathan picked clean by unknown carrion-eaters.

A car was parked beside what appeared to be a drained pool in front of an immense structure.

"The funhouse," Hatch said, for he had seen it before through other eyes.

It had a roof with multiple peaks like a three-ring circus tent, and disintegrating stucco walls. She could view only one narrow aspect of the structure at a time, as the headlights swept across it, but she did not like any part of what she saw. She was not by nature a superstitious person—although she was fast becoming one in response to recent experience—but she sensed an aura of death around the funhouse as surely as she could have felt cold air rising off a block of ice.

She parked behind the other car. A Honda. Its occupants had departed in such a hurry that both front doors were open, and the interior lights were on.

Snatching up her Browning and a flashlight, she got out of the Mitsubishi and ran to the Honda, looked inside. No sign of Regina.

She had discovered there was a point at which fear could grow no greater. Every nerve was raw. The brain could not process more input, so it merely sustained the peak of terror once achieved. Each new shock, each new terrible thought did not add to the burden of fear because the brain just dumped old data to make way for the new. She could hardly remember anything of what had happened at the house, or the surreal drive to the park; most of it was gone for now, only a few scraps of memory remaining, leaving her focused on the immediate moment.

On the ground at her feet, visible in the spill of light from the open car door and then in her flashlight beam, was a four-foot length of sturdy cord. She picked it up and saw that it had once been tied in a loop and later cut at the knot.

Hatch took the cord out of her hand. "It was around Regina's ankles. He wanted her to walk."

"Where are they now?"

He pointed with his flashlight across the drained lagoon, past the three large gray canted gondolas with prodigious mastheads, to a pair of wooden doors in the base of the funhouse. One sagged on broken hinges, and the other was open wide. The flashlight was a four-battery model, just strong enough to cast some dim light on those far doors but not to penetrate the terrible darkness beyond.

Lindsey took off around the car and scrambled over the lagoon wall. Though Hatch called out, "Lindsey, wait," she could not delay another moment—and how could he?—with the thought of Regina in the hands of Nyebern's resurrected, psychotic son.

As Lindsey crossed the lagoon, fear for Regina still far outweighed any concern she might have for her own safety. However, realizing that she, herself, must survive if the girl were to have any chance at all, she swept the flashlight beam side to side, side to side, wary of an attack from behind one of the huge gondolas.

Old leaves and paper trash danced in the wind, for the most part waltzing across the floor of the dry lagoon, but sometimes spinning up in columns and churning to a faster beat. Nothing else moved.

Hatch caught up with her by the time she reached the funhouse entrance. He had delayed only to use the cord she had found to bind his flashlight to the back of the crucifix. Now he could carry both in one hand, pointing the head of Christ at anything upon which he directed the light. That left his right hand free for the Browning 9mm. He had left the Mossberg behind. If he had tied the flashlight to the 12-gauge, he could have brought both the handgun and the shotgun. Evidently he felt that the crucifix was a better weapon than the Mossberg.

She didn't know why he had taken the icon from the wall of Regina's room. She didn't think he knew, either. They were wading hip deep in the big muddy river of the unknown, and in addition to the cross, she would have welcomed a necklace of garlic, a vial of holy water, a few silver bullets, and anything else that might have helped.

As an artist, she had always known that the world of the five senses, solid and secure, was not the *whole* of existence, and she had incorporated that understanding into her work. Now she was merely incorporating it into the rest of her life, surprised that she had not done so a long time ago.

With both flashlights carving through the darkness in front of them, they entered the funhouse.

All of Regina's tricks for coping were not exhausted, after all. She invented one more.

She found a room deep inside her mind, where she could go and close the door and be safe, a place only she knew about, in which she could never be found. It was a pretty room with peach-colored walls, soft lighting, and a bed covered with painted flowers. Once she had entered, the door could only be opened again from her side. There were no windows. Once she was in that most secret of all retreats, it didn't matter what was done to the other her, the physical Regina in the hateful world outside. The *real* Regina was safe in her hideaway, beyond fear and pain, beyond tears and doubt and sadness. She could hear nothing beyond the room, most especially not the wickedly soft voice of the man in black. She could see nothing beyond the room, only the peach walls and her painted bed and soft light, never darkness. Nothing beyond the room could really touch her, certainly not his pale quick hands which had recently shed their gloves.

Most important, the only smell in her sanctuary was the scent of roses like those painted on the bed, a clean sweet fragrance. Never the stench of dead things. Never the awful choking odor of decomposition that could bring a sour gushing into the back of your throat and nearly strangle you when your mouth was full of crushed, saliva-damp scarf. Nothing like that, no, never, not in her secret room, her blessed room, her deep and sacred, safe and solitary haven.

Something had happened to the girl. The singular vitality that had made her so appealing was gone.

When he put her on the floor of Hell, with her back against the base of the towering Lucifer, he thought she'd passed out. But that wasn't it. For one thing, when he crouched in front of her and put his hand against her chest, he felt her heart leaping like a rabbit whose hindquarters were already in the jaws of the fox. No one could possibly be unconscious with a thundering heartbeat like that.

Besides, her eyes were open. They were staring blindly, as if she could find nothing upon which to fix her gaze. Of course, she could not see him in the dark as he could see her, couldn't see anything else for that matter, but that wasn't the reason she was staring through him. When he flicked the eyelash over her right eye with his fingertip, she did not flinch, did not even blink. Tears were drying on her cheeks, but no new tears welled up.

Catatonic. The little bitch had blanked out on him, closed her mind down, become a vegetable. That didn't suit his purposes at all. The value of the offering was in the vitality of the subject. Art was about energy, vibrancy, pain, and terror. What statement could he make with his little gray-eyed Christ if she could not experience and express her agony?

He was so angry with her, just so spitting angry, that he didn't want to play with her any more. Keeping one hand on her chest, above her rabbity heart, he took his switchblade from his jacket pocket and popped it open.

Control.

He would have opened her then, and had the intense pleasure of feeling her heart go still in his grip, except that he was a Master of the Game who knew the meaning and value of control. He could deny himself such transitory thrills in the pursuit of more meaningful and enduring rewards. He hesitated only a moment before putting the knife away.

He was better than that.

His lapse surprised him.

Perhaps she would come out of her trance by the time he was ready to incorporate her into his collection. If not, then he felt sure that the first driven nail would bring her to her senses and transform her into the radiant work of art that he knew she had the potential to be.

He turned from her to the tools that were piled at the point where the arc of his collection currently ended. He possessed hammers and screwdrivers, wrenches and pliers, saws and a miter box, a battery-powered drill with an array of bits, screws and nails, rope and wire, brackets of all kinds, and everything else a handyman might need, all of it purchased at Sears when he had realized that properly arranging and displaying each piece in his collection would require the construction of some clever supports and, in a couple of cases, thematic backdrops. His chosen medium was not as easy to work with as oil paints or watercolors or clay or sculptor's granite, for gravity tended to quickly distort each effect that he achieved.

He knew he was short on time, that on his heels were those who did not understand his art and would make the amusement park impossible for him by morning. But that would not matter if he made one more addition to the collection that rounded it out and earned him the approbation he sought.

Haste, then.

The first thing to do, before hauling the girl to her feet and bracing her in a standing position, was to see if the material that composed the segmented, reptilian belly and chest of the funhouse Lucifer would take a nail. It seemed to be a hard rubber, perhaps soft plastic. Depending on thickness, brittleness, and resiliency of the material, a nail would either drive into it as smoothly as into wood, bounce off, or bend. If the fake devil's hide proved too resistant, he'd have to use the battery-powered drill instead of the hammer, two-inch screws instead of nails, but it shouldn't detract from the artistic integrity of the piece to lend a modern touch to the reenactment of this ancient ritual.

He hefted the hammer. He placed the nail. The first blow drove it a quarter of the way into Lucifer's abdomen. The second blow slammed it halfway home.

So nails would work just fine.

He looked down at the girl, who still sat on the floor with her back against the base of the statue. She had not reacted to either of the hammer blows.

He was disappointed but not yet despairing.

Before lifting her into place, he quickly collected everything he would need. A couple of two-by-fours to serve as braces until the acquisition was firmly fixed in place. Two nails. Plus one longer and more wickedly pointed number that could fairly be called a spike. The hammer, of course. Hurry. Smaller nails, barely more than tacks, a score of which could be placed just-so in her brow to represent the crown of thorns. The switchblade, with which to recreate the spear wound attributed to the taunting Centurion. Anything else? Think. Quickly now. He had no vinegar or sponge to soak it in, therefore could not offer that traditional drink to the dying lips, but he didn't think the absence of that detail would in any way detract from the composition.

He was ready.

Hatch and Lindsey were deep in the gondola tunnel, proceeding as fast as they dared, but slowed by the need to shine flashlights into the deepest reaches of each niche and room-size display area that opened off the flanking walls. The moving beams caused black shadows to fly and dance off concrete stalactites and stalagmites and other manmade rock formations, but all of those dangerous spaces were empty.

Two solid thuds, like hammer blows, echoed to them from farther in the funhouse, one immediately after the other. Then silence.

"He's ahead of us somewhere," Lindsey whispered, "not real close. We can move faster."

Hatch agreed.

They proceeded along the tunnel without scanning all the deep recesses, which once had held clockwork monsters. Along the way, the bond between Hatch and Jeremy Nyebern was established again. He sensed the madman's excitement, an obscene and palpitating need. He received, as well, disconnected images: nails, a spike, a hammer, two lengths of two-by-four, a scattering of tacks, the slender steel blade of a knife popping out of its spring-loaded handle. . . .

His anger escalating with his fear, determined not to let the disorienting visions impede his advance, he reached the end of the horizontal tunnel and stumbled a few steps down the incline before he realized that the angle of the floor had changed radically under his feet.

The first of the odor hit him. Drifting upward on a natural draft. He gagged, heard Lindsey do the same, then tightened his throat and swallowed hard.

He knew what lay below. At least some of it. Glimpses of the collection had been among the visions that had pounded him when he had been in the car on the highway. If he didn't get an iron grip on himself and stifle his repulsion now, he would never make it all the way into the depths of this hellhole, and he had to go there in order to save Regina.

Apparently Lindsey understood, for she found the will to re-press her retching, and she followed him down the steep slope.

The first thing to attract Vassago's attention was the glow of light high up toward one end of the cavern, far back in the tunnel that led to the spillway. The rapid rate at which the light grew brighter convinced him that he would not have time to add the girl to his collection before the intruders were upon him.

He knew who they were. He had seen them in visions as they, evidently, had seen him. Lindsey and her husband had followed him all the way from Laguna Niguel. He was just beginning to recognize that more forces were at work in this affair than had appeared to be the case at first.

He considered letting them descend the spillway into Hell, slipping behind them, killing the man, disabling the woman, and then proceeding with a *dual* crucifixion. But there was something about the husband that unsettled him. He couldn't put his finger on it.

But he realized now that, in spite of his bravado, he had been avoiding a confrontation with the husband. In their house earlier in the night, when the element of surprise had still been his, he should have circled behind the husband and disposed of him first, before going after either Regina or Lindsey. Had he done so, he might have been able to acquire both woman and child at that time. By now he might have been happily engrossed in their mutilation.

Far above, the pearly glow of light had resolved into a pair of flashlight beams at the brink of the spillway. After a brief hesitation, they started down. Because he had put his sunglasses in his shirt pocket, Vassago was forced to squint at the slashing swords of light.

As before, he decided not to move against the man, choosing instead to retreat with the child. This time, however, he wondered at his prudence.

A Master of the Game, he thought, must exhibit iron control and choose the right moments to prove his power and superiority.

True. But this time the thought struck him as spineless justification for avoiding confrontation.

Nonsense. He was afraid of nothing in this world.

The flashlights were still a considerable distance away, focused on the floor of the spillway, not yet to the midpoint of the long incline. He could hear their footsteps, which grew louder and developed an echo as the pair advanced into the huge chamber.

He seized the catatonic girl, lifted her as if she weighed no more than a pillow, slung her over his shoulder, and moved soundlessly across the floor of Hell toward those rock formations where he knew a door to a service room was hidden.

"Oh, my God."

"Don't look," he told Lindsey as he swept the beam of his

flashlight across the macabre collection. "Don't look, Jesus, cover my back, make sure he's not coming around on us."

Gratefully, she did as he said, turning away from the array of posed cadavers in various stages of decomposition. She was certain that her sleep, even if she lived to be a hundred, would be haunted every night by those forms and faces. But who was she kidding—she would never make a hundred. She was beginning to think she wouldn't even make it through the night.

The very idea of breathing *that* air, reeking and impure, through her mouth was almost enough to make her violently ill. She did it anyway because it minimized the stink.

The darkness was so deep. The flashlight seemed barely able to penetrate. It was like syrup, flowing back into the brief channel that the beam stirred through it.

She could hear Hatch moving along the collection of bodies, and she knew what he had to be doing—taking a quick look at each of them, just to be sure that Jeremy Nyebern was not posed among them, one living monstrosity among those consumed by rot, waiting to spring at them the moment they passed him.

Where was Regina?

Ceaselessly, Lindsey swept her flashlight back and forth, back and forth, in a wide arc, never giving the murderous bastard a chance to sneak up on her before she brought the beam around again. But, oh, he was fast. She had seen how fast. Flying down the hallway into Regina's room, slamming the door behind him, fast as if he'd flown, had wings, bat wings. And agile. Down the trumpet-vine trellis with the girl over his shoulder, unfazed by the fall, up and off into the night with her.

Where was Regina?

She heard Hatch moving away, and she knew where he was going, not just following the line of bodies but circling the towering figure of Satan, to be sure Jeremy Nyebern wasn't on the other side of it. He was just doing what he had to do. She knew that, but she didn't like it anyway, not one little bit, because now she was alone with all of those dead people behind her. Some of them were withered and would make papery sounds if somehow they became animated and edged toward her, while others were in more horrendous stages of decomposition and sure to reveal their approach with thick, wet sounds. . . . And what crazy thoughts were these? They were all *dead.* Nothing to fear from them. The dead stayed dead. Except they didn't always, did they? No, not in her own personal experience, they didn't. But she kept sweeping her light back and forth, back and forth, resisting the urge to turn around and shine it on the festering cadavers behind her. She knew she should mourn them rather than fear them, be angry for the abuse and loss of dignity that they had suffered, but she only had room at the moment for fear. And now she heard Hatch coming closer, around the other side of the statue, completing his circumnavigation, thank God. But in the next breath, horribly metallic as it passed through her mouth, she wondered if it was Hatch or one of the bodies moving. Or Jeremy. She swung around, looking past the row of corpses rather than at them, and her light showed her that it was, indeed, Hatch coming back.

Where was Regina?

As if in answer, a distinctive creak sliced through the heavy air. Doors the world over made that identical sound when their hinges were corroded and unoiled.

She and Hatch swung their flashlights in the same direction. The overlapping terminuses of their beams showed they had both judged the origin of the sound to have come from a rock formation along the far shore of what would have been, with water, a lake larger than the lagoon outside.

She was moving before she realized it. Hatch whispered her name in an urgent tone that meant *move aside, let me, I'll go first.* But she could no more have held back than she could have turned coward and retreated up the spillway. Her Regina had been among the dead, perhaps spared the direct sight of them because of her strange keeper's aversion to light, but among them nevertheless and surely aware of them. Lindsey could not *bear* the thought of that innocent child held in this slaughterhouse one minute longer. Lindsey's own safety didn't matter, only Regina's.

As she reached the rocks and plunged in among them, stabbing here with her light, then there, then over there, shadows leaping, she heard the wail of distant sirens. Sheriff's men. Hatch's phone call had been taken seriously. But Regina was in the hands of Death. If the girl was still alive, she would not last as long as it would take the cops to find the funhouse and get down to the lair of Lucifer. So Lindsey pressed deeper into the rocks, the Browning in one hand, flashlight in the other, turning corners recklessly, taking chances, with Hatch close behind her.

She came upon the door abruptly. Metal, streaked with rust, operated by a push-bar rather than a knob. Ajar.

She shoved it open and went through without even the finesse that she should have learned from a lifetime of police movies and television shows. She exploded across the threshold as might a mother lion in pursuit of the predator that had dared to drag off her cub. Stupid, she knew that it was stupid, that she could get herself killed, but mother lions in a fever of matriarchal aggression were not notably creatures of reason. She was operating on instinct now, and instinct told her that they had the bastard on the run, had to keep him running to prevent him from dealing with the girl as he wanted, and should press him harder and harder until they had him in a corner.

Beyond the door in the rocks, behind the walls of Hell, was a twenty-foot-wide area that had once been crowded with machinery. It was now littered with the bolts and steel plates on which those machines had been mounted. Elaborate scaffolding, festooned with spider webs, rose forty or fifty feet; it provided access to other doors and crawlspaces and panels through which the complex lighting and effects equipment—cold-steam generators, lasers—had been serviced. That stuff was gone now, stripped out and carted away.

How long did he need to cut the girl open, seize her beating heart, and take his satisfaction from her death? One minute? Two? Perhaps no more than that. To keep her safe, they had to breathe down his goddamned neck.

Lindsey swept her flashlight beam across that spider-infested conglomeration of steel pipes and elbow joints and tread plates. She quickly decided their quarry had not ascended to any hiding place above.

Hatch was at her side and slightly behind her, staying close.

They were breathing hard, not because they had exerted themselves but because their chests were tight with fear, constricting
their lungs.

Turning left, Lindsey moved straight toward a dark opening in
the concrete-block wall on the far side of that twenty-foot-wide
chamber. She was drawn to it because it appeared to have been
boarded over at one time, not solidly but with enough planks to
prevent anyone entering the forbidden space beyond without effort. Some of the nails still prickled the block walls on both sides
of the opening, but all of the planks had been torn away and
shoved to one side on the floor.

Although Hatch whispered her name, warning her to hold back,
she stepped straight to the brink of that room, shone her light into
it, and discovered it was not a room at all but an elevator shaft.
The doors, cab, cables, and mechanism had been salvaged, leaving
a hole in the building as sure as an extracted tooth left a hole in
the jaw.

She pointed her light up. The shaft rose three stories, having
once conveyed mechanics and other repairmen to the top of the
funhouse. She swung the beam slowly down the concrete wall
from above, noticing the iron rungs of the service ladder.

Hatch stepped in beside her as the light found its way to the
bottom of the shaft, just two floors below, where it revealed some
litter, a Styrofoam ice chest, several empty cans of root beer, and
a plastic garbage bag nearly full of trash, all arranged around a
stained and battered mattress.

On the mattress, huddled in a corner of the shaft, was Jeremy
Nyebern. Regina was in his lap, held against his chest, so she could
shield him against gunfire. He was holding a pistol, and he
squeezed off two shots even as Lindsey spotted him down there.

The first slug missed both her and Hatch, but the second round
tore through her shoulder. She was knocked against the door
frame. On the rebound, she bent forward involuntarily, lost her
balance, and fell into the shaft, following her flashlight, which she
had already dropped.

Going down, she didn't believe it was happening. Even when
she hit bottom, landing on her left side, the whole thing seemed

unreal, maybe because she was still too numb from the impact of the bullet to feel the damage it had done, and maybe because she fell mostly on the mattress, at the far end of it from Nyebern, knocking out what wind the slug had left in her but breaking no bones.

Her flashlight had also landed on the mattress, unharmed. It lit one gray wall.

As if in a dream, and though unable to get her breath quite yet, Lindsey brought her right hand slowly around to point her gun at him. But she had no gun. The Browning had spun from her grip in the fall.

During Lindsey's drop, Nyebern must have tracked her with his own weapon, for she was looking into it. The barrel was impossibly long, measuring exactly one eternity from firing chamber to muzzle.

Beyond the gun she saw Regina's face, which was as slack as her gray eyes were empty, and beyond that beloved countenance was the hateful one, pale as milk. His eyes, unshielded by glasses, were fierce and strange. She could see them even though the glow of the flashlight forced him to squint. Meeting his gaze she felt that she was face-to-face with something alien that was only passing as human, and not well.

Oh, wow, surreal, she thought, and knew that she was on the verge of passing out.

She hoped to faint before he squeezed the trigger. Though it didn't matter, really. She was so close to the gun that she wouldn't live to hear the shot that blew her face off.

Hatch's horror, as he watched Lindsey fall into the shaft, was exceeded by his surprise at what he did next.

When he saw Jeremy track her with the pistol until she hit the mattress, the muzzle three feet from her face, Hatch tossed his own Browning away, onto the pile of planks that once boarded off the shaft. He figured he wouldn't be able to get off a clear shot with Regina in the way. And he knew that no gun would properly dispatch the thing that Jeremy had become. He had no time to wonder at *that* curious thought, for as soon as he pitched away the Browning, he shifted the crucifix-flashlight from his left hand to his right, and leaped into the elevator shaft without any expectation that he was about to do so.

After that, everything got weird.

It seemed to him that he didn't crash down the shaft as he should have done, but glided in slow motion, as if he were only slightly heavier than air, taking as much as half a minute to reach bottom.

Perhaps his sense of time had merely been distorted by the profundity of his terror.

Jeremy saw him coming, shifted the pistol from Lindsey to Hatch, and fired all eight remaining rounds. Hatch was certain that he was hit at least three or four times, though he sustained no wounds. It seemed impossible that the killer could miss so often in such a confined space.

Perhaps the sloppy marksmanship was attributable to the gunman's panic and to the fact that Hatch was a moving target.

While he was still floating down like dandelion fluff, he experienced a reconnection of the peculiar bond between him and Nyebern, and for a moment he saw himself descending from the young killer's point of view. What he glimpsed, however, was not only himself but the image of someone—or something—superimposed over him, as if he shared his body with another entity. He thought he saw white wings folded close against his sides. Under his own face was that of a stranger—the visage of a warrior if ever there had been one, yet not a face that frightened him.

Perhaps by then Nyebern was hallucinating, and what Hatch was receiving from him was not actually what he saw but only what he imagined that he saw. Perhaps.

Then Hatch was gazing down from his own eyes again, still in that slow glide, and he was sure that he saw something superimposed over Jeremy Nyebern, too, a form and face that were part reptilian and part insectile.

Perhaps it was a trick of light, the confusion of shadows and conflicting flashlight beams.

He could not explain away their final exchange, however, and he dwelt upon it often in the days that followed:

"Who are you?" Nyebern asked as Hatch landed catlike in spite of a thirty-foot descent.

"Uriel," Hatch replied, though that was not a name he had heard before.

"I am Vassago," Nyebern said.

"I know," Hatch said, though he was hearing that name for the first time, as well.

"Only you can send me back."

"And when you get sent back by such as me," Hatch said, wondering where the words came from, "you don't go back a prince. You'll be a slave below, just like the heartless and stupid boy with whom you hitched a ride."

Nyebern was afraid. It was the first time he had shown any capacity for fear. "And I thought *I* was the spider."

With strength, agility, and economy of motion that Hatch had not known he possessed, he grabbed Regina's belt in his left hand, pulled her away from Jeremy Nyebern, set her aside out of harm's way, and brought the crucifix down like a club upon the madman's head. The lens of the attached flashlight shattered, and the casing burst open, spilling batteries. He chopped the crucifix hard against the killer's skull a second time, and with the third blow he sent Nyebern to a grave that had been twice earned.

The anger Hatch felt was righteous anger. When he dropped the crucifix, when it was all over, he felt no guilt or shame. He was nothing at all like his father.

He had a strange awareness of a power leaving him, a presence he had not realized was there. He sensed a mission accomplished, balance restored. All things were now in their rightful places.

Regina was unresponsive when he spoke to her. Physically she seemed unharmed. Hatch was not worried about her, for somehow he knew that none of them would suffer unduly for having been caught up in . . . whatever they had been caught up in.

Lindsey was unconscious and bleeding. He examined her wound and felt it was not too serious.

Voices arose two floors above. They were calling his name. The

authorities had arrived. Late as always. Well, not always. Sometimes . . . one of them was there just when you needed him.

3

The apocryphal story of the three blind men examining the elephant is widely known. The first blind man feels only the elephant's trunk and thereafter confidently describes the beast as a
great snakelike creature, similar to a python. The second blind
man feels only the elephant's ears and announces that it is a bird
that can soar to great heights. The third blind man examines only
the elephant's fringe-tipped, fly-chasing tail and "sees" an animal
that is curiously like a bottle brush.

So it is with any experience that human beings share. Each
participant perceives it in a different way and takes from it a
different lesson than do his or her compatriots.

In the years following the events at the abandoned amusement
park, Jonas Nyebern lost interest in resuscitation medicine. Other
men took over his work and did it well.

He sold at auction every piece of religious art in the two collections that he had not yet completed, and he put the money in
savings instruments that would return the highest possible rate of
interest.

Though he continued to practice cardiovascular surgery for a
while, he no longer found any satisfaction in it. Eventually he
retired young and looked for a new career in which to finish out
the last decades of his life.

He stopped attending Mass. He no longer believed that evil was
a force in itself, a real presence that walked the world. He had
learned that humanity itself was a source of evil sufficient to
explain everything that was wrong with the world. Obversely, he
decided humanity was its own—and only—salvation.

He became a veterinarian. Every patient seemed deserving.
He never married again.

He was neither happy nor unhappy, and that suited him fine.

Regina remained within her inner room for a couple of days, and
when she came out she was never quite the same. But then no one
ever is quite the same for any length of time. Change is the only
constant. It's called growing up.

She addressed them as Dad and Mom, because she wanted to,
and because she meant it. Day by day, she gave them as much
happiness as they gave her.

She never set off a chain reaction of destruction among their
antiques. She never embarrassed them by getting inappropri-
ately sentimental, bursting into tears, and thereby activating the
old snot faucet; she unfailingly produced tears and snot only
when they were called for. She never mortified them by accidentally flipping an entire plate of food into the air at a restaurant
and over the head of the President of the United States at the
next table. She never accidentally set the house on fire, never
farted in polite company, and never scared the bejesus out of
smaller neighborhood children with her leg brace and curious
right hand. Better still, she stopped worrying about doing all
those things (and more), and in time she did not even recall the
tremendous energies that she once had wasted upon such unlikely concerns.

She kept writing. She got better at it. When she was just fourteen, she won a national writing competition for teenagers. The
prize was a rather nice watch and a check for five hundred dollars.
She used some of the money for a subscription to *Publishers
Weekly* and a complete set of the novels of William Makepeace
Thackeray. She no longer had an interest in writing about intelligent pigs from outer space, largely because she was learning that
more curious characters could be found all around her, many of
them native Californians.

She no longer talked to God. It seemed childish to chatter at

Him. Besides, she no longer needed His constant attention. For a while she had thought He had gone away or had never existed, but she had decided that was foolish. She was aware of Him all the time, winking at her from the flowers, serenading her in the song of a bird, smiling at her from the furry face of a kitten, touching her with a soft summer breeze. She found a line in a book that she thought was apt, from Dave Tyson Gentry: "True friendship comes when silence between two people is comfortable." Well, who was your best friend, if not God, and what did you really need to say to Him or He to you when you both already knew the most—and only—important thing, which was that you would always be there for each other.

Lindsey came through the events of those days less changed than she had expected. Her paintings improved somewhat, but not tremendously. She had never been dissatisfied with her work in the first place. She loved Hatch no less than ever, and could not possibly have loved him more.

One thing that made her cringe, which never had before, was hearing anyone say, "The worst is behind us now." She knew that the worst was never behind us. The worst came at the end. It *was* the end, the very fact of it. Nothing could be worse than that. But she had learned to live with the understanding that the worst was never behind her—and still find joy in the day at hand.

As for God—she didn't dwell on the issue. She raised Regina in the Catholic Church, attending Mass with her each week, for that was part of the promise she had made St. Thomas's when they had arranged the adoption. But she didn't do it solely out of duty. She figured that the Church was good for Regina—and that Regina might be good for the Church, too. Any institution that counted Regina a member was going to discover itself changed by her at least as much as she was changed—and to its everlasting benefit. She had once said that prayers were never answered, that the living lived only to die, but she had progressed beyond that attitude. She would wait and see.

Hatch continued to deal successfully in antiques. Day by day his life went pretty much as he hoped it would. As before, he was an easy-going guy. He never got angry. But the difference was that he had no anger left in him to repress. The mellowness was genuine now.

From time to time, when the patterns of life seemed to have a grand meaning that just barely eluded him, and when he was therefore in a philosophical mood, he would go to his den and take two items from the locked drawer.

One was the heat-browned issue of *Arts American.*

The other was a slip of paper he had brought back from the library one day, after doing a bit of research. Two names were written on it, with an identifying line after each. "Vassago—according to mythology, one of the nine crown princes of Hell." Below that was the name he had once claimed was his own: "Uriel—according to mythology, one of the archangels serving as a personal attendant to God."

He stared at these things and considered them carefully, and always he reached no firm conclusions. Though he did decide, if you had to be dead for eighty minutes and come back with no memory of the Other Side, maybe it was because eighty minutes of that knowledge was more than just a glimpse of a tunnel with a light at the end, and therefore more than you could be expected to handle.

And if you had to bring something back with you from Beyond, and carry it within you until it had concluded its assignment on this side of the veil, an archangel wasn't too shabby.